φ φ
ORLOK

ORLOK

DON DANDREA

PINEAPPLE PRESS, INC.

Inquiries should be addressed to:

Pineapple Press, Inc.
P.O. Box 3889
Sarasota, Florida 34230

www.pineapplepress.com

The Library of Congress catalogued the hardcover edition as follows:

Dandrea, Don.
    Orlok.

    1. Sabutai, ca. 1172–1245—Fiction. 2. Genghis Khan, 1162–1227—
Fiction. 3. Mongols—History, Military—Fiction. I. Title.
PS3554.A523507   1986   813'.54
          85-23251

ISBN 978-0-910923-22-4 (hb)
ISBN 978-1-56164-553-4 (pb)
ISBN 978-1-56164-554-1 (e-book)

First Edition
10 9 8 7 6 5 4 3 2 1

For Rosalind,
Rachel and Judith

ORLOK is a work of fiction. With the exception of actual historical personages and events, characters and events herein are imaginary.

Although the story is structured within an essentially accurate historical context, historical purists will immediately detect the departures in this novel from what has come to be generally accepted data concerning Genghis Khan, Subotai, and the Mongol military operations of the 13th century A.D.

It is the author's sincere hope that the resulting story makes up for these deviations from currently accepted historical views.

The author wishes to thank June Cussen and Pat Tucker for their energetic and professional editorial treatment of the original manuscript. I am indebted to them for their encouragement and insistence upon excellence.

φ φ
ORLOK

PROLOGUE

The old man sitting his horse atop the slight rising of the knoll could see in the distance the yurt, the round felt tent that had been his home for the past three years. The simple dwelling was a lonely anomaly on the wild steppe which surrounded the man and his animal like an earthen, grassy ocean. The steppe grasses were brittle and brown, for the season was late. Had he known anything of the Christian calendars, the old man might have known that it was the year 1245 A.D.

The old man had not seen another human being for nearly three cycles of the sun, not since he had left the Blue Lake after being informed that the new Kha Khan's Chinese ministers had denied him audience with the successor to Temajin and to Ogadai. It had been the Chinese ministers' subtle conspiracies and the death of Ogadai, not Christian might, as the vainglorious leaders of Europe liked to believe, that had held the Mongol army at the Danube and finally engineered its recall. Now they had curtained Ogadai's successor and—the old man sighed—they would make this new ruler more Chinese than Mongol.

But all that had slipped out of his life. He had been assigned out of the military cadres and pensioned with a handful of livestock and just four horses. And the world had turned its back on him.

The old man had been known by many names: Bahadur, the Valiant; orkhan; yes, even orlok of tumans, the Eagle of Temajin, who was the Genghis Kha Khan. He had also been known as father, husband, and yes, even lover.

If he had had harshness and humanity, savagery as well as serenity, at once in his nature, it was because the Light and the Dark, the swirling, entwined Yin and Yang had come to near fullness in him.

Soon his dharma, his spiritual duty, would be accomplished. Then the last veil would fall from his consciousness and he would go to Her—She who had caused him to fall in love with one of Her physical forms. She, behind all the loves of all the women he had known. She, the very Light of Mind, his Cosmic Beloved.

But now, while there was still a little time, he would remember his life and mark the souls who had assisted him in Snow, Desert,

1

Death, and Battle. And even before that—the Solar Warrior had taught him the technique—he would venture back along the Way through the dimness of subconscious memory to when he first held the Blue Sword.

Slowly and stiffly, the old man got down from his horse. Tying the pony's reins to his ankle in the Mongol way, he lay back on the dry, crisp grass and closed his eyes.

In time his mind lightened. Then he began to dream the dream of incarnations.

φ φ

THE
BLUE
SWORD

*O*ld Mizushima seized the red-hot metal billet with bone tongs and brought it quickly to the cylindrical anvil. Then, hammering and turning the sparkling billet in accordance with ritual—even the exact number of hammer blows was prescribed for each of the anciently preserved phases in the process—he gradually doubled the bar over upon itself.

This was to be no ordinary sword. Prince Sadazumi, the Sixth Lord and said to be the favorite of the Emperor Seiwa, had come himself to the smithy of Mizushima.

φ   φ   φ   φ

The prince had arrived with a great retinue of his most trusted samurai, who were without armor in the unseasonable warmth of an unusually dry autumn. Mizushima, ancient and wizened, and recognized even in his own lifetime as one of the greatest artisans of the blade, prostrated himself before the prince. After the required formalities, the household women quickly brought herb tea for the prince and Mizushima.

Seated on a rice-shuck tatami, Prince Sadazumi presented the commission to the swordsmith: a perfect blade, to be prepared and sanctified with the purification of the ancient Shinto ceremonies throughout, and to be made to extra length, an additional reach of steel equal to a man's forearm, elbow to wrist. It was to be a gift for the prince's greatest retainer, whom the prince had named Yama-Arashi—Mountain Storm—to match the man's violent and courageous nature.

Time was short, but the prince condescended to tour the work area. He appeared not to notice the swordmaker's apprentices in their frozen prostration, his samurai always close to his person. The flat, watchful eyes of the warrior-born seemed to give off in an unreflecting way the cool and untainted courage and self-possession within each man.

But even in the company of this elite of the soldier caste, the prince was one apart. His quick intelligence and good humor were a radiant harmony surrounding his person, and it was well known that he was one of the greatest samurai of the age. He was a perfect master of Yawara, the martial art thought to have been anciently borne across the roof of the world from the land whence the Lord Buddha had sprung, and then brought to the Rain Islands, to Dai Nippon, by the monks bringing the hope of the blessing and freedom of Gautama Buddha.

The prince hastened past the furnaces, forges, and tool areas. He was garbed no more richly than his military retainers in his plain black hakama and a grey top, with a katana anchored in his heavy cloth belt and a shorter tanto on his right side. Only the six-leaved chrysanthemum symbol above his heart betrayed Sadazumi's imperial status.

When the prince and the samurai were gone at last and the household and the apprentices could again relax, Mizushima sat alone, and, in the deep concentration of the artisan, contemplated, sketched, and styled the imaginary blade in his mind's eye. Then, satisfied with the mental parameters he had ascribed to the blade, he called his aged and faithful wife and directed that she prepare rice and vegetables for him to carry on his way. He knew instinctively that this sword would be his last and he intended to make it his greatest. When his dead flesh was returned to the moist soil of the mountainside above the paddies, the blade would be the material testament and monument of his life and of his mastery of his craft.

Early the next morning he was on his way. It was painful for him to walk now, but with his walking stick, his bo, he struggled at last to the little fishing village on the Inland Sea and, by sharing his portion of rice with a fisherman, he gained passage to the green island standing a league away to the east.

The fisherman, steadying the boat with one hand against the outgoing tide, helped the old man over the side with his other hand. He watched Mizushima wade slowly ashore in his slow and bent way. Then he rowed back toward the main island.

It was night before Mizushima beat his bo on the barred monastery gate. The monks, carrying their flimsy spherical lanterns, recognized the swordmaker and admitted him in silence. The night was dry and Mizushima slept on a small patch of grass beside a stone walkway. He spoke briefly with one of the elders the following morning. Then he adopted the customary silence and the routine of the monks, joining them in their zazen in the long meditation hall and squatting with them to share their simple repasts. For a fortnight he continued his retreat, purifying his mind and his motives for the task ahead.

Upon returning from his retreat, he met his wife and attentive daughters garbed in their best kimonos, standing on the pathway in front of the row of assistants and apprentice swordmakers. The dignified bowing at last completed, Mizushima went immediately to the forges and began selecting steel and iron stock. He called for the novices to begin firing the furnaces and to renew the supply of charcoal. Then he began, working without rest, combining the ritual process and his own consummate art.

The finest of the already steeled stock was heated red-hot in the furnaces and then brought to the forges for the expert carbonization technique employed by Mizushima. The swordsmith squinted into the forges, testing each billet, hammering, quenching, and subjectively tempering them to ascertain the best quality among the stock billets.

For two days and two nights, the assistants and the apprentices labored in shifts. Then, when the forces and the rightness of time and steel had come into harmony, the young disciples stood away in silent respect, and the master took up the hammers.

φ φ φ φ

Mizushima seemed a man possessed. Silent, except for the most curt instructions to those fueling the forges or bringing oils for the quench baths, his thin body appeared to be incapable of the energy and untiring effort demanded of it.

The hours passed as Mizushima doubled and reheated the ever-flattening material, bending the steel, then hammering the bent steel into a single glowing and lengthening slab. And there was always the art, balancing hardness with ductility in the heating, quenching, and tempering as the steel was bent and rebent. The steel layers mounted by powers of two until they numbered more than two hundred thousand.

The old man had to be helped away when it was finally done. His gentle womenfolk tucked the spent and aged man into a futan. The long blue blade lay immersed in its final bath of oil drawn from the skull of a sperm whale.

Mizushima never awakened from his exhausted sleep. The sword had indeed been the seal upon his life. And the dark blue steel with its exquisite curvature, the faint gray rippling in its texture, stood as the epitome of his life-dedicated art.

φ   φ   φ   φ

A lone samurai was sent by Prince Sadazumi to acquire the sword. The grim Japanese warrior gruffly informed the old widow and the daughters that they were now under the protection of the Sixth Lord, and that a pension would be forthcoming as well as periodic stipends to maintain the production of Mizushima's armory.

Prince Sadazumi marveled at the beautiful weapon. Throughout the gray and wet winter, whenever affairs of his provinces and demands of his Emperor allowed, he would take the blade from its silk wrappings, slowly unsheathe it, and inspect its compelling artistry. In the majesty of his consciousness, the tall, ascetic nobleman perceived the beauty and the regularity of the latticed crystalline structure within the metal.

Prince Sadazumi presented the sword to the Yama-Arashi during the celebration of the Spring Blossoming, as a token to be carried by the chosen soldier on his mission to the Yamato clan in their enclave on the peninsula of Silla, northwest across the Sea of the Setting Sun. The winter storms had at last subsided and the ship carrying the Yama-Arashi could be on its way.

Prince Sadazumi accompanied the Yama-Arashi to the jade-reflecting cove where the small sailing vessel awaited the spring dispatches and the voyagers bound for Silla. His voice grave with the power of a premonition, the Yama-Arashi searched the black eyes of his prince and asked, "Shall we meet again, my lord?"

Sadazumi let his gaze linger on the line of rain squalls against the western sky before he replied. "If that is your desire, then the turning of the Way will surely draw us together again."

φ   φ   φ   φ

The memory of those words was the last glimmering in the Yama-Arashi's mortal consciousness as his blood-drenched body seemed to grow distant from him. But even in the surprise of the Hwa Rang warriors' ambush, only short hours after his debarkation on the lonely beach, the Yama-Arashi had proven the worth of the blue sword in his hands. Of the five soldiers of Silla who had lain in wait, knowing of the secret dispatches he carried, one lay decapitated by the master stroke of the blue sword, another would expire from his pulsing arterial wounds within the hour, a third was hamstrung for life.

Darkness was falling and the two remaining able Hwa Rang warriors quickly stripped the short, muscular body of the dead samurai. They found the messages in a narrow reed tube cleverly hidden within the handguard of the blue sword, instead of in the samurai's rectal orifice as they had expected. Gathering up the weapons of their dead comrades, they bound the leg of the wounded Hwa Rang, helped him onto his horse, then rode swiftly north along the beach, avoiding the steep hillsides of the mountainous terrain on the inland side.

That violent day, in the last remaining year of the ninth century after Christ, was drawing to a close. The three Hwa Rang hid in cold silence in a sea cave for the night, relying on the running tide to wash away their horses' spoor. They were well away into the safety of Silla-controlled land before the Yamato samurai found the dead courier and mounted a pursuit.

The blue sword was given to the crippled Hwa Rang as a symbol of his service to the queen of Silla. The man cared for the hypnotically exquisite weapon daily over the years, until the oiling and wiping down of the steel merged in his mind with and became an adjunct to his regular practice in the Buddhist faith.

As the lame Hwa Rang grew older and matured in statecraft and administrative ability, he began to gain notice and rapid promotion in the civil arm of the Kingdom of Silla. He privately attributed his advancing status in the world to his wound and to the blue sword, which he came to regard as a sacred charm. When he died at a great age, he went to his grave with the unshaken conviction that the sword had been the bearer of the fortune and honor attained in his old age for himself and his family.

When the lame Hwa Rang had been a rising young minister, the queen herself had bonded him in marriage to a fresh and lovely Korean woman, who in the untroubled years that followed, had borne him a single son. The dark blue weapon passed to that son, who, like his father, was trained in the military and moral ways of Hwa Rang Buddhism.

But the lineage of the lame Hwa Rang did not go forward. In the great jealousy of a rivalry with a fellow Hwa Rang over a young noblewoman, the son and his adversary both perished in a duel. It was an emotionally pointless affair since the woman was already promised to a Chin border lord to ensure certain military commitments between the Silla and the Chin concerning lands which reached to the Manchu forests.

She was informed of the tragic duel in an oddly cruel manner. She never learned who had done the thing, but someone brought the bloodied swords of both of her hopeless suitors secretly into her chambers and left them in plain view with the wet, caking evidence drying on them. The openly spoken rumors running through the court and the cruel surprise of discovering the blades had brought her immense grief and, in her secret womanhood, a grand satisfaction which lasted throughout her life, for do men, she asked herself, sacrifice their lives for an ordinary woman? She hid the stained weapons away after cleaning them, storing them amongst the packing in a great wooden chest.

With iron self-control, the lady veiled her grief. She finished her premarital preparations and packed for her journey to the north and her future life with the Chin warlord. She did so with some misgivings, since it was rumored that the warlord, in the grand Chinese fashion, already kept numerous concubines and continually terrorized his domains in his demented search for young and unspoiled women to feed his lust.

On her journey north, she found herself only one more item in the large array of gifts and articles of trade sent out from Silla to finalize treaties and satisfy the bribe demands and the formal tributes exacted by the border warlords of the powerful Chin Empire and the neighboring allied region of Koryu. When she was finally installed in the fortified holding where the warlord headquartered, the demon winter had settled upon the land and in the foreboding of her anxious heart.

Her worst fears materialized almost immediately. The wedding ceremony became a travesty. In a sudden and inexplicable rage, the drunken warlord, cursing and spitting food through his blackened and broken teeth, overturned a feast table, struck one of his guards senseless and strode away to the concubines' wing of his stronghold. She fortunately saw little of the man thereafter. Preferring the constantly renewed wares in the concubine wing, the maddened Chin only graced her bed a single night. Almost a year after her arrival from Silla, her marriage was consummated in rape. Her husband came into her bedchamber while she slept and nearly blotted out her senses with his unwashed alcoholic body, putrid breath, and prurient appetites. She lived thereafter in terror of any renewed interest in her by the loathsome drunk, but he let her alone.

However, she quickly came under the thumb of his disgusting mother. The mother seemed the only one who could control, or generally redirect, the lunatic urges and waves of raging madness which beset the warlord. In hateful, scheming, and perfidious ways, the vile old woman conducted and obstructed all the details of life within the walled compound where the young wife now existed as her chattel and virtual prisoner. But the wife watched, listened, and learned from the tormenting domination of her foul mother-in-law, and eventually began to compete with her for the upper hand in manipulating the insanity and sex-fiendishness of the warlord.

To her great relief, her mother-in-law and then her husband died in quick succession. But the power vacuum left by the two deaths was quickly filled, first by the arrival of a hard Manchu soldier sent by the emperor of the Chin, then by the bloody assault of a wandering band of mercenary soldiers led by a bandit from the Hsi-Hsia region to the west. The wife, considered old by this time, fell as booty to one of the principal lieutenants of the wandering bandit warlord, as did all of her now scanty possessions including the blue sword. The lieutenant did not keep it long. The first time the Hsi-Hsiang warlord saw the marvelous weapon, he commandeered it for himself.

The Hsi-Hsiang warlord occupied his time in pillaging the surrounding country and in squeezing and coercing the populace out of their pitiable wealth and their hard-won crops. His tenure was abruptly ended by another military expedition sent by the Chin. The Hsi-Hsiang leader escaped in the middle of a cold, moonless night by riding boldly straight through the beseiging Chinese forces. His hapless soldiers, unaware of their leader's flight, remained within the walled compound and died, many of them pleading for life after an ignoble surrender. The woman of Silla was also slain during the indiscriminate slaughter after the Chinese broke into the fortification, but they did not find the treasure she had brought from the south. The blue sword had been borne away by the Hsi-Hsiang in his reckless flight.

φ   φ   φ   φ

The Hsi-Hsiang fugitive rode his horse to death that night. Being a ruthless and totally selfish creature and therefore given to unblemished practicality, he sawed off one of the haunches of the still twitching animal, using the blue sword and his dagger. He then hoisted all the raw meat he could carry into a bloody bag made from some hide he stripped from the horse, and set off afoot into the safety of the Manchu forests.

A few hours later he happened to look back as he was recrossing a shallow stream and saw a mounted Chin patrol stopped where he had crossed before. Several Chinese had dismounted and were examining the mud he had trodden. With the animal wiliness imbued in him by a life of wandering savagery, he quickly broke a heavy branch from a nearby tree and carefully backed across the mud into the water again. He scooped a hatful of water and backed out of the stream, disfiguring his telltale tracks with the branch. Then he splashed water over the branch streaks, totally obscuring his trail to the edge of the forest, where he stopped to watch the Chin. After some moments, he saw them remount and divide into two groups, one group going upstream and the other downstream, to resume their search.

The Hsi-Hsiang did not linger on the edge of the trees but plunged deep into the forest, wading in erratic and deceptive ways in the many small streams. Pausing momentarily, he reached into the skin bag and thrust a slab of horse meat under his leather coat and into his armpit before continuing on through the thick undergrowth. He stopped only after it had become too dark to fight the thick brambles and the treacherous ground. He retrieved the now-warmed horse meat and using his dagger and his yellowed teeth, tore, slashed, and bolted down the precious food. Withdrawing his arms from the sleeves of his pullover skin coat, he huddled in the warmth of his body heat and let himself drift into a light and wary sleep.

Several days later, the horse meat long gone, the Hsi-Hsiang was plodding through the forest when he thought he detected, faintly at first, the undeniable odor of wood smoke and the stronger smell of cooking meat. His sensitive nostrils quivering, he tracked the wafting smoke and the saliva-inducing aroma of the hot meat. When he was near enough for the wood smoke, hanging like frail, layered veils, to burn his eyes, he dropped to the earth and slithered on his belly toward its source.

He would have missed the tiny clearing and the little conical branch huts had it not been for the fire. He lay unmoving, watching like a predator in the undergrowth. When he was sure that a single old man and two younger women were the huts' only inhabitants, he stole with great caution to the edge of the tiny camp to a point behind the squat, huddled man. He waited until the women left the clearing with their primitive fishing seines and the man was dozing as he watched the hot fat drip into the flames from several heavy chunks of spitted, blackening meat. The man roused and was turning his head to one side to clear his nose when the Hsi-Hsiang drove his filthy dagger into the base of the old man's skull. The gross body twitched for some seconds, venting gaseous excrement and urine before it lay still in open-mouthed, wide-eyed death.

The Hsi-Hsiang resheathed his blade without wiping it, seized the skewer over the fire with his bloodied hands, and tore off a great slab of the fat-marbled flesh. He ripped a mouthful of the rare meat and chewed it savagely. He was not worried about the women; they would understand quickly enough when they returned and found him with the stiffening body of the old man. He could make good use of them. After all, a man needed several women to do the heavy labor—fishing, skinning, and tanning—and to keep his bed warm during the cold night.

It was just as he anticipated. When the two short, heavy women returned carrying several silver-gray fish on a sinew stringer, their straight, lank black hair still dripping water, they did not seem at all surprised to find their old kinsman lying dead and a stranger devouring their meat. They set to smoking the fish near the fire, fueling the blaze and cautiously watching as he ransacked the huts. When he emerged from the last hut, having found little of value, he turned his glittering black eyes on them. The women quickly fled into the trees and brush.

They returned in the dead of night as the Hsi-Hsiang dozed fitfully in front of the open fire. One came with a sharpened stick, the other with a heavy rock. The Hsi-Hsiang awakened, but only for a moment, when the wooden point entered his throat and thrust upward into his lower brain. The other woman then calmly crushed his skull with heavy, systematic blows of the stone.

The older woman pulled and worked the blue sword from beneath the Hsi-Hsiang's body. It was loose and partly drawn from its scabbard when it finally came free. She shoved it home in its wood and bone scabbard and placed it in the center of her bundle.

Then the women sat down to wait out the darkness around the fire. In the first light of dawn, they dragged the old man's carcass into the forest and, as was the custom of their people, the Yakut, they built a simple raft and set the dead man adrift on a nearby river. Returning to the clearing, they fired their huts.

The two women traveled afoot for a week's time, hurrying with a low, simmering anxiety brought on by the cooling air of the approach of autumn. Frost had formed on the thickets and branches of the dense forestland on the very morning of their arrival at the main encampment of their tribe. In the total informality of their primitive people, they were welcomed by kin. They offered the blue sword as a gift to the male head of the family, then promptly merged into the simple survival-oriented existence of the little hut village in the midst of the northwestern reaches of the Manchu forests.

The Yakut elder, having little to occupy his time during the long winter, took an artistic interest in the strange weapon he had been given. The steel of the blade itself and the lovely curving symmetry of its design he knew to be beyond any native technology he had ever encountered. The generations-old hilt of the weapon, originally of hardwood, was cracked and worn to an incongruous shabbiness against the perfectly preserved and unmarred metal of the blade.

On one of the icy, shimmering days of deepest winter when his very breath congealed and crystallized, rainbowing in the brightness of the sun reflecting from the snow in the forest clearing, he vaulted onto a reindeer and rode the swift-trotting animal north to the frozen bogland.

His memory served him correctly. He went to the remembered location and dug through the drifted snow. The huge prehistoric mammoth skull was mottled and streaked with brown mineral stains, as were the two enormous ivory tusks. He could see only the base of one; the rest of its length was mired in the frozen bog. Pounding his primitive flint chisel with a hand-sized stone, he gradually worked the circular rooting of the tusk out of the mighty skull. He heaved and strained, sweating profusely in spite of the aching cold, and finally broke the nearly ten feet of ivory free from its bone mooring. It almost smashed his leg when its great mass toppled ponderously onto the icy surface of the bogland.

The day's sunlight was almost spent when he finished lashing the tusk with long hide lines and secured the ends of them to the reindeer harness. Then he led the beast, dragging the hundreds of pounds of tusk through the bitter twilight back to the village.

It took him the better part of three days, using his simple bone files and flint saw blades, to saw through the tusk in two locations, releasing the choicest section of ivory. With an inherent artistic genius, he now sawed and worked with the ivory, matching the contours with those of the worn and ragged remnants on the grip of the blue sword. He hollowed the inner sides of the ivory pieces until their concavity closely matched the steel base of the sword's haft. He had extracted especially thick slabs of ivory, intending that the final cross-sectional dimensions of the new handle would slightly exceed the maximum width of the blade. After stripping away the old wooden grip and making sure the four ivory sections of the new handle would fit the sword exactly, he put the weapon aside and began carefully to abrade the surface of the ivory with fine sand and rough boiled leather.

When all of the superficial stains and irregularities had been removed and the essential ivory glistened in the dim firelight he worked by, he laid out his three small iron carving tools. After musing in thought for some time, he arose and withdrew a stiff leather roll from a pile of old reindeer harness, scrap hide, and wood. He rolled out the long-dried, wood-hard scroll and anchored it flat with rocks at each end. He studied the image of the strange beast inscribed on the leather. The depicted animal reared up from a thick and cumbersome body to a head heavy with two straight tusks jutting from the mouth. The animal's feet resembled the simple paddles his people used in negotiating the swift streams and rivers on their rafts of birchwood. Comical whiskers adorned the beast's sagging face, and the eyes had a dreamy heaviness which was almost manlike.

He painstakingly inscribed the general outlines of the animal's form on each of the ivory segments. Then, heedless of the passage of time, he carved and concentrated by the light of the fire inside the little timber and hide shelter while the subarctic winter-shortened days passed outside.

When he was finished, the carved creature stood out from the material in perfect representation of the animal pictured on the leather. After he had affixed the pieces of the new handle to the weapon, bonding them to the bare steel with an ingenious amalgam of a variety of pitches and resins, he carved a number of miniature copies of reindeer in selected locations on the now firmly set handle. The crafting of the snowy ivory created a startling contrast against the deep blue-gray, shimmering steel.

The Yakut elder spent the waning days at the end of the winter rehabilitating the fine wood and whalebone scabbard of the blue sword. He soaked the old, well-seasoned hardwood in fatty oil and burnished it with his palms until it shone and his hands were blistered from the labor. He alternated ivory sections with the existing whalebone to toughen the scabbard, and carved miniature flights of wood grouse above outlines of evergreen trees on the ivory.

The elder took the sword into the natural light of the sun only after all of his work was completed. Winter still held the dense forests of high Asia, but a subtle intensification of the day's light proclaimed that spring was near. The marvelous steel of Mizushima and the ivory art of the Yakut were sharply displayed between the frosty blue sky and the light-scintillating purity of the carpet of winter snow.

The Yakut lived on for two more decades, attaining an age virtually unknown among his tribe and kinfolk. Upon his death, all of his possessions were distributed among the little family group. The blue sword passed back to the old woman who, so many years before, had slain the Hsi-Hsiang. She in turn passed it to her grandson, a master trapper, who used the fabulous blade in a curiously skillful way to skin out the mink and sable he caught.

And it was the grandson who lay alone during one of the bad years, alone in his barren shelter and alone in the little settlement. All the others had starved to death. Hunting and fishing had yielded little throughout the previous summer and fall, and then a sickness had run through the herd of reindeer. The few surviving animals had been slaughtered for survival before the worst of the winter weather set in.

The young Yakut knew he must conserve all his strength, expending it only to fuel the fire. The rest of his time he lay nearly motionless, sucking on old hide strips for whatever nutrition they might yield.

Then during one night of utter cold, he felt a strange warming sensation come into his body. He sat up and, as though he had no choice in the matter, he carefully cleaned the blue sword. Taking the last remaining cube of fat, the one he had saved for so long in the agony and delirium of starvation, he thoroughly greased down the samurai sword and then resheathed it. He did not bother to place more wood on the fire. After bolting what little remained of the fat, he simply lay down, fell into a calm sleep, and died.

φ   φ   φ   φ

Generations passed. Snow and spring. Rain and rebirth of the forest. The simple shelters decayed and crumbled and were overgrown with grass and saplings. The bones of the dead were gradually scattered by the scavenging forest animals.

φ   φ   φ   φ

The felt-coated horseman guided his mount slowly over the old mounds he encountered. The ground seemed to be heaped in places, lacking the natural roll of the forest land. The horse pawed gently in the grasses and cropped a mouthful of the vegetation.

A flash of white under the animal's hoof caught the man's eye and he dismounted. Probably just a stone or a bone, he thought. He stooped to pick it up, but it was larger than he had thought and firmly lodged in the earth. Then he saw the carved ivory starkly set off by the damp soil in the creases of the animal forms.

The blue sword came out of its earthen sleeping place with some difficulty. After the man scraped and wiped the handle and the scabbard free of most of the muddy encrustation, he forced the blade from its sheath and held up the rusted metal for inspection. He grunted with satisfaction when he saw that when the weapon was cleaned there would be little pitting from the rust. He could already imagine the envy when he showed his lucky find to his fellow tribesmen in the hunting party.

By the time the hunters rode west-by-southwest out of the wooded regions several weeks later, the man had removed all the rust from the steel exteriors of the blue sword and had carefully scoured out all of the embedded dirt from the elaborate carvings.

The band of Kuraits, their dozens of pack horses heavily loaded with meat from their forest kills, rejoined their nomadic tribe camped on a shallow and clear-flowing river.

And thus it was that the blue sword found its way onto the steppes of Eurasia in the second half of the twelfth century after the birth of Jesus Christ.

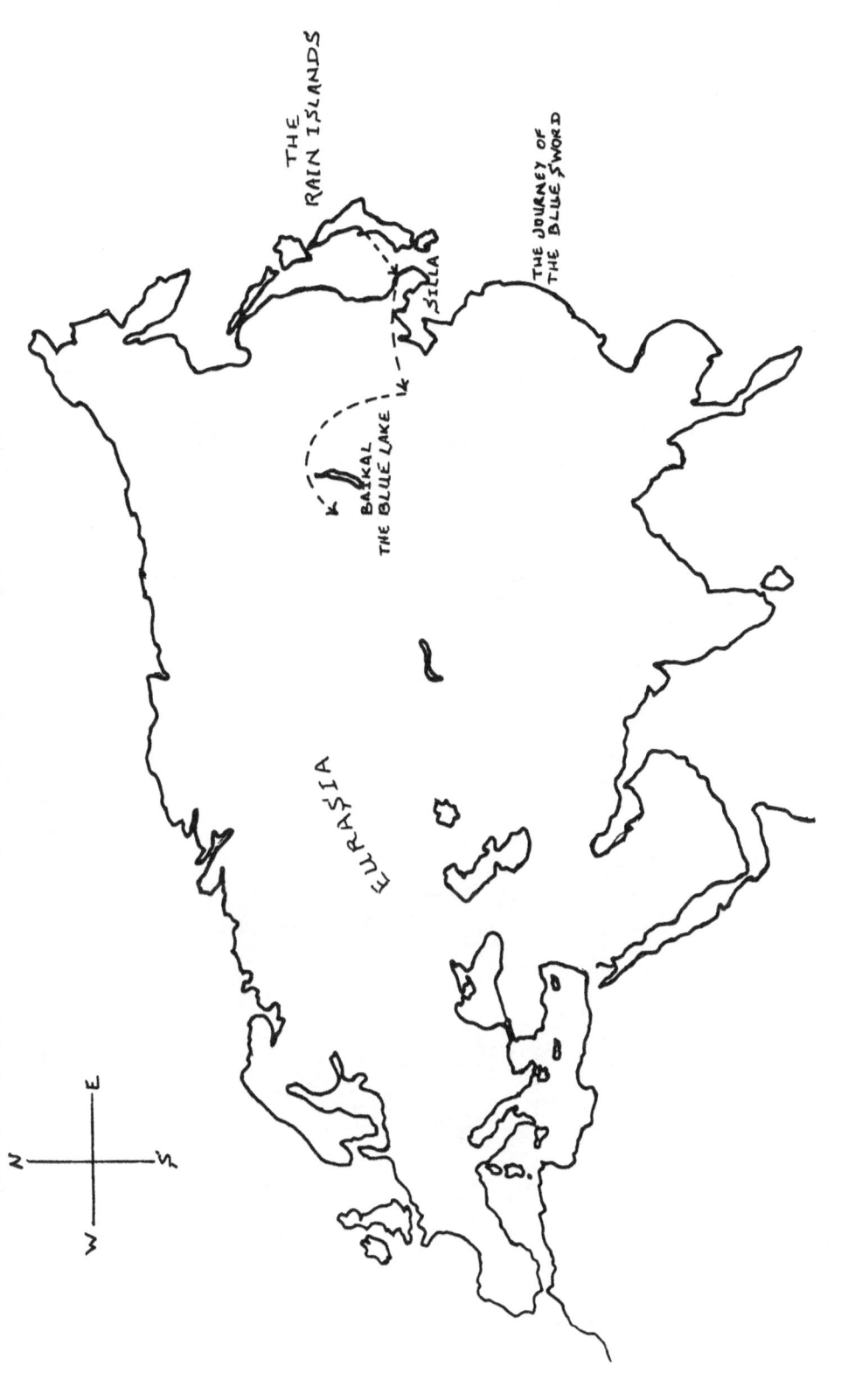

THE RAIN ISLANDS

THE JOURNEY OF THE BLUE SWORD

SILLA

BAIKAL
THE BLUE LAKE

EURASIA

N E S W

ϙ ϙ
THE
SNOW

*H*is earliest memory was the great, arching endlessness above the wide expanse of white ice on the Blue Lake. The Sky in winter seemed to draw off any vestige of warmth in the bitterness of the great Siberian cold.

He came early to know the strangeness, his hair drawn out by the magic forces which came with the Northern Lights. Their appearance, the mysterious warping of their ascending sheets of brilliance, first set in him an unsureness, a vague sense of lack which in later years would descend to despair—and in an even later time, with the growth of understanding, flame into a glorious hope. Although dim at first, it was this hope that would compel him through the dharma which had befallen him.

The snow and the time of hunger set the cycles of nomadic life in high Asia during the twelfth century after Christ. But for him, as he grew, the snow was always a marker in time, a clear, clean gift to him from the Sky. The early light snowfalls in autumn, crystalled and dusty white or shimmering in the light of the almost arctic sun, timed with the flights of the migratory waterfowl, were the natural states with which he was most harmonious.

He did not remember his mother, nor could he recall ever feeling the loss of her. She had died after weeks of increasing pain in her belly when he was just over a year old. Since she was without husband or kin, her wasted body had been consigned unceremonially to a hasty and shallow grave on the steppe with only a token place-ment of rocks on the grave to delay the carnivorous excavations of the steppe wolves.

An orphan ward of the clan, dependent upon his own com-petitiveness in the squabbling contests with the other children for food, he clothed himself in the throw-away leather and tattered scraps of felt provided by the rare charity shown to him. There was never enough food. Children of the clan frequently died, even those with caring parents. During the cold winter nights, he sometimes wondered if his would be the small stiffened body next found dead from hunger or cold.

His mother had given him a different name, but he came to be called Subotai, a name not commonplace among the Mongols, but neither was it one of distinction or derision.

As with all Mongol boys, he early became caught up in the role of herdsman. Almost as soon as he could walk he was placed in the saddle to adapt to their herding way of existence, an existence which seemed always to have been. Although there were traditional legends and sagas of ancient days told about the campfires when the Mongols—the People—had once been hunters along the great ice, their livelihood now, as it had in living memory, always centered about their flocks and horses.

In his early boyhood he rode only culled mounts, ponies of advanced age or broken beyond other use. Then, as his skill as a steppe rider and drover grew, he earned good mounts of his own.

The horses which Subotai rode and herded and guarded, the tough ponies which made the astonishingly mobile life of the Mon-gols possible, were a swift and shaggy and durable breed evolved in the climatic extremes of the northern steppe lands. Mongol and horse had become an inseparable life-unit over the timeless nomadic cycles of life in that hostile land and barbarous time. The horses and flocks, as much as the men—Mongol, Tartar, Turk, Hun, Avar, or Kipchak—were the cause and the way of the continuous rounds of steppe warfare.

There was the danger. Grasslands and flocks, horses, women, and the austere belongings of the clans were so fiercely fought over that, over the centuries, entire nations were driven from the steppes, always to the west and to the south, by the more competitive, the more militarily capable. On any day a tribe, a clan, could be overwhelmed by a superior enemy war-band. In lost and unremembered places the steppes were littered with skeletons and molding felt rags, the unrecorded remnants of slain clans. Subotai and his clan lived in a simmering tension. Would they see a new sunset? A new sunrise?

And now in this time, as Subotai grew toward his young manhood, there was a new threat. The pasturelands which supported the nomads were beginning to disappear. Long drought and the pressures of too many flocks and herds wore away the more and more limited grazing. The steppe fighting had once been characterized by small-scale hit-and-run raids by small bands from different clans, but this had been altered by the growing demand for living space. Confederations of clans were now pitted against one another in desperate conflict over their own marginal sustenance and for the survival of their herds.

Subotai's once small clan now moved with other larger family groups and traditionally allied clans who spoke the Mongol tongue. They were oddly diverse in physical appearance, but basically homogeneous in custom and language. Some even resembled the exotic reindeer people of the cold forest, the Taiga; others were given to tallness and to fairness of hair and complexion. All were marked as masters of horsemanship, men and women alike.

But there was also, for the orphan boy, the loneliness. Outwardly, even in his boyhood, Subotai always appeared rather distant, as though permanently distracted by some inner thought of great perplexity. For the most part, his face bore the changeless, expressionless mask characteristic of the wanderers of the vast Eurasian steppes, but his eyes somehow betrayed the active mind beneath the mask.

And the glad times. During the good times, when the flocks were abundant, when the clan had dominated in the endless steppe warfare for the good grass, when there was a great feast, he seemed to break past all others in a vast and individual enjoyment. His laugh was the heartiest and the loudest, his consumption the greatest. His sheer joy in the riding and archery competitions seemed a thing of wonder to the Mongol women. Those women with the tragic

faces lined and leathered by the outdoor steppe existence of baking
and freezing and starving, of being eternally on the move to follow
the grasslands that were now decreasing and dessicating in this the
ninth decade of the twelfth century after the birth of Christ, the
strange Man-God who, the Mongols had heard, was worshipped by
remote and alien nations beyond the beginnings of the wind.

Although light hair and light eyes were not uncommon among
the Mongols at this time, they were essentially a brunette people.
Subotai's hair was black with highlights of reddishness. He kept it
shorn to a length which allowed it to fall just below the shoulder,
and secured it behind with a strip of rawhide. His eyes had the
Asiatic slant. They were blue, gray, or blue-gray, their color at a
given moment determined both by his mood and by the prevailing
conditions of light. Stocky and in good times inclined toward heaviness, his physique was swiftly becoming powerful and capable. In
the practice of the mounted military arts of the Mongols—horse-
archery with the short, powerful, double-bent saddle bow of the
nomads, and with the lance—he was among the best of his peers.
In the dismounted forms of fighting, the lightning unarmed methods used in the vicious steppe wrestling, he was quickly becoming
adept and gaining an unpolished expertise. His ability derived from
a capacity to absorb both instruction from the warrior teachers and
punishment from the older boys.

φ   φ   φ   φ

There were the lessons.

"Step over the arm, just above his elbow, Subotai. That's it—
now lean back toward his shoulder and pry up on forearm and wrist.
This is a good lock on the ground against a man who's belly-down
to the dirt, but make sure he doesn't roll under himself with a knife
in his other hand."

Subotai moved in accord with the instructor's guidance. He
covered his unsureness and boyish lack of confidence by acting with
great decision, hoping his application of the lock would appear expert
and prove effective. In consequence, he bent his opponent's arm
back somewhat farther than was really necessary in a practice lock,
forcing a yelp of pain from the bigger boy beneath him. Subotai
quickly released him.

The taller, slimmer boy got up, grimacing and rubbing his slightly strained elbow, and shoved Subotai. "You pile of pony dung!" He started an angry punch at Subotai's face, but his aim was deflected by the well-aimed kick delivered by the teacher to the center of his breeches.

"Get over with the other group, Talalkh!" Talalkh knew better than to argue about it. He slunk away with an evil sideways look at Subotai. He was about three years older than Subotai and the leader of a group of bullying older boys. Subotai did not mind the occasional harassment by Talalkh and his friends. What he found to be nearly intolerable was Talalkh's compulsive domination of any conversation. Along with being boorishly loud, Talalkh had the obnoxious trait of maintaining his egoistic blustering by filling in any lapse in his barely intelligible speech with long drawn out "ughs" to lock out the possibility of interruption to his bellowed and mindless thoughts.

Subotai had applied his ready mind and developed an appropriate set of nicknames for Talalkh and his motley followers. The humor in these names was seized upon by the teen-age youths on the threshold of becoming full-fledged warriors. Talakh had been aptly dubbed "the North Wind." His henchman, a tall, skinny, thick-haired lad with a protruding stomach and the nervous habit of clasping and reclasping his hands, was "Stuck Paws." Subotai knew it was only a matter of time before Talalkh and the others recognized the derision in these nicknames and that they would then find a way to retaliate.

Subotai's icy disregard for the Talalkh group and the originality and spirit shown in applying the nicknames generated approval among the older boys who were on the verge of becoming men. Subotai became their mascot and protégé. The senior boys took special pains to tutor him from the lofty regions of their superior experience. At this time being only about nine years of age and living alone in a dilapidated and previously abandoned bachelor yurt, Subotai found some of their confidences concerning girls and women mystifying.

φ   φ   φ   φ

And there was the shaman, thought to be the oldest man in

the entire clan. Everyone in the clan, child and adult, treated the old man with a deference motivated by a uniform fear of his much discussed powers with potions and charms and trances. It was even said that during the dark winter when the Door of the Sky was open, when the sheening and twisting lights brightened the black north, he sallied in spirit form through the portal of light and conversed with the Sky itself.

Subotai, like all the other youngsters in the little yurt society, gave the old shaman a wide berth. Sometimes he would run completely outside the encampment to avoid proximity when the old man made one of his infrequent appearances at the fires. The shaman did not even speak with the women, hardly even acknowledged their existence. The grown warriors evaded his gaze and grunted reluctant greetings only when they could not avoid the spirit-worker. His eyes, on the rare occasions when he was seen in the daylight, were slitted and unreadable. His wisps of white mustaches and long, thin beard gave him the visual aura of patriarchal power and the Asiatic elder's authority.

Subotai was walking head down, intent upon the water droplets beaded on the grease in his worn lambskin boots. Although it was already well past midday, the clear dewdrops diamonded the sunlight, still clinging to the green shoots of steppe grass as they had hours before during the early spring morning. He was also feeling the aftermath of a bloody nose and a chipped tooth he had received in a general melee with Talalkh and his friend in which he had been unable to inflict any damage and had received the bulk of the leather when the fight was broken up by two clan matriarchs wielding ten-foot herding whips. He looked up just as he collided with the still-standing form of the shaman.

Suddenly a shaft of cold force shot up Subotai's spine. He turned to run, but a long arm collared his ragged and sleeveless skin tunic, and he was dragged through the wet grass until he at last managed to scuttle his feet back up under himself. The shaman pulled the flapped covering of the yurt entrance aside and hauled Subotai in, then sent the youngster sprawling onto the felt flooring with a trip and a shove which made Subotai's shins ache from the contact with the old man's sharp bony leg.

The shaman pointed to a place by the yurt fire centered in the shelter. Subotai moved cautiously on his hands and knees to the position the old wizard had indicated, and sat in silence and trepidation.

In the past Subotai had almost frantically avoided the shaman. He could think of no earthly reason the shaman might have for dragging him into his mysterious and odorous yurt. Was the wizard going to turn him into a slimy fish or set him bucking like an unbroken stallion, crazed by those potions he had heard quietly discussed among the clan? Or something worse, something so dreadful that he could not even imagine it?

The putrifying stench of decomposing entrails and the smell of herbs and mushrooms burned by the shaman in his secret animistic rites made the interior of the yurt sickening to Subotai. His longing for clean air to breathe, the pressing odors, and his child's fear made the saliva surge in his mouth. He scuttled to the entrance and vomited outside.

The shaman seized him roughly from behind while he was in the midst of his violent regurgitation, dragged him back inside and deposited him with a thud beside the low burning fire once again.

The old wizard ignored the misery of the boy's condition and seated himself opposite Subotai with perhaps a yard separating them. They sat facing each other for a long quarter of an hour, the shaman silently appraising the forlorn youngster in front of him. Subotai's nausea rolled up again until he gagged and vomited once more, but the wizard took little notice of it.

The shaman rubbed himself briskly across the chest and spoke in a voice which was both gravelly and whispery. "Subotai, you are alone. You have no blood kin in this clan, and probably none that can be found anywhere among people within our knowing. Until you are a blooded warrior, you will be forced to live on the scraps of others. When that gift horse of yours becomes spavined what will you do?"

The boy sat unanswering. The meaning of the words would not come home on this day. Their full impact would come only later with the transition into manhood.

"I'm going to give you a gift, young man. One no man should ever be without. Long ago when I was a boy it was an initiation all warriors received from their fathers. For a soldier, it is the only beginning of knowledge. For you—and I say this to you alone—

have only one purpose in life. I have knowledge of this. I have gone with the Bogdo of Light, the Sky Traveller, beyond the top of the Iron Mountain. Your days will be spent at war; no rest or peace will be yours. You will not have herds, nor flocks which will increase, nor—for long—a woman to warm you, nor sons for your old age as shields against your enemies."

The shaman paused to sniff, then pulled several times on his nose before he continued. "Riches and lands for grazing, and women—ah, that will be your weakness—women of all ages, shapes, and shades. All these things that are now beyond your ken, you will gain for others, but you will have none of them. And the tall woman of sun-gold and ice-blue—she will belong to another as well." The elder was quiet for a long moment; then he said, "When the One Made of Good Steel is gone, when the world is shaken, when the geese come from the north to the Blue Lake, then will your end come."

At length the shaman drew up from his sitting position and knelt in a posture with his buttocks resting on the backs of his calves. He gestured for Subotai to do the same. Then he reached behind and to his left and produced in one hand a yellowish, spherical orb embossed with symbols whose secret meanings, Subotai thought, must be apparent only to the wizard. Reaching again, the old man brought out a wooden wand about three feet in length and a quarter-inch in diameter. Both of these objects were laid out in front of the shaman's right kneecap.

Slowly and with an hypnotic, sleight-of-hand movement, the shaman began rolling the ball on the floor in front of him from hand to hand. Indifferent to the passage of time, and seemingly indifferent to Subotai's presence, he sent the orb, left to right, right to left, in a continuing routine, his entire attention apparently lost in the slow, wobbly, rolling motion of the sphere.

Suddenly, with no outward cue of anger, he took up the stick and struck the boy savagely across the shoulders. Subotai recoiled from the stinging surprise of the whippy wand snapping over his lightly protected upper body. His startled look sought out the shaman's slitted eyes for some clue to the reason for the blow, but the shaman's unchanging face betrayed nothing. The wizard lapsed into his solitary game, rolling the balled totem back and forth with an unbroken, annoying, and unnerving calmness.

Subotai became conscious of a new discomforting feeling rising within himself. The closeness of the yurt and the irrational behavior of the shaman caused a latent claustrophobic emotion to emerge and grow in his young mind. The shaman was going to kill him, he was sure of it. And in some slow and fiendish manner.

The burning pain of another blow of the wand, this time bruising and welting the left side of his face, made him edge backward for flight through the yurt's flap door behind him. But the wizard took him in a clawlike grip, pinching the nerves and blood vessels of the right side of the boy's neck. The breathtaking pain immobilized the boy.

With an infuriating repetitiousness, the wizard began rolling the orb again. His interest centered on the randomly nutated patterns the embossments made as the orb wobbled across the matting on the yurt's floor. The wand flashed again, followed by another maddening silence as the totem ball passed slowly from one hand of the old man to the other.

Then Subotai's hate of the shaman flamed up, the heat of anger reddening his entire face to the color of the burning streak on his left cheek and rendering it unnoticeable. The wizard struck again, but this time the boy grabbed the bony arm and bit down on the flailing wrist like an animal, hanging on to the flesh like a stoat as the old man yelped and rained down blows on his head. The wiry and strong wizard finally dislodged the teeth and sent the boy hurtling against the felt of the yurt's inner wall. Subotai crouched, his back to the felt, defiance flaring in his gray-blue eyes. He crouched back even farther when the shaman reached into his leather lambskin-lined vest and then thrust out his right hand. The open hand offered something to him. "Take it, boy." The wizard spoke quietly, but Subotai's hackles rose in fury. The old man was firm now. "Take it, I say. Eat it."

The authority in his voice made Subotai do as he was bidden. It was a piece of hardened, sweetened fruit. The Mongol lad had never eaten anything sweet before, nor had he ever had fruit of any kind, dried or fresh. The incredibly pleasant taste of the sweet astonished him. Its goodness made his pain and anger vanish. Its rewarding effect was enhanced by the smile which now split the leathery, seamed face of the wizard.

The shaman held the door flap aside. "Remember this day. Remember the taste of a warrior's defiance." He spoke impatiently now. "Go on. You know all you will ever need to know."

The yurt's entrance flap fell closed behind the lad as the shaman shoved him rudely into the brightness of the afternoon.

φ   φ   φ   φ

And there was the splendor of the steppe summers, and the days when the Mongol boy was a glad solitary spirit. Choosing to be alone when he could, he accepted the herdsman's task on the most remote grazing grounds. The herds and flocks were often quiescent during the warm breezy days, the infinite Sky always there. Clouds were pinkly golden with the dawn, white like the clean snow of winter in the midst of the days, then golden, amber, and pink again with the sunset. The beauty of the Sky would sometimes dispell even the need for his cautious watchfulness against enemies, man or wolf. But that awareness of potential danger never left him for long.

He noticed and wondered about the diminishing of those clouds during the drought that lasted longer each year, but he always welcomed the sudden rain showers which would occasionally break above him, flashing lightning and great bursting cracks of thunder around him. Then the storms would pass on like torrential moving mushrooms of cloud, downpour, and electricity, renovating the steppes as they slowly drifted across the land, leaving the Mongol lad sodden, cold, and refreshed.

On pleasantly warm afternoons he would tie his pony's reins to his leg and lie on his back to soak in the blue and white hemisphere of the Sky, the sun and the season a brief blessing before the heat became a searing curse to men, flocks, and grasslands. His heart was filled with an inner joyful gladness in these times.

Cooling autumn would envelope the steppes, great flights of water birds reaching almost from horizon to horizon were bound south from unknown northern places. A grimness would pervade the clan, rooted in the stark knowledge of the hardness of the inevitable winter to come: hunger, and the hopelessness of their condition, the turning remorselessness of nature.

In gray and bitter winter, the meagerness of the flocks demanded of the clan a fearful self-control, balancing present starvation against the future of the livestock and the maintenance of a critical breeding mass of the herds and flocks. For mortal danger could come from within the clan, from any desperate slaughter of the breeding stock essential for the herd's regeneration. The Mongol shamans—and Subotai—looked to the Sky for strength and relief.

Then came hopeful and blessed spring, the birth of the spring kids and lambs, and the foaling of the mares. Subotai sensed green patching on the land even before all the snow was gone under the heightening sunlight. Finally the short summer returned.

And so did Subotai's boyhood slip by with a slow grace, it seemed to him, in spite of the hunger and hardness, into the first unexplainable restlessness of adolescence he would feel when the big white-gray moon hung over the vast steppes.

φ   φ   φ   φ

During the past two years the congregating of the Mongol clans had brought more and more unfamiliar people into the loosely organized, traveling society. Subotai, although only about sixteen years old, was often on one of the mounted patrols which the Mongols kept circuiting as far out as a fast day's ride to detect and raise the alarm against raiding parties of other tribes. The older warriors often chose him because of the quiet competence he showed in his developing years and the reliableness of his character. And for his willingness to take the risks involved on the long, lonely patrols—risks of attack and death, or worse, capture and torture.

He had just returned from one of these patrols, having been finally located and relieved by two other tribesmen after four days in the open steppe. It was late summer—Subotai always remembered the quiet warmth and the perfection of that evening. He had stopped at the edge of a small reedy pond, a rarity on this part of the range, just beyond the main Mongol encampment. He let his pony dip its muzzle for a short drink, and slipped off the back of the animal and knelt for a drink from his cupped hands to assuage his two-day-old thirst.

When he stood up, taking in the balmy air, his habitually scanning gaze fell on the woman—a maturing teenage girl really—

who was standing quietly on the opposite shore of the pond. He was looking into the clearest blue eyes he had ever seen. He knew at once that she must have come into the camp since his departure for his roving guard mount. Then he was struck and overcome by the perfection and the blonde, patrician beauty of the young woman. Her lightly tanned complexion was completely unblemished and sweetly fresh, and her straight and generous smile radiated a magnetism which dazzled the young man. Her gloriously golden hair, unstreaked with any shading of other color, was parted in the middle of her lovely head. The long, light yellow braids had been bunned up on either side of her face and caught by small silver combs and hair clasps. He had never seen a person of such blondeness before in his life, nor a woman with such an overpowering loveliness and presence. He thought she must be taller than he, perhaps a whole hand taller. She was the first woman or girl he had ever seen in a dress. She was wearing an ankle-length gown of coarsely woven wool dyed a dark blue color. It showed the curving outlines of her superbly healthy body and a womanly figure of extraordinary beauty. The nobility of her face and bearing drew the breath from Subotai and froze him to the place where he stood.

In the sure knowledge of all truly beautiful women, she smiled again, not so much at the young man as at her effect on him, before she turned and walked back toward the cluster of yurts and carts on the encampment. He stood unmoving in his silent way until she passed out of his view within the Mongol camp.

The sight of her had somehow dissolved the bone-deep weariness of his long watch on the steppe. Dissolved, too, his relationship with space and time until his tired, hungry, and impatient pony nipped his elbow sharply, allowing some reassertion of reality to creep into the young Mongol's head. His mind filled with a swirl of questions. Where had she come from? And her name—surely she must have a name? And then his first torment: Could she be?...He tried to stifle the thought...She must not be, and he gritted his teeth, she could not be married. He willed her not to be married.

He led the horse some distance away from the little lake, rope-hobbled it, and let it out to pasture. With his saddle, coat, bow and quiver loading his shoulders and arms, he hiked back toward the yurts. Inside his solitary, dilapidated shelter he threw down his gear, stared blindly for a moment, and then turned and went back out, ignoring his lynx fur pallet-bed and the sleep he had yearned for in the saddle those long nights on watch.

As usual there were several large outdoor cooking fires burning in various locations about the camp. He sought out the one tended by the older widowed women, the one where he always got the choicest cut from the spitted goat or mutton roasting over the flames. And the camp gossip was always available there. He would have to remember to give the women a sheep or two from the small flock he had built up over the years from his hard-earned recompense as a herdsman.

"Ah, Subotai." The old woman smiled, showing her only tooth. Her skin was hardly distinguishable from the leather of her coat and riding breeches. "Talalkh said you were gone on watch in the steppes." She patted his arm, reached for his belt knife, and sliced a well-done slab of goat meat from the animal carcass that was being turned over the blaze. "Watch out for that Talalkh. He is jealous of you because you are the one the warriors treat like a man." Impervious to the hot fat on her hands, she jabbed the blade through the meat and handed the knife to Subotai.

His hunger had gone dormant at the sight of the blue-eyed girl, but the hot meat in his mouth reawakened his appetite. He finished the meat and started on another slab before he spoke. "There seem to be more strangers with us now. Have you seen the tall girl with hair the color of dry grass?"

The old woman moved to take her turn rotating the spit. She flashed her gummy grin again. "Caught your eye already, has she? That one will cost plenty. Her father will grow wealthy with her bride-price." She closed her eyes against a shift of smoke toward her, waited for it to blow another way, then spoke again. "You would need all the flocks of the Tartars to buy her. Best you look elsewhere, Subotai."

The old woman wiped her watering eyes. "Her father is the noyon of their clan." She gestured toward the southeast. "Most of her clan have their yurts in that direction to keep their flocks from mingling with ours. They call her Mursechen—Lovely Wisdom." The old woman was sarcastic now. "Wisdom indeed!" Then looking intently at Subotai, she said, "Don't set your hopes on that one.

You are to serve the Good Steel and the Sky. You will never have enough stock to trade for a woman like that." Her look was knowing as she spoke.

Subotai started at her words, but he knew the old crone was the only woman, indeed one of the few of either sex, who associated with the shaman. He jammed the last morsel of the meat into his mouth and strode away from the fire pit without speaking. Since the painful day with the shaman years before, he had wondered at the import of the words "Good Steel" which the shaman had spoken. Fatigue and the hot meat in his belly at last overtook him. He went back to his ragged yurt and, feeling for the pallet in the darkness, threw off his boots and fell asleep.

The gentle ruffling of the siding of the yurt in the wind awakened him at first light. He stepped out into the morning as in the eastern Sky a wide flare of scarleted gold announced the coming of the sun.

φ   φ   φ   φ

It took him some time to locate the shaman's yurt, for the banding together of the Mongols had steadily increased congestion in the camp. He stopped outside the yurt and pondered exactly how to attract the elder's attention. Finally he threw aside the entrance flap and looked into the tent. He saw the huddled form of the wizard almost straight across from the doorway of the circular shelter, seemingly asleep there.

With the boldness of youth Subotai entered, walked straight to the prone form, and shook the bony body. But the old felt quilt was cold to the touch and the shaman did not stir. Nor would he ever. It took Subotai a long moment to realize the wizard was dead. He should have known at once, since the fire was also dead and cold. And Subotai, who came seeking the meaning of the shaman's words to him, now knew the wizard had taken their cryptic significance to the grave with him. The old woman who had spoken to him was, he knew, only mouthing fragments of what she had overheard from the shaman years before: "Good Steel."

The death of the shaman was received in the camp as an event of ominous consequence. There was no successor to assume the mantle of spiritual leadership. And the old women, grave in their barbarian superstition, foresaw an evil future for flocks and events, a future soon manifested in burgeoning disputes between the uniting clans over pasture and grazing.

Councils around the evening fires became a nightly occurrence. The councils were as much a search for leadership as a forum for venting the creeping anxiety about the pasture space for flocks and herds the clans were now constantly quarreling over. There had never been an over-khan, a Kha Khan, for any assemblage of Mongol clans. The councils were attended by all the clans' warriors, each body of men from a given clan headed by an elected noyon with the rank of clanate khan. Strategy was thus developed in a representative and democratic context.

And it was in this way that a major group of the Mongol nation began planning and preparations for moving onto the superior grasslands occupied by the Kurait nomads and some of the easternmost Tartars. The decision was not taken lightly. They had warred with the Kuraits and Tartars before, and only the younger hotheads among the inexperienced warriors spoke open disregard for the risks involved.

Subotai sat at the evening councils with the rest of the unblooded young men. At the meeting fire, the nearness of each concentric ring of men to the flaming dung and peat blaze was prescribed by status. Noyons and distinguished warriors occupied the innermost circle and were the only ones to speak. Behind them sat the younger and less noted warriors, age and rank decreasing as the circles spread outward. The peers of Subotai, young men of no status, made up the outermost ring.

In fact, there was little choice. The Kuraits had good grazing land which the Mongols required. The question of hereditary rights was ignored. With the existing pasturelands becoming more and more marginal with each passing year, a rapid and violent process of natural selection would have to transpire, leaving either the Mongols or the Kuraits in possession of the coveted grazing lands.

A series of raids against the western areas of the Kurait domain was proposed. The plan was that the raids would draw the bulk of the Kurait clans to the west, lessening resistance when the Mongols moved west with their yurts and livestock onto the Kurait's eastern grass.

They would strike before the chill of autumn, giving the Kuraits the dark winter months in which to assess the raids and—the council hoped—mount a mass move to the west to guard against their recurrence when the warmer months returned.

The strategy and its assumed outcomes were simple. But by the time all the more seasoned and reasonable warriors had spoken each man knew that even if the strategy succeeded, they would have traded grass for a ferocious rekindling of the long-dormant but generations-old blood feuds with the Kuraits and the Tartars.

φ   φ   φ   φ

He must get control of and focus his mind where it belonged, Subotai thought.

He had volunteered to scout the Kurait camp's readiness and defenses. It took all of his willpower to keep from shivering in the autumn night after he had crawled through the ice-cold, shallow stream bordering one side of the Kurait lodges. He had to grit his jaws and hold his face in a rigid grimace to stay the chattering of his teeth. The unromantic indoctrination on Kurait torture of captives given him by the more seasoned Mongol warriors reinforced his self-control.

Still he let his imagination drift back to thoughts of the beautiful Mursechen. Since the evening he had seen her by the pond, he had thought of little but the lovely blonde girl. He had glimpsed her from a distance on several occasions, but the preparations for the forthcoming raids soon demanded most of his time and energy along with that of the other able-bodied men. When, at the last moment, he was called out to accompany one of the warrior bands on the very morning of the campaigners' leaving, he had been set in an emotional quandary, the desire to remain in camp near the golden-haired girl warring with his powerful cultural yearning to be given at last the opportunity to advance to manhood as an accepted warrior. He had had no choice but to leave with the other warriors, praying that he would return to capture the affections and somehow find the bride-price of the lovely Mursechen.

A mole slithering through the dark grass made him jerk with alarm. One of the Kurait camp dogs trotted to the edge of the sleeping tents and set up a yammering bark. The breeze held into Subotai's face, and the cur, losing interest in the night scents that came to its nose, returned to the embers of a fire and, settling its nose within its paws, fell back into its fitful dozing.

Subotai remained motionless in the dewing grass until he was certain nothing moved in the darkened tents. Then he retraced his wet route through the shallow water, slithering backward in slow motion without a splash.

Subotai could not make out their features in the darkness, but he felt the skepticism in the older warriors when he related his findings to the huddled group of men.

"You're sure? No sentries at all?" The warrior leader spoke in a near whisper. "We heard the dog. Did it find you?"

"No."

"All right. Just before first light."

Then all the muted talk ended. Only the quiet shuffle of a pony's hoof and the mild breeze disturbed the night.

In the black and cold waiting time, Subotai searched himself for his fear. But he found none. He was even a trifle dismayed that after his period of introspection he was more discomforted by his wet clothing than by the tensions of the slow-moving night before the raid. He seemed to have slipped into a mental state where the fear of death was something he sensed only as might a distant spectator. Yet he knew that with the coming of daylight his world would be filled with death.

There were almost toxic, cold sweats on the faces of some of the Mongol warriors from the waiting when several youths of Subotai's age slipped away through the stream toward the picketing stakes where the Kuraits kept their animals tied. Unless the raiders could achieve control of, or at least scatter the enemy horses, the Mongols would be plunging into a self-made trap from which there would be little or no chance of extrication or even survival. If the horse-pickets were guarded, if there was an alarm, the Mongol raiders would face failure and probable annihilation. But the attack had to begin before the main Mongol force could know if the Kuraits' mounts had been successfully led away or if the raiding party had been discovered just at the critical moment when they were committed to the attack.

Then, with the east to their backs, the Mongol skirmish line galloped into the unstirring Kurait camp. The air filled with the notes of Mongol bowstrings as Mongol shafts raced through the early morning light to cut down emerging figures still slow with sleep and dazed with shock. Time and motion seemed to take on a curious clarity and a slowed distinctiveness for Subotai. He saw some of the Kurait yurts already in flames, and Kurait women running and splashing across the stream to escape the violence of the Mongol attack.

Subotai was wheeling his mount about when he heard the bloodcurdling battle scream of the Kurait warrior and saw the man brandish a magnificent sword as he sprang to launch himself bodily, knocking Subotai out of the saddle across his animal's withers onto the ground. But even the surprise and the impact of the fall had not loosened Subotai's grasp on his bow. Stunned for the barest moment, he sprang to his feet, then rolled under the savage horizontal sweep of the Kurait's mighty sword and twisted to loose a shaft at his attacker.

The Kurait did not attempt to strike again. Other Mongol riders, seeing that Subotai was afoot, loosed their shafts at his attacker. The Kurait suddenly stood erect as half a dozen arrows seemed to sprout from his neck and arms with a single sound of impact. The Kurait reeled backwards like a man losing his balance, then fell into the naked, ribbed siding of a blazing yurt.

Without a second's thought, Subotai leaped into the flames after the dying Kurait, mesmerized by that spectacular sword. As the Kurait's eyes rolled upward in glazed finality, his death-tightening grasp relaxed enough for Subotai to jerk the weapon from his hands. Clutching his prize and shielding his stinging eyes, Subotai lurched out of the thick and foul smoke of burning felt. He ran to find some clean air, dizzy now and almost down from smoke inhalation. Gasping, he fell on all fours and heaved in the freshness outside the periphery of the Kurait camp, while the rest of the Mongol war band quickly looted and set fire to the remaining yurts.

With his eyes burning but his lungs beginning to clear, Subotai got up and, half-jogging, half-galloping, managed to seize the rein of his frightened horse. The animal had been running in lunatic circles around the fire and confusion of the raid. Subotai regained control of it and struggled into the saddle again, still clutching the beautiful sword, and followed after the last whooping Mongol stragglers who were now riding like demons to overtake the rest of the retreating Mongol raiders. They could not afford to tarry in Kurait territory however rich the booty, for vengeance was swift on the steppes. The smoke would bring enemy riders as quickly as horseflesh could carry them.

They rode on, first toward the south, then swinging westerly for some hours. They had driven their horses to the narrow edge of tottering fatigue throughout the day and into the night before they came upon the first of the fresh mounts left in carefully chosen locations along their long retreat route. They rested briefly in the middle hours of the nights, then pressed on toward the safety of the Mongol zone, the blinding sunrise of each morning holding them to the eastward course they had assumed after their evasive ride to the south and west.

It was during a short watering stop at midmorning on the day of the raid that Subotai had had his first opportunity to examine at close hand and in a good light the great sword he had won from the Kurait. First he hefted it. The grip was sized for a two-handed grasp, the ornate handle set with elaborately carved ivory. It slid into his hands as if it belonged there. The marvelous balance of the weapon made it handle lightly for all its length and power. Just to balance it in his two hands gave Subotai an intoxicating sense of power, akin to the vibrant feeling he got when lightning struck nearby.

Next Subotai turned his attention to the carvings of reindeer and walruses which stood out in relief from the ivory hilt. The walruses were animals as mysterious to the Mongol as they had been to the Yakut elder who had carved them. Subotai appreciated the cunning artistry that had carved the figures to run from the butt to the circular handguard so that they offset the slipperiness of the material and gave human hands a firm grip.

But it was the steel itself that drew his interest like a magnet, seeming to absorb his very being so that he and that blade became, in some mystical way, one. The long, slightly upcurving blade was dark blue streaked with beautifully jagged gray tones in the metal. Subotai would never know the origin of the superb weapon, or its religious crafting by a superb metalsmith and artisan in the Rain Islands hundreds of years before. Nor could he know how the steel had been forged and doubled upon itself time and again until the metallic sandwiching had given it an almost unbreakable temper and the capacity to take an edge of amazing keenness. But his hand rubbing along the blade could sense the harmony of the carbon and iron atoms in its beautiful inner crystals vibrating as part of him, imparting a sense of tremendous power. With the sword in hand he felt as he thought he would feel if he had Mursechen by his side as his—dare he think it?—his wife.

The power stayed with him when he sheathed his treasure and hung it on his saddle. The weariness that had overtaken the war party left him. Anticipation of their arrival at the great circle of Mongol yurts surged through him, fed by memories of the admiration accorded the warriors as they rode back to their people in their proud, almost unseeing manner after a successful raid. Visions of Mursechen's eyes on him with the great sword at his side filled his mind. Somehow, the blue sword promised fulfillment of every impossible dream. He glanced up at the sun, now low in the sky; surely before sundown they would come to the Mongol camp.

Then the tormenting doubt crept into his mind. Mongol clans and families came and went as they chose—would she be there? It troubled him that every pleasant thought he had of Mursechen was balanced by an agonizing one.

They slowed their mounts now, walking them for longer and longer intervals, though a Mongol never dismounted when he walked his animal. Then, with the sun a bloodlike ball just tangent to the horizon behind them, they saw the smoke of the Mongol camp and the yurts, tiny in the distance. It was still light when the first riders from the camp circled them, calling names, yelping their pleasure at the return of the war band. The women waited on foot at the edge of the yurts and fires, waving and smiling as they held up spitted hunks of hot mutton and goat meat and cups of mare's milk for the warriors.

Subotai looked for Mursechen's tall, golden presence among the Mongol girls. He even dropped the haughty, head-up posture the returning warriors had assumed upon their homecoming in order to search the throng, but she was nowhere to be seen.

He got down just inside the line of tents. Long habit and the law of nomadic survival made him look to his mount first. He pulled off the saddle, slipped the bridle, and sent the beast off to pasture with a peremptory slap on the rump.

"So the mighty warrior is returned at last."

It was Talalkh, looking somewhat less smirky and overbearing than usual. Subotai made no secret of his dislike for the taller, raw-boned, and dark-haired youth. They had fought on several occasions while growing up together. Talalkh had always won when they were younger, but in the years of transition into their early manhood, Subotai had come to dominate because of his maturing mastery of combat wrestling, the great strength of his arms compounding his science in the bone-twisting, Yawara-like techniques.

"You look as though someone hamstrung your horse, Talalkh."

The tall youth looked at Subotai, a slyness mixed with his downcast attitude. "You've been away, Subotai the Stout. You haven't heard. Mursechen has been given in marriage by her father to a foreign noyon. From some tribe we'd never even known until they rode up one afternoon with a herd of the finest horses that ever were. Their noyon swapped the entire herd for her almost as soon as he laid eyes on her. Threw in a great weight of silver to boot."

Subotai almost buckled. Talalkh and the noisy knots of people around the yurts and fires suddenly seemed at a great distance across the steppe. He couldn't hear their voices for the hot swelling of blood in his head.

Like words spoken faintly from afar, Talalkh's question reached his mind. "You didn't think you were the only one sweating under your lambskins for her, did you?" Subotai didn't want to believe what he had just heard, but Talalkh continued. "They left about half the time of a moon ago."

"Who is he?" Subotai's voice was husky. "Who are they? Where is their pastureland?"

"Kipchaks." Talalkh was enjoying this. "They told us by sign language where they had come from, so far it sounded like the last shadow of the Sky in the west. She belongs to one called Kotyan, a noyon. Why don't you track them down? There are only about thirty of them." And Talalkh, his own sharp disappointment blunted by Subotai's bitter reaction, strode away.

Subotai had never known such a quandary. It was as though the coming of Mursechen had split his life in two. Now and what had gone before were of no importance—only a future with her had meaning for him now. He had no experience that would help him deal with this feeling, no knowledge of what his options were, or even if he had any. He knew only that he could not, would not, face the thought of never seeing Mursechen again.

Subotai spent a miserable night forming and discarding wild schemes. Finally, with his hand on the blue sword, he began to take stock of his situation realistically. Of the old women to whom he felt an obligation because they had fed him and given him cast-off leather and wool garments while he was growing up, only two were still alive. His psychological makeup allowed him little or no emotional linkages with men; what he felt for most of them was essentially tolerance. So he was little bound to his people by emotional ties. As for companionship, he cared nothing for the drinking and carousing that was the social life of his peers. His unquestioned ability with the bow and saber and in unarmed combat had permitted him to maintain his loneness and his distant attitude, and he preferred it so.

Then there was the matter of his future status. Only moments after Talalkh had barbed him with the knowledge of Mursechen's departure, the master of the leading warrior yurt, the Snow Arrows, had announced that he was commending Subotai for investiture into the warrior order. It was the goal longed for by all young Mongol men. If he should leave his own clan, he well knew how slight his chances were of ever being even accepted into any other, much less of achieving any kind of status. But did even that matter now? Subotai found nothing in his situation that could overcome his yearning for Mursechen, nothing to hold him from following her.

Casting aside the old sheep-and-horseskin quilt before daybreak, he drew on his boots, fueled the glowing embers of the yurt-fire for light to see by, and began assembling his scant belongings. The blue sword seemed to urge him on as he slung it over his shoulder. With his quiver over his other shoulder, he took his light nomad saddle in one hand, his bow in the other, and walked to the horse enclosure. The drowsy guards only grunted in their sleepiness as he walked by them. Just like those unwatching Kuraits, Subotai thought.

He heaved the saddle onto his pony's back and looped the quiver

and bow in its skin sheath over the pommel, then skillfully secured
the girth. He spun with the blue sword in hand at the sound of
booted feet on the brittleness of the late autumn grass. Even in the
dark, he recognized Talalkh.

"You should stay here with the People, Subotai."

Subotai was taken aback by words so softly spoken by Talalkh.

"Let her go. What could you do even if you could find the
Kipchaks out there? They'll butcher you if you catch up with them,
there are too many of them."

Subotai completed his saddle adjustments and then said with
more youthful bravado than confidence, "When I find them, then
I'll know what to do."

"Subotai, you didn't know her, but the rest of us did. She
asked us about you when you left with the warriors. But she thought
it strange when we told her you rarely seemed to speak." Talalkh
paused. He seemed about to say more but apparently thought better
of it.

Subotai said nothing. He unlooped his stirrups and let them
fall on either side of the pony. Talalkh put his hand on Subotai's
shoulder and said, "Someday... I don't know why I am saying this,
but I feel that someday the People will have need of you. Stay..."

Subotai had never thought he would see the day, but he offered
his hand to Talalkh. They shook long and firmly, Talalkh reluctant
to release Subotai's strong, square hand.

φ   φ   φ   φ

The forcing wind grew in its gusting power. Icy sleet in broken
sheets drenched and abraded man and horse. The hardy steppe pony
doggedly moved on into the storm in the gathering darkness.

Subotai had tied down the earflaps of his furred hat, and he
hunched into his heavy sheepskin-and-felt coat embossed with the
stiff, lacquered leather plating which passed for armor on the primitive steppes. He lowered his head against the fiendish wind and
sleet. Before the onset of the storm he had been generally following
a west-by-southwesterly course, but now he had no way of deter-
mining in which direction he was headed. In the storm-darkness
which shaded what little remained of the day, he strained for the
sight of any break in the terrain or even a scrub tree which might

serve as shelter. The increasing cold would bring a blizzard and the fresh, clean snow from the sky. But better to not be frozen to death and miss the beauty of the glistening, snowy steppe when the sun reasserted itself.

Night settled swiftly upon the storm, and Subotai was beginning to shiver in the driving sleet when there, half an arrow's flight away, was the dim outline of a traveling yurt mounted on a wooden cart bed. No draft oxen were visible which could have brought this seeming apparition to this place, although Subotai could make out four saddle horses hobbled and tied to the downwind side of the cart-yurt.

The Mongol rode closer. From the trappings on the horses' bridles and the jagged blue trim of wavy diagonals on the central circumference of the yurt, he surmised it belonged to the Yakka clan of the Mongol nation, a clan not noted for its conviviality or willingness to coexist with other steppe peoples, not even other Mongols.

He drew the curved, two-handed sword from its soft leather scabbard, dismounted beside the tied horses, and secured the reins of his own mount to the cart bed. Cautiously, he walked to the entranceway of the yurt. Its felt door covering was untied and flapping crazily in the peaking wind gusts. There was light within, and even from where he stood he could feel the inviting heat from the yurt.

He shouted a greeting in Mongol and stepped quickly back into the wind and to the blind side of the yurt entrance. Nothing. He moved farther out to where anyone emerging from the tent could see him, called again, and held his breath. Still no response of any kind.

His choice was clear. He could risk turning back into the storm that was now reaching lethal ferocity. Or he could hope the yurt-dwellers, whoever they might be, would greet a stranger with questions instead of a quick death.

He waited in the wet wind until his intuition, seeming to transcend his waking consciousness, gave him an unmistakable impulse. With that he slipped a rawhide loop over the butt of the sword and hung it over his neck and shoulder, blade dangling over his back in a clear indication of peaceful intent. Feeling naked and vulnerable, he pushed aside the felt curtain and entered the shelter.

The heat within was a pleasant bath, laving over the being and the cold-teared eyes of the Mongol youth. It took him some moments to adjust to the surroundings and to the warmth, questioning all the while the wisdom of moving into this completely unknown situation without his weapon at the ready.

"Sit and eat this."

It was a woman's voice. A woman nearly as striking as the blonde girl of his fixation, but dark and slightly shorter than he. She was dressed in leather riding trousers and a sheepskin vest over a colorful underblouse of Chinese origin.

Her hair was long and deeply black and braided on both sides of her beautifully symmetrical face. Her pinkish-brown complexion seemed to have a glow, and her eyes were like a steppe wolf's— brown, basically, but from the center of each iris startling streaks of gold-amber radiated.

She spoke again. "I am Bourtai, and this is my lord, Temajin."

Subotai's eyes leapt to the tall man who now stood up on the opposite side of the yurt. He dared not relax his concentration for even a second in order to remember what it was the shaman had said, but "temajin" was the word for *good steel*. He looked up into the man's green eyes, almost a head above his own, then at his face. He saw a handsome, almost Grecian-classical face surrounded by thick and long light brown hair braided almost exactly as the woman's on each side of his head. Stripped to the waist in the heat of the yurt, the man's upper body showed wide-shouldered, sinuously muscled, and flat-bellied.

"I am Subotai of the Alynquar Mongols," he announced in a voice as calm as he could make it.

"You are out on a bad night," the man said conversationally. He appeared to be some years older than Subotai, possibly as many as ten or twelve years older. "As my wife has just invited you, please sit and eat. Not very good mutton but hot, and enough for a night such as this, don't you think?"

Subotai nodded in agreement. As a symbolic gesture of his appreciation for the couple's hospitality, a hospitality he knew had in all likelihood saved him from a freezing death on the open steppe, he slipped the sword loop from across his thick neck and heavy shoulder and set the weapon next to the entrance with the blade's edge toward the wall of the yurt. He also slipped out of his soaked coat and laid it beside him along with his fur hat.

The young woman beckoned for him to come to the dung-fueled, iron cooking brazier. When he was seated on the rugged felt in the warm glow of the brazier, she handed him a chunk of hot mutton impaled on a hardwood stick. As he began to devour the fatty mutton ravenously, the woman, Bourtai, set a stone cup of clear drink beside his knee and then moved graciously and gracefully to her husband's side and sat down next to the green-eyed man.

The youth took a cautious sip from the cup, tasting for the bitterness of a drug or a poison. It tasted strange, but he could detect nothing suspicious in the pleasant taste. A liquor of some kind—the Sky knew the great weakness of the lonely and beset peoples of the hostile steppes—and it was good of them to offer it.

"Rice wine." It was the man who spoke, seeming to understand and be amused by the young man's confusion of conflicting suspicion and gratitude. "It comes from the country of the Chin emperors below the Great Wall. Aside from making you drunk if you take too much, it will not harm you."

"What is rice?" Subotai asked with characteristic bluntness.

"It's a crop the Chin grow in water ponds," his tall host answered.

Since Subotai had no idea what a crop might be, or how the word related to growth, he did not pursue the subject.

"Have you ever seen the Great Wall?"

"No, but I have heard many speak of it," Subotai answered.

Temajin was quiet for a moment, then he laughed softly, as though to himself. "The Chin think that because their wall cannot be broken or climbed, it cannot be breached in other ways—or ridden by."

Subotai finished his mutton and was warmly aglow with the effects of the rice wine, but his suspicion that poison or a sleeping potion might have been included in his cup had not entirely left him. But when Bourtai refilled his cup from a leather water pouch heavy with the inviting liquid, he drank again, taking too large a swallow, so that the wine burned a cough from him. In the relaxing warmth of the yurt, his stomach full for the first time in several days, the rice wine worked its soporific magic on him. He struggled somewhat weakly to remain awake, but the long days in the saddle and the food and drink in the luxurious heat overcame him. The wolf-eyed woman covered him with a lambskin quilt as he fell innocently and unceremoniously asleep on the floor of the cart-yurt.

For a long while the man and the woman sat together, she huddled in the man's long, muscular arms, watching the younger man in his deep sleep.

"Do you know him, Temajin?"

"I remember him from before."

And that was all that was said.

When Subotai awoke he was surprised to find the wife of Temajin talking and laughing in low tones with a healthy young boy. The boy had been asleep when Subotai arrived, and the Mongol had not been aware that there was a child in the yurt.

"This is our son, Juchi," she said. "He is nearly ten seasons now."

Subotai could see that Juchi strongly favored his handsome mother, but seemed destined also to have his father's tall frame.

Outside, the blizzard was a full, gale-blown, swirling demon blotting out the world around the little islet of life and warmth within the cart-yurt. Bourtai roasted more mutton for the morning meal. By this time Subotai's wariness and fear had faded.

When they had finished eating, Temajin and Subotai went outside the shelter to see to the horses, which were nonchalantly poking their noses through the accumulation of snow in search of any grazing that might be had within the arcs permitted by their rope-ties.

After shifting the rope-ties to give the horses new pasture ground, the two men returned to the yurt and spent the snowy day in talk. More accurately, Subotai, Bourtai, and the young boy Juchi spent the day listening to Temajin. The woman seemed mildly shocked that he could discourse so, and interrupted on several occasions during the day to announce that she had never heard him speak so much. Temajin, she assured Subotai, was usually a silent man.

Sitting or reclining in turn about the warm brazier, the youth and the boy listened raptly as Temajin recounted adventures of his boyhood and his youth. Subotai had never heard such a stirring and heroic telling before, although his host spoke in relatively unspectacular terms and frequently made himself appear as the object of some ridicule or the unwitting victim of a humorous circumstance.

"My father was Yesakai, a noyon of the Yakka clan," Temajin began. "We treated with the Tartars when I was a boy. They are a short, dark people with eyes like those of the yellow Chin to the south of us. I well remember that night when my father returned from a feasting with them. He complained of a great burning in his belly, and died before the night was out. It is well known that the Tartars are adept in the use of the most subtle poisons, and I have no doubt that they fed one of their vile potions to Yesakai.

"As I was not yet a grown man, our kinsman, Turgatai, seized the opportunity presented by my father's death to take the leadership of the clan. I remember my mother riding after the yurts when the clan deserted us to go over to Turgatai, but she could not persuade any to remain with us."

Temajin drank frequently from the skin with its rice wine contents. He offered it several times to Subotai, but Subotai declined.

"You are wise to abstain, Subotai. We drink too much as a people." With a smile, Temajin pulled from the skin again and then said, "But who can keep from getting drunk sometimes?"

The tall man wiped his mouth with the back of his hand and continued, "Rice wine is better than our sour milk. Perhaps if Bourtai heated the wine, you would drink? No? We have another skinful of it outside on the cart. It never freezes, no matter how cold it gets."

Temajin seemed grave now. "After we had been left alone on the steppes with only our horses and our yurt and with so many mouths to feed—there were seven of us: my mother; my three brothers; and the two sons of my mother, my half-brothers—we lived on what we could find. Mostly rabbits and ground squirrels." He laughed. "I remember once my brother lay beside a squirrel burrow for most of the day waiting for it to poke its head above ground, and when it finally did, he was so startled that the squirrel ran one way and he ran the other."

Temajin's somber mood had suddenly turned lighter. "Sometimes we even ate fish when we could catch them." Subotai was thunderstruck. He had never heard of Mongols eating fish. They were considered corrupt and unclean, no matter how freshly caught they might be.

"Does that surprise you, Subotai? It is one thing to make do on a mouthful or two of mutton in the winter and another to starve completely." But Temajin's pleasant humor held, and he seemed to have borne with him no bitterness from the bleak experience.

"I was fast asleep in the yurt when Targatai and his men came for me. All the others had gone to the river to fish and hunt." Temajin leaned back against the yurt wall and crossed one of his long legs over the other. "As I have since learned, Targatai had to be rid of me because the grumblings over his leadership were growing loud, and even leading to outspoken sentiment for returning to the fold under my mother until I was a man grown. But I didn't know that then. I did know that Targatai and his riders had come to kill me. They collared me and locked my arms in a kang. And—remember I told you about Mongols and drink—they had brought several skins of fermented mare's milk for celebration if they caught me, or, I would suppose, consolation if I had happened to elude them."

The mention of the kang, the heavy, wooden yoke, told Subotai just how hopeless Temajin's situation had been. It also lit Subotai's memory. Of course, he thought, I have heard the story of the outlaw prince of the Yakka clan told around the campfires for years.

The green eyes had a glint of hidden mirth. "By nightfall they were all roaring drunk. The wood bars which locked the kang in place were behind my neck, and my hands were tightly lashed. But the mare's milk had lured them off before anyone had thought to hobble my legs, so when I saw that enough of them were sprawled out or lurching around the fire, I took my chance. It seemed that I ran for most of the night. Just before daybreak I ran right over the edge of a steep hillside and fell and rolled into some brushy cover, where I hid."

Bourtai handed cold, dried, milk curds to the men and to Juchi. Subotai saw the mothering fondness in her eyes when she hugged and caressed the youngster. The sight of it gave him an aching behind his eyes and in his heart.

Temajin's straight teeth showed white against his weather-seasoned complexion as he bit into the hard curds. He went on, speaking through the food in his mouth. "They scoured the brush for most of the morning. I could hear their horses stirring the growth, and their shouts. I knew that several of them had seen me.

"The worst part of it by then was the worry over my mother and my brothers. I had given up hope for myself and was sweating for their safety." Temajin took another milk curd from Bourtai before he continued, biting into it as though speaking through the food made the memories easier. "Finally, after nightfall, after Targatai and his warriors had given up the search, one of his men came back and slipped the holding bars out of the kang. Together, after Targatai and his band were gone, he and I found my mother and the others hiding not far from our yurt, which Targatai had neglected to burn.

After that my brothers, my mother, and I went to the wooded lands near the Iron Mountain to hide. Targatai made several forays to capture or kill me in the years after I escaped from the kang. Thanks to the Sky and his own drunken ineptitude, he failed. Salgan-Sheer was the warrior who set me free from the kang. Some moons after we had gone into hiding in the forest, Salgan and several other younger men sought me out and swore to me as their noyon. Since then more yurts than I can count have joined us."

Subotai did not think to ask Temajin why he was isolated here in the only yurt within the distance of several days' flight of a hunting eagle.

"But, for all the yurts which now follow me, this is my real treasure, my Bourtai." Temajin drew the handsome young woman into his sheltering arm. "And my son. I almost lost them both once."

Bourtai put her hand to Temajin's lips. "Please do not speak of it, Temajin. It is all past now."

But the tall noyon put her hand aside and spoke anyway. "She was just swelling with the first signs of my son. I was away at the time, making a summer game drive to load the meat-drying racks before winter."

Just then Juchi came into the yurt from his solitary playing in the blowing snow. His clothes were wet through, but in the incredible hardihood of the nomads, he was neither harmed nor distressed, not even by the icy snow packed between the toes of his bare feet. Bourtai stood the boy near the warmth of the brazier, stripped off his damp leather and fur, and dried him briskly with a soft marten pelt.

Temajin's eyes always seemed to be level and unwavering with an unnerving penetration, but Subotai noticed that they somehow caught a softer gleam of light whenever he looked at his wife and his handsome son.

"While I, and most of the menfolk were away on the hunt, the Merkits overran our Yakka camps and Bourtai and many other women were taken by the raiders." The Yakka noyon's jaw was a hard line.

Subotai listened, riveted, although he already knew the story. The bards of the steppe had made this Temajin a legend, telling and retelling and embellishing the noyon's deeds in their singsong fireside recitations. How Temajin had gone to the Kuraits, the enemies of the Mongols since time immemorial, and bargained their wily khan into a hasty and temporary alliance against their mutual enemy, the Merkits. How Temajin, using a new steppe tactic of wielding his combined Mongol and Kurait force as cavalry in depth against the thin, single-strand Merkit force, broke them and devastated their camps.

Temajin took his naked son on his lap and, reaching over to tousle Bourtai's shining black hair, said, "She was just standing there with that long knife in her hand when we reached the women. She didn't say anything, but I was told later by the other women that while the fight was raging out on the steppe, she slipped the blade away from their guard and..." But here Bourtai interrupted him.

"Please, my lord, it would be best if you did not say more."

Temajin would not be stayed. "...slit him from chin to chine."

Bourtai's gaze was directed down, and when she looked up her she-wolf eyes made Subotai's skin tingle with a knowledge of women unknown to all but a few, very perceptive males. She stood up and left the yurt, returning with dried animal dung to build up the brazier's heat against the night. The short winter day had flown on the fascination of Temajin's tale-telling, and Temajin retreated into the habitual silence attributed to him by his wife as abruptly as he had begun talking.

Bourtai lit oily stone cups for light, and soon there was meat roasting over the brazier. They ate the food quietly and, in the way of nomads, sat in silence listening to the creak of the cart beneath them in the buffeting wind of the blizzard. Then all four of them, with unspoken thankfulness to the Sky for meat and shelter in the grim time of winter, fell into contented sleep.

φ   φ   φ   φ

Morning found Bourtai once again roasting breakfast meat. Temajin and Subotai tended the horses by scraping any dead vegetation they could find under the heavy snow into little, white-crowned piles for the animals. The vicious wind propelling the blizzard had abated somewhat, but the snow still swirled, and occasionally wind-driven ice stung their faces.

In the midst of chewing Bourtai's morning mutton, Temajin caught Subotai's eyes with his own, nodding at the sword lying against the framing of the yurt. Without interrupting his eating, Subotai slowly handed the weapon, hilt first, to Temajin. To have moved abruptly with the sword would have been a serious breach of weapons-courtesy, as would allowing the sharpened side of the blade ever to face a trusted host.

Temajin examined the blue sword, picking at a few rust pits along the blunt ridge of the blade. He returned the weapon. "Bourtai..." He looked from his wife to Subotai. "...See, the steel of the blade and Subotai's eyes are very nearly the same color."

She turned from tending the brazier and slid closer to Subotai and looked into his wind-burned face. "No," she said, "I think his eyes are a little lighter." She looked into Temajin's face, then back to Subotai's. "You two are the only ones I have ever seen with green or blue eyes."

As if to draw him out, Bourtai addressed Subotai. "Have you seen many Mongols with eyes as light as yours?" Both Temajin and Bourtai waited for his reply, as though the question had been pre-arranged between the two of them.

Subotai, seated on the cart-yurt's floor as they were, turned back to them after replacing the blue sword against the ribbing and felt of the yurt-wall. His head was lowered for a long moment.

"Aye. I have seen one with eyes that rival the hues of the Great Sky itself." Then the emotional tide of his feeling for Mursechen poured out. "Her hair is the color..." He searched for something within his experiences of the wondrous outdoor world of the steppes and the blue lake, something adequate to describe her. "...like the moment of the sun, the breaking of morning when it turns the steppe lightest yellow before even the gray leaves the Sky."

Bourtai was amazed. "You have actually seen a Mongol woman with yellow hair?"

"Aye." His lovesickness showed plainly, and Bourtai's eyes softened with sympathy for him. Then he told them everything.

Early winter darkness had crept upon the cart-yurt by the time he finished the telling of his encounter with Mursechen and the raid and the taking of the blue sword. Like Temajin, he fell silent when his story was ended. Bourtai tried to make him eat the evening meal, but his appetite was lost in his longing for Mursechen. So she fueled the brazier and rocked quietly to and fro with Juchi upon her lap until she saw that the entire yurt was asleep except for herself.

Three nights and two days after he had been taken in from the blizzard by Temajin and Bourtai, Subotai saddled his mount, saddle-sheathed his two-handed, curved sword, and said his good-byes to the handsome family so strangely marooned in the middle of the snowbound steppe.

Bourtai had given him two sizable chunks of cold mutton to take with him, and now offered him a stirrup cup of rice wine she had heated. "Are you sure you won't stay over with us?" she asked. "It may snow again and this cold won't break for a long time."

Temajin had a knowing smile on his face as he said, "You're on a wildly hopeless quest, you know that, don't you? I have only vaguely heard of the Kipchaks. Only the Sky knows what they were ever doing in this country, even a small band of them. I know for certain that they live farther into the west than any man has ever gone in my recollection."

Subotai could only shrug his shoulders. Any further rest or delay in his search was out of the question. He was fate-bound to it. The eyes of the two men locked for a moment, a gleam of admiration plainly visible in Subotai's gray-blue eyes. Subotai again thanked Bourtai and silently envied any man who could have such a woman. He gripped Temajin's sword-hand—his left—and turned his faithful animal toward the west again.

"Come back someday, Eagle," Subotai heard the tall Yakka say. He wondered why Temajin would call him an eagle.

When the isolated cart-yurt was almost out of sight in the distance, Subotai turned for one last look back across the snowy plain, still warmed by the cordiality and unaffected pleasantness of the family. He could just make out the man, now a barely visible speck, standing away from the yurt. He didn't think Temajin could see the gesture at this great distance, but he lifted his sword arm in farewell anyway.

As he rode on into the freezing day he wondered, and not for the first time, how the Yakka cart-yurt came to be isolated and blizzard-bound. Surely no man in command of his senses would purposely place his family in such apparent jeopardy. He looked back once more, but only a snowy wasteland lay behind him now. Then he was overcome by the feeling that somehow the man had been waiting on the steppe for him to ride out of the storm.

φ   φ   φ   φ

The mutton vanished before nightfall of the first day after he left the yurt-warmth behind. Light snow fell during the next two nights, and he slept in his fur greatcoat beside his horse as the powdery stuff drifted over him. At first it was difficult to get the animal to lie on its side for such an extended period of time with snow piling up on them, but once the horse experienced the relative warmth of the snow's insulating properties, it responded readily when Subotai tilted its muzzle as a signal to lie down.

The snow eventually ceased, but the cold grew day by day until it seemed an almost living, predatory thing that sought his life-warmth remorselessly. Hunger and cold dulled his loneliness and his misery with its overriding interminable demand. He knew that death, an invisible stirrup-companion for any lonely rider on the steppes, was drawing ever closer to him now. Why had he been such a fool, abandoning the shelter and safety of Temajin's camp to press on into this frozen hell?

Then, almost miraculously, after days of nothing to eat, he

sighted a lone, stringy gazelle. Flattening himself across his mount's back and neck so that the horse's silhouette looked almost natural, he managed to get close enough to the wary creature for a single, hasty bow-shot. He cursed as the gazelle sped away, but speckles of blood told him his shot had been lucky. He and his worn pony plowed wearily after it, breaking the crusted snow and slipping on the hidden ice. The speckles of blood showered into a red mist, and half a league beyond, Subotai came upon the drained creature lying dead in a shallow, pinkish depression in the snow.

Subotai controlled his savage hunger. He fought back the urge to slash open the gazelle's belly and devour the warm heart and liver raw. He heaved the still-quivering carcass over the pony in front of the saddle and swung himself up. The pony staggered on while Subotai swept the horizon for any sign of shelter or possible fuel for a fire. He could see only the open, white flatness stretching to the north, the west, and the east. But to the south he thought he could make out the minutest rise in the landscape. Perhaps only a break in the dull, winter light of the overcast day?

"No, I can still see it." He said the words aloud.

He coaxed the nearly exhausted pony toward the south. The low upsweep in the land seemed at first to keep receding into the distance, but eventually he came to it and discovered that a gullied, nearly snow-filled watercourse slashed along the base of the vague upturn in the terrain. A small grove of stunted trees grew along the more open side of the gully, invisible unless looked at from almost immediately above.

Subotai almost leaped from the saddle and quite literally dragged his horse down into the soft, drifted snow in the ravine. He threw the gazelle onto the snow and turned in a near panic of starvation to warm and feed himself. But a cautionary state of mind again forced him to suppress his raging hunger. A consciousness above himself bade him hobble his mount where it might find winter grazing under the snow, forced him into rational selection of a site for a campfire, steadied his numbed, nearly frostbitten fingers as he broke twigs, laid in his fuel, shaved tinder from the driest bark, and struck sparks from the two dense stones and the small, jagged piece of steel he always carried.

It took Subotai an eternity to get the tinder smouldering, his fingers bleeding near the nails from his desperate efforts with the flinty stone and the steel. His fixed mental state willed the fire into existence. With an unbroken patience, he nursed the flames with larger and still larger twigs and branches he stripped from the trees.

Then he could no longer control his haste. He rolled the dead gazelle over and stepped across one of the now stiffening forelegs. With one deft, drawing motion of his knife he opened the stomach, then began jerking and cutting loose the entrails. The guts did not steam when they hit the snow. Already the unspeakable cold had extracted the lingering life-warmth of the gazelle.

Then Subotai dragged the heart, liver, and kidneys from the disemboweled animal and skewered them over the flames on a makeshift spit, a thin branch which promptly burned through and dropped the meat into the fire. He took the great sword and impaled the internal organs and braced the blade over the flames with smooth stones he pried from under the snow in the bed of the watercourse. As the meat began to sizzle, he carved away the cooked outer layer and, burning his mouth, gorged on the rare flesh. He added the gazelle's tongue to the roasting chunks beading the weapon.

When he had blunted the fiercest edge of his hunger pangs, he foraged for branches substantial enough to serve as a proper spit, then flayed off a rump of meat and spitted it above the fire. All the while he kept feeding the precious fire with bark strippings and larger twigs and broken birch branches he found mounding the snow under the trees.

With the darkening grip of winter firmly upon the steppe land, Subotai knew that farther travel without food and warmer garments would doom him to a premature trip through the Doorway of the Sky.

When the fire was going well, Subotai set about constructing a shelter. He began with a temporary lean-to structured from a framework of branches tied off with sinews stripped from the dead animal's legs and covered with its hide.

His hobbled pony seemed content to browse with its muzzle below the top of the snow, dragging out and vigorously chewing dried grass and leaves from the fallings of the autumn season.

φ   φ   φ   φ

Over the short days of the winter weeks which followed, Subotai set his cunning snares and deadfalls along the length of the watercourse. He began with snares of sinew baited with suet he had set aside from the gazelle. He trapped first song birds, weasels, big-footed hares, and then a snowy owl which he freed because of some natural aversion within himself to eating a bird of prey. As his open-aired, naturally cooled food larder became stocked with the frozen carcasses of smaller animals, he began to set heavier deadfalls for wolf, lynx, and fox, using inedible portions of the game for bait.

He began acquiring larger pelts to add as coverings to his improvised shelter, and used the more luxuriant furs to cover his own back. His appearance became shabbier and more bulky as he donned additional hides, which either flapped over his shoulders or became aprons about his waist, increasingly greased and grimed as they accumulated the stains and leavings of skinned animals and the fat-dripping feasts he devoured before his open, ever-burning fireplace. When his boots wore through, he covered them with a rough set of mukluk-like foot-mittens, and leggings he fashioned of richly thick lynx fur.

And he passed the cold season in this way, talking to his horse and talking to his fire in the lonely, freezing nights; describing countless times to the flames, to the softly down-drifting snow-flakes, and to his patient pony, the beauties of the blond Mursechen and his idealized fantasies of how they could live together through the sharp seasons and the years he saw warmly ahead of them in his lovesick boy's mind.

But one night of savage cold he woke from his always fire-conscious sleep in the midst of a dream of the shaman. The hated old wizard's words had branded his soul: "And the tall woman of sun-gold and ice-blue, she will belong to another as well."

He did not sleep again for nearly three days, hating the dream, hating the inner truth that the lovely Mursechen was lost to him forever. He trod his gray trap-line thereafter with a deadening depression shrouding his being. He thought himself dissolved in a world of whitened gray, his mind and his hurting soul immersed and one with the gray dead season surrounding and dominating him.

When he came to the snare with the flapping and beak-snapping eagle owl in it, he set about freeing the bird, oblivious to the taloned feet and the ramming beak that were tearing at his wrists and hands. With the owl finally held down and its leg cleared of the snare's loop, Subotai looked at the big yellow eyes, their black pupils etched with fear and instinctive defiance, and he longed for the unpained simplicity of the bird, envied its naturalness and cyclic involvement with the wild world. And he wondered why he did not have such a correct and harmonious place in his own world which would take the longing, desirous pain from his mind.

Subotai released the bird's wings. Then, rolling and flapping up a miniature snow-haze, the owl flew quickly upward above the watercourse and silently flew away following the snowy stream bed. Then it turned, wheeling up and to the right, and disappeared over the rim of the ravine's wall-like embankment.

φ φ
THE
TRAPPER

*W*ater was trickling under the snowpack in the ravine. Subotai awakened with a start; the attunement of his mind to the moods and needs of his fire had alarmed him into wakefulness. The lapse in the vital sounds of the snapping fire caused him to jerk upright, ready to feed the blaze from the kindling stack he replenished daily from the fallen logs and growing trees along the stream bed.

He thought he must have slept past his usual rising time because the sun was higher than it seemed to him it should have been. Nursing the flames to a more substantial level, he noticed that while the air was cool, the chill had departed. The sun was more northerly, as well. It no longer kept to the southern sky in its winter course. The gradual lengthening of the days and the sun's northward shift had gone essentially unnoticed by Subotai, lost in thoughts of Mursechen on his continual rounds of subsistence trapping and hunting.

Throughout the morning, the flow of water from the warming snow perceptibly gathered in volume and in sound. Spring had gentled the time of the blizzards again. He knew he must resume his search at once. He stuffed skin pouches full of smoked game and rolled a mound of choice furs into a bedroll. With his mount saddled and loaded, he quickly scoured the campsite for anything else worth carrying away and then took a fond, parting look at the limb-and-hide shelter he had expanded from the scant protection of the original gazelle skin lean-to. As he mounted, the moistening earth about the dying fire was already making the embers hiss and emit steamy vapors.

The pony's fetlocks were dripping with wetness from the snow dissolving under the early spring sunshine. Subotai, squinting at the sun's position for orientation and narrowing his eyes against the brutal snow glare, turned the animal westward.

As he persisted in his westing travel during the days of the maturing season, the snow succumbed and disappeared, and the steppe, green in its spring glory, reemerged. The mud began to dry and the mire that had clung to his horse's hooves solidified and was gone, along with most of the short-lived spring ponds which dotted the steppe at the end of each winter.

The scarcity of winter forage had taken its toll of his pony, and the disappearance of the snow-water ponds forced horse and rider into longer periods of thirst. Mongols rarely viewed their beasts of burden with affection or formed emotional associations with any animal which would eventually become food. But when the once sturdy, once stocky pony could go on no longer, when it lay down on its side in the steppe grass and expired, Subotai was shocked to feel a grieving emptiness—not one of selfishness because of his dependence upon the horse for survival, but one of losing a close familiar to whom he had confided his most intimate thoughts and desires.

Subotai lingered near the dead pony through the light of the summer afternoon, sorting half-heartedly through the little pile of weaponry, fur, and saddle which the animal had carried so willingly. He would have to proceed on foot, and knowing he could not himself bear the wood-and-leather nomadic saddle, he fashioned a pair of thong-tied and heavy-soled sandals from it and abandoned the rest. He was short of food, but his unexpected feeling for the pony kept him from butchering the carcass. He swung up his load of bedroll and weapons, and with his precious boots secured within the sleeping furs, hiked swiftly away from the horse's carcass before the onset of darkness brought the inevitable arrival of the vicious steppe wolves.

He thought at first that the rolling vibration which drew him awake one morning several footsore days later must be a thunder-storm. But when he opened his eyes, the dawn sky was cloudless and promised another day of heat to plague his slow-marching progress. The sound was not sporadic like thunder, and the tremor he heard in the ear he pressed next to the earth gathered in volume.

The vibration blended into an audible sensation. Horses. He could discern their sounding hooves in the undisturbed air of early morning. He knew he must make the most of the miraculous appear-ance of horses. And he knew there would be armed men with them. There was little point in attempting to take cover since none existed on the flat steppe. Dropping his gear on the ground, he pulled his bow from its skin sheath and strung it. With an arrow nocked, he stood his ground as the earth began to shake beneath him.

Subotai turned the herd's lead stallion with a yell and a sharply thrown rock which whacked on the big stud's neck. Then he was caught in a raceway of horses, smelling their hot foam as they thundered past him.

A horseman sped by him, then pulled his animal up in the dust, wheeled, and halted to survey the fur-clad Mongol standing with strung bow and an arrow at the ready within shooting range of both him and another rider who had stopped to join the first.

"Is that a man?" the astonished horseman called to his com-panion. Neither of them had ever seen a live man alone on the merciless steppes, and certainly not one on foot. They scanned the area. Where were his companions? Where was his horse? They spoke excitedly to each other in the Seljuk dialect of the Turkish language. What they were seeing was a logical impossibility. Even with a horse, no man lived for long alone on the steppes. They were so taken aback at the sight of Subotai, erect and solitary on the plain, that they did not even bolt out of arrowshot.

They were joined by two other riders. Subotai singled out one that seemed older than the others, and noted that he was accom-panied by what Subotai took from that distance to be a brown-haired boy. The riders had suddenly realized their error in stopping where the reach of the lone man's bow could empty saddles. The older man spoke to the other three.

"Even if we run now, one of us at least is dead."

Then the middle-aged Turk did something which, on the steppes in the twelfth century would normally be regarded as so utterly foolhardy as to approach an act of simple-mindedness. He rode slowly over to where Subotai was standing by his bedroll, halted, and made gestures of greeting in the hand-sign language which was used steppe-wide to transcend the language differences between the nomadic tribes of high Asia.

Subotai withdrew his right hand from the feathered end of the arrow, but held the bow and nocked shaft ready in his left. He returned the greeting with clever, flying fingers. The months and months of loneliness had made the usually withdrawn Mongol feel abnormally gregarious, and he conveyed in the sign language the paramount events of his winter and spring journey from the region near the Blue Lake—omitting, of course, the reason for his undertaking such a monumental trek across the open wilderness of the steppes.

Then the lean Seljuk Turk turned in his saddle and called to his companions. One of the men kicked his animal in the flanks and sped after the small herd of horses which had galloped past the drovers when they stopped. The brown-haired boy rode up to the Mongol, and when Subotai met the hazel eyes he laughed aloud at himself for mistaking such a pretty young woman for a boy. She pursed her lips in a piqued expression when the Mongol laughed. But she could not break her gaze away from him. His catlike eyes reflected the splendid blue of the summer sky and his cool and good-natured presence caught her in a second surprise greater than that of just finding a lone man on foot on the steppes as if he had fallen from the stars themselves.

Subotai, returning their trust, thrust the arrow into the quiver he had left leaning against his bedroll. He scrutinized the Turks with his wide-set, intelligent eyes until the man who had set off in pursuit of the horse herd returned leading a young, coal-black mare at the end of a rope.

The older man, obviously their leader, hand-signed for the Mongol to mount the mare. And Subotai, heavy as he was with weapons and his furry bedroll, took the lead rope offered by the other Turkish herdsman and sprang to the mare's back, equally at home bareback or astride a saddle. Then, fanning out, the group of riders galloped after the herd, Subotai riding with them. Their progress in regaining control of the herd was a marvel of unspoken coordination arising from experience acquired almost from birth.

As Subotai guided the black mare in an arc to his right and then reined in close to the herd which had slowed into a lazy gallop, he remembered the words he had heard so often around the Mongol fires. "On the steppe, no man encounters a friend."

That night after the Seljuks had shared cold meat with him, Subotai lay unsleeping until daybreak, watching the three men relieve each other on the night watches with the horse herd. He was grateful that they hadn't promptly deprived him of his life or even his weapons, but he kept the hilt of the blue sword in his right hand so that he could bring it up in a savage slash if any of the Turks should try to take him by surprise in the darkness.

He spent the next day's drive still wary but weary, and frequently caught himself dozing in the saddle. He managed to ride so that the Turks were always in front of or flanking him, letting his horse straggle from time to time to keep from having any of them at his rear.

At midmorning they dismounted and, sitting in the shade of their animals, shared with him meat and hard, black bread. The Mongol watched the Seljuks tear at the coarse-grained bread, then took one bite of his portion. Bearing their generosity in mind, he kept himself, but just barely, from gagging it up. He put the rest inside his jerkin, feigning the intention of holding it for another time.

"You do not like it?" The Seljuk girl conveyed the question by means of the glimpses of understanding the sign language permitted them.

Subotai shifted a piece of dried horse meat to his left hand and signed back, "What is it?"

"Bread," the young woman answered in the Turkish tongue.

The word meant nothing to Subotai who wondered if her tongue was as sharp as the deft jabbing and finger-crooking of her sign work.

"Do you have a name?" she signed.

"Subotai."

She repeated the spoken name. Then pointing to the leader she said, "Balankar," then signed, "he's my father."

Here Balankar intervened. He pointed back at his attractive daughter and said, "Narslana." His brown fingers wove a mosaic of communication as he gestured toward the other men. "My kinsmen." Pointing to the southwest, he signed, "We have a trading camp near the Sea of the Ravens." He used the sign for a large expanse of water to convey the notion of a sea.

Balankar signalled another question. "Who are your people?"

Subotai signed back, "The People."

The Seljuk leader grinned, and turning to his relatives, said in Turkish, "But are we not all people?"

Their brief repast finished, the Turkish men drew off to one side of the ground-reined horses and spread cloth mats on the grass. The Seljuk girl followed suit, first separating herself from the men by some distance. Then the Mongol was amazed to see them all kneel down and, facing toward the southeast, prostrate themselves several times. The thought occurred to him that this might be ritual preparation for a sacrifice with himself dedicated as the victim, and his hand crept toward the hilt of the blue sword, still reassuringly at his side. But soon they began to stand up and shake out their prayer rugs, and Subotai forced himself to appear relaxed. Balankar remained for some time at his devotions after the others had finished, then, upright but still on his knees, called three times, "Allah Akbar...Allah Akbar...Allah Akbar." Lowering his upstretched arms he stood and rolled up his mat and tied it behind his saddle with his sleeping roll. Subotai breathed again as they all mounted and resumed the drive.

Subotai slept fitfully that night, still conscious of the warning implicit in the old Mongol saying. But the night went as the one before except that when one of the Turks returned from his slow-riding guard around the picketed horses, Subotai went out on the midwatch and let Balankar sleep the night through.

The land was changing now as they rode. The steppe was extraordinarily flat and Subotai sensed that the terrain had taken on a long, shallow descending tilt toward the south and the west. He thought at first that the shimmer of water on the horizon was one of the mirages that came and went on the steppes, ever receding, lingering to taunt a thirsty man, then disappearing into dust.

But late in the afternoon the sky filled with large white birds with trim, pointed wings, and soon after, they reached the water's edge. The vista of choppy water stretched as far as he could see. The late summer heat was stifling and they led the herd into the water for a cooling swim. The thirsty Mongol atop his wading mount scooped up a cupped handful of the water, but its salty bitterness nearly forced it upwards through his nostrils. He found it utterly amazing that so much water could be undrinkable.

The Seljuk girl had watched him try to drink the brine, and was covering her pink-lipped mouth to hide her amusement at his reaction to his first gulp from the sea. Her gestures indicated that this great water was named for the ravens. The Mongol quickly responded that all the birds he could see at the moment were white, then queried, through signs, as to where the ravens might be. Narslana said the Seljuk word for it, "Winter." She made the steppe season's sign at the same time.

For five days they followed the coastline of the great, salty body of water southward. On the fifth day they rode into the bustle and vigor of the Seljuk trading camp, which was situated on the sandy shores of the Caspian Sea—the Sea of the Ravens. Subotai was wide-eyed at the color and the permanent log dwellings interspersed among plain and gaudy tents of all dimensions and geometric configurations. His fears, which had gradually subsided in the camaraderie of the trail, stirred anew. He felt for the blue sword and looked again at the girl riding confidently beside him. She smiled reassuringly. There seemed to be a continuous uproar in an unidentifiable medley of languages. Buyers and sellers parleyed loudly beside the trade goods, chiefly cloth, wine, and grain, but also slaves.

This was the first time Subotai had seen a slave market. He well knew the fate of captives taken on the warring steppes, but he had never seen the actual bartering and was unprepared for the sight of the systematized and coldly commercial institution of slavery. Light-skinned younger women were being offered for the most part, and they were being eyed and pruriently handled unmercifully by dark and richly garbed traders who, to the Mongol's surprise, wore no fur. But there were also young men for sale, and Subotai, picturing himself exhibited naked on the block, forced himself not to grip the handle of the sword at his side.

Balankar was hailed on sight by nearly everyone within the confines of the outpost. His return to the camp drew a mounted group of armed bodyguards who quickly formed a shielding escort for him and Narslana. When the Turks dismounted in front of the largest of the log halls, Balankar started through its entranceway, then, remembering Subotai, called the Mongol by name and crooked his head inward toward the interior of the wooden building. Subotai slid off the mare, and with his sword handle and quiver knocking in rhythm with his walking gait, he joined Balankar and his daughter within. The Seljuks had not attempted to disarm him. Perhaps, Subotai suspected, they did not think it worth the probable casualty rate.

"Teach him the trail tongue." Balankar looked over his shoulder at Narslana. "He can sleep at the stable. I've been needing a man to double the watch there. Perhaps he is unspoiled enough to avoid the temptation of theft."

Subotai, who had already picked up enough of the Seljuk language to get the drift of Balankar's instructions, unclenched his hands and tried to breathe naturally as his mind doggedly returned to the purpose of his long ordeal. Narslana started to convey her father's words to Subotai in the steppe sign language, but Subotai interrupted her with a one-word question. "Kipchaks?"

Balankar and Narslana looked quizzically at each other. Then, tired from his long journey on horseback, Balankar shrugged and repeated, "Kipchaks." And Subotai interpreted his shrug and his inflection as the answer of a man who did not know of what he spoke. The sense of imminent danger he had felt when coming into the riotous trading camp was lost in a wave of dejection which plummeted into the pit of his stomach when Balankar seemed to be ignorant of the existence of the Kipchaks.

After Subotai and the Seljuk girl had left the log hall, Balankar accepted hot food from a serving woman. Kipchaks had come in the past to the Seljuk camp to trade and sell of their stock or booty from their far-reaching raids. Tracing through his memory, Balankar realized he had not seen or heard of any Kipchaks for several years; then he recalled that they had federated with some of the Rus princes to the west and had shifted their grazing grounds onto the Russian steppes. The Turk finished his meal, then lay down for a rest. He would not reveal the general whereabouts of the Kipchaks to the Mongol. Unless, of course, the lad proved of no use to him; in that case he would bless the boy on his way and probably rid the trading post of another disruptive element.

φ   φ   φ   φ

"Come on, I'll teach you how!"

Subotai was always slightly dismayed at the unflagging ebullience of the Turkish girl, and he had never known anyone in his life who knew how to swim.

She proved to be a patient teacher. As she well had to be. Subotai's disinclination to go into water deep enough to swim in was similar to that of a yurt cat's. But gradually she had him floating on his back while she hovered at his side, her reassuring arms buoying and leading him. In the warmth of the summery Caspian water, the Mongol, a natural athlete, soon graduated from dog-paddling to an elementary side-stroke which made Narslana laugh with accomplishment at her instructive feat.

"See, I told you I could teach you." Her voice was filled with her smile.

The Mongol had proven his worth to Balankar as a sentry at the prosperous Seljuk's stables. The losses the Turk had come to expect from his unreliable mercenary watchmen suddenly stopped. Intentional slips in herd accounting, sharp transactions involving animal substitutions, and outright theft disappeared under the Mongol's uncorrupted guard. Subotai lived at the stable and, totally unfamiliar with coinage, accepted his meals as his remuneration for carrying out his duties while he waited for a clue to how he could continue his search.

Narslana visited him daily. She was fascinated by the strange barbarian. And she painstakingly taught him the functional lingua franca of the caravan trails and the trading camps, a simplistic child-talk used from the steppes to the inner reaches of the great empire of the Chin.

Summer should have been ending, but the stables were still an inferno of moist stench on one particularly hot day. Narslana and the Mongol, at Balankar's bidding, had taken most of the horses which remained after the summer's trading out to pasture to relieve the beasts of the oppressive heat. That done, they were cooling themselves with a swim.

Narslana and the Mongol were identically clothed up to their waists with linen loin cloths and the Seljuk girl had bound her young and ample breasts with the material. The soaking cloth clung to her mature form when they came out of the surf. Subotai was too inexperienced to detect the knowing seductiveness in her glances at him. And his natural male protectiveness, nurtured in the framework of Mongol society and untarnished as yet by the raw debasements of life and disillusionments which often accompany carnal knowledge, was a powerful governor over his youthful urges.

They lay down on the sandy shore under the midafternoon sunshine. Narslana fluffed out her hair to dry behind her upturned face. Subotai, his chunky body soon glistening with perspiration, fell asleep beside the murmuring shore of the Sea of the Ravens.

He was certainly fully aware of the nature of relations between men and women, but he had retained his innocence and his celibacy into this, his seventeenth year. He had always had a healthy interest in the more comely girls of the Mongol clans; and the remembered vividness of the blondeness, the clear blue eyes, and the lovely form of Mursechen caused him arousals so powerful that they were an anguish to him. The singularity of his desire for the young blue-eyed girl had restrained him from the unlicensed behavior of his peers among the young men of the clans. And from their even more unlicensed bragging. Many an idle sexual boast in the nomadic and feuding Mongol society resulted in swift, painful, or even fatal visitations by male relatives noted for extremely narrow points of view and an almost total lack of humor with respect to aspersions cast upon the reputations, chastity, or sexual worth of their kinswomen.

The sun was gone and the breeze across the water had cooled when Subotai awoke. He shook Narslana awake, and watched with interested silence as she quickly dressed beside her hobbled horse. His tongue twisting awkwardly around the unfamiliar language, he said to her, "Ride for the camp."

Lifelong use of the trail tongue had made her fluent. She gave him a parting smile and said, "I'll bring you out some food in the morning. If it rains, I'll bring you a skin for shelter." She stepped into his cupped hands and swung up onto her mount. Then she kicked it into a flat-out run and woman and animal vanished into the undulations of the Caspian steppe.

Summer lingered that year and Subotai spent more than a fortnight with the grazing herd. He possessed an unspoken communion with the animals although few of them had been saddle-broken. A true son of the steppes, he slept as he circled or, with the trusting consent of the horses, mingled with them, rarely dismounting, as was the Mongol way when herding. And the Seljuk girl came each day with food, stayed until just before sunset, then returned to the trading camp.

When she asked him on several occasions why he had come so far from his people, he feigned misunderstanding and shifted the conversation to areas where he made her think he was more proficient in the pidgin language. Obeying an intuitive feeling, he had abandoned his characteristic bluntness for the first time in his life. He masked his quick acquisition of the trail language and even much of the Turkish the girl and Balankar used. But the girl in her womanly feeling detected his mental parrying of her questions. She did not press him, though, having now come under the influence of his manly calmness and his centered and self-assured presence.

Balankar and three men of his private camp guard came one morning without the girl. The Turk and his mercenaries took the horses and, directing Subotai to return to the Seljuk trading post to maintain a protective surveillance of Narslana and his servant woman, they rode off into the northwest with the herd.

The Mongol moved his bedroll into one alcove of the log hall, much to Narslana's delight since she knew her father would be away for some time. She had schemed and, appealing to Balankar's liking for the Mongol, had finally forced his agreement to allow Subotai to serve as a house-watch, provided the serving woman remained in the hall.

She was fully aware that her father would give her in marriage to a distant relative she had never seen after the coming winter. Resigned to the fate of women in a Moslem culture, she knew her days would be short—shorter still if her brood-mare efforts did not produce male issue for her husband.

And the old servant woman—she rid herself of the chaperoning crone one afternoon by administering an overdose of the poppy drug which was freely used and traded about the camps along the Sea of the Ravens. When the toothless mouth wheezed in its deeply doped sleep, Narslana dragged the servant into her father's alcove and dropped the heavy Persian curtain over the alcove door to insure privacy.

"We get it from the Venetian traders on the coast of another sea to the south of here," she said as she handed Subotai a block of soap. Subotai was briskly splashing in the great oaken tub into which Narslana had first poured heated water and then lured the Mongol for the first tub-bath of his life. The slippery feeling of the soap lather was ticklish.

The Seljuk girl was aglow with a seductive mischievousness. With quick command she took the soap and began to scrub his broad back. He was surprised and, in the almost puritanical natural modesty of some barbarians, momentarily overcome when she slipped into the tub behind him completely bare. He started to make a protest but then, of course, thought better of it.

The sensuousness of their young and healthy bodies, the warm water, and their frankly carnal attraction for each other soon overrode their beginning bathing playfulness, and an urgency grew between them. The Seljuk girl's face was flushed and slightly swollen with demand, her hazel eyes sleepy with her passion, the pupils dilated. Kneeling in the warm bath to face him, she kissed him on the mouth in the Greek manner. This utterly new sensation dissolved Subotai's last vaporous reluctance and the last thin barrier of his sexual restraint. Beyond self-control now, he lifted her wet body up and out of the tub.

On the fur-thrown floor, his manhood a rigid inferno pulsing in rhythm with the erotically tormenting shafts of her tongue on his, he was driven to seek her lower sweetness. Her body pink from the warm bath fired his brain and nervous system, as yet unconditioned to the sexual experience with the newness of an excruciating pleasure enhanced for him by the knowledge of the sharing, the transfer of the satisfaction from man to woman.

They joined again and again, each somehow knowing that this encounter would never be repeated and that their time together would be drastically foreshortened. The afternoon light faltered as they slept in their youthful satiation. Once Narslana heard a muffled stirring behind the Persian curtain and slipped from Subotai's unwaking embrace. She found the old woman trying to rise from her drugged sleep. And Narslana, speaking soothingly to the faithful servant, held another brimming cup of honey beer and opium to her lips. The servant woman drank thirstily, then sank back into her stupor.

Subotai and Narslana dressed before morning light and walked through the camp, now quiet after its usual night-long carousel, to the sandy bluffs near the murmuring coastline of the Sea of the Ravens. They watched the water turn from gray to yellow-silver in the late summer dawn, but the wind off the water carried away the last warmth of the green season, and they knew that autumn had once again conquered the fair summer.

φ   φ   φ   φ

The Turk's stables were nearly empty after the season's trading, leaving Subotai at loose ends. Attracted by the ringing sounds of a smith's hammer, he wandered to the edge of the semi-permanent village. The Mongol knew the origins of the hammer noise. With his ears and wit always garnering even the most trivial information and gossip around the camp, he had heard about the Englishman's arrival only minutes after the newcomer had unpacked and set about erecting his tent.

Subotai watched with a tingling fascination as the huge man from the mysterious west sweated, hammered, and shaped glowing metal spikes on a great metal anvil. The blacksmith was the biggest man Subotai had ever seen. His smooth efficiency at the forge gave the smith's labor an almost dancelike character that enthralled the simple lad from the steppes.

The big, fair man had stripped to the waist and rolled up the sides of the tattered, although once richly appointed, traveling tent. The late fall day was nearly freezing, and Subotai was wearing every stitch and fur he possessed, but the smith seemed impervious to the cold, seemed literally to steam in his efforts when he moved away from the heat of the forge into the chillier air. He looked at Subotai with a long, unblinking blue gaze, a twinkle barely glimmering in the pleasant eyes, then continued his work until he had made several dozen metal nails of different lengths.

The arts of the metalsmith were not unknown on the steppes,

but the clan from which Subotai sprang were herders and horse trainers only. His people relied on outside clans for metal and any other goods produced by the ever-traveling home industries of the other tribes of the steppes, goods which they either took in raids or obtained by trade during the rare truces between the various nomadic clans.

As Subotai's interest in the blacksmith's work grew, he edged his way into the tent until he was standing in the work area with a wide-eyed look that was too much for the smith to resist. The big man, a Saxon from a little known island country called England, gestured to the lad to hold out his hand. Then, with the inferential humor of his race, he said in the Saxon tongue, "Here, hold this." With his tongs he placed one of the still hot nails in the gullible, outstretched palm and roared with hoarse laughter when the youth flung the nail away and gripped his branded hand in an effort to ease the burning pain.

Something shifted in the Mongol's mind above his pain and anger, compelling him to an action as inevitable as the seasons. Instantly he was out of his furs and at his mount sliding the blue sword from its saddle-scabbard with the tender hand now rendered painless by his righteous anger. But the Englishman was just as fast. He faced the steppe warrior with his great, gray battle-ax, slowly swinging it in a dully glittering windmill before him.

Subotai leaped to the attack. When his quick, straight feint was parried as he expected, he circled his blade up and slashed it downward in a powerful, diagonal stroke as he moved with lynx-quickness to his right. The edge nicked the Englishman on his exposed left shoulder. Subotai now expected the bearded giant to rage at him for drawing first blood, and stepped back in his icy manner, awaiting the inevitable blind charge which would give him his lethal opportunity. But the Englishman stepped back too, and circled to his left, his eyes now aglow with the battle fury of the northern berserker, but also somehow coolly controlled, not in the detached, almost indifferent way of the young Mongol, but in the manner of a professionally disciplined soldier.

Warily the tall, graying warrior circle-stalked the shorter, dark-haired and massively built young man. Suddenly, with an astonishing agility, the Englishman moved in, the ax-blade a nearly invisible cleavage in the light. Swifter than the eye, the giant rent with sweeping death the place where Subotai had stood an instant before.

The Mongol had stepped obliquely into the attack, turned out in a complete circle, raised his sword in the same flowing coalition of movement and struck down and to his right at the vulnerable back of the big man. The Englishman, feeling his charge and master stroke meet nothingness, reacted with the conditioning of a warrior who has survived in a world of brutal and unforgiving warfare. He let his momentum go on to evade the fatal stroke aimed at his undefended back so that Subotai's blade also found only space and whispering air. Circling anew, the grimness of the affair now overshadowing both their first angers and their impulses of self-preservation, the two men measured themselves against the end of the thing they must now pursue with all their skill, mind, and force. Each man knew that one of them would have to kill the other.

The combat had drawn a small crowd of delighted onlookers from every corner of the Seljuk trading camp. Subotai knew the Turkish girl was there, but he also knew the least deviation in his concentration would stow his bones in the cold earth forever. Subotai's respect for the Englishman was that of a skillful trainee for an experienced warrior who has survived in the fearful psychological cauldron of mortal combat for many years. Subotai did not need anyone to tell him the origin of the purplish welted scars on the man's arms and across his broad chest. He knew that only concentration, skill and luck could save him now.

The Englishman moved deliberately. He was unsure whether the younger man facing him was as veteran as he seemed or merely the product of an exacting and expert schooling. He knew the lad learned like lightning as he went. It dawned on him that that great, thirsty sword might well drink his life in the next few seconds.

In the way of all bystanders at the carnival of blood, the crowd taunted and urged the combatants on, screaming and bellowing with displeasure at the intent, cautious attitudes of the two warriors.

Narslana was away like an arrow as soon as she saw who the combatants were. Streaking breathlessly into the log hall, she blurted out to her father what was transpiring between the Mongol and the Englishman. On his feet with the litheness which is the gift of spare men, the Turk shouted for his camp guard mount as he dashed outside and ran toward the gathering of spectators around the two fighting men. He saw the flash of steeled weapons as he ran. Catching up behind him came four riders responding to his summons. Glancing back, Balankar shouted to them to press ahead and break up the fight.

The horsemen scattered the pedestrian mob and came between Subotai and the Englishman. Two mounted guards to each man, the Seljuk Turks herded the combatants apart and kept them at bay until Balankar jogged onto the scene.

"My friends, put up your weapons. The loss of either of you would pain me. What has brought this about?" With lowering motions of his hands and arms, he went on, "Disarm yourselves and we will talk this out. Come...come now..." He motioned for Subotai to lower his sword, fearing the lad might not understand everything that was said in the pidgin language of the trails and camps.

Subotai, seeing that the Englishman's ax was now hanging from his wrist by the thong through its handle, lowered his blade. And when the older and wiser Englishman walked into his tent-smithy and replaced the ax next to his anvil, the Mongol resheathed the blue sword in its scabbard, which was still hanging from his horse's saddle.

Balankar sent one of his horsemen spurring off for bread and meat and a skin of wine, then followed the Englishman into the tent-smithy, calling for Narslana to bring the Mongol. She responded by tugging Subotai along, using both of her hands to haul on his leather sleeve. Mutterings and spat curses of disappointment from the bystanders followed them into the Englishman's traveling tent before the motley mob began to disburse.

Balankar and the Englishman sat down cross-legged on a worn carpet within the radiant range of the smith's forge. The Seljuk glanced at the standing Subotai and then spoke to the big man in Turkish. "How did it start?"

The Englishman laughed under his breath, then said, "It was just a little sport I was having with him. I tonged him a cooling nail and when it singed his paw, he took it more seriously than I expected. And when he came at me with that grand blade of his, well, the old body is not young anymore, but still the only one I can be lord over, so I thought I would chop him down before he served me up in succulent style."

The Englishman grinned widely at the Mongol. He turned back to Balankar. "He surprised me, though. I am not sure I would care to reopen the contest with him. Frankly, I had not thought it possible a man that young could be so accomplished with any weapon. Not a damn scar on him that I can see, either. How do you suppose he became so proficient?"

Balankar shrugged. "Only Allah knows. We came across him on the steppes just after the land had dried. Without a horse—just that extraordinarily beautiful sword and his bow and some badly tanned furs he used for a bedroll." Then changing the tack of the conversation, Balankar swept his hand toward a disjointed pile of saddlery and baggage thrown near the Englishman's set of more than two dozen riding and pack horses. "You are preparing to travel to the north again?" It was more a statement than a question.

The blacksmith nodded in the affirmative. Balankar's face took on a grave cast. "Each time you are gone nearly two whole years. Sometimes you come back with never a thing to show for the hardship. Why do you follow such a path? Why not come in with us here in the camps?" Balankar raised a restraining hand. "Do not tell me that old threadworn tale about my kinsmen not accepting you because you are a Christian. They all know the truth—and I have not forgotten my manners and my gratitude to the Lord Muhammad and to you, my great friend, for saving my life and the lives of my servants in the Grecian passes."

The Englishman sighed loudly, his mind going back to when, fleeing the stifling tyranny of the Normans in his fondly remembered, rain-cleansed and greenly sweet and cool England, he had first ventured to Constantinople to enlist in the Varangian Guard. "Let that old bone rest undisturbed, Balankar. It was only after that incident that I started to understand the Byzantine perfidy. When I saw that the Greeks paid the hillmen to ambush the Seljuks just after that treaty, I would have counted myself a poor man not to have warned you and your party. And, as you well know, I took my mustering-out share there and then. I could well have finished my twenty suns in the Varangian Guard and had my hectares of farmland, but my stomach was nigh full with the oily bastards by then. The life is freer here along the Sea, and, I don't know, but perhaps this will be my last ride to the inlet."

Balankar knew the answer to his question, but he asked anyway. "Do you travel alone this time?"

The Englishman looked mildly startled. "After the two brigands I carried last time—one took the birds and the other everything else he could carry when we encountered our first caravan—I think so."

Then the Seljuk's face lit with a thought which almost made him blurt out the beauty and convenience of it. "That young swordsman over there that my maiden daughter seems so intent upon protecting is the most honest creature I have come upon in Allah's creation. And now that you've tried him, I think you'll agree he would be worth his rations in a fight."

"I doubt the boy would take to my company after the activities of this day." But the Englishman took a long, direct look at the stocky youth. He noted how the Mongol returned his gaze with a calm, reserved confidence.

Balankar was not to be put aside from his plan. "Let me talk to him. His capabilities in the trail language are somewhat confined. If I can bring him into agreement, why not take him along?"

"If you can, then, by Our Lady, I will take a chance on him. He can communicate in the sign language, can he not?" Balankar nodded. "All right, but be sure he has some notion of just what he is getting himself into. Tell him I travel in the snow, tell him about the bear-people of the forest whom no man has seen. Balankar, rid yourself of that skeptical look. I know of what I speak. They are there, they kill for no reason, taking nothing but the life itself, leaving no traces, no tracks of their passing."

Balankar feigned seriousness at the mention of the bear-people; naturally he would not speak of them to Subotai. He knew it was time to separate Subotai from Narslana. He had seen the kind of looks which his daughter and the Mongol exchanged before. It was best to proceed in this way. And, of course, he would avoid mentioning any realistic estimate of the time the Englishman was usually away whenever he journeyed to the north.

Motioning for the Englishman and Narslana to remain, Balankar led Subotai out of the tent-smithy. He strolled by the side of the Mongol, stepping gingerly around fresh deposits of horse dung. "The ax-man is a traveling trader," he said. "And," he looked inquiringly at Subotai, "he needs a trained fighting man to travel with him on a trading journey. Needless to say, he—like the rest of us— is impressed with your exceptional abilities." Balankar saw the light of understanding in the nomad's eyes and knew that the Mongol's quick intelligence had penetrated, at least to some extent, the complexities of his Seljuk and trail tongue words with the Englishman. He had suspected for some time that Subotai could comprehend virtually all of a Seljuk or a trail talk conversation.

Balankar suspected other things as well, and this caused him to press on with Subotai. "I cannot tell you exactly where the Englishman goes on his ventures or in what goods he trades," he lied, "but I can tell you that he always has plenty of arms, horses, and furs and money to throw away at the races and games when he returns." A great shout emphasized his point as three horses raced by some distance away followed by a wagering throng.

Subotai was intrigued by the proposal. But would the Englishman lead him to, or at least perhaps know of the whereabouts of, the Kipchaks? Almost as if by clairvoyance, the question Subotai had put to him some moon-months earlier came to Balankar's mind, and he said, "Perhaps the Englishman knows of the Kipchaks."

φ   φ   φ   φ

Subotai crouched in the shallow, salty water behind the blind of reed and cattails he had matted and tied and then anchored with mud. The marshes and the meandering waterways were still hazed with an early morning winter mist. The Mongol could hear the honking cacophony of the in-bound waterfowl growing louder. The Englishman had directed him to several such reedy areas where stragglers and lay-overs were likely to spend the cold months after the gigantic flocks of ducks, swans, and geese had gone farther south to balmier wintering grounds. Subotai could hear the wind in their wings as the snow geese braked from their fast-descending glides to splashing landings on the water's surface. He waited, holding his breath to a shallowness, maintaining his frozen posture to allow the geese to settle in and begin their dabbling feeding. He knew he must wait until the marsh mist rose slightly before he could see well enough for fair shooting.

Drawing the bow as he slowly came erect from his stooped position, he brought the arrow's guide-feather back until it touched below his right eye on his high cheekbone. He was already reaching behind his right shoulder for another shaft from his quiver before the first arrow took the big white gander fair in the head, killing the bird instantly. The air and water exploded with the flock's frenzied wing-flapping flight. But another of the Mongol's arrows had tallied, and taken a snowy goose, just airborne, through the heart, its air-shivering shaft tumbling the bird into the dark water.

Subotai carefully chose his footing step by step through the murky slime of the marsh bottom until he could retrieve the floating geese. Two were enough. He had actually hoped for but one, but in the still, heavy air of the cold morning his bowmanship was more solid than he expected.

When he emerged from the chill water he tied one dead goose to each end of a leather thong, then looped the thong over his saddle pommel with a goose on either side of his horse's shoulders. The blood on the white feathers began to glisten redly as the sun asserted itself through the dissipating fog. Subotai turned his mount, the black mare which Balankar had given him, across the oozing and slightly quaking land adjacent to the marsh.

The Englishman grunted a greeting when Subotai came into the tent-smithy with the morning's quarry. Then the big man turned back to his sewing as he continued to fashion leather rain cloaks and furry mittens with knife, needle, and sinew. The Mongol laid the heavy birds on the Englishman's burn-scarred workbench, then plucked the birds clean and carefully sorted and piled the feathers and the soft down. He gutted the naked carcasses and dropped them whole into a soup cauldron the Englishman always left simmering over a wood fire.

Subotai returned to the workbench and carefully eyed the various lengths and textures of the goose feathers. He chose several of the long wing feathers of the geese, selecting only the smoothest of those with unbroken quills and with the fabric of the feather undivided. With a razor-sharp blade, he split each of the selected quills almost its length, then carefully, by free-hand, cut each half into a set of three guide-feathers of exactly equivalent size. He took

care to take the three guide-feathers in each set from the same side
of a feather to insure that each fletching would curve in the same
direction. Once glued to the arrow and viewed from the rear of the
shaft, each set of fletchings would clearly show a uniform direction
of curvature. Thus the fletching would impart a spin to the arrows
in flight that would prevent random tumbling and provide the basis
for accurate bowmanship.

When Subotai had finished the careful cutting he turned his
attention to the bundle of wooden shafts he had turned on the crude,
foot-powered lathe in the Englishman's smithy. He laid out the
shafts, balancing them one by one across two of the Saxon's small
anvils. From each he hung a small iron weight from a line hooked
over the shaft, and eyed the bend the wood took. In this way he
began sorting out those shafts with approximately the same tendency
to bend. Long ago he had learned that his shooting would be more
consistent if each arrow, when launched into flight, bent about the
same amount from the shock of the released bowstring.

Using his finger, Subotai dabbed up a small amount of a gluey
substance from a small earthen pot. The glue was the sticky by-
product of boiled-down goat sinew and horse hoof. He smeared this
bonding onto the flat quill side of each guide-feather and, with his
breath expelled, he glued it to the shaft, slowly turning the arrow
and its newly attached fletching. He did this part of his work closer
to the smithy fire so that the heat would hasten the setting.

When each shaft had been fletched, Subotai finished fabri-
cating the missiles by jamming and gluing on one of the barbed
steel points the Saxon had so generously forged for the Mongol's use
after the two men had agreed on their joint venture.

Then from his quiver Subotai drew four shafts of the type he
had used that day. These were made of dark gray horn. After examining their feather mountings, he stripped the guide-feathers from
two of them and replaced them with white guides from the snow
goose quills. He mounted new steel heads on all four of the horn
shafts of the arrows. When this was done, and when the glue had
dried, he put a small amount of sawdust in the soft leather quiver
as an anchor for the arrows, loaded them point-down in the quiver,
and capped their feathered ends with a soft leather casing which
fitted over the top of the quiver.

That night by the glow of the forge, Subotai sat unspeaking as the Englishman laboriously went down the list of supplies inscribed on a skin scroll, and watched as the big man got up now and again to poke into a piece of tied baggage and assure himself of its actual contents.

Subotai noticed that it was starting to snow in the night outside the tent-smithy, but the Englishman seemed not to notice, in fact did not even look up from his manifest when the Mongol untied and dropped the sides of the tent and went outside to secure them to the stakes.

In the morning they waded ankle-deep in the new snow as they pack-loaded a dozen and a half tall and heavy-hooved horses. Subotai had never encountered horses as big as these prior to the Englishman's coming to the Seljuk trading camp. As the Mongol, acting on the signalled bidding of the Englishman, brought out each load item, the big man hoisted it up to the pack frames and lashed it securely in place. With the pack horses burdened, they took their saddles from the ground where the traveling tent-smithy had stood only an hour before and carried them to their waiting mounts.

Just as they finished cinching their saddle girths Balankar rode up alone, got down into the snow and kicked a small area free of the wet fall. He took a silver decanter and some hard cheese and bread from one of his saddlebags, then reached again into the leather bag and brought out three wooden cups. With the cups set on the ground from which he had foot-scraped the snow, he poured into them steaming hot wine along with raisin and apple chunks and lifted a warm wooden container to each of them. With a salute, he brought his own cup to his lips and cautiously tested the heat before he took a longer drink of the vintage. Subotai could feel the wine and fruit warm him downward through his gullet and into his belly.

Lowering his cup, Balankar looked up at the giant Englishman and spoke in Turkish. "Naturally I know why you must leave at this time. I will try to keep an accounting of the time you are away. On your return journey will you stop where you usually do on the big river with the green sand?" The Englishman, still sipping the hot drink, nodded. "Then I will dispatch some supplies about six moons after the beginning of next winter, and have them stored in your ground cache by the river. I remember the year you came down from there nearly snowblind and starving."

Subotai noted this talk, the first he had heard of danger and hardship, and wondered again about the purpose of the journey he was undertaking with the Englishman. He could hardly ask now without revealing his comprehension of the Turkish tongue, and that he was not yet willing to do. Subotai's face showed nothing of these feelings, nor of the inward mental shrug with which he dismissed these questions. Danger and hardship had been an integral part of his life as long as he could remember, and it made little difference to him why or even where the Englishman was going. His own purpose was perfectly clear in his mind, and his chance to accompany the Englishman now seemed not only convenient, but a genuine windfall.

The Seljuk's voice now took on a note of urgency. "Why must you go alone? Generations ago when the Rus Vikings found those breeding grounds, my great-grandfather said they went in great expeditions, sometimes hundreds of trappers in a single band, and even then many times the entire expedition was lost to a man."

The Englishman interrupted with a booming laugh. "Where would I find a hundred men to go on such madness as I do? Remember, they had the tribal impulse then. Besides, the division of profits is not appealing to me. And who knows," here he glanced at Subotai, "this master of the sword may well be worth the hundred you suggest."

Balankar tore bread and cheese for both of them and urged them to eat. He refilled their cups and let the last drops from the decanter fall into his own. Then he stood in silence as the Englishman and the Mongol stepped onto their horses and, taking the lead lines of the pack train between them, started at a walk into the gray northeast.

φ   φ   φ   φ

Subotai had not said so but he privately thought the Englishman's brains must be as white as his skin for beginning a long journey at the start of winter. But the other's knowledge of where he trailed made the cold night camps at least endurable. The ex-Varangian guardsman seemed to be able to pace most of the trailing to bring them to night stops that offered a source of fuel for a fire. Always they carried a load of emergency kindling and dried dung, and a metal fire box with smouldering punk in it with which to light the evening blazes.

And the brutal, numbing, bone-reaching, and lung-torturing cold of high Eurasia settled upon them. And the wide rivers froze solid. Undelayed by the overwhelming obstacles the rivers would have been in the warmer months, the pack train plodded on day after day and into the fiendishly cold nights. Like the Mongol, the Englishman was given to long silences. The weeks of winter travel with their cruel demands made both of them even more taciturn than ever as they reserved the energy it would have required to talk for maintaining their slender margin of body heat.

φ   φ   φ   φ

With the feet of the pack and saddle animals wrapped in coarse leather, the Englishman sometimes followed the flat surfaces of frozen rivers for great distances, depending on the reliability of the smooth, snow-covered ice in preference to the treacherousness of the snowy steppe ground.

They followed the course of one such river for a number of days. When they reached a turning of the ice where the river bent its birch-lined shores back almost due west, the Englishman headed the ambling pack train toward its eastern shores. Suddenly a jarring crack ripped the air. Neither man needed any prompting from the other. With the Englishman roaring and kicking his mount and hauling on the lead ropes, Subotai dropped back, then ranged up the line of pack animals shouting and slapping rumps to urge them up to a ponderous gallop.

The air was echoing now with the thunderclaps of splitting ice. The shore and the safety of dry ground were near now, but the Mongol suddenly felt the ice crack and slide away just behind his mount's hind legs. Without a conscious thought, he drew the blue sword and in two ruthless strokes severed the tie-lines of the last two draught horses which were now foundering in a slush of rotten ice and cold water. Then he gave the black mare her head and raced for the tree-lined banks. He looked back for an instant and saw the abandoned animals lose their fight to paw up onto solid ice. Then, dragged down by their great loads, they disappeared below the chunks and floes of ice that were breaking off and being carried along by the river's swift current.

Once safe on the far shore, the Mongol and the Englishman stepped off their mounts and watched the white ice islands race downstream on the thawing river. The Englishman made the hand and arm sign for luck or fortune. Subotai chopped his right shoulder in the gesture for emphasis.

The freak onset of balmy spring weather had surprised the Englishman, but his timetable of travel still held. Their luck had enabled them to cross the last of the major watercourses before the spring breakup, and there was no recurrence of colder days after the initial thawing. The steppe mud dried more swiftly than in normal years, and the Englishman began to break his long silences.

"It's a good living, lad." The big man knew Subotai spoke only some heathen jibberish and a smattering of the pidgin tongue of the trading camps and the caravan trails. But the Englishman continued in the rough, gutteral Germanic language of the Saxons in his native land anyway. "No sweating for Greek pay in the Varangian armor, no clawing in dirt or pigsties for a Norman overlord, and we're not hungry, either."

Subotai was still not privy to the Englishman's destination and purpose. Once he had mentioned his own purpose, the Kipchaks, but the smith put him off with a smile and the trail sign for "later." Subotai was wearying of this trip which seemed to him to have no goal nor any end. When the smith did talk, he maundered in unintelligible languages, drifting between Saxon, Greek, and Arabic, much to Subotai's annoyance. Once when the Englishman spoke directly to him in Saxon, Subotai slapped the hilt of the blue sword and responded with a universally obscene gesture, but that only made the big man laugh and return the gesture in kind.

Their way passed now from the open steppe lands into a slightly rising region of scrubby growth and yew trees. The yews prompted the red-faced, yellow-and-gray bearded man to remark, once again in his native language, "Best wood there is for bows. Bends like gristle. Why when I was poaching game in the fens..." On these words he abruptly fell silent and rode that way for the rest of the warming afternoon.

As they were making their night camp while dusk spread over the departed brilliance of the afternoon blue and the lingering violet of early evening, they noticed a dark line, horizon to horizon, like a ragged wall in the immediate north.

"Taiga, the forest," the Englishman signed and tried to get this notion across to Subotai, but to no avail. The signs for trees and big, great, or wide and their pidgin equivalents, and what they might mean in relation to each other and to the dark line, were simply beyond Subotai's experience and hence his comprehension. He learned the meaning the next morning when they rode into immense gloom and the misty, sun-shafted, snow-patched coolness of the great forest.

Riding in the green glades the Englishman's silence seemed to deepen. They cold-camped after entering the Taiga, partly because there was no dry wood—the springy forest floor was still wet from the melting winter snows—and partly, Subotai knew, because the big man feared something.

Days passed into a fortnight of quiet passage through the vast Taiga. And still no end, nor any evidence that the trees might have an end. Always the cold camp, cold, dry milk curds, dried camel jerky for their brief meals. They slept under leather sheets against the dew, underpinned with the same kind of slick leather sheeting to protect themselves from ground seepage.

It was as they rolled from their rough fur beds that Subotai sensed the presence. Not the danger the big man feared, something different. Something, Subotai recognized, that was much like himself—a silent, secret, deadly, inexorable thing.

The Englishman, on his knees, was frozen with a rooting fear so great he seemed unable to breathe or blink his eyes. Then Subotai saw it too. The pale, snowy orange fur, the blackish-gray stripes, sitting on its haunches in the underbrush like a tame cat inside a warm yurt. The green, unblinking eyes encompassed both men and their animals, missing nothing.

The Englishman was in a shock of terror, unable to move, incapable of speech. One of Subotai's great gifts was a quality of mind which allowed him perception and recognition of danger but blocked any fear from rising above the subliminal boundary of his consciousness. Fear, genuine, gut-watering, will-freezing, sickening fear would strike at Subotai only once in the life to which he was fate-bound. Without haste or undue caution, the Mongol stood up, then bent and picked up his saddle bow sheathed in an ibex-skin covering. He slid the bow from the water-protective leather while stringing it smoothly in a graceful flow of young strength. The cat-eyed Mongol stared across perhaps forty English yards into the cat eyes of the great Siberian snow tiger.

Somehow the Englishman controlled himself, and with amazing presence of mind handed one of the beautiful horn-shafted arrows to the Mongol from the lidded quiver which had lain next to the double-curved bow.

Subotai blinked his eyes. The tiger had moved, or rather it was now in a different place. Subotai knew no words for it, but the great cat had instantly altered the geometry of the confrontation. The blurring shift had changed the angles, narrowed the distance between the men and the magnificent predator.

In the instant of the charge, in a seeming unity, the tiger and the Mongol acted as one. The small cat-brain was arrow-pierced in mid-leap, the central nervous system of the savage killer fatally wounded. But its bounding flight carried the fearful, flailing carnage of fangs and claws onto Subotai.

Wrenched from the grip of his fear, the mighty Englishman was instantly on the beast with his great, wide-bladed war ax, crushing the snarling cat skull with the flat of the ax head in powerful strokes.

Subotai lay stunned under nearly six hundred pounds of dead weight, the tiger's bloody death-drool pooling on his shoulder. Straining and bucking against the heavy carcass, the Englishman at last freed the semi-conscious Mongol from the pressing weight.

The Englishman could see that though the Mongol's heavy leather jerkin was in shreds, the tough material had shielded the youngster from the worst of a horrible flaying by the dying beast, but blood was showing through the ragged places ripped by the snow tiger's piston-legged and razor-clawed assault.

Subotai groaned and tried to get up, but the Englishman restrained him. "Lie still there, lad." He spoke in the Saxon tongue. "And a cool one you are, too," he added as he went sorting through the pile of loads until he found a pouch of salt. But before rising from his kneeling position beside the baggage, he turned and stared at the prostrate Mongol. The Englishman had never seen a colder demonstration of courage. He remembered the ones, now long dead, who might compare with this strange lad. There was only one, really, a medium-sized man, warrior, who spoke even less than the Mongol yonder. Killed in that set-to with the Knights of Malta. The Englishman could not remember the man's name or the features of his face. All he could remember was his unwavering behavior in the battle-stress. Yes, that was it. He had a pure valor. The Englishman walked toward Subotai. The word came hard to his mind, it carried religious connotations, but it seemed appropriate for this lad. Yes, by Christ, the boy was pure.

φ   φ   φ   φ

"We'll lay up here a day or so, lad." The Englishman had liberally applied salt to the open wounds on the Mongol's shoulders, arms, and chest, and then gone on a search in the forest for suitable fungi with which to poultice the gashes. He was still bewildered by the silent, ungrimacing, and unmoving way the young man had reacted, or rather not reacted, to the sting of the dousing with salt. But the Englishman could have known nothing of the life of the steppes and the deserts from which Subotai sprang, where suffering was a condition without obviation, and death at most times hardly less desirable than the harsh, nomadic, warring life.

At the Englishman's insistence, the Mongol rested throughout most of the day. While the Mongol napped fitfully propped against a saddle, the Englishman swirled a butchering knife against a whetstone, then began skinning the snow tiger. When all the mandatory cuts had been made he hitched a draft horse to the hide and stripped the fur in a bloody fat-glistening sheet from the red carcass. He made a wooden stretcher frame and secured the hide to it. Then he spent most of the afternoon scraping and cleaning the hide. He salted the skin and, noting that Subotai had fallen asleep, he went into the trees again to search for the proper bark to use in tanning the large and luxuriant fur. He would soak the hide in a tanning solution drawn from the bark he was gathering, but that would be done later. He packed the bark, then rolled the hide tightly and packed it, too.

The two men remained for another day after their encounter with the snow tiger. The days were warming now, and the occasional hum of insects could be heard in the tree-shaded wilderness. The Englishman did not press him, but on the third morning, the Mongol signaled that he was ready to travel again by stripping off the fungi from his cuts and saddling his own mount. Then he helped the Englishman load up the pack horses.

When it was only midafternoon, the Englishman halted and wordlessly set about making the evening camp. After the pack and saddle animals had been divested of their burdens he took a crude saw and a two-handed wood ax and strode off into the trees. The Mongol tagged along behind, feeling the pleasant healing itchiness of the wounds inflicted on him by the snow tiger. The afternoon was comparatively warm and the early stop seemed to have a naturalness about it, a correct synchronization of place and time coherent with the buoying spirits of the two unlikely companions.

The man from that distant island, England, chose a number of low-hanging branches of evergreen trees and sawed them off. He also chopped down several armloads of young larch trees, each about seven or eight feet in length. Some of these he directed Subotai to saw roughly in half or into thirds, silently indicating the desired length by spanning his arms and the numbers of each by raised fingers.

Darkness was falling when the labor was finished. Subotai felt his strength returning, the resiliency of his young body asserting itself. Once again he felt the joy of his youthful power. And he wondered if he would ever find Mursechen, or the Kipchaks who were her people now. Or what he would do even if his improbable search succeeded. He hadn't thought much about that. What if she were content in her new life? After all, he had to admit to himself, only a single smile had ever transpired between them. He laughed aloud to himself. Always a realist, he nevertheless seemed unequal to the task of placing the handsome memory of the perfect young woman out of his mind. Only a man touched by the fevers of the northern darkness would persist in this kind of behavior. But it was Subotai's curse to be ever obsessed by his wanting thoughts of the fair girl, Subotai's curse to be one of those rare men, one of those tormented men, who, at a given period in his life, can ever only really admire or give complete mental allegiance to a single woman. An oddity when the times and customs of these dark ages set women for the most part far down in the scale of social value. The notion of a spiritual loving between man and woman was beyond the mental evolution of the times.

For the first time since leaving the steppes the Englishman struck sparks from two ratcheted pieces of steel onto tinder, re-igniting the source in the fire-box. A cooking fire blossomed against the night. They boiled some of the dried camel jerky to an almost chewable consistency and then, both of them quietly reveling in the warmth of the meat in their bellies, went off to sleep in the primeval silence.

The long trek through the Taiga was ending. They came now to the edge of the barren grounds. Farther to the north they would come onto the mosquito-swarming tundra lands, but here early summer dominated and the treeless northern ranges were verdant with life. Never had Subotai seen such an abundance of food for the taking. Foolish ptarmigan, which could almost be seized by hand, were easily felled by a well aimed rock. Eggs of all kinds seemed to litter the landscape. Both men grew sleek and cheerful as they pressed on into the almost constant, late-spring daylight of the high arctic regions.

At times it seemed all but impossible to take their animals farther into the boggy land they encountered after they left the northern edge of the Taiga. After nearly a week of the harsh labor and gut-wearing distress of moving the saddle and pack animals across the sucking and trembling peat of the lower barren grounds, the land began to take on more of a roll, and the footing gradually firmed. Two more weeks of the swifter travel this terrain afforded and they arrived at a watery inlet that widened and stretched to the horizon in the shimmering north.

This, apparently, was the goal of the Englishman. He swept his hand toward the reaches of the inlet where icebergs floated in eerie, spectral silence, their pure white and translucent blue mirrored in the quiet waters. Then he spoke in the trail tongue. "See those high cliffs? The ones with white splashed across their faces are the seabird rookeries. The peregrine falcons rarely nest on the rocks in the rookery. The peregrine eyries will be easy to find because the parent birds will come after us like Saracens when we get anywhere near the nesting areas."

So that's what it is, the Mongol thought. This English black-smith—this warrior—is a falcon trapper.

In recent days the scope of the pidgin conversations between the two men had expanded and richened through the use and under-standing of a growing infusion of Saxon, Norman-French, Greek, Mongol, Turkish, and Arabic words and expressions.

The Englishman dismounted and, holding his reins, sat down on a granite boulder that jutted up from the tundra. He squinted across the watery scene, then pointed into the north as he dipped up a handful of water to taste. The water of the rocky and cliff-edged inlet tasted even saltier to Subotai than that of the Sea of Ravens.

"There must be a great salt sea to the north of here," the Englishman said. "Sometimes I wish I could follow the inlet on until I see for myself, but there isn't the time. Without that, we'll be damned lucky to be away from here before the cold sets in again."

They established a camp and hobbled their horses, which were soon feeding in the lush tundra grass of summer. Then the English-man set himself and Subotai to work. When the carefully selected wood they had brought up from the Taiga was set out, the English-man began measuring, cutting, and roughly shaping the pieces into structures which puzzled Subotai.

"Cadges," the Englishman answered Subotai's unspoken ques-tion without looking up from his intent labor. "For the falcons to perch on. The pack horses will carry them until we can get to the caravan routes and sell them off."

Subotai readily understood what had to be done, and although he had had no acquaintance with carpentering or the tools used for working in wood until he met with the Englishman, he was soon an invaluable assistant in the building of the cadges.

The wooden perches themselves with their diagonal cross-sup-port struts and the back mounts for loading them onto the horses were now nailed together with the steel spikes which Subotai had seen the Englishman forging in the tent-smithy at their first meeting.

Other tasks followed the completion of the cadges. Rolls of soft leather were laid out onto relatively flat rock surfaces. Subotai

quickly fell into the job of cutting the leather with a set of metal
pattern plates and a small, keenly honed knife. Some of the patterns
were for hoods, soft coverings which, when fitted over the heads of
the falcons, would keep the birds in darkness, keep them quiet,
and avoid damage to the creatures and to their potential value as
an economic cargo. Others were patterns for jesses, leg straps which
would fit loosely and, with swivels on their trailing edges, would
be attached to a long leash to tether the birds to the çadges. The
remarkable humanity of the arts of falconry and its accoutrements
and furnishing belied the overall barbarism and mindless cruelty
of the age and conditions into which Subotai and the Englishman
had been born.

The leather work done, the falcon trapper launched himself
and the Mongol into one final construction task. He took the remaining wood and scrap material and quickly fashioned and hammered
together a number of small, slatted, boxlike cages of indifferent
but sturdy appearance.

"We'll fill these boxes up with ptarmigan just as we go into
the trees to provide the hawks with a supply of fresh meat until we
get south of the Taiga." He spoke in Saxon, then he signed and
used pidgin words to communicate this to Subotai.

Their preparations ended with the advent of the summer sol-
stice. Now they went on foot around the great inlet, seemingly an
extension of an unknown sea, and began to scout the eyries, the
nesting sites, of the arctic peregrine falcons. The falcons habitually
chose high ledges on the sea cliff faces, ledges which commanded
a view of the water and of the rookeries which had been used by
the aerial colonies of seabirds since time immemorial. The birds in
the rookeries and the ground-level congregations of nesting waterfowl were the prey of the peregrines.

The Englishman was checking that most reliable indicator of
full maturity in a first-year falcon: the final growing out of the
feather quills. After the feathers reach their full, adult length, they
no longer need nutrients, so they seal themselves off from the bird's
blood supply. By the time this occurs the falcon has usually become
a fairly accomplished flier and is ready for the passage, the fall
migration. Trappers must wait until the peregrines are just ready
to glide off the nesting ledges before taking them captive. The

Englishman could tell that these young peregrines in the nest—eyases—would not be ready for any serious attempt to fly for about another fortnight.

After they had checked some half-dozen falcon eyries they returned to their camp. To hasten the passage of the waiting time they busied themselves repairing clothing and harness, and checked the leathern climbing rope they would rely upon when they descended to the nesting ledges to capture the young falcons.

They slept and ate a great deal. The energy requirements of their outdoor existence made them constantly ravenous and, with a natural abundance of food at hand, they now sated their appetites. They feasted on puffin and murrelet eggs lifted by the armload from the more readily accessible areas of the rookeries, and gorged on duck and goose eggs taken from the waterfowl nests which congested the flatter shores of the inlet, throwing in an occasional ptarmigan egg for variety. They cooked the eggs over fires built from driftwood which had found its way onto the shores of this far northern and woodless land, wood which floated to the inlet on a wide river whose mouth Subotai had discovered emptying into the inlet on one of his scouting trips which he undertook, always alone, in order to break the boredom of waiting.

It was as he was riding back from one of these exploratory sojourns, a far-ranging traverse to the west of the inlet, that it came upon him for the first time. He had reined in and dismounted on a promontory above the blue inlet, and was standing there watching it glitter brightly with the light of the ever-transiting sun of the far northern summer. The clearness of the air, the powerful contrasts of colors and conditions of ice, the water, the green land, the buff-colored and lichened rock, and the unbroken sweep of vision in every direction—all these suddenly seemed to coalesce, come together, first unify and then widen out to some unknown limit in his consciousness. At first he felt odd, but joyously so, and then Subotai, unable to move, sensed with perfect clarity his mind and his being suffused and lifted into a towering, drawn-up majesty of his own existence.

How long he remained in this state he could never recall. And later, upon his return to their camp, the big falcon trapper looked at him long and with great intensity.

"Is there anything ailing you, lad?" He spoke softly, for he saw the silvery, gray-blue of the Mongol's eyes still alive with the overpowering experience.

φ   φ   φ   φ

The time came for the taking of the eyas peregrine falcons. The two men systematically worked around the eyries they had previously scouted, some of them located no farther apart than an English mile.

Taking turns, since there seemed to be little difference between the weights of the two men, one would belay the other over the rocky top of a sea cliff above a nesting site. Once the roped man reached the nesting ledge, he would quickly seize each young, hissing, and fear-fluffed nestling by its ankles, hood it, brail the wings to secure the valuable wing pinions and prevent the flapping that might damage them, and then stuff the prize unceremoniously into a soft leather bag. When all the nestlings were in the bag the top man would draw the bag up by the line to the top of the cliff and then anchor the rope while the other man scrambled back up the cliff.

At some of the eyries they came too late. At those ledges, the branching peregrines were advanced enough to take wing at the first sound above them and glide out over the water, returning to perch on a different, usually inaccessible ledge on the same sea cliff.

On a ledge they had overlooked on their earlier scouting of the nests they discovered the treasure of treasures—an eyrie of great and beautiful black gyrfalcons, the largest of the falcon species. Gyrfalcons rarely strayed south of their far northern habitat, and these birds literally represented a king's ransom, for they were highly prized by the nobility both of Europe and of the Moslem emirates.

The trapper hoisted up the bag with the three prizes: one male, the tiercel; and the two larger females, the falcons. The big Englishman yelled with glee, clapping his forehead in uncontrolled delight, but keeping a hand on the rope that was looped about Subotai's waist. Then, hastily throwing a loose loop of the climbing rope around his waist and catching another loop around his left thigh, the trapper shifted hands from the rope to gentle the position of the bag containing the eyas gyrfalcons, and in doing so inadvertently slackened the line just as Subotai started back up.

Subotai, beginning to scramble hand-over-hand back toward the clifftop, felt the line slacken and swung himself desperately across the cliff face to try for a handhold, but the rock was wet with sea-damp and his fingers slid over it. When Subotai's full weight hit the slackened rope, the line burned and whirred about the trapper's waist and leg and nearly dragged him over the precipice before he could clear himself of the loops and let the line go.

For a long moment Subotai looked straight up into the blue arctic Sky. He even had time for a wordless prayer. Then as he fell, he caught a glimpse of the trapper, staring down at him from the clifftop and bellowed a Mongol curse as the freezing water slammed into and knocked the breath from him. His head and right shoulder hit the water first. The double shocks of impact and icy water numbed him almost to the point of unconsciousness.

As Subotai hit the water some seventy feet below, the trapper turned for his spare rope just at the moment the kicking gyrfalcons had jerked their confining bag along until it was teetering on the cliff edge. He dove for the bag, sliding belly down, to catch it on the very brink. Then, falcon-bag in one hand and legs dangling over the edge of the cliff, he clung for his life to a tuft of tundra grass with his other hand. As he swung his torso to the left to get a better grip on the grass, he saw Subotai coming up like a great bubble from deep beneath the surface of the crystal clear, frigid water of the inlet. Heaving the falcon-bag to safety, the trapper just managed to edge his chest up over the cliff edge before the grass tuft he was clinging to ripped out of the rocky soil.

The trapper cursed and swore for long seconds, pausing only briefly to roar through the sweat on his beard, "I'm sorry, Holy Mother." What flashed through his mind was a drunken night in Constantinople when he and other Varangian soldiers had carved their names as best they could on a marble balustrade within the cathedral of Saint Sophia, their efforts limited more by illiteracy and inebriation than by the marble.

Subotai was aware and not aware of breath returning to him, of seeing the trapper's legs finally kick over the clifftop above, of his boots heavy with water, and of the clinging, soaked weight of his leather clothing. Treading water, he strove to muster the will to begin side-stroking toward a natural jetty of rock some yards away. Halfway there he had to jettison his water-logged boots, but finally hauled himself from the bone-achingly cold salt water, privately thanking the Sky, his lucky stars, and Narslana who had taught him to swim. He had almost recovered his breath when the end of the trapper's spare climbing rope whipped across his head.

"Grab on, lad."

As Subotai tied a loop under his armpits, the trapper yelled, danced, and sang his own distillated versions of Greek and old Saxon folk songs. The trapper bellowed down at the Mongol, his voice clear in the still, arctic air, "We're rich, lad. By old William Bastard's blood, if we get these gyrs back to the trade routes we'll buy our own landhold!"

Subotai scrambled as best he could with his nearly frozen limbs to keep from banging against the rocks as the exultant trapper hauled him back up to the clifftop, then closed his eyes and sank back to the ground in the comparative warmth of the arctic sunlight, his teeth chattering uncontrollably from cold and shock.

"Get those wet things off of you, lad."

But the trapper's attention focused more on the gyrfalcons than on his shivering, sodden companion. Picking up the bag of eyases, he said, "Coil the rope and bring it along, that's a good lad," and marched away. Subotai limped behind him on his bare, bruised feet.

Dried by the campfire, redressed, and rebooted, the Mongol completed the rounds of the remaining falcon eyries with the trapper. As with the black gyrfalcons, they returned each day's catch of eyases to their base camp where the young birds were quickly jessed, swiveled, leashed, and perched on the cadges which were now resting on the tundra turf. Starting when the optimum time for trapping had arrived, the two men had worked with a fevered energy. Before it was over they had covered a circuit of about twenty-five miles along the inlet. In the unchanging light of the arctic summer they had worked continuously for three days and two nights without pause. They now prepared to set out on the return trip with their wild treasure—more than eighty peregrines and now the three black gyrfalcons.

With glowing eyes, the trapper spoke in the trail tongue. "We must start down this very moment, lad, else we'll be snowed in before we get clear of the Taiga. We can sleep in the saddle till first camp."

"Perhaps we can trade these to the Kipchaks." Subotai said it like an order to the trapper.

The Englishman turned with a surprised smile at this suggestion. "Aye, we might do just that...if they are the first to barter with us." The blue-eyed Saxon and the blue-eyed Mongol locked eyes for a long moment. Then the trapper, feeling the overwhelming superiority of consciousness within the Mongol, averted his gaze.

They lined the still downy, hooded falcons in neat rows on the cadges and securely tied each leash to its perch. The carefully constructed cadges were then mounted on the pack horses so that they extended at almost right angles from the sides of the beasts to make the perch-boards ride parallel with the ground. They finished loading in the twilight period of the day, a twilight that was growing in duration with the passage of the season, and immediately set out for the south.

As they pressed on day after long arctic day, the Englishman oscillated between deep, silent depression over the possible fate of their living cargo and states of ebullient, grandiose daydreaming of the riches to be had when they at last reached a caravan trail or a trading camp.

Subotai assumed the duty of feeding the precious birds. It was essential to keep the crops of the falcons satisfied with fresh meat, and fresh meat was easily had on the tundras in this season. The Mongol was kept busy rocking game birds for falcon food and shifting himself from the back of one cadge-horse to another so that he could feed the hawks while the pack train plodded on toward the tantalizing south. The young hawks could not be left the least bit hungry lest weakened lines appear across the tail and wing feathers, unsightly hunger streaks that would lower their market value.

The pack train with its scores of cadged eyas falcons made swift progress in its almost flightlike trailing across the tundra until they reached the Taiga. By this time summer was drawing toward its end, and nights and mornings in the great forest were cooling and misty. And it was there that disaster struck the trapper's hopes.

Within a single night all three of the gyrfalcons were taken by eagle owls which came and departed on soundless wings. Subotai made it a special point to remain far behind the Englishman during the next day's trailing. The big trapper was mostly quiet with hard-set jaws, but at times he would pull up his mount, shake his fist at the Sky, and scream curses and oaths in half a dozen languages. Thereafter the two men stood constant watch over the falcons, relieving each other by the night fire to ward off visitations of other predators seeking the hooded and defenseless falcons.

The larch and evergreen trees and the matted floor of the forest were stark and white with frost in the early mornings before they at last reached the southern edge of the mighty Taiga. Thereafter the trapper held them to a southwesterly trail, intending to intersect the most northerly of the caravan routes where he could trade off the falcons. Conveying the birds across the enormous distance to the Sea of the Ravens in the snow would have been an impossibility. Even now they had to slaughter one of the older pack animals to feed themselves and the precious birds.

φ   φ   φ   φ

"You must be a lucky charm, lad." The Englishman watched the caravan disappear into the snow flurries and listened to the distant camel bells and the shouting of the drovers that still came faintly to them over the wind.

The transaction had been extremely favorable to the English-man. Their pack train was loaded with well seasoned and tanned ermine, sable, and otter furs, and with a great weight of amber. And the Englishman held a heavy sack of silver weights and gold and silver coins struck in the Russias, in the Byzantine empire, and in nations unknown. The peculiar appearances and logos of the coins were of no interest to the Englishman; only the inherent value of the precious metals in the monies interested the solidly practical trapper.

Subotai had taken no part in the bartering between the caravan merchants and the trapper. He had merely loitered in the background near the falcon cadges with his sheathed sword slung over his shoulder and a hand on his bow strung with a nocked shaft at the ready. He had done this instinctively, not at the trapper's bidding, and he saw the sparkle of approval in the trapper's eyes when he did so, but he did not hear the Englishman say softly to himself, "And you know the nature of men, do you?"

Subotai's voluntary act of providing security for the falcons while the trapper bartered with the caravan traders strengthened the growing bond between the two men, a bond they both knew must now carry them through the savage steppe winter settling about them.

φ   φ   φ   φ

"Water only makes it burn more fiercely. Fire of the Greeks, lad. It's a secret, though. All I know is they mix some crushed white stone with something they call naphtha. When it's lit, watch out. We used it in a campaign in the north of Africa."

Subotai turned his cool gaze toward the big trapper reclining beside their night fire. "Where is Africa?"

They had wintered near the river with the green sandbars, and early spring buds were now appearing on the trees, even though snow still lay in shaded patches beside the river and in the ravines on the steppes. If Balankar had had a cache of supplies set for them, they had not been able to find it. When the snow made the search impractical, they abandoned attempts to locate it. They had to rely on Subotai's extensive trapping and hunting skills for food after they camped at the river.

"One thing at a time, son. I was soldiering with some other Varangians from Scandia in the Guard at the time. But only the Greeks—call themselves Romans, they do—handled the fire. It was shot off catapults. Too dangerous to use at sea, though. Two of the Greek galleys burned themselves to hulks when the stuff got loose. It will make a city or a walled citadel quit quick enough. We burned out one Saracen fort easily enough when we landed a catapult or two. Didn't do any good, though. They whipped us for fair three days later when their relief force caught us with our tails to the Mediterranean and our sunburned snouts to the desert. I was damn glad to be on the last boat out of that hole."

The Mongol yawned openly. "Where is Africa?"

With a look of feigned exasperation, the Englishman picked a glowing stick from the fire. He began to sketch in the dirt. "Now this is the Sea of the Ravens. I have come upon it from the north, from the east, and from the west, but I have never traveled all the way around it. Altogether, I think it must look like this. I have sailed on the Mediterranean and on another sea, an arm of it really, to the north of the Byzantine lands."

The trapper drew another representation of a sea like a ball to the left and slightly below the Sea of the Ravens. Then he drew a larger, more oblong figure beneath the ball-sea. "That is the Mediterranean. Here, about here, is the Byzantine capital." He pointed with the stick at the juncture of the ball-sea and the Mediterranean. "Now the land south of the Mediterranean is Africa. I have only seen a very small part of it, I am pleased to say. The Saracens are not hospitable, to say the least, toward my ilk—toward fair-skinned Christians, that is."

Subotai's association with the widely traveled and intelligent Englishman had begun to strike sparks of curiosity from an intellect which had largely lain dormant during Subotai's rude life, and Subotai began to wonder. Somehow the big trapper always seemed to know more or less where he was, whether on the monotonous steppes or within the thick sameness of the Taiga. Somehow he knew how to travel for moons between the Sea of the Ravens and the inlet and arrive at the intended destination.

Subotai remembered the days, even weeks, when he had wandered alone on the steppes, trying to stay in a westward course but knowing intuitively that he was often circling widely. There were days on the unbroken landscape when he could not tell whether he had even moved at all, even after a full day's ride.

Finally Subotai asked the trapper outright, "How is it that you know where you are going? How do you travel so straightly?"

In the polyglot mixture of languages he and the Englishman used, Subotai could not make the questions precise, but the trapper knew what he wanted. Without getting to his feet, the Englishman stretched and pulled one of his saddlebags toward him. He fumbled amongst its contents, then drew a hand-sized, opaque stone from the depths of the pouch. This he tossed to the Mongol. It's shape was irregular, but one side of it was partially flattened. Subotai scrutinized the runic symbols which were inscribed in meandering, circling bands about the stone.

"Do these have meaning?" he asked, pointing at the runes before handing the milky-crystal stone back to the trapper. The trapper ran his palm across the runes.

"The Scandians make markers and writing in this manner, or they did long ago. The Norsemen I knew in the Guard could no more make out these markings than I could, but I'm sure this stone belonged to a Viking sea-rover." He noted the Mongol's waiting look. "The Vikings and the Norse were one and the same at one time. Long before I was born they sailed from the lands above and east of Britain. I am sure they used stones like these to guide them when they crossed the open seas. In the morning I will show you how it is used."

"Where did you obtain such a thing?" Subotai's eyes had the same knowledge-lusting look they had shown the first time he entered the trapper's tent-smithy by the Sea of the Ravens.

"A gift—one of the kind of baubles the Byzantines throw in with the gold to bribe barbarians like myself into their Varangian Guard to do their killing and protect their effeminate hides. But the old Greek who gave me that wasn't too bad a sort. He had been a physician with the army for ages. Told me that when he was a young man himself, he was given the stone by a Norse Varangian."

The trapper replaced the stone in the leathern pouch. "I also guide on the stars." Here the Englishman stood up, walked to the entry way of the traveling tent, and looked out and up. Subotai joined him, but the night sky was obscured by clouds.

Returning to the fire, Subotai retrieved the stick the trapper had been using to map in the dirt. He threw aside a ragged carpet used as flooring for the tent and began to sketch by firelight. He carefully and accurately drew a reasonable schematic of the heavens of the northern hemisphere, while the Englishman looked on and grunted his approval. For some time they traded Saxon and Mongol names for the North Star and each star cluster, drawing and redrawing the relative positions of some constellations as they would appear at different seasons above the English fens and above the steppes near Lake Baikal, the Blue Lake.

The following morning dawned gray and cloudy. The Englishman produced the runed stone once again and spoke through a morning mouthful of roasted meat. "Look into this stone, son. That's it. Now hold the bottom, the side with the markings, on a line with the horizon. Now slowly turn. When it happens, you will know."

Subotai, following the trapper's instructions, faced the northwest and began to turn slowly to his left, pivoting on his feet but holding them to the same spot. As he swung to a point facing almost due east he suddenly uttered an exclamation, "The sun!"

"Keep turning, lad. Right. As you can see, the stone only flares when you point it into the sun. The Vikings called it the sun-stone. Now you know why."

Subotai made several more revolutions, smiling each time the light-polarizing property of the sun-stone lit up when it was aligned with the direct rays of the morning sun, although the sun itself was hidden in the overcast sky.

"With the stone, you'll always know east and west. You don't go wandering in circles if you can keep a constant check on the sun's position."

Subotai bounced the dense sun-stone in his hand and gave it back to the trapper, but the trapper put out a halting hand.

"It's yours, son. I've another. Not so fancily carved, but it still does the same trick with the sunlight."

The Mongol was silent for a moment, then he said, in almost perfect Saxon, "For this special gift I will remember you always, even to the day when I shall pass through the door of the Sky."

The Englishman's dumbfounded expression slowly dissolved into a broad grin. He looked Subotai over with narrowed but twinkling eyes. "You have more surprises and ambushes in you than any man ought to have. Damned if you wouldn't make a general in the Guard. Well, probably not. I would guess you'd be more for the battlefield than for planning campaigns, plotting, and seducing Greek noblewomen with the correct political connections. But enough of that. We had best finish loading and push on to Balankar's camp." They both turned to dropping and folding the tent.

The Englishman was thoughtful while they packed and loaded the animals. All of the great rivers they had to cross were behind them now, rivers which Subotai had apparently been able to stay south of on his trek from the Blue Lake to the Caspian Sea. Then he looked up from lashing the rolled tent and said, "You must be closer to your own people here than along the Sea. I know you never tell why you left them, but listen to an old campaigner, lad. If they will have you back, well then, go. The life you are used to, away from the cities and trading camps, following your herds, is a cleaner and better one." The trapper turned back to his work. "That way when you die you will at least have fresh air and a starry sky over your head." But he knew his words were wasted.

Subotai said nothing. Once they were back at the Sea of the Ravens he would resupply and search again for the Kipchaks. The thought of Mursechen in another man's yurt...in his bed. He glanced at the blue sword. Surely destiny had put that matchless weapon in his hand for the express purpose of setting her free.

With the pack horses loaded, they both stepped up onto their saddle mounts. The trapper turned in his saddle. "Damned if I don't think there must be a woman behind your behavior. That's usually at the bottom of most varieties of lunacy."

Then the trapper pretended impatience. "Move that nag. I need to get this load back to the trading camp where I can grow my profits even taller."

Narslana was gone, of course. Balankar had met the trappers at the entrance to his log hall at the trading camp. He embraced the big Englishman and threw a welcoming arm over Subotai's shoulder. After the boisterous greeting he turned a serious face to them and asked, "Did my men get through to meet you at the river? Remember, I said I would dispatch them with relief supplies."

The Englishman glanced at the Mongol, then answered, "No. We were at the green-sanded river earlier than we anticipated. But we did not find your supplies, nor did we come across your people on the way from there to the coast of the Sea of the Ravens."

Balankar lowered his head. "These times! There is no order anywhere. Even in the lands of the Prophet where the law should be observed there is corruption and violence. And from what you tell me," here the Seljuk looked at the trapper, "great hatreds and enmity are everywhere also among those who follow Jesus Christ."

"Aye. In Christendom the Holy Father, the Holy Roman Emperor, and all the kings and princes spend their days and energies at war and in pillage and destruction. But let us not dwell on that this evening. I have waited near onto two years for a deep quaff of that honey brew for which you are famous. Now would there be a keg of it about?"

"Yes, and more. I set a great amount aside just for your coming. But come in—by the Prophet if I shall not set a great feast for your safe return. You both shall sleep here under my roof." And at this point Balankar's look turned even more joyous with a sudden excitement which came over him. "And while we eat there is something I must tell you."

Later the three men lounged in the relative luxury of the Seljuk's hall on the raised floor spread with thick carpets and furs. The trapper and Subotai were relaxed, their faces reflecting their satisfaction after a hearty indulgence in the roast goat and lamb served with hot fruit and nuts in a sweetened sauce brought by Balankar's servants. All three were drinking thirstily of the Turk's honey beer.

Subotai was waiting for Balankar to mention Narslana, but the Seljuk said nothing concerning her. Anxious as he was to resume his search for Mursechen, Subotai still wanted to be reassured of Narslana's well-being.

Balankar drew his sleeve across his mouth and stifled a belch. "Some ten days or so ago, a caravan arrived here from the Shallow Salt Sea. There is a dark and very wealthy man with a large retinue of guards and retainers who came with that caravan and camped about half a day's ride from here." The Seljuk placed a familiar hand on the trapper's shoulder. "He says he has journeyed a great distance just to see you. I have talked with him but briefly, but he told me he is either a servant or an agent of a great lord of the region of the Hindustan. His lord has heard of your reputation as a hawk trapper."

"And what if he has?" The Englishman reached for another morsel of the greasy lamb and washed it down with a long uninterrupted draught of the amber-colored beer.

The Seljuk shrugged. "I told him I would send him word when I learned of your whereabouts. He intends to remain here until just before snow flies. If he has not found you by then, he and his party plan to return whence they have come." Then he added, "He also told me there is a lucrative commission he is empowered to offer you."

The trapper turned interested eyes in the Turk's direction at the hint of money. "I have to trade or sell the loads I have just brought in with me. After that, well, then I will go and see this agent. Where is it that he comes from?"

Balankar was extracting a piece of meat lodged between two of his teeth. "The Hindustan—India."

φ   φ   φ   φ

Morning found the trapper with his head athrob from the overindulgence of the previous evening. The Mongol watched in silent amusement as the trapper got through a protracted period of groaning and head-holding which was at last followed by a face-dunking in cold water. The giant, sputtering and leaning over a rain barrel, slowly forced himself into a completely upright posture, then seized his brow in a futile attempt to squeeze the drum in his forehead into silence.

The trapper's voice was irritable. "Come on, lad. Don't just sit there looking smug. I have to get my goods to market. I would be more than pleased if you would hoist your lazy rump and help me before my cursed head goes off like that Greek fire I told you about. And hurry, or I'll throw that rich man's sword you sleep with into one of my trade bargains."

The trapper, with Subotai accompanying him, quickly converted the weights of amber and the tightly tied packets of thick pelts into more coinage to add to the already bulging money sack he had carried away from the caravan they intersected south of the Taiga. Most of the golden and silver monies he gave into the safe-keeping of the Seljuk Turk who, as camp master, with his kin and his armed mercenary force, represented law and stability in the tumultuous settlement. The remainder the Englishman promptly lost in games of chance and in wagers on the almost daily horse races on the steppe outside the trading camp.

Subotai was standing in the morning sunshine currying the black, gleaming withers and sides of his mare when the trapper managed his usual lurching and painful morning exodus from the Seljuk's log dwelling to throw cupped handfuls of water from the rain barrel adjacent to the hall into his swollen face. He spent an inordinate amount of time tilted over the barrel, hanging onto the rim as though fighting for balance.

Once he looked at the Mongol with eyes which blinked back

the ache of the sunlight from his head, then returned to his reverie over the rain barrel. Finally Subotai interrupted the trapper's preoccupation with his roaring brain.

"Is it time to go onto the steppe and see the trader who came seeking you?" It was more direction than question. Subotai had discovered a disliking within himself for the camp. Perhaps, he thought, it was because of the pleasant memory he had of it in his relationship with Narslana. Balankar had finally volunteered that Narslana had been married to a distant cousin in the Armenian lands. She had mothered a son and was pregnant again. Bearing the son had elevated her to senior wife status in the cousin's harem. The news of Narslana's apparent well-being seemed to resolve the conflict he had experienced between his concern for her sake and his undampened devotion to Mursechen. And it was time for him to press his search for the Kipchaks, although something within him bade him remain silent as to his true intents while he traveled with the trapper.

The Englishman scooped a handful of the water into his mouth. He turned from the barrel and, with hands anchored on his knees, dry-heaved until his throat was red and corded from the exertion. He wiped the strings of saliva hanging from his mouth with the back of one of his huge hands.

"Aye, lad. I need to have the clean breeze of the steppe in my face. We had best be off from here lest I lose all I have struggled for. Thank Christ I gave the bulk of my hoard to Balankar, else I would be a pitifully thin kestrel again."

He started for the entranceway to the hall, but turned and said, "Saddle my mount, that's a good lad, whilst I hoist just a smidgin of a tankard to see if a growl won't cure the bite of my flaming head."

Subotai had both animals saddled and waiting when the Englishman emerged from the Seljuk's hall. The giant's eyes were somewhat clearer, but he moaned out his distress as he swung himself slowly up onto the large gelding he used for a trail horse.

Following the directions provided by Balankar, they located the temporary campsite of the trader before midday. The armed guards outside and circulating within the confines of the half dozen tents seemed to recognize the pair immediately. The trapper's gigantic stature easily identified him as the man Balankar had described. To Subotai, even the guards and the servants seemed exotically and richly dressed. The cloth turbans wound about their heads were stark white against their brown and bearded faces. Their weapons were oddly carved and multi-pointed in ways totally unfamiliar both to the trapper and to Subotai. Only camels were to be seen in the stock picketing area, which was heavily guarded.

The trapper turned to Subotai after they dismounted. "Professionals, son. And as watchful as the devil himself. From the looks of this lackey approaching us, he will take us to his liege lord."

The man the trapper had dipped his head toward was brown and beardless. He stopped before them, placed his hands together before his face with the fingers pointed skyward in a pronam, then turned on his heel and gestured for them to follow. He led them to a large pentagon-shaped traveling tent with three of its sides rolled up to allow the steppe wind to sweep through its interior.

Inside sat a lone man frowning over the writing on a scroll, who turned intelligent brown eyes on the trio that entered. The servant spoke softly to him and then withdrew. The man put the writing aside and slowly appraised his guests. Then, smiling, he spoke in a dialect of Turkish. It was not the Turkish of the Seljuk, in which both the trapper and Subotai were now fluent, but they could understand most of what the Hindu was saying. The Englishman also noted with surprise that the Hindu mixed a number of Greek words and expressions into his speech.

"You are the Christian trapper, are you not?"

"Aye, I am that. And I have heard you seek me. My services are available at the moment. For the right amounts, of course."

The Hindu's expression was one of patient understanding. "Of course." He reached into his cotton tunic, took out a small bag which clinked metallically, and placed it in front of the standing trapper, then indicated that they should seat themselves on pillows facing him. The Hindu waited until his two guests had settled themselves before he spoke again.

"My lord the Maharawal of Amrithistan bade me make this long journey to find you and offer you an opportunity, a commission if you like, which you may find agreeable."

For some reason, the Hindu looked directly at the Mongol

while speaking of the opportunity as though reappraising the stocky, gray-eyed young barbarian.

"What would be the nature of such a commission?" Although some of the early morning bloatedness still showed in the trapper's face, he focused his bloodshot, pale blue eyes on the Hindu intently. The Indian pointed at the money pouch he had laid at the Englishman's feet.

"In our homeland there is a falcon we call the red-naped shaheen. Not as large as a saker, nor for that matter as the more northern peregrines, although my master the Maharawal thinks the northern peregrines and the shaheen may be very closely related. He bids me request that you undertake a trapping expedition for his benefit to bring him northern peregrine falcons. But mark you, he does not want any screaming eyases. He wants only first-year passage birds or young haggards trapped during the fall migration. And he wants them manned, but no other tampering. He does not keep a falconer, only bird handlers and mews attendants. He trains the birds himself in a way which you, perhaps, might consider religious."

The Maharawal's emissary paused, then clapped his hands and spoke in quiet tones to the manservant who responded to his summons. When he had given the man some instruction, he went on. "The Maharawal desires the northern peregrine falcons for his own sport, of course, but also to study the closeness of structure and behavior between them and the Indian shaheens."

The servant returned offering a platter of dried dates and sweet raisins, which interested Subotai much more than the proposition that was being offered to the trapper.

The Hindu picked up the money pouch in one hand and raised the other in a cautionary gesture. "One other thing. This is a retainer for you. You are to keep all of it if you trap and send at least a score of these falcons to my lord by caravan under the care of one of Balankar's agents. You may, however, consider this coinage as only an advance if you yourself bring the birds across the Macedonian Gate into the Indus valley and deliver them to the city of Sarghoda. If you do this thing for the Maharawal, he will pay you in worked gold a piece solid, about this size, for each healthy peregrine in good plumage."

The Hindu measured with his fingers a size that made the

trapper whistle then raise his brows in joyous contemplation. The Hindu went on.

"Sarghoda is on one of the caravan trails which shunts off between the Roof of the World and the small salt sea, which I believe you call the Shallow Salt Sea. In fact, the last portion of the route into India is under the military protection of my lord the Maharawal."

The Englishman liked the prospect of what he had just heard. With one eyebrow raised, he lapsed into quiet thought. Then he said, "I will have until the migration season to get the dho-ghazas, my trapping nets, made. And I will have to get a flock of live doves or the like to use as bait. Allow a month or more to get out on the northern steppes just south of the Taiga. I would guess the passage falcons coming from the shores of the cold seas will be fairly hungry after crossing the forest. I do not see how a long-winged falcon could do much successful hunting over those woods." The trapper clapped Subotai on the left shoulder. "How about it, son? It will be better than racing the winter back down from the inlet."

The manner in which the Englishman voiced the question made Subotai think that his decision depended upon the Mongol's participation in the venture. He had heard the Englishman refer to "the northern steppes just south of the Taiga." That meant they would probably travel straight north from the Caspian Sea. Subotai hesitated, weighing the time involved against the prospect of being able to scour another sector of the steppes for the Kipchaks.

Subotai nodded his head in the affirmative, and for a moment his broad grin revealed his still-perfect teeth whitely contrasted with his clean and healthy and somewhat brownish skin.

The Hindu's face was set in thought. "It will take you from four to six moons' travel, if you go under the protection of a caravan, just from here to the Indus valley."

The trapper frowned. "That means we will have to keep the birds unexercised for up to half a sun's time." His face brightened. "But I have seen older birds such as your master describes kept healthy on the block during the moult for as long without ill effects." The big man's enthusiasm returned. "Return and tell your lord," he said, "that I willingly undertake this task, and that, God willing, I shall bring as many peregrines as I am able to Sarghoda."

The Hindu was silent. He looked piercingly first into the trapper's eyes, then into those of the Mongol as if seeking the lurking light of deception or insincerity. He saw none. "Let it be so," he said, and handed the bag of gold to the trapper.

φ   φ   φ   φ

When Subotai and the trapper finished setting up the irregular grouping of dho-ghazas on the open plain and tying a flapping white dove behind each net, they climbed back into their saddles. They led the pack animals, loaded with the trapping paraphernalia, including the rest of the jostling cages of cooing and fluttering doves, to a slightly higher node of ground at a considerable distance from, but still within sight of, the dho-ghazas. Here they dismounted, hobbled the horses, and sat down in the cold and declining light of the late afternoon to keep the nets under surveillance.

The trapper produced the inevitable camel meat jerky and sliced a piece into halves, extending one portion to Subotai. The tedious task of chewing the meat, which seemed of an ironlike consistency, helped to take their attention away from the cold wind and their general overall misery.

"You are sure this is better than going up to the inlet in the summer?" The shivering Subotai spoke through his mouthful of unyielding camel meat. The trapper ignored the question and ground away at the jerky in his mouth with English stolidity.

Before total darkness settled on the steppe they returned to the trap site. They found the nets empty. The doves had been slaughtered by foxes.

The Mongol's eyes were fish-colored in the dusk. "Is this the way you usually go about it?" he asked. The question drew a noncommittal grunt from the big man. They rode back to their cold camp, wrapped up in their fur camp beds, and without making a fire, passed into a welcome but cold sleep.

They awoke before dawn. At the trap site the freezing wind slowed their fingers, making a tedious nightmare of the simple act of tying knots to secure the living bait behind each net. Each dho-ghaza was adequately attended to as the first light of morning crept over the eastern horizon.

Back at their vantage point on the distant knoll, they saw in the clearing light that preceded the sun's upper curvature a big female peregrine—a mere speck in the cold sky to the northwest, but there was no mistaking the rapid wing-beats as the bird stooped on down the wind toward the dho-ghazas. Faster than the fastest arrow, the sickle-shaped hawk swept low across the ground, intent on the hapless doves, straight into the collapsing dho-ghaza net in front of one of the desperately leaping doves which tugged with futility against the tie-downs that secured its legs to the earth.

They swung into their saddles, their excitement a contagious, nearly hysterical joy. The trapper bellowed the long-forgotten war cries his ancient, seafaring warrior ancestors had used when they first splashed ashore into the wildly beautiful fens of Britain. Subotai rode with equally wild abandon, laughing his loud laugh, feeling the peaking power of his young manhood.

They were stepping off even before their horses skidded to a stop and they sprinted together to the tangled net with the trapped falcon in it. The peregrine, its beak open in fear, was a first-year passage bird, feather-perfect, brown across its back and deck feathers. The tears of color surrounding and reaching below its brown eyes—the most remarkable distinguishing feature of the bird's head—were dark, blackish brown.

The trapper quickly grabbed the bird, holding its wings tightly against its body. "Cut the netting around the bird, son. We can sew the hole back with an awl faster than we can sort this falcon out of it." Long experience had taught the trapper that it was more profitable and effective to repair the cut net later at his leisure than to risk damaging a valuable falcon fouled in the net by trying to untangle it.

Subotai sprinted back to his mount and returned with the blue sword. Deftly he drew the razor-sharp blade across the net cording surrounding the trapped peregrine while the trapper held the wild bird.

The peregrine was hooded and carefully slid into a soft cloth sheathing which fitted the bird like an open-ended glove. This would hold the creature safely and prevent its escape until it could be jessed, swiveled, and leashed at the camp site.

The peregrine falcon captured on that morning was only the first trickling of the dozens of migrating falcons which left the arctic in the fall. Others followed it across the steppes in their annual fall flight to the shores of the warmer salt seas to the south in the wake of the flocks of ducks and shore birds which were their livelihood. For days thereafter, hardly a moment passed when a survey of the air above them did not reveal at least one of the pointed-winged falcons drifting toward the south. Sometimes several were visible at the same time.

Then one morning there were none to be seen in the sky. The migrating waterfowl and the pursuing falcons were all south of them now. The northern steppes were growing colder with the approach of winter.

The Englishman and the Mongol had captured more than five dozen peregrine falcons and seventeen of the large Eurasian goshawks of the Taiga, also coveted by falconers. And all of them in perfect condition.

They cadged the hooded hawks and began the month-long journey back to the Sea of the Ravens. They paused for only hours at the Seljuk trading camp, learning that a caravan, headed by the Bulgar agent in Balankar's service, had departed for India two days before their arrival at the camp. There was time only for a solid meal with the Seljuk Turk and hasty farewells as they hastened on toward the southeast to catch up with the caravan ahead of them. It was easy to follow the broad, plodden track laid down by the caravan's camels and horses.

They were challenged six and a half days later by the rear guard of the caravan, and passed on into the relative safety of the armed column for the rest of the journey to the Macedonian Gate—Alexander's Gate—and India.

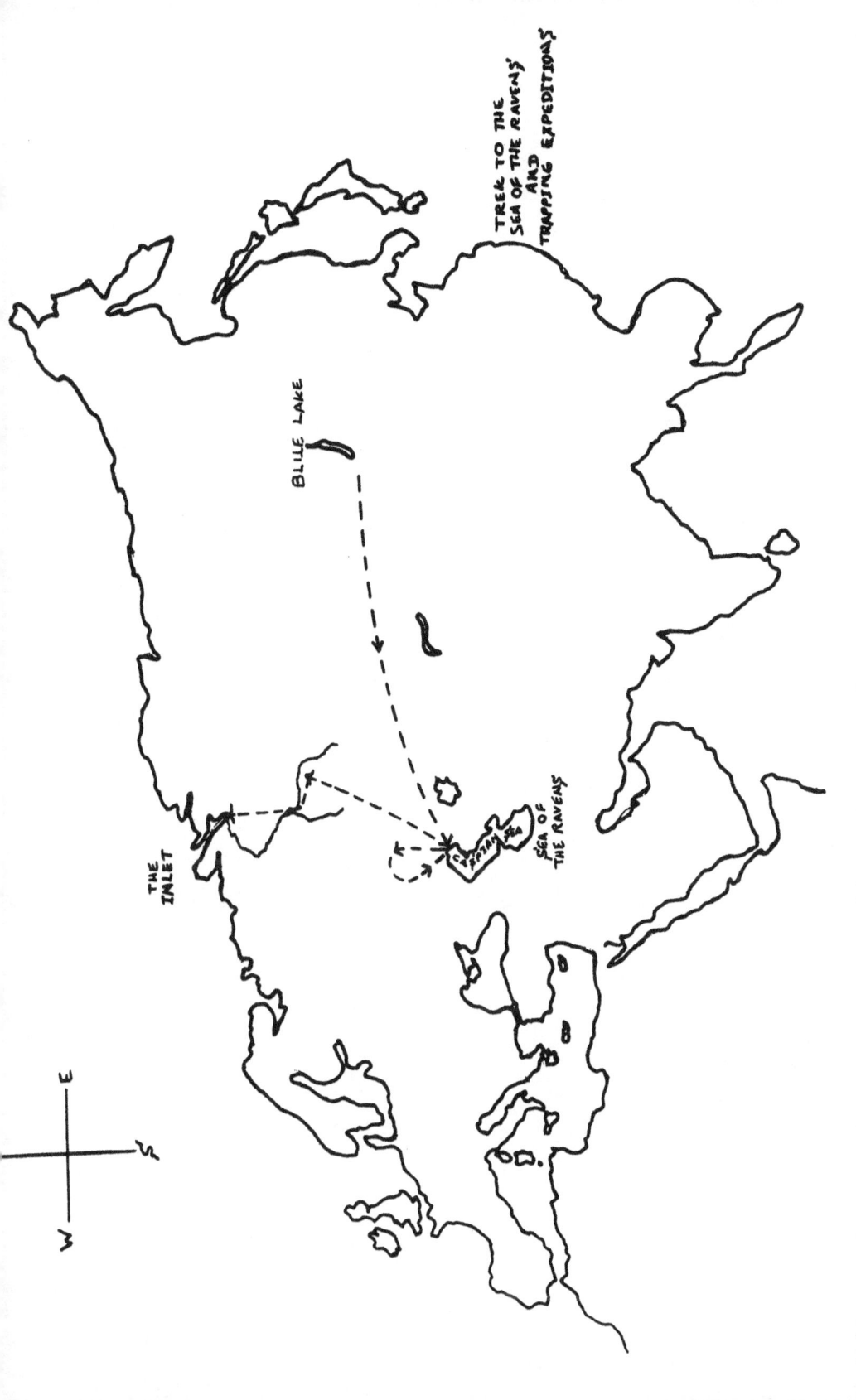

φ φ
THE
SOLAR
WARRIOR

*T*he swift, torrential runoff of the spring melt had held the caravan northwest of the awesome mountains and the pass, the Macedonian Gate into India, for almost a full moon-cycle. The trapper had fretted and worried about the long idleness of the hawks. Then, as much to relieve the boredom as to exercise the birds, he and Subotai began flying them with the creance, a long cord attached to the bird's swiveled jesses. The creance prevented the falcon's escaping before it had become conditioned to flying to the meat scraps tied to a padded leather lure. Although this was unquestionably a step in the falconer's training process which the emissary had warned them the Indian lord wanted left to himself, the Englishman was sure this intrusion would be discounted since it was for the welfare of the birds.

Late one afternoon Subotai burst into the traveling tent. "The pass is open. The Bulgar is back and says we start over in the morning." His voice was tinged with the excitement and anticipation now running like a fever through the caravan camp.

The trapper was quick to ask, "And the tariffs? Did the gate-keeper accept the amount the Bulgar squeezed out of us?"

"I forgot to ask," the Mongol said indifferently. He had little notion of the economics of the world.

"Damn!" The Englishman ran an irritated hand slowly across his brow. "I wonder if you will ever be good for anything except tiger hunting."

The Mongol turned toward the tent flap. "If it will make you an easier companion than a den snake, I will go and find out." He shook his head. The Westerner's avariciousness was foreign to Subotai's nature and to his background. The Mongols knew of gold and silver, of course, but in their essentially bartering economy, there was little if any place for a medium of exchange, and no coinage. The Mongols—and Subotai was typical in this—were generous to a fault. Their society, composed of primitive groups based on families and clans, had its prices at times, usually measured in flocks and stock and horses, but generosity, valor, and loyalty were counted as the real social assets.

Subotai heard the trapper's footfalls coming behind him. "I will come with you, son. Just so you won't forget." But the grizzled ex-mercenary was smiling. Like the Mongol, he had caught the contagion of the moment, glad at the prospect of at last leaving the lethargy of stagnation in the encampment behind, glad at the prospect of at last crossing the great, snowy Hindu Kush into the fabled India, the India he had been hearing about since his early manhood. The trapper, searching his memory, recalled now that he had heard India spoken of even as a youth in England. And that was before he had first ventured to flee the stifling tyranny of the Normans for Constantinople for the strict but less oppressive discipline of the Varangian Guard.

The burly Bulgar caravan master was emerging from his own tent as the pair strode up.

"How did it go with the bargaining on our cost to cross the pass?" The trapper spoke as though he expected the worst.

The Bulgar said nothing, but only untied and opened a leather money pouch and, still wordless but with a spreading smile he failed to restrain, began counting out coins from the purse. The smile broke into a wide grin which seemed to reach over the bald curvature of the trailmaster's hairless scalp. Retying the pouch to his belt, he reached for the Englishman's right hand, turned the palm up, placed the coins in a clinking pile, and closed the fingers back over the money. Still smiling but now conspiratorially, he said, "Come inside."

Bewildered, they followed the Bulgar into his tent. He gestured for them to sit on the felt-carpeted ground. Then the Bulgar opened a small traveling chest and produced a trio of small and exquisite Chinese bronze drinking cups without handles. He filled all three of the cups with a purpled stream of spiced wine from a camel hide water skin. He handed the cups around, then seated himself on the ground facing the two falcon trappers.

"It started out badly. I was afraid at first that it would cost me twice as much as I paid for safe passage four sun-cycles ago, the last time I cargoed for the Hindustan. But then—I don't know why I even mentioned it—I remarked to one of the gatekeeper's officers that I had a consignment of falcons with the caravan. Everything changed from that moment on." The Bulgar swallowed down his wine, wiped his mouth on his sleeve, and went on.

"The troops who hold the gate have been watching for you for moon months. They are in the service of the Maharawal of Amrithistan, the lord to whom you are taking those birds." The Bulgar laughed heartily, shaking his head in disbelief. "After I told them the birds were in good condition—they look so to me—the gatekeeper not only lowered the tariff for the whole caravan but offered to give us a military escort down the other side after we crest the Macedonian Gate."

Later, after nightfall, and after a pleasant, wine-warmed afternoon with the trailmaster, the Englishman and the Mongol bedded down in the cold night, both of them having forgotten to eat an evening meal. Even for the trapper it would be a night of unworried rest, of sweet respite from anxiety for the hawks and from the troubled and violent memories of his life.

Four days later, with the gatekeeper's stone custom house at the bleak and wind-chilled summit of the Macedonian Gate behind them, the caravan slowly descended toward the sunny land stretching out panoramically below the steep trail. The cadge horses picked their footing down the treacherous and rocky way, jostling the hooded peregrine falcons and goshawks perched on their cadges with their feathers fluffed out against the cold that had lingered into the spring.

The air grew warmer as they carefully descended toward the lower plains, and was made even warmer by the inspired cursing of the caravan's camel drivers. Then, as the days of trailing into the

Indian subcontinent passed, a feeling of familiarity overtook Subotai which mounted from dawn to dusk. The scenes before him, the sun-darkened country people encountered along the way, their peaceful and friendly manners as they waved shyly at the caravan—each incident stunned the Mongol with the remarkable sense of being accustomed to this place, a place he knew he was seeing for the first time.

The Bulgar, afoot on the bank of a wide, placid river, wiped the sweat from his bald head. "The Indus River. Once you cross, I will turn you onto the trail toward Sarghoda. After that you will have to travel alone," he told them. Flat ferry barges poled by slim, brown men clad only in the briefest of loin cloths stood ready to convey the drivers, horses, and camels across. The camels grew balky and bad-tempered in the increasing Indian heat, but the Bulgar maintained a rudimentary order in the loading of the beasts onto the ferry rafts. Then at last it was the turn of the trapper and Subotai to board the cadge horses.

But on the far side of the Indus, a striking, hawk-faced soldier rode up to the re-forming caravan with a detachment of mounted lancers at his back. When their leader dismounted, the cavalry squadron fanned out behind him. The leader walked over to the hooded peregrines on the cadge horses and looked the birds over quickly. When he turned toward the trapper, they saw that his eyes were hard and white-gray in the irises, giving the man's face the disconcerting appearance of an eyeless copper mask. Somewhere between the Englishman and the Mongol in height, he was lean and had the appearance of whipcord toughness. He wore baggy cotton riding breeches tightened at his ankles just above heavy sandals made of leather and wood. His upper body was vested with a sleeveless white tunic, beautifully adorned with embroidery work in patterns that combined flowery and geometric designs in a peculiar blend. In his left hand he carried a sheathed katar, the straight Indian sword with a complete, hand-protecting grip cover. His turban was yellow with a steel ring hung around it diagonally like a rakish tiara. To those level with him, the narrow steel band was almost invisible because it rested against the turban on one edge, its width pointing outward from the man's head. It was a moment before Subotai realized, with something of a start, that the outer edge of the steel band was honed to razor sharpness.

Subotai backed to his mount to get the blue sword in easy reach when he saw the heavy armament of the Hindu cavalrymen. The mounted squadron winked with sunlight reflected from burnished steel weapons. Colorful green and ocher ribbons fluttered from the lances pointed upward toward the hot Indian sun. The Mongol noted that some of the glitter came from steel bands identical to the leader's, which most of the Indians were wearing about their turbans.

A group of four plainly clothed men with the cavalry column detached themselves from the other horsemen, dismounted, and joined their commander at the cadges. They spoke softly among themselves, pointing at the falcons and drawing out the wings of some of the birds to check the plumage and bone condition. The birds were showing distress in the unfamiliar heat by panting through their open beaks.

The trapper stood by silently, then said to the Mongol, "Those brown ones without weapons must be the bird-handlers of the Maharawal."

As if to emphasize the trapper's deduction, two of them returned to the mounted soldiers to fetch cotton cloth and wood, from which they quickly fashioned sun shades and mounted them above the falcons. Then all four of the hawk-handlers began to circulate about the cadges with bowls of river water which they blew in gentle sprays from their mouths onto the overheated peregrines and goshawks.

"Why didn't I think of that?" The trapper watched the Hindus with a half-smile of respect for their ingenuity.

The Hindu horse-commander walked straight up to the perspiring Englishman and the heat-wilted Mongol. He seemed to appraise the pair with a single glance. Subotai thought he detected a fleeting trace of a smile on the narrow, bronzed face as the Indian surveyed them.

The trapper started to speak in the trail tongue, thought better of it and said simply, "Maharawal of Amrithistan?"

The drawling sound of the white giant's use of the words made the Hindu smirk, giving his face a diabolic cast which instantly alienated the two wayfarers. The trapper held his tongue with difficulty as the Hindu turned his back arrogantly on them and ordered his troops to commandeer the cadge horses. The Englishman looked at Subotai, then with a shrug, mounted and trailed northwestward after the Indian horse squadron with the Mongol following.

The rich, well tended garden farms which lined the banks of the Indus River were quickly left behind and the land gave way to a reddish desert, and a cloud of fine dust raised by the horses added another miserable increment to the northerners' discomfort in the heat pressing down upon them.

Subotai and the trapper had had the foresight to fill their waterskins at the Indus. And well that they had, for although the troop rode for nearly three days farther into the desert region, the white-eyed captain of the mounted troop offered them neither food nor water during the journey. They were left strictly to their own devices in other ways as well, ignored as if they they were not there.

Then on the third afternoon, they caught sight of a walled stone fortification wobbling in the heat-tormented light of the mid-afternoon sun against grayish-black granite cliffs in the distance. The citadel dominated the surrounding desert. Its high sheer walls mimicked the native granite cliffs within which they were set. The skill of the military engineer who had conceived this fort on this site was immediately evident to the Englishman.

A single trail leading up the sloping gradient of the rocky hills and cliffs seemed to provide the only access to the fortification. The trapper had seen fortifications in Europe and all across the Mediterranean world where he had served as a Varangian, but the one set before him exceeded in cunning and defensibility any he had ever encountered. The ascent from the dusty plain to the entranceway of the massive structure itself was an unbroken struggle. The animals were often forced into a single file by the narrowness of the trail and its unrelenting steepness. In some places the great granite cliff walls pressed in so close together that they bruised and skinned the legs of the riders as their mounts squeezed through the narrows.

The last barrier to the huge bronze and iron gates into the fort was a man-dug chasm, deep and wide, with a bottom studded by great sharp boulders. A wooden, railless bridge that crossed the chasm could apparently be withdrawn to the far side by men or draft animals to leave the gulf unbridged.

The resonant clatter of hooves fell away as they entered the gates. Then the heavy, metal-plated teak gates boomed closed behind them, and they dismounted in the dust and confusion created by the Hindu troops. The cadge horses were taken away by male servants in white turbans and dhoti-like loin coverings, their brown torsos uncovered and their feet and legs bare to the knees. Their baggage animals had also been taken in hand by other brown men who seemed to appear in numbers for each little task without any evidence of having been summoned.

And then their trail horses were suddenly gone, smoothly and quietly removed before either of them could react. Their weapons, all of them—sword, ax, and bow—were now out of their reach. Subotai, his eye on the blue sword, took a hasty step toward the departing rumps of their saddle animals, but the Englishman laid a restraining hand on his shoulder.

"Hold, son. Let us go at this gently." But without his arms close at hand the ex-Varangian felt as naked as did Subotai without the blue sword.

The Englishman turned to survey the inner sides of the fortification. The lower walls of the inner fort were a long arrow-shot from the stabling and mews areas where they had dismounted. The Englishman's practiced military eye gauged the entire width of the irregularly bounded compound at about three-quarters of an English road-stone. An inner citadel, much like the Norman donjon of the Englishman's early experience except for its much greater expanse and circumference, stood in the northwestern corner of the walled enclosure.

The white-eyed Indian captain signed for them to come along, and they followed him through the late afternoon heat toward the second wall. No military gate, not even a barred sallyport, blocked the portal into the second entryway.

To Subotai and the trapper, red and thirsty, their faces, necks, and arms streaked with sweat-muddied dust, the sudden drop in temperature in the gardened area just within the secondary walls came as a physical shock. The sound of falling water and a heavenly haze of damp spray dewed them as they followed the Indian along a path flagged with granite slabs through a garden lush with melons and flowers and mango trees in this astonishing oasis. Both travel-weary men marvelled to see water streaming out of the living rock to form waterfalls that fell in spouting and misting cascades down the cliff faces at the side of an ornate white marble palace.

The mansion itself rivaled anything the trapper had seen in Greece. Its outer ground-level veranda was fluted with delicate white columns rising up through a second veranda covered by an extensive flat, shading roof beamed with heavy black teak logs and gray granite slabs. Most of the palace was constructed of stone which, with its high specific heat along with its watery surroundings, created a deterrent to the stifling heat outside.

The Hindu warrior walked straight through the well guarded but undoored entrance. The trapper and Subotai followed close behind him, exchanging quizzical looks.

"Shanti." A tall, walnut-complexioned man of thin and seriously noble bearing offered the greeting. The cosmopolitan trapper met the greeting silently, but with a warm smile and upraised right hand opened in peace. Then the trapper hand-signed in the trail manner his pleasure at having been invited within the confines of the palace.

The enclosure they entered was apparently an anteroom of some kind. The big trapper gazed about the carved and silk-curtained chamber. "Sarghoda?" he questioned.

The slim Indian laughed pleasantly. He responded, surprisingly, with the trail signs and indicated that Sarghoda was until recently a great city under the direct protection of his lord.

"It must have been quite recently." The trapper had boldly launched into the spoken trail tongue, hoping the man would be conversant in it.

The tall Hindu did not answer immediately. He looked first at the arrogant troop commander, then spoke sharply to him in Hindi. The blank eyes of the brown warrior seemed to freeze, but he turned in obedience to the tall palace official's abrupt dismissal.

The tall Hindu easily dropped into a variant but understandable form of the trail pidgin and answered the trapper. "Yes, the Moslems of Kharesmia have been troubling the upper Indus region again, the first military activity on their part for more than seven suns of time. The Maharawal still holds Sarghoda under his influence, but he has been forced to evacuate his household from the city and retreat to this more easily defended locale."

The Indian paused briefly, noting the light of understanding on the faces of this strange-appearing and strangely matched pair. "Please," and he extended a long, slim brown arm toward a lovely arched doorway on his right. "The Maharawal would be happy to see you bathed and rested after so long a journey. He also suggests you join him and his other guests for an evening repast. I shall come for you at his pleasure."

No doubt it shall be at his pleasure, the trapper thought to himself.

They were shown into a spacious stone chamber with low, wood-shuttered and wood-latticed window openings which made the room light and airy and, as Subotai discovered in his immediate inspection, extended to offer a walk-through onto the lower veranda. Their host left silently, letting the curtain which veiled the doorway drop quietly behind him.

The Englishman had seen the luxury of the Byzantine Empire, but to the young Mongol it was the first sight and experience of the rich trappings of a civilized culture. There were scarlet cloth draperies hung and tied back in all corners of the room which could be undone to muffle the walls in colder weather. Three wide and thick sleeping mats were lined against one wall, and each was covered with cotton material for comfort in the heat. Cold water sprang continuously from a bronze spout above a large oblong basaltic bathing pool set into the stone floor against another wall.

Clapping and rubbing his hands together, the trapper stripped off his dusty trail leathers and plunged into the pool. To his pleasure he noted that it drained constantly in equilibrium with its rate of fill.

"You will just have to wait your turn, son." The sunburned Englishman dunked and sputtered in the water as he spoke. He seized and unstoppered a green pottery decanter standing beside the pool and let a stream of golden-pink oil splash into the bathwater.

Subotai, reminded of his bathing with the Seljuk girl, smiled and turned to give the elaborate guest quarters a more leisurely inspection. He was baffled by the ornateness, his simple nomad's mind having been conditioned to an appreciation for only the barest, most practical—and portable—essentials of existence.

His nature allowed him only an unspoken contempt for what

he saw; his claustrophobia simmered just below conscious level in the confinement of the chamber. It felt to him like a stone dungeon such as the trapper had described to him. He saw use for only the sleeping mats and the bathing pool—somehow he let slip from his mind that his taste for bathing had been only recently acquired. He compared this stony rigid room with the coziness of a felt yurt when the black and icy wind raged over the steppes. The yurt in its softness and its protectiveness was easily opened to the great Sky, never harshly and permanently closed in like this place. Subotai turned as he heard the trapper's splashing emergence from the bath. He surveyed the dirty foam fouling the pool as the trapper began toweling his great sunburned frame, and decided to let the pool clear itself before taking his turn in the bath. He had long since stored his felt-lined boots in one of the saddlebags now gone with the pack horses. He kicked off the leather sandals he had hastily cobbled for himself on the trip and stripped off his heavy clothing, anticipating the delight of the cooling water after the dust and the heat of the desert.

He let himself sink slowly into the sensuous coolness of the pool up to his neck, then, holding his breath, ducked under the water's surface to prolong the heavenly chill of the clear water. He eagerly poured the amber-colored liquid from the vase as he had seen the trapper do, savoring this new experience as he scrubbed his dusty scalp and cleansed his muscular body in the fragrant softness of the frothy, bubbling water. Then he lay back in the bath until it had run itself clear.

Subotai rinsed himself thoroughly and stepped up and out of the pool just as the trapper sent a heavy cotton towel flying across the chamber into his face. Subotai retaliated by adroitly launching most of his pile of dirty clothing back at the trapper with an expert Mongolian front-fighting kick. With an easy dodge, the trapper ducked the flying leathers and slid down on one of the sleeping mats in the same careless and athletic movement. He rolled over with his back to Subotai and fell asleep almost immediately. Subotai threw the wet towel back toward the pool's side and followed the Englishman's example, the trail weariness and the refreshment of the bath conbining to overcome the closeness he felt in the rich confinement of the sleeping chamber.

φ   φ   φ   φ

Subotai's finely attuned warrior's senses brought him awake. The merest whispering sound had triggered the long-conditioned alertness arising from the very center of his self-preservative instinct. He caught the barest glimpse of a woman's back as the curtain-drop fell behind her withdrawing figure.

As he rolled to his feet he noticed the neatly folded white garments placed at the foot of each sleeping mat. The dirty trail clothing and the damp toweling had been removed. He was cha-grined that anyone could have entered and left the chamber so quietly that he had been unaware of it. Here again was the same smooth deceptiveness with which they had been separated from their weapons.

The Englishman now stirred and yawned greatly, grunting and scratching the sleep from his body. He said "Humph!" when he saw the garments and cloth slippers set on the ends of the mats, then seized the clothing and stood up to put it on. He seemed to be familiar with such apparel.

Subotai watched as the trapper slipped the cotton robe over his head and picked up a black cord from the bedding which he tied about his waist, then followed suit. At least he thought he was doing the same until he heard the trapper's roaring laugh and felt helping hands turn the front of the robe around from the back. The hems of the loose and cool cotton robe fell midway between Subotai's knees and ankles. In Subotai's experience only women wore skirted garments, and very few even of the women. He well remembered Mursechen's lovely shapeliness in her long blue woolen skirts, and felt rather foolish at being similarly robed. He tied the cord around his waist with a square knot as the trapper had done, pleased that his cord was a vivid scarlet in color. The Mongol had never seen such a vital hue. The slippers went on tightly at first, but seemed a fair fit by the time they had completed their dressing.

The trapper seemed quite at home in his robe. "The Greeks in Byzantium wear clothing like this, lad, only shorter. The men, that is. The women wear ankle-length gowns. Noble ladies, I mean. In the country, well..." and he laughed heartily and mischievously, "...they wear, oftentimes, little or nothing, especially in the hot harvest time." He pulled thoughtfully on his gray-streaked, blond beard and, looking Subotai over with joking eyes, he added, "And a lovely lass, you are too, lad." And he roared again with ribald laughter as Subotai crimsoned in anger and embarrassment.

"Now what is it that we do?" The Mongol's face was still reddened.

The Englishman answered with a diffident tone in his voice the Mongol had never heard him use before. "Easy enough. You heard the Maharawal's seneschal, or whatever he might be titled—'at the Maharawal's pleasure,' he said—and that's how it is." He lowered his voice. "Remember, lad, we are in his country and his castle. I can feel you itching to have that blue steel lady of yours at your side. Trust me. We are better off without any sign of weapons. Try to show this lord we are merchants, not mercenaries. We came for the gold. We will mind our manners and pray to the White Christ, and to Our Lady, and to the Sky, old Wotan, and Freya for good measure, that there is no treachery afoot here. We would not be the first who ever turned over their goods and received only a poisoned flagon or a sharp blade in the ribs for payment."

Still, the Mongol wished he had one of the short Grecian daggers like the Englishman's to hide in the folds of his white robe. They turned from their hushed conversation as the thin, turbaned seneschal swept aside the curtain in the doorway and, uninvited, stepped within.

"Noble travelers," he used the respectful greeting in the trail tongue, "my lord the Maharawal awaits you for the evening repast."

Although not vain, Subotai nevertheless took one parting glance at his image in a sheened, bronze reflecting disk before following the trapper and the seneschal through the chamber's portal. Unlike the fair, nordic Saxon, Subotai had darkened under the Indian sun. The white material of the robe set off his high-toned complexion and further emphasized his slanted, blue eyes which were now in brilliant contrast with his clothing and deeply tanned skin. His massive, rippling and sinewed arms were exposed by the sleeveless garment, and the scarlet belt-cord drew attention to the flatness of his stomach and the expanse of his deep chest and wide shoulders. His bare calves were thick and muscularly contoured, especially so for one who had spent nearly his entire life on horseback. Health and youth shone through his clean tan and, combining with the barbarian purity and the wild magnetism of his natural spirit, made him a figure of unusual and striking dominance.

φ   φ   φ   φ

Subotai and the trapper were led into a spacious and high-ceilinged dining chamber. Serving women, all clad in spotless saris, stood silent and attentive in two lines, one line to the left and one to the right of a low, bow-shaped feast table with its open side facing the dining hall's entrance. The feast table was heavy with fruit. Bananas, mangoes, jackfruit, and melons were heaped at precise intervals around the curved dining board. Exquisitely crafted gold and silver wine cups were set in an adorning circle about the base of a large, two-handled wine chalice so massive that it would require two persons to carry it with any sureness.

Heavy, rich, and tasseled cushions, deeply purple in color, lined both sides of the table, but only three were presently occupied. Two men and a vibrantly beautiful dark young woman looked up from their conversation as the Englishman and the Mongol entered behind the lean Hindu seneschal.

It was before the smaller of the two men that the seneschal dropped to his knees, then placed hands and elbows flat on the stone work in a smooth and incredibly low obeisance, and awaited the recognition of the Maharawal. At a signal from the Maharawal, the seneschal regained his feet and half-turned as he gestured with his right hand, open-palmed, toward Subotai and the Englishman. Melodic Hindi flowed from his lips as he described the two guests to the Indian Maharawal.

The trapper seized the opportunity of a lapse in the seneschal's introduction to bow, as he had learned to do in the Varangian Guard, from the waist. Subotai followed suit in a stiff and ungraceful imitation of the trapper's movement. Their untutored and rather shy acknowledgment of the introduction brought smiles to all three of the Indians seated on the cushions.

Subotai looked with interest at the young, pleasant-faced Maharawal. He wore a gold and brown turban seeded with pearls and small rubies. About his throat hung a heavy gold chain bangled with tiny idols, exact duplicates of Hindu carvings of temple dancers. His tunic and full, baggy dhoti were of yellow raw silk. Subotai noticed that he was warding off an early corpulence and wondered if the vigorous exercise entailed in hawking was to compensate for an excessive fondness for food and his cups. With a slightly inebriated smile and a wavering motion of his braceleted arms, the Maharawal invited the northerners to be seated opposite himself. The seneschal went around the curving table and knelt just behind and to the left of the Maharawal to act as interpreter. Subotai and the trapper settled on the cushions on the stone floor in silence.

The Mongol turned his nearly unblinking gaze on the other two Indians, staring in frank approval at the young woman. He guessed she was perhaps three years older than himself, in the bloom of her womanhood. She was garbed in a light blue silk sari which served to highlight her slim yet full femininity. Her wrists were heavily encircled with gold, and her graceful neck and ankles were banded with gold set with jade, diamonds, and emeralds which caught the light with eye-holding shades of deep green. The shawl of her sari was drawn up half over her head. Her hair was black, the Mongol thought, as the wings of an arctic raven, so black the light gleamed in a rainbow of reflected hues about her lovely head. The woman's eyes were brown, now black, now liquid brown again. Her perfect skin was olive-brown, and the features of her face were a totality of loveliness and natural harmony. But it was her dark, pooling eyes that drew the Mongol. They sparkled with a sweet intelligence and a youthful mischievousness which seemed at the same time to be under enormous self-control.

While the Maharawal and his servant conversed in Hindi, Subotai turned his attention to the taller Indian man. The Mongol was startled for a moment—but no, it was so, the man had nearly the same masculine counterpart of the woman's facial features. Their coloring and the sameness of their faces left no doubt they were natural brother and sister, suggested they might even be twins. But the man's eyes were even more extraordinary than the woman's. They held the Mongol's gaze with a vibrant power that set Subotai's head humming with an energy he could recall experiencing in its fullness only once before. The exchange of consciousness between the two men was like the mighty gathering of the hair-lifting forces which vortexed about the northern lights.

Subotai's edgy concern at being completely unarmed returned when he looked over at the turbaned and rigid guards stationed behind the servant women in the shadows beneath flickering wall torches and saw the white-eyed Hindu captain come quietly into the dining chamber. The captain moved to take a place behind the seneschal silently and with an uncanny unobtrusiveness in the deceptive and visually offset way of those who are masters of Ninjutsu. Although the man had made his entry behind the Indians, Subotai sensed that the troop commander's presence had not gone unnoticed by either the woman or her brother. Nor had it escaped the trapper, although the Englishman did not break stride in his interpreted conversation with the Maharawal. Listening to the trapper describe experiences of his life as a hawk-merchant, the young Maharawal burst into burbling laughter at the story of Subotai's plunge into the icy salt water of the inlet. The tall Hindu also laughed pleasantly, and the young woman smiled at Subotai. Then she selected a lush mango from the piles of fruit and with a grace of hand and arm motion which riveted Subotai into a frozen fascination, peeled it, divided it, and offered part to the Mongol.

As Subotai was savoring the juicy sweetness of the fruit, the seneschal, at the Maharawal's bidding, introduced Subotai and the trapper to the Indian guests, Dharayan and his sister Gauri. The seneschal did so in the trail language, knowing that both brother and sister were quite familiar with the pidgin. When Dharayan replied, he too used the pidgin, and embellished some of the childish trail expressions with Greek words. After that he and the ex-Varangian were diverted into a two-way conversation in the ancient language.

Subotai shyly ventured to speak to Gauri, to thank her for the peeled mango, then asked, "How is it you speak the language of the caravan trails?"

Her answer was colored by her Hindi accent and spoken in a voice of pure femininity. "My older brother is in the merchant trade of the trails. He has a small caravanserai in the city of Sarghoda. Since the deaths of our parents and our grandmother, I have been helping with the accounts of the ladings." Then she added, "It was through him," and here she lifted an arm toward her brother, who was still lost in a garble of bad Greek with the Englishman, "that the Maharawal sent his agent to the end of the northwestern trail to barter for the falcons."

After her first few words, Subotai was hopelessly smitten. For all his life he would be obsessed with the image of Mursechen, but this black-haired and enchanting woman was flesh and blood and reality only an arm's length away. And, in her contrasting darkness, she rivaled the fair northern beauty of Mursechen in every way.

"And you," she caught his eyes with the questioning intensity of her look, "you are not like him." She turned her head toward the huge white Englishman, then back to the Mongol. "Where do you come from?"

Subotai tried to frame an answer that would convey something of his hard-won knowledge of the Eurasian steppes between the Sea of the Ravens and the Blue Lake, tried to structure in the pidgin-talk some idea of the vast land-sea of the steppes beyond the high, snowy mountains and below the Taiga and the barren grounds; but the simple trail language and his fluency were inadequate.

"From the north," he said finally, "from the cold lands." And he added, almost with embarrassment, "Where men cover themselves with animal furs and grease to fend off the bitter wind."

Her face was alive with childish interest. "Have you seen the water when it falls from the cold sky, when it is white and fluffy?" She made rounding, upheaving movements with both hands to imply the meaning of her words.

Subotai laughed his pleasing but nearly always roaring laugh. "You mean snow." He used the Mongol word for it.

"It covers those great mountains not far from here." She went on in her lively way. "I am going to see it when Dharayan and I return to Sarghoda. The caravans will be on their way before the coming of the monsoon and we are going into the mountains to the lamasery to buy lamps for trade."

Subotai could make little of what she said, but the low timbre of the young, womanish voice made his skin tingle with arousal. Their growing feeling of intimacy was interrupted by the Maharawal. Now deeply in his cups and in an obviously good humor, he called his seneschal to his side and issued instructions in a voice slurred by both the wine and his jovial mood. As the thin servant hastily left the dining chamber, the young Indian nobleman called for the refilling of the wine cups and, lifting a finely crafted gold goblet encrusted with glinting gems, enjoined all of his guests to imbibe.

Subotai noticed that the merchant, Dharayan, did not even lift his wine cup, but instead saluted the Maharawal with a piece of luscious, yellow melon. There was an apparently humorous exchange between the Indians, the Maharawal nearly choking with laughter at a remark Dharayan made.

The seneschal reentered the dining hall followed by two armed soldiers bearing between them a heavy wooden chest covered with the carved likenesses of the dancing Krishna surrounded by the storied milkmaidens in their enraptured adoration. The chest was placed on the dining board next to Dharayan, who slid easily back and away from the ornate box and moved across the table from Subotai closer to his handsome sister to give room for the Maharawal and his servant.

The chest was opened, and from it the Maharawal chose several doeskin bags tied at their tops with strangely intricate knots. He laid eight of the bags in front of the Englishman, then opened and spilled the shimmering golden contents of one bag onto the table. The gold measures bounced and rang together like miniature ingots as they cascaded onto the table top. With a quizzical and thoroughly intoxicated smile, the Maharawal held out his left hand, palm upward, toward the trapper. The trapper threw back his head with its long gray-blond hair and laughed with gusty delight. Then, mimicking the Indian salutation, he placed his hands together in a respectful pronam and profusely thanked the Maharawal for his unqualified generosity.

Subotai watched the proceedings with his barbarian indifference to the gold, but he did not fail to notice the sickly evil look which came over the face of the white-eyed Indian captain when the Maharawal loosed the gold pieces. The wavering light of the socketed torches and the hanging lamps lent an eerie and demonic cast to the man's face. The knife-edged steel band encircling the man's turban caught some of the torchlight and reradiated the fire with a glassy dullness.

Assisted by the seneschal, the Maharawal got heavily and unsurely to his feet. Smiling in sodden satisfaction and fairly reeling from the drink he had taken, the Maharawal groped for support. Both of the northerners noted the quickness with which the tall merchant and the seneschal moved to assist the young rajah, interdicting the

too hasty approach of the Hindu captain. The Englishman caught
the Mongol's eye for an instant. Something was surely amiss in this
place. The captain had been literally and rudely shoved aside by the
two men who were now half leading and half carrying the Maharawal
from the hall. The white-eyed man sullenly retreated into the shadows with the rest of the guard mount. Gauri followed after the trio,
her gliding departure a graceful, whispering silkiness. Subotai started
to speak, but the trapper raised an index finger in the sign for
silence. After a few moments one of the older serving women came
to the pair and beckoned for them to follow her. She led them
straightway back to their quarters.

When the curtain had fallen behind her, the trapper went to
the entryway and held the curtain back enough to scan the outer
hallway for eavesdroppers, then over to the latticed windows to look
outside. Satisfied that their talk would be private, the big man
spoke in a husky whisper.

"Lad, I don't like the smell of this pot of herring. Did you see
how swiftly Dharayan and the old major domo were to keep that
fish-eyed devil's hands off the Maharawal? This has the feel of
Byzantine palace intrigue about it. God's blood, our animals need
rest and so do we, but unless my nose has dulled in these long years
since I left the Greeks, we had best be off at our first opportunity.
There are those here who do not match their faces. That Dharayan
now, made my hair stand up on end when I first looked at him.
And did you see how he moved when he got up?—like a stallion—
brown, big, and lightning fast. Son, I have seen them all—Normans, Germans, Saracens, Turks—but that is the fastest man, and
mark my words, the deadliest, I have ever seen."

Subotai nodded in agreement. "Lovely sister he has, too."

"And I noticed the lady could not keep her eyes off you either,
son." The trapper spoke in the ribald tone he used whenever a woman
was the subject of the moment.

At midmorning of the day following the festive evening meal
with the Indian rajah, the palace seneschal reappeared. He led the
two travelers to the outer compound and assured them they had
total freedom of movement throughout the citadel. He walked with
them to the mews and let them inspect the birds of prey of all
varieties which the Maharawal kept both for his hawking pleasure

in the fields and as a private aviary. The northern hawks were in mews attached to stone cliff faces cunningly cooled by spray from the waterfalls.

Three days later, as the northerners were finishing a midday repast of fruit and chappatis and savoring the last drops of a cool melon juice brought to them by the ever-attentive legions of women servants who seemed to swarm the place, the seneschal once again swept aside the door-curtain and strode in. They were pleasantly astonished to see that he had brought their weapons to them—the blue sword, the battle-ax, and the bow and quiver—concealed in a rolled sheet of shabby leather.

"Noble travelers, the lord Maharawal knows you will wish to begin your return journey soon. There are servants ready to assist you with the mending and care of your harness and baggage, which I have kept under watch by my own staff rather than the usual guards." The thin, brown man paused for a moment and seemed about to say more concerning his military retinue, but apparently thought better of it. As he turned and started for the doorway, he said, "Whenever you like I shall send a servant to lead you to the stables."

They spent the better part of a week repairing tack, airing the traveling tent, and directing the docile and smiling servants, mostly women, who were sent to sew their tattered leathers and cloth. Without being asked, the women completely lined the inner side of the traveling tent with raw silk, assuring the two northerners that this would enhance the water resistance and the wind-breaking character of the folding shelter.

When all was in readiness, the trapper spoke with the grave and reserved seneschal, requesting that they be allowed to take their leave on the following morning. The old servant made a pronam.

"You are free to go as you wish, but your haste makes it impossible, at this time, to arrange for your passage with a caravan." Then the Hindu placed a thoughtful, bony finger to his lips and said, "But perhaps not. I shall speak with His Highness. He is not without influence in matters within his domains. Will you reconsider and wait for a time to be assured of traveling with a caravan?"

The Englishman gave his great, leonine head a negative shake. The Indian smiled.

"But of course you would not," he said.

The Englishman waited until the Hindu was gone before saying, "Let's look to our weapons, lad. But remember, we go about unarmed until we load. Whatever is stewing amongst these dark schemers is none of our affair."

They awoke next morning before daybreak, bathed, and donned their leather riding clothing. Then, slinging sword and battle-ax over their respective shoulders, they went to the stable area. Quickly, in the habit that was their second nature, they loaded their pack animals and saddled their mounts. Subotai hung his quiver and his sheathed bow over the pommel of his old saddle. The trapper consigned to his saddlebags the gold-filled pouches which he had been carrying with him wherever he went and keeping overnight beneath his sleeping mat.

While they were loading and tying the last of their baggage onto the pack horses, the Maharawal, his seneschal, and Dharayan entered the stable trailed by half a dozen armed soldiers. Subotai saw the Englishman's jaw clench, heard and clearly understood as the trapper cursed to himself in the Saxon tongue. "The bastards! They've come to take back the gold." But the trapper's fears were allayed when the tall merchant spoke with an even sincerity.

"The lord Maharawal wishes you to accompany him to the mews before you take to the trail."

The young rajah himself, smiling, took the arm of the Englishman and led the group outside. Subotai looked about for any sight of Gauri, but in vain; she had apparently chosen to remain within the confines of the white palace.

Dharayan, dropping back behind the rajah to walk beside the Mongol, announced to both Subotai and the trapper, "The Maharawal wishes, if it also be your desire, that you remain here in his service. You have tasted his generosity. He is greatly impressed with the honesty and courage which both of you have displayed in making such a long and hazardous journey at his behest. And he is rightly pleased at the expertise you have shown in maintaining the condition and feather-quality of the falcons and hawks over such a difficult and lengthy travel. He surmises that both of you are skilled fighting men as well as seasoned falconers."

The merchant broke off to speak to the Maharawal in the Hindi language. Subotai and the trapper looked at each other, wondering if they would be given a chance to discuss this astonishing proposal before an answer was demanded of them. Dharayan turned back to them and, putting a hand on the Mongol's shoulder, said, "My sister and I will travel with you to Sarghoda where, if you wish, I shall arrange for your departure with a caravan for the northwest pass, which I believe some call Alexander's Gate in honor of the great conqueror. Consider the Maharawal's proposal while we journey to Sarghoda. It is only about three days' travel by camel from here, so it would be but a brief return if you decide to enter his service."

Inside the cool mews, the Indian lord led them down the long rows of perches and spoke at length of the exotic birds of prey which he had collected. Since his long dissertation was in Hindi, the northerners could understand none of it.

The Maharawal had paused in front of a large saker falcon brought from the far Arabian peninsula and launched himself on a lengthy discussion of it when a loud jingling of hawk bells made Subotai turn toward the sound. Dharayan had turned also, and in the act of turning, his speed of perception had so exceeded the Mongol's that he was already pushing the Maharawal to the earth before Subotai even registered the gleaming flight of the circular razored steel band from the captain's turban. The sailing weapon nicked Subotai's right cheekbone, ricocheted off a wooden post, and sheared off the head of the saker falcon. The bird flapped and spattered blood as it hung suspended from its perch by its jesses and leash.

As Subotai reeled back from the sharp, screeching pain of his grazed cheekbone, he heard the trapper roar, "Fight, lad! We're on a side whether we like it or not."

The immense Englishman, battle-ax in hand, charged like a mighty bull through the staved, wooden siding of the mews dragging the confused Maharawal with him. Dharayan, pulling the momentarily pain-blinded Mongol along, backed out of the enclosure through the splintered opening the trapper had made in the wall of the mews.

Outside they found themselves in a desperate situation. Some of the Maharawal's guards had joined the assassins in their treachery. Others were dying. The defenders who were still on their feet were disorganized by an emotional quandary of divided loyalties. Among the already dead lay the lean seneschal, his stomach opened and his entrails hotly smearing the mews floor. He lay where he had fallen before he could reach Dharayan and Subotai. The white-eyed guard captain and the dozen or so troops with him in the mews seemed to be making corpses or hasty recruits of the rest.

The four were outside now, and the rebel troops were maneuvering them away from any cover. The Maharawal was weaponless, but the trapper and the Mongol had their arms. Dharayan seized a wooden stave almost a fathom long from a stack of wood intended for falcon perch construction.

As the Mongol's pain began to dull and his vision to clear, he reached over his shoulder and drew the blue sword. In that moment, the fleeting instant before combat when life is somehow sweet to cling to but exhilarating to release, the beautiful two-handed weapon made Subotai a whole despite his wound. It was as though he had been born for that moment, a moment gone like dying sunlight but preserved in his soul and his consciousness across the everturning cycle of his lives.

The trapper was already swinging his war ax to meet the first attack. And Subotai, even in his heightened state, in his love of it, was glad he was not facing that Saxon battle-ax.

The mutinous troops and their treasonous captain were attempting to encircle the four men. Instinctively, the two Indians, the trapper and the bleeding Mongol formed a defensive perimeter, each assuming responsibility for a quadrant of their protective circle.

"Look to your left, son."

Subotai, still trying to focus one eye, could not block the crazed attack of one of the soldiers. The man, apparently wild from hashish, drove in and grappled with the unarmed Maharawal, stabbing at his victim with a tri-pointed dagger. The Maharawal, worth his salt, reacted like a veteran. He seized the knife-arm and clamped it into his right armpit, and at the same time reached around his attacker's neck to bring his left hand raking across the soldier's eyes.

Then Dharayan was there. He rang the steel cap under the turban of the Maharawal's assailant with a blurred stroke of his wooden cudgel. The Maharawal released the limp body, which sagged from unconsciousness to death before it dropped to the earth. A cleaving stroke of Subotai's blue sword shivered off the man's spinal column at the top of his shoulders.

The bright blood enflamed the wild Norse cells of the Englishman and drove him to the verge of berserking. One of the old rallying cries of the Varangians came back to him, and he roared, in the private language he and Subotai had devised, "They've got us surrounded, the poor bastards!"

"It's the Maharawal they want." Dharayan's voice was a husky whisper to Subotai. "We must keep baiting them with him so they will attack, or they will stand off and send for bows and spears."

Subotai, seeing that the mutineers carried only daggers and swords, the weapons of court assassins, recognized that Dharayan had assessed them correctly. Without further prompting, the Mongol feigned dizziness, pressing his right hand to his sliced, bleeding cheek. Dharayan lowered his stave from the on-guard position and seized Subotai under one arm as though to steady him.

The white-eyed captain's reaction was instantaneous. He touched the shoulders of three of his troops and pointed. They charged toward the Maharawal. Dharayan seemed to appear in the midst of them as they sprinted. His lathi movements were so swift they were almost invisible. In spite of their mortal peril, Dharayan's three allies gawked in open disbelief at the blinding speed and perfection of the tall Indian's stave work.

When Dharayan stepped back toward his place in the defensive circle one of the three attackers lay jerking on the ground with a crushed windpipe, the other two were sprawled awkwardly on their backs with cracked skulls. The white-eyed captain was assembling his remaining forces. Dharayan stooped to gather up all the weapons littering the arena of the fight, then tossed them toward the trapper and Subotai. Seeing that his staff was now nearly broken in two, he snapped it over his knee and cast the wooden pieces aside before rejoining the others.

Some of the mutineers were slinking away, but the white-eyed captain still faced the Maharawal's group with a hard core of seven men. Dharayan, using gestures and whispers, positioned the other three defenders to take maximum advantage of the bodies ringed about them so that any assault by the mutineers would run the risk of tripping on their own casualties. For the moment it was a stand-off. Time had seemingly gone rigid. The only sound was the heavy breathing of exertions and fear. The merciless Indian sun made them all, the righteous as well as the wrongful, sweat as though even the sun knew in its natural way that there was no discerning good men from evil, that no man was completely either.

Then the sudden stillness was as suddenly broken by the arrival of horses. The white-eyed captain swung up onto one of the two mounts a lackey had brought from the stables for the mutineers. One of his followers struggled to get his foot in the stirrup and mount the other horse, his sword wobbling in the same hand he was using to grip the pommel of the saddle.

The Maharawal seized one of the mutineers' swords proffered by Dharayan and, leaping the body of the man who still gasped through his crushed windpipe, ran at the fleeing mutineers with wild yells. The noise and his jerky, unorthodox swings with the sword startled both horses into bolting, and the half-mounted soldier was flung into the dirt.

Subotai and Dharayan were hard after the escaping captain, but the Englishman scored ahead of them. A mutineer who was aiming a stab in the back at the Maharawal was cloven through the ribs, heart, and lungs with the Saxon battle-ax.

With the numbers now nearly equal, the defenders went over to the attack at close quarters. Subotai slashed across and nearly through the sword-hand of one soldier, and then finished the man with a thoughtless stroke across the throat. But as he turned in the steel-ringing confusion of the melee, he sustained a hammer blow on his right temple from the back-handing swing of a sword hilt. He could not feel himself fall, but when he felt the ground and breathed its dust, he tried desperately to get a grip on it to keep from spinning into black unconsciousness.

His dreams of victory and a throne dissolving into death and desertion, the white-eyed captain got his horse under control and headed toward the fortress gates, intending to ride over the Englishman who was now running to block his escape. But the disastrous starting odds and the hand-to-hand fighting had so roused the Englishman's wild Saxon blood that the battle had become for him something terrible and sexual. Now possessed by the northern battle madness, he hewed the living beast to its knees as it charged him.

The white-eyed captain soared over the head of his stricken mount as it skid-tumbled, and died of a broken neck just as the berserk trapper delivered an exultant coup de grace.

φ   φ   φ   φ

Subotai was rudely brought out of his unconsciousness by a cold and unceremonious dunking in the basalt bathing pool administered by the trapper. The Mongol's head fairly roared with pain and throbbed in blinding synchronization with his heartbeat. Aided by Dharayan and one of the female house servants, the trapper stripped off Subotai's riding leathers and again plunged him into the cold water. Then Subotai, spluttering and incongruous of thought and vision, was hastily dried and laid on his sleeping mat. He promptly fainted into a deep and nightmare-shattered sleep filled with fiery lights and troubled with wind demons.

More than a day passed before Subotai drifted back into knowingness. One eye opened to see the sleeping chamber filled with yellow light from a hot afternoon sun. His right eye was swollen shut, but he could feel a cloth tied over it and wrapped clear around his head. The outside of the wound wrapping felt sticky where an ointment of some kind had soaked through. His head still ached, but he was able to focus one eye, and he coherently recalled the desperate fight of the previous day.

"So, you have finally awakened? And in good time, too." The trapper was lounging on his own sleeping mat, amusing himself by piling and caressing the little golden ingots. He began pouring the gold back into the pouches. "I'll wager your skull feels like a Saracen drumhead, though. Whenever you feel that you can sit a horse or, Our Lady forbid, a camel, we will be on our way."

Subotai sat up slowly and waited for the sickening ache in his skull to subside. "What about the Maharawal?" He glanced at the packets of gold. "He seems to have what you want."

The Englishman grinned merrily. "Oh no, lad. What we had yesterday is why I quit the Varangian Guard. Intrigues, murder, palace politics, assassination—part and parcel to this kind of life. No, I will have no more of this, thank you. Yesterday we were caught standing fair on one side of the battle lines. Them or us. Although it seems, all things considered, old Thor and Mother Mary put us with the right contingent."

Subotai held his head in his hands, elbows propped upon his knees. The grizzled but still mighty Englishman looked the young man over, noting his hurting and hang-dog look.

"Bye the bye, Dharayan and that sister of his..."

Here the Mongol interrupted, "Gauri."

"Yes, Gauri, to be sure. They departed with their servants and about ten camels early this morning. He will make the arrangements for us to travel out of the Hindustan from his caravanserai in Sarghoda."

The Englishman's face had a more thoughtful cast now. "When...if...we get back to the Sea of the Ravens..." He let the words die, then seemed to brighten. "Lad, here in this India they have a custom, I am told, called 'swayamvara'. Seems turned about to me, but what it amounts to is that the young women here, under certain circumstances, select from among their suitors the one they will have to husband." He pulled at his thick mustaches for a moment. "Dharayan's sister has spoken to him about you." The English blue eyes were aglint with humorous interest. "It seems the lovely lass would be content to wed you."

Then, before Subotai could respond, he went on, "I think myself she is taken by the lightness of your skin and your blue eyes. And the mystery of that big sword of yours. She told Dharayan and me she watched yesterday's hurly-burly from the upper veranda of the palace. In fact when we brought your swooning body in she wanted to tend you herself. She and Dharayan had some very sharp words over it. One of the household women who speaks the trail talk told me later that Dharayan advised Gauri it would be unseemly for her to nurse you since she had already made her intentions known to him."

The trapper laughed as a look of complete discomfiture spread over Subotai's face. The Mongol squinted through his uncovered eye. "I thought we were going back up to the inlet once again, and then you were planning to travel to Scandia or return to England, wherever those places may be."

The trapper reflected for a moment on the shortness and the unreliability of life and the obvious advantages being offered to Subotai by the marriage arrangement. He spoke again from a genuine fatherly interest in the young man.

"This India is warm and peaceful. And Dharayan will make a merchant of you. You could see some of his wealth around the dear neck and ankles of his sister. I know—you could also see that he himself lives simply enough. That, and what we saw yesterday— although I still cannot seem to believe I really saw a man move that swiftly—show that he has plenty of sand in his craw. And the young woman, Gauri, is as pretty, slim, and lively and feminine as I have ever seen. Go ahead, lad. The steppes, Europe, yes even England, are savage and filthy compared to the life you will have here. You've a good head, son. Someday I will be too old to travel through the cold to the north. And so will you—that is, if you don't have your throat cut or freeze or starve to death first." For a moment the trapper seemed to search for words, then he went on. "Don't worry about me. With the gold I have now, well, perhaps England or the Scandias are not for me any longer. You have heard me curse the Byzantines enough, but I know an imperial administrator or two, and I know the way around those people. I will try the Sea of the Ravens for a while, as Balankar has asked. If it doesn't work out, well, then I will go back into Greece." He winked at Subotai. "A little oil in the palms, as the Greeks say, and I will have a comfortable farm and a woman or two myself."

The trapper reached down and, seizing two of the bags of gold, bounced and squeezed them in his hands. "Your part of the gold— I am giving you one quarter part. If it is agreeable to you, I shall ask Dharayan if he will take it as a sort of a dowry for you."

They both laughed at the notion of a reverse dowry.

"It will serve to get you into the family enterprise. You won't feel like a dependent."

They had not spoken of a division of the payment for the falcons and goshawks. It had not occurred to the Mongol in his utter simplicity that anything was due him. It had all been the trapper's know-how and his equipment. Subotai's unspoken purpose in joining the Englishman had been his continuing search for the elusive Kipchaks. So much the better that he had been fed and equipped, and he knew his informal apprenticeship to the trapper had greatly enriched his life, for not even the most scholarly of men during these barbarous times had a larger grasp of the geography of the enormous Eurasian land mass, or a better capability for intuitive navigation and dead reckoning from the stars of the northern hemisphere, than Subotai of the Mongols had gained at his relatively tender age of some twenty-two years.

And Subotai could not deny to himself the powerful emotional surges he had felt just sitting in close proximity to the beautiful, dark Indian woman. He had great sexual desire for women, but what he now felt for Gauri was something different, akin to the as yet unassembled spiritual, emotional, and sexual segments of the grand feeling he had nurtured for the fair Mursechen. Subotai's new feeling for Gauri came as a temporary relief for him, relief from the obsessive, preoccupying love that had been constantly burning him since he had seen Mursechen on the steppe. Yet it had been years since that momentary encounter.

The trapper broke into Subotai's reverie. "Whatever you are looking for out there..." The trapper nodded in the general direction of north with a half-grimace and half-smile. "I have heard you murmur a name in your sleep, lad. You know what is up there: vastness and cold and death. Whatever, whoever, she is, you could search forever. You know that, don't you?"

The Mongol let out a heavy sigh. "Aye."

Subotai felt entirely at ease with the trapper, trusted him without fear of any misunderstanding, potential deviousness, or treachery. He admired the Englishman, and appreciated that through him he had acquired not only knowledge and practical skills but also the redeeming gift of a personal and expanding sense of humor.

Subotai focused his unbandaged eye on the Englishman and asked, "Will you stay for the binding?" He used the Mongol word for wedding or family gathering.

"I can't hold the caravan. If it doesn't leave beforehand, I will be there. And in my finest. Dharayan has promised to take me through the bazaars of Sarghoda when we arrive."

φ   φ   φ   φ

At the Maharawal's suggestion, the northerners remained at the desert citadel until Subotai returned to better fettle. The Mongol with the blessing of youth, recovered swiftly. The gash had closed and was healing cleanly, and the purplish discoloration about his eye and temple began to fade into the normal texture of his skin.

Less than ten days later they rode out of the fortress after a warm leave-taking from the Maharawal. Two camels went with them, loaded with great weights of dried fruit and finely woven cloth, wedding gifts for Gauri and Subotai from a grateful Maharawal of Amrithistan. One of Dharayan's servants who had remained behind after the merchant's departure served as their guide over the desert trail to the city of Sarghoda and to Dharayan's caravanserai.

They reached the caravanserai in the dead of night. The compound used for lading and staging the long camel trains was surrounded by a low wall constructed of mud bricks into which, at intervals, flaring torches had been thrust. Late as it was, they were greeted in the yard by a host of brown people sounding gongs, ringing camel bells, and waving more torches. Dharayan was there, but Gauri was apparently in seclusion until the wedding.

The tall merchant approached them as they dismounted. He was followed by a small group of young men, each of whom, even in the torchlight, seemed to have the same level and knowing gaze which Dharayan possessed.

"Shanti—peace, welcome," the Indian said.

Morning revealed that the living quarters of the caravanserai were actually a part of the outer wall of Sarghoda. Upper level windows with cleverly worked stone lattices overlooked the band of desert between city walls and the fringes of the irrigated gardens stretching to the banks of the Indus River. Windows on the opposite side of the wall-house overlooked the colorful, noisy, and aromatic life of the Hindu city, the first city Subotai had ever seen.

Dharayan took the trapper and Subotai into the bazaars during the cooler mornings for the next several days. The trapper reveled in the incredible variety of fine cloth and wares filling and spilling out of the stalls and shops.

"Nothing like this, lad, in Constantinople," he remarked on several occasions. He converted some of his golden treasure into bolts of silk which had come over the high and freezing Tibetan plateau from China. At his language-scrambled direction, the wives of some of the cloth merchants were induced to tailor to his rather bizarre personal specifications a number of unique silk and brocaded costumes which, the Englishman assured the Mongol, would rival even the Eastern Roman Emperor in his finest.

When the trapper's material tastes had been temporarily glutted he and Dharayan turned their attention to garbing Subotai for his wedding and his future role in life. His brother-in-law-to-be, looking the stocky Mongol over with an intensely critical eye, voiced a suggestion which, although all his words were softly spoken, seemed to bear the force of natural law.

"Gauri intends to wear a red and gold sari. Our religious tradition dictates that you wear at least something of saffron color. Perhaps silk and cotton, a long outer coat of yellow silk, about knee-length, with open Chinese sleeves reaching past your elbows. And yellow cotton for the rest. And Subotai, you must bring some of your divided riding bottoms for the women to copy. Have several pair sewn, since much of your work and mine involves camel riding."

Subotai agreed with everything. Hindi traditions and appropriate wedding clothing were inconsequential compared with the delightful fantasies he was conjuring in his mind around Gauri. He was inclined to mutter affirmative answers to any question or issue that was raised so that he could continue his imaginings uninterrupted. He had not seen Gauri since the evening of the Maharawal's banquet, but one hot afternoon when he was standing at one of the inner window balconies hoping for a relieving breeze, he caught sight of her briefly. She was leaving with an escort of chaperoning women whom he took to be a mix of servants and kinswomen. All the women's faces were covered, but Gauri's elegant and graceful walk betrayed her identity.

She was gowned in a white sari beautifully worked with gold thread about the skirt hems. Some of the women with her were bright splashes of color in saris of four and five colors, blending gold, green, yellow, orange, and white in a startling gaiety under the bright Indian sun. He learned later that what he saw was Gauri being escorted to the great stone temple of Kali for a traditional bridal dedication ceremony.

Subotai was left more or less to his own devices for the remaining few days before the wedding. Dharayan and the trapper had gone into the city once more. The trapper shrewdly exchanged his golden hoard for an array of expertly cut jewels—rubies, emeralds, and sapphires—and these he sewed into his heavier equipment and saddlery to secure them from at least the thieves of opportunity.

Dharayan was occupied from dawn to the hours past sunset in staging and scoring the lading logs for a camel train soon to leave.

In the early morning hours of Subotai's wedding day the camel train departed for the pass in the northwest, the Macedonian Gate, and through it to the trail that debouched onto the southern steppes.

The trapper traveled with it, since another caravan would not venture from Sarghoda in that direction again for nearly a sun-year. Subotai helped him load his pack animals, both men working in silence and avoiding each other's eyes.

"I will never ride one of those accursed creatures," the trapper said jovially as he pointed at the ugly-natured camels and started to swing up onto his trail horse. Instead he turned with a brusqueness not typical of his nature and shook Dharayan's hand. Then he faced the silent Subotai and placing both of his overlarge hands on the Mongol's shoulders, gently shook him.

"You are a strange one, son. Sometimes you and your new brother both have that distant look of knowing what others do not." With that he dropped his hands, took his reins, and mounted. Looking down at Subotai with eyes that were suddenly misty, he said earnestly, "Stay here in this place. The sun always shines and the bazaars are rich and heavy." Then in a whisper, he said, "Lord Christ and Wotan guard you, son."

Subotai watched the caravan until it was gone in the deluding heat waves.

φ   φ   φ   φ

Subotai had bathed and was half-dressed and tying back his shoulder-length, reddish-black hair when his quarters were invaded and he was good-naturedly set upon by the same group of younger men who had been with Dharayan on the evening of his arrival in Sarghoda. They hauled him down the stone steps of the wall-house inner stairway and thrust him into a waiting palanquin. He was garlanded with flowers before the litter was hoisted onto the strong brown shoulders of the laughing and shouting group.

All of this seems puzzlingly familiar, Subotai thought to himself. Borne along in the palanquin by the boisterous young men he felt the rightness of the moment. And for the present, the burning, preoccupying desire for the blonde Mongol woman was obscured by the more immediate reality of the imminent marriage ceremony and the prospect of the lovely and graceful Indian woman with whom he would soon share life and lodging. For an instant he wondered at the precise and peculiar chain of thoughts and events, conditions and pressures, which had brought him to this rich land and this rich moment.

The procession hastened on to the stone-blocked temple of Kali amid the blowing of conch shells and clashing of gongs and cymbals and the soft, timbrous resonance of the famous camel bells of India. Subotai's senses were nearly overloaded with the color of the scene. He was filled with a warmth he felt for everything living, and sent glowing thankfulness in a soul-mind expression to the Sky. Brown faces smiled up at him. Every passerby offered him a pronam, the gentle and graceful greeting of the subcontinent.

At the steps of the temple with its elaborate, carved friezes two Brahman priests who would officiate at the wedding joined the celebrating parade and strode with it on the return to Dharayan's and Gauri's home where the wedding would be performed. At the wall-house the Mongol was pulled out of the litter and thrust into his new yellow wedding coat while one of the priests lifted the multi-colored circlet of flowers from about his neck.

A mandap—a wedding tent with saffron-colored siding and curtained drops—had been erected in the largest inner hall of the wall-house. Large, shield-shaped carmine banners hung from the ceiling, suspended above a sacred Vedic fire. The priests went immediately to tend the orange and almost smokeless ceremonial flame.

Dharayan came forward and led Subotai to a low cushioned seat before the fire. Then Subotai caught his breath as Gauri, heavily veiled and richly gowned in a carmine silk sari, banded and heavily embroidered with golden thread, was led to the fire and seated beside him. He saw that the upturned palms of her hands had been carefully painted in spiraling patterns with henna.

At the moment judged most astrologically propitious for their union, a Brahman priest tied their right wrists together in the Kautuka rite. Then the priests began reading and reciting in Sanskrit from the Vedic texts, Dharayan gently cuing the couple at the proper times for their responses to the vows. Subotai was absorbed in the ceremony and the sound of the Sanskrit words. The haunting syllables of the ancient language brought to him a vague and indistinct longing, a reaching toward something in the deepest dimness of his being which he could not quite bring to the surface of his consciousness.

At the end they took the ritual steps together around the sacred fire that sealed the oneness of their future. Subotai tenderly lifted the veils which shimmered with a gauzy, wavering golden sheen and looked at his bride. Gauri had colored her lips a lush crimson. Tears stood in her deep, dark eyes. The gathered onlookers—men, women, and children—gave a hushed murmuring of exultation at her darkly lustrous beauty.

The entire lower level of the wall-house was then opened for the wedding feast. Gauri and Subotai were placed on a low dais, and from there received the blessings and the well-wishes of the Indian women, who praised Gauri's loveliness and the exotic handsomeness of her foreign husband. Subotai endured it all numbly, still wondering at that strange feeling of familiarity, never taking his gaze from Gauri.

The astonishing assortment of gifts that had been arriving at the household for nearly a moon-cycle were on display. Dharayan's relatives and associates in his trading enterprise had unloosed their massive Indian generosity upon the young couple. There were staggering quantities of dried fruits, cotton, silk, and brocaded cloth, as well as silver plate and matched drinking cups of extraordinarily artistic workmanship. There was also a late addition to the gifts from the Maharawal—a pair of tumbling and playful cheetah cubs.

Rousing himself from his musings, Subotai went to sample the assortment of dried and sweetened fruits. His memory of the old shaman and that bitter but instructional day marked by the first taste of a sweet in all his cold, wandering young years, made him marvel at this deluge of plenty.

The rooms filled with guests delighting over a variety of hot curries, bowls of fresh and dried fruit, heaping sweetmeats and chappatis. All the arrangements had been made by Gauri herself with the loving assistance of her serving women and female relatives.

After tasting his way through the sweets and fruits, Subotai, without a word to Gauri, left the wedding celebration and ascended the stone stairway. He returned moments later with a long and heavy roll wrapped in coarse jute.

"My gift to you, Gauri," he said as he set the jute unwinding on the stone before the nuptial dais.

The menfolk abandoned their feasting and their talk of crops and goods and profits at the sight of the huge, pale, and perfectly preserved Siberian tiger skin. Utterances of amazement at the size of the pelt were followed by further notes of astonishment at the thickness and pleasing softness of the striped fur. Gauri, with her captivating femininity, stood, lifted the skirts of her sari above her ankles, and stepped off the dais, an act which made Subotai almost visibly pulsate and caused him to go suddenly dry-mouthed and feverish. Gauri knelt and ran her lovely woman's hands through the luxuriant fur and then looked up at her husband with a gleam of admiration and a warming of desire on her flawless face.

"It is said by the Ramayama, 'Without my lord, my life to bless, where could be heaven or happiness?' " She stood and came to his side, sat by him, and took his square, powerful hand in her own.

The feasting and goodwill visitations would continue for days. As the Indian darkness stole over their wedding day, Gauri and Subotai, trying vainly to slip away, were followed to their bedding chamber by a throng of noisy well-wishers. Within, however, there was quiet relief from the social strains of the afternoon. Servants had set lamps ablaze and loaded a table with food and drink. The wedding bed was white with fresh coverings. The flames in the lamps bent gently with a soft, cooling breeze from the Indus River.

Gauri crossed the room and stood by one of the open windows which offered a view of the desert floor set below a jet black sky lightened with star swarms like cosmic snow. She heard Subotai pour and drink deeply of the stone-cooled water. He came to her in his warrior-trained silence, and slowly took the shawl from her shoulders. She turned into his embrace and felt the fiery need in his hard body through his seeking lips. Then she spoke in Hindi so he would not understand.

"My Subotai. My Warrior of the Snows. I have always known thee. Companion of my sleeping dreams. My wandering Soul. I knew thou wouldst come to me in time. Together we were before. Together we shall be again. I will make thee forget the other one—for a time."

She helped him undo the clasp at her shoulder that held her flowing sari and it settled about her feet noiselessly. She sat on the edge of the nuptial bed with her underskirt draping her invitingly at the middle of her softly curved thighs. She unbound her full bosom and slipped off her remaining clothing as Subotai lay down beside her, his heavily-muscled body almost alight with his vital force and his enflamed desire for this enticing and mysterious dark woman.

They came to their marital knowledge in a bursting and sensuous craving for each other. They slept, bathed, then in their enormous wanting, they shared and satisfied their needs together again and again. His northern vitality and energy swirled and was satiated and absorbed into her warm seductiveness. Each time it was complete, it seemed to both of them that they had never truly rested as they now rested in arm-and-leg-entwined sleep.

φ   φ   φ   φ

"It is so cold, Subotai!" Gauri frolicked like a young doe in the early fall snow above the lamasery which was perched atop a gigantic natural granite balustrade. Steep, rock-strewn, and snow-covered mountain slopes fell sharply away below the base of the high fortress rock and the walled building that crowned it. Behind the gray-white and dark-windowed lamasery with its peculiar Buddhist turrets, lotuslike in their bulbousness, the massive and soaring upthrust of snowy Himalayan peaks caught the narrow and stony and bleak valley in a sun-blocking encirclement.

The snow fields sprawling down from the higher elevations reached to the uphill side of the lamasery wall. The snow piled against the outer side of the wall was darkened with ash from monastery fires, but only a short distance uphill it became white again.

Gauri and Subotai careened recklessly down a snow field, tobogganing on his Mongol greatcoat. Gauri, dizzy from the wild, sliding spin they were in, glimpsed the jagged, gray boulder jutting up through the snow in the path of their high-speed slide.

"Subotai, look out!"

"For what?" But his breathy laugh choked off when the rock they were speeding toward blurred across his spinning vision. He tried to skid his legs into the snow to brake their descent, but the action tore him from the greatcoat and rammed him head first into the snow.

"Subotai-i-i-i..." Gauri's howl broke with a gasp when the greatcoat skittered up on the boulder, knocking the wind from her. Then the greatcoat sailed up and over the top of the boulder like a magic carpet and crashed into the snow. Its spinning momentum dug Gauri under the snow surface while the greatcoat spun and slid down the snow slope.

Gauri struggled painfully to regain her breath while Subotai waded and slid to her side. Her eyes were still closed as he lifted her head and shoulders out of the snow and into his lap. He began rubbing her hands and wrists briskly, then lightly slapped and pinched her cheeks, but still she lay like a dead weight. He put her head down gently and stood up to raise a desperate shout to the lamasery below, but as he opened his mouth he saw one alert and mischievous brown eye wink open for an instant.

Gauri heard him move away from her, and opened her eyes a slit, looking toward the monastery, but did not see him. She wondered where he had got to, and sat up to look. Just as she did so, a lightly packed snowball exploded on the back of her head. She seemed stunned for a moment, and began to cry. At that the experience of guilt ripped through Subotai for the first time in his life, and he rushed back to her, only to be greeted with a handful of snow in his face and her triumphant laugh in his ear.

Their exertions in the thin air on the gently sloping snow field left them breathless. Gauri's eyes were alight with her first experience of snow. And, after the hot lowlands of India, the Mongol was in his element. The crisp air and the fresh bite of the cold seemed to uncoil and surface his dormant energy. A few hours in the high chilliness had banished a dulling lassitude he had begun to feel in the dusty heat of Sarghoda. Both of them were atingle with delight in this exploration of newly licensed, intimate playfulness.

φ   φ   φ   φ

The last of the wedding guests and the wreckage of the marriage feast had been still in evidence when Dharayan had pressed the Mongol into service in the caravanserai. The last camel train to be outfitted before the onset of the muggy and swamping monsoon had kept the brothers-in-law laboring across a week of long days in the darkening tropical heat. Subotai's experience with the trapper came to the fore, and he was soon rendering yeoman service in organizing, packing, and securing the freight and, in the critical hours of loading the spitting and biting camels, overseeing the manhandling of the goods onto the beasts.

"No rest yet, Subotai." Dharayan spoke with anticipation when the caravan was ready to leave. "Don your trail leathers. You, sister, and I are going with them."

They had trailed generally north following the course of the Indus River and entered the disputed lands now under the sway of the Kharesmian general, Kutub-Ud-Din. When the tribute exacted by the officers of that Islamic commander had been paid, the caravan was allowed to continue on into the hill country. And on one of the strange, humid days with the monsoon sky rumbling behind them and the snow peaks of the Himalayas seeming as far clouds on the horizon, they came upon the hunting camp of the great general.

Kutub-Ud-Din, galloping by the swaying file of camels with half a dozen companions and bodyguards, pulled up when he caught sight of Dharayan and hailed the tall merchant. Subotai did not learn until later that Dharayan, due to his genius for languages and his native dignity and integrity, had served as emissary of the Maharawal of Amrithistan when a boundary treaty had been successfully negotiated with Kutub-Ud-Din. The treaty had, at least temporarily, halted the powerful Islamic military thrust across all of northern India.

That evening, with the two camps side by side, Dharayan and Subotai attended a meal at the general's hunting tent. Gauri remained behind since, at Dharayan's insistence, she wore the typical male caravaner's clothing and her presence was known only to the brothers-in-law and to some of the trusted and long-dedicated family servants traveling with them.

The fare at the supper included the day's bag—partridge and wild pig. Clear water from the many cool streams in the hilly region was drunk from dripping water bags passed around the circle of men on the carpeted ground. Much to Subotai's relief, since he had neither a genuine taste nor a weakness for it, no wine was served, as the great Moslem soldier held strictly to the admonitions of the Koran concerning strong drink. Since leaving the colder climes of the steppes, where a welcome draught of heated wine or fermented mare's milk brought the quick sweats and the pleasing dissipation of a chill, the Mongol found little pleasure in, and put little reliance on, the grape and barley drinks fermented in the ancient Indus River valley.

The general seemed a man given to long silences. After the meal, he questioned Dharayan about deep religious matters, and listened with singular attention to Dharayan's answers. Their talk lasted until dawn. Subotai sat most of the night in an uncomprehending silence, sharing the relaxed energy of the Moslem and the Indian but remaining alertly awake although the paladins of Kutub-Ud-Din dozed around him. He noted that the Kharesmian general had lost his left hand and wondered how the general could manage a bow or a shield without it.

In the always quiet majesty of that moment when darkness departs and the first shafts of the promised morning appear, the Islamic general had ushered them past his sleeping officers—his war dogs, he called them—and blessed them on their way, handing Dharayan a small, official scroll bearing the flowery signet of Kutub-Ud-Din which guaranteed safe passage and relieved them of further payment of duties.

During the following days they had trailed on into the hill country with the upsweep of the Himalayas looming closer at each sunrise. For the climb into the precipitous and rocky highlands sure-footed donkeys had replaced the camels, a trade they made at a Tibetan settlement where yaks, donkeys, and camels mixed in an integrated stock enclosure. Here they also traded for long coats, peculiar flat-peaked Tibetan hats with earflaps, pants, and boots with upturned toes, all of yakskin and wool-lined against the high, cold air they were climbing into.

They had traveled afoot thereafter, toiling beside the heavy-laden donkeys. Always they were breathless and aching with fatigue, stubbing and tripping against the sharp rocks along the narrow pathway which was all that was left of the once spacious trail. Subotai came to feel great respect for Gauri's toughness in her uncomplaining and resilient battle with the thin air and the rough trail. She had quickly shown her lean strength and endurance in the wearing ascent as the pack train struggled up, always up.

They had finally reached the summit of the pass far above the treeline on the high and bleak trail. And still the mountain peaks towered in white remoteness above them. They could see wind-driven plumes of snow on the mountain reaches sent roiling against the severity of the Himalayan Sky by unimaginable winds.

On the far side of the pass they could see lying beneath them at the rock-strewn foot of the cliff face the lamasery and its Tibetan village which was their destination. Embankments of prayer stones now marked the center of the trail in its descent to the village. Buddhist prayers were scratched on many of the flat stones. Their Tibetan trail guide assiduously kept the donkeys descending with the rounded wall of prayer stones constantly on their right side. They moved along glacier-fed streams, white and ice-cold, that raced down the stony slopes, feeding an Indus-tributary river in the bottom lands of the small valley below the village and the lamasery.

φ   φ   φ   φ

And so it was that Gauri had come to be in the high snows she had wondered about.

They lodged in the lamasery itself. A red-robed Lamasitic monk, silent and moving with a studied and contemplative slowness, led Subotai and Gauri to a small, cell-like room where they could spread their trail bedding and sleep on the floor. After seeing Dharayan to his guest chamber, the monk returned to them with hot yak milk. Its warmth and the yellow butter fat melted in it sent them off to a contented sleep with satisfied bellies.

The following fortnight they spent in the village negotiating with traders in the marketplace for the fine Tibetan wools and the silks and musks of China which came to this trail terminus over the long, dangerous route across the Tibetan plateau. Their own wares of Indian indigo, spices, and cotton cloth created a yammering demand among the slant-eyed, hard-faced merchants of the high mountains.

There were many Tibetan women living in the village, and Gauri felt relieved that she could put aside the fur hat and let her hair down in the marketplace. She was glad of the chance to mingle with others of her own sex. She loved Subotai and Dharayan, each in an appropriate way, but she found there can be such a thing as too much male companionship.

The traders seemed to Gauri to be of the same people as her new husband, lacking only his exotic blue-gray eyes and slightly lighter skin and the reddish luster in his long black hair.

Dharayan had made an outright gift of much of his merchandise to the monks of the lamasery and, in return, had received, in addition to shelter in the hostelry, numerous brass lamps of intricate design and a variety of sizes, some for hanging and some fashioned to be set upon a floor or table. All the lamps combined a practical lighting function with the beautiful ornateness the Buddhist monks had imparted with their crafting and their expert metalsmithing. Filled with oil or yak butterfat and wicked with jute or cotton, the lamps put forth a light that was both warm and bright.

New snow had fallen—in secret, it seemed to Gauri—while they had slept in the lamasery throughout the cold mountain night. The days since their arrival had not dulled her fascination with it, and now, with her breath steaming in the freezing air around her, she romped and slid in the white newness. Subotai thoroughly enjoyed initiating her into the snow-games of his boyhood. He explained all the esoteric techniques for making snowballs of varying hardness, and described the skis used by the Reindeer People when they traveled with their herds. Then, wet and shivering from their snow-play and worn from the thinness of the atmosphere, they went panting back to their little lodging in the peaceful lamasery. Within, the heat was delicious, and Gauri set to warming yak milk over a yak dung blaze confined in a sunken, stone fire-hollow in the middle of the floor. They stripped off their wet clothing and huddled together naked in front of the fire-glow, sipping the rich, hot milk. They knew they must start the slippery and dangerous trek back down to the Indian lowlands the next morning. Dharayan had carefully moved ahead of the gathering monsoon to get here, and now they must travel down the Indus trail before winter came on the mountains and before the possible onset of winter rains which sometimes come to northwestern India.

Gauri fluffed her hair near the fire to dry it. It had grown very long, and some of the black strands which she flipped back with a toss of her head led Subotai's eyes to the classic, brown curvature of her hips and down the precious thighs and calves. Before his marriage, Subotai had not been afforded views of the legs of many women, and now he had become obsessed with Gauri's. When he reached out his still-cold hand and caressed one inner thigh, she slapped it gently. "Warm those a little first," she ordered.

But he would not be stayed. "You will have to turn back into a man tomorrow."

She twisted one of his ears lightly. "And do you like me in pants and heavy coats?"

He answered after he had drawn her down to his side, his voice thick with arousal. "The first time you even lifted your skirts briefly, I felt as though I had been sword-hammered on the skull."

Her smile was knowing and slightly wicked. "Perhaps we'd better wait. This is a monastery, you know." But then she realized that he probably knew nothing of what she meant.

"There will be no waiting," he said. Then he covered their feet with one of the Tibetan coats and they began their love play.

It would be a hard day tomorrow on the rocky trail with no sleep for them this night.

φ   φ   φ   φ

On a marvellously clear and snow-glittering morning, they left the lamasery behind, the long-drawn chants of the lamas at their meditations murmuring ever more faintly behind them. Soon the freezing wind and the digging hoof steps of the donkeys and the squeaking strains of the baggage tie-down lines were the only sounds they could hear above their labored breathing.

They arrived at the Tibetan herding settlement with the loss of only three donkeys which, with their expensive cargoes, had been swept off the narrow mountain trail by a sudden, slamming rockfall. Retrieving their camels at the settlement, they persevered on their way from dawn to dusk, and came trail-sore and muddy to Sarghoda in the early drizzle of the beginning winter rains.

As the caravanserai had been left in the capable and trustworthy hands of intelligent servants whose families had served the family of Dharayan and Gauri for many generations, they found all in good order. They set about renewing life within the familiar confines of the comfortable and large dwelling set so uniquely with its one side looking out upon an almost unspoiled natural view and its inner, city side open to the active and always changing panorama of human life.

Their relaxation in their homecoming was short-lived. Within hours, merchants or their agents from the city began arriving to appraise the goods freighted back from the Himalayas. The shrewd brown men felt the texture of the wools baled and piled in storage sheds on great wooden shelves, hid their delight at the assortment of lamps, and silently calculated profits from the bolts of silk which always seemed to have an eye-catching sheen even on cloudy and dreary days.

Dharayan and Gauri were both kept busy checking manifests against goods and striking bargains of exchange or coinage with the Hindu merchants. Most of the agreements were in terms of accounts receivable—young camels from the following spring's birthing, spice loads expected from the sweltering south of the subcontinent or vouched for with partial payments in gold or mortgages to be held as collateral. Except for the wares that had been contracted for prior to the expedition into the mountains, the caravanserai's stalls and shelves emptied in a few days' time. The remaining goods would be delivered throughout the city at leisure by Dharayan's staff.

Spring and early summer were the seasons of greatest activity at the caravanserai. Subotai had quickly found his calling as loadmaster and trainer of the young camels. He found that he had an even greater communion and understanding with camels than with horses. Before his first trailing season was done, he was a functioning and necessary part of the trading and fitting-out at the caravanserai. But his complete illiteracy and his indifference to gain made him balk at both Gauri's and Dharayan's efforts to teach him enough of written language and of the Hindu number system and mathematics so that he could assist them in the accounting. He would listen patiently but with deafened ear to their discourses, then simply walk away.

Winter—although Subotai, with his memories of the life-and-death bitterness of winter in the savage northlands, could hardly recognize its existence in warm Sarghoda—was the period of calm and relative inactivity in the commerce of the caravanserai. And during this first winter, Gauri, the product of an intricate culture thousands of years of age, and Subotai, the orphan son of the barbarous steppes, took their first steps on the long and demanding path of marital understanding. As Subotai's grasp of the Hindi language expanded, tensions grew between them, but then subsided in their mutual need for each other, cauterized as much by their magnetic pull for one another as by Subotai's vigorous response to Gauri's demands in their sleeping chamber.

After the sweet hotness of their early days of marriage eased a little, Subotai began to discover one of the subtle complexities of Indian domestic life. Unused to the rigid nature of Hindu society flowing from a tradition of great antiquity, he found his wife's dominance of the household something of a shock. Mongol women, to be sure, occupied an established level in the more democratic nomad society, but their social condition had always been below that of men in every aspect of life and below that of able-bodied warriors in particular. The Indian woman's position was quite different. Graceful, sweet of voice, attentive to husband and children, rich in religion and strong in family traditions, the Indian woman was nonetheless an integral and forceful influence in all affairs save war, and took an active part in direct and tangential ways at all levels of life including government and trade. It took the Mongol some time to adjust to being treated rather like a feeble-minded rajah in his own home. His wife's loving corrections of his behavior and habits left him in a speechless state of semi-pleased conformity.

And there was the spiritual dimension of Indian life, so different from that of the steppes. At first Subotai held back somewhat, but he was happy to busy himself helping Gauri host the many people who came, on all days and at all hours, it seemed, seeking Dharayan's counsel.

Gauri's spiritual nature made her every movement, her words, her every act an artful event of holiness and sweet devotion to her goddess, the Mother Kali, whom she worshipped daily in Sarghoda's massive temple. Her flowing, soft mannerisms and her quiet energy hypnotized the savage man from the steppes, and gradually he began to become, if not civilized, at least presentable by Indian standards. Eventually Subotai's mind was profoundly altered through his daily contact with this extraordinary woman. Her high spiritual vibration, while not more advanced than Subotai's, nevertheless affected his willingness to conform to her social attitudes.

Nor did he, in the beginning, join in the daily walk Gauri and Dharayan took into the city to the temple of Kali for their devotions. But after he accompanied them once, this became as much a part of his life as of theirs. He liked the dim interior of the temple with its lamp-lit altars, and the stony coolness of the place. The high, darkened ceiling of the temple suggested to him the farness of the night Sky of the steppes for which he sometimes yearned.

Their first son was born about ten moon-cycles after the colorful Hindu wedding ceremony. The squalling brown bundle of life and demand burst the peace of the pleasant house, but it was a disturbance full of promise and purpose. And for Subotai the event provided a respite from the surfacing tension he had developed under the Gauri's gentle, guiding harassments, as she was now devoting most of her time and her energies to her first concern, leaving Subotai more breathing space.

It was during the hot days, while Gauri nursed and cooed over the child and recovered from the birth and the clumsy aid of some unfortunately inept midwifery, that Subotai and Dharayan took the full measure of each other. The cycle of commerce was at a low ebb and both men were seeking outlets for their energies. Dharayan had come upon the Mongol one morning as he sat sharpening and oiling the fine steel of the samurai sword. His bow lay beside him glistening from the hour's labor he had invested in rubbing fine oil into its wood.

"The air is heavy, but I judge the monsoon is still a week, possibly two, away." Dharayan nodded his head toward the southeast as he spoke, noted the Mongol's careful whetstoning, then asked, "Do your people have many weapons as fine as that one?"

Subotai smiled and squinted into the morning sun over Dharayan's shoulder. Not for the first time, Subotai became consciously aware of his feeling of calmness when he was in Dharayan's company, aware that somehow everything else—sound, emotion, tension—dropped away from him. He laughed pleasantly as he answered, "No, I took this from a dead man from another tribe. As to where he got it, I do not know since his people, the Kuraits, do not usually have blades as tough and keen as this either. See the grip? I have never seen beasts of this kind. Have you?"

Dharayan took the sword and slowly inspected the superb carvings, then handed it back to Subotai. "No, although the stags look somewhat familiar." He looked thoughtfully at Subotai for a moment before he spoke again. "Have you been trained to fight with the lathi?"

"You mean the long stick like the one you used so effectively that day at the citadel?"

"Yes."

"On the steppes we used long poles with horse-tail nooses on them for capturing wild ponies and sometimes for hunting. I knew men who were adept in fighting on horseback with them. I have always concentrated on the sword. It is, I think, more useful, whether one is either mounted or dismounted. I don't think there is much a stick-fighter could do against a good swordsman—if both of them were afoot, I mean."

"Would you care to try a little exercise?" Dharayan asked, knowing the answer. He walked into one of the mud warehouses and came out with a long, polished lathi.

Subotai slid his blue blade into a leather scabbard for safety. "I'm hopelessly stale," he said, then tied a leather thong around the scabbard to make sure the blade would not slip out in the proposed scrimmage.

Dharayan spun the lathi above his head until it dissolved into a blur, then he dipped, spinning the lathi diagonally, criss-crossing the cudgel in front of him. Subotai merely took some loosening swings with the long sword. Then both came on guard several yards apart, respecting the principle of distance. The Mongol advanced one cautious linear step. With the sword held directly before him in both hands, he let the point of the weapon inscribe small, deceptively lazy circles in the air.

Dharayan moved to his right and seemed suddenly to disappear. Subotai felt a suctioning force and two quick, light blows, one on his upper left arm and one to the back of his head. He first thought he had been caught flat-footed, but then realized that he had actually started a thrusting attack which Dharayan had blended into, then had turned to the outside of the Mongol's forward-moving body and delivered the irresistible counterstrokes. Had the encounter been deadly serious, Subotai realized he would be down—either dead or unconscious.

Several times more, with slight variations, Dharayan repeated his unbelievable performance. At times it seemed to Subotai that Dharayan actually faded away from the physical plane and rematerialized in another place. Subotai was not able either to attack successfully or to counter the amazing art of his tall brother-in-law's attacks with the Indian staff. Subotai, the product of a martial people in a martial age, was awestruck by Dharayan's ability. Baffled, the Mongol lowered his weapon.

"How is it that you can have such skill?" Subotai made no effort to hide his wide-eyed admiration.

Dharayan, always good-natured, laughed and laid the lathi aside. "I am the very incomplete apprentice of my late uncle, my father's brother. As doubtless Gauri has told you, we are members of the Kshatriya caste, the caste of warriors."

Here Subotai interrupted him. "And I do not understand that either. Being Kshatriyas, why or how do you live as those in the merchant class? I have seen how deferentially those people you trade with treat you and Gauri. She told me the name of the merchant class, but I have forgotten it." Subotai's barbarian contempt for the obsequiousness he often found since leaving the northern steppes showed plainly.

"One mystery at a time, Subotai. Let it suffice for the moment to say that the castes were never meant to impose a lifelong condition. In the teaching my uncle gave me, it was supposed in ancient times that men would vary their personal quality, and that personal quality, rather than birth alone, would govern their position and caste in life. We had best go inside, or into the shade, Subotai, unless you prefer short answers. The summer sun is not tolerant of lengthy discourses."

They went into the large lower hall of the wall-house and seated themselves on the stone flooring. Dharayan called for a servant to bring fruit and milk. Then, closing his eyes, he mused for a few moments, searching for the best beginning.

"Longer ago than there are written records to verify, this region of India came under the sway of a group of related ruling families. They were Kshatriyas, and the spoken tradition given to me by my uncle relates that they came to be called the Solar Warrior dynasty. After a period of many centuries the dynasty disappeared, but the tradition of that clan, or group of clans, lived on through a military order which retained the structure and theory of the spiritual and martial teachings of the original warrior families. Their methods and their sciences were also preserved and carried on by the order."

Subotai started to speak, but the Indian made a silencing mudra with the fingers of his right hand and went on. "You were about to ask what a military order is. Consider it much like the social and warrior councils of your own people in organization and purpose. You once spoke of them as 'warrior yurts,' as I recall. The Order of the Solar Warriors was, naturally, an exclusively male body. Only Kshatriya men could be invited to enter the order. My uncle stated to me on several occasions that when he passed through the final initiation into the secrets of the order, he went alone, and that in the years after he entered the order no other young warriors were asked. Those Solar Warriors who taught him and advanced him in the secrets, he said, were very old men."

Dharayan had grown distant-eyed as he related the story to the Mongol. He was so completely preoccupied that his singular state of mind held Subotai in fascinated silence. "My uncle came to live with us, and as I grew toward manhood, I came under the influence of my uncle much more than of my father. He was a very old man, even in my earliest recollections of him. He was, however, enormously vigorous, and undertook to train me in all the weapon and unarmed fighting systems he had been taught by the Solar Warriors. He was exacting. Even on the day of his death, he put me through a stringent and demanding exercise, requiring me to demonstrate all the traditional forms with all the weaponry. It was on that day, his last, that he allowed me knowledge of the secrets of the order. He told me then that I was to be the last Solar Warrior until the revival of the order in the far-distant future."

Dharayan abruptly stood up. "On days like this I sometimes go to the river to bathe and take the sunlight. Can you swim?" He made paddling motions with his arms.

"Yes." Subotai also stood up and, indicating the northwesterly direction behind him, said, "I learned in the Sea of the Ravens." With boyish enthusiasm, he bounded up the inner stone stairway toward his and Gauri's bedchamber. "I will tell Gauri where we are going," he called back.

It was just before midday when they began the long walk to the Indus River, and well past the noon position of the sun when they reached the sandy banks stretching down to the water.

Subotai looked questioningly at Dharayan when he saw that huge crocodiles littered the beaches and sandbars. Dharayan simply threw rocks at the long, slim-snouted crocodilians.

"Gharials. They are harmless to us."

For all their immensity, the gharials were inordinately shy, and scrambled in their fast, swaying, high-legging manner into the river.

Dharayan hurled a few more stones after the creatures as the last ones slid into the water. "They live on the rougher fish. That narrow jaw makes it difficult for them to hang onto anything very large. But if it will comfort you, bring your bow and keep it close by when we come again."

The handsome merchant gave Subotai an appreciative look. "Your friend the trapper told us about the snow tiger. By the size of the hide you gave to Gauri I would judge the northern cats are even larger than our Bengals."

With his suspicions of the evil-looking reptiles temporarily allayed, Subotai stripped down and waded into the coolness of the Indus up to his waist. Then he struck out in his steady side-stroke until he felt the main current's strength and changed course to veer along its down-stream vector before turning back toward the shore.

Refreshed from the water and the swift evaporation of the moisture in the Indian heat, Subotai sat down and watched Dharayan use a long, alternating overhand crawl to cross the entire breadth of the Indus River in less time than the Mongol had taken just side-stroking out to the main channel and back to the sandy riverside.

The tall and magnificently proportioned Kshatriya came dripping out of the water like some river god, it seemed to Subotai, and seated himself on the sand in the half-lotus position. Subotai closed his eyes, lifted his face toward the sun's rays, and said, "The next time we come, will you teach me that swift way of swimming you have?"

At sunset they walked away from the Indus. The day creatures of the river were giving way to the rising crescendo of noises made by the now-awakening nocturnal birds, insects, and animals which cohabited with the great river. The rhythmic cycles of diurnal and nocturnal life were interchanging above, beside, and below the water. The last bronzed light of the disappearing sun was chopped into a mirroring mosaic of countless reflections when the dancing lightness of a cool evening zephyr disturbed the smoothness of the boundary between air and water.

"Gauri will be wondering where we are," Subotai murmured, more to himself than for Dharayan's hearing.

Dharayan laughed. "Already the perfectly trained husband! I suppose I should have told your English friend a little more about what you were getting into when I first discussed with him the arrangement with my sister. You were fairly unconscious at the time, and I was concerned with getting Gauri safely out of the citadel before there were any more revolutionary exhibitions." He laughed again. "But if I had confided in him so fully, then I, rather than you, would have had to continue bearing the brunt of her daily fussing and polishing. I have no doubt that you will be a perfect specimen when she is at last satisfied with you."

Subotai smiled, anticipating the sweetly stern reception that would mask Gauri's concern for both of them. Dusk began to settle around the tropical warmth of the day as they walked on through the beautiful evening.

"Why are you not married, Dharayan?" Subotai's barbarian bluntness still charmed his brother-in-law as well as his wife.

"Because I am a monk."

Subotai was clearly uncertain of the exact meaning of the Hindi phrasing and words, so Dharayan went on. "A monk. When my uncle initiated me into the mysteries of the Solar Warriors, I took the vows of monkhood. I have sworn never to marry, and to commit my energies and time to more spiritual pursuits than ordinary family life. I do have to make my own way, like almost everyone else. The trade we are in is ideal for me. It allows me...us—you, Gauri, and now the boy as well—to live in relative comfort without harshly consorting with the world. My time is generally my own, and when I make trading journeys to the mountains or down country, I can use them for pilgrimages. An armful of mangoes with one shake of the tree, if you take my meaning."

They walked the rest of the way in the darkness which had swiftly ended the twilight, guiding themselves by the lamps Gauri had set in the upper windows for them.

ϕ   ϕ   ϕ   ϕ

The second son came some two years after the birth of the first. Both of the children strongly resembled Gauri and Dharayan, and both were brown and healthy from Gauri's careful and intelligent mothering. They had been lusty from birth and well nourished at her breasts with pure mother's milk before passing on to the milk, fruit, and cereal diet to which she adhered.

After the birth of the second child, Gauri seemed at last fulfilled. She came to a complete acceptance of her life. She further diminished her guidance of her outwardly rough yet inwardly gentle husband as their lives tracked the yearly cycles of the caravanserai's trade. As for Subotai, the peaceful and warm days of the Indian months slipped into years unmarked by the seasons of the north for his accounting. He found contentment in watching the two boys playing, growing, and being tutored by Gauri in numbers and in reading as she sewed or embroidered in the sunny upper level of the wall-house or in the coolness of the lower hall with its stone flooring.

While still breast-feeding the younger child, Gauri took both children with her and went into the city with Subotai and Dharayan to participate in the spirited ritual for the offering of the crops during Agrayana, the harvest festival. The festival, sanctified by innumerable religious ceremonies, drew an enormous crowd of country folk into Sarghoda. The farming people brought great measures of grain, cotton, fruit, and vegetables along with their cottage wares to display for trade or sale in the several bazaars set aside for the fair.

For a period of ten days, Sarghoda was a colorful and vibrant scene of bazaars with harvest plenty overflowing the stalls onto the ground around them. Naked holy men, each with a staff in hand, roamed the streets or recited the Ramayana to circles of rapt listeners on the temple grounds. Huge wrestlers vied in a dusty arena for a prize of gold sent by the Maharawal of Amrithistan. The Maharawal sponsored both the wrestling tourney and the festival, this being the most practical way for him to gauge the year's productivity so he could adjust his taxes accordingly.

Subotai and his older son were fascinated by the charmers and their lidded wicker baskets heavy with kraits and cobras. The hypnotic oscillations of the upright snakes slaving to the sway or the rhythmic hand movements of the charmers were irresistible to both father and son. Gauri literally had to drag them away from the charmers at the end of each day of the festival.

The final night of the Agrayana, the night of the full harvest moon, was celebrated by the lighting of thousands of lanterns, lamps and candles. The Temple of Kali, bathed in moonlight, was ablaze in the light of the countless flames lit in thanksgiving and devotion to the Mother Kali.

Morning found the city emptying rapidly, farm families in their high-wheeled carts, and the roving theater, mime, and dancing troupes all eager to leave before the heat of the day. Giant wrestlers strode side by side in the stream of traffic with wandering sannyasis, the monks and holy men, many of them headed north toward the Himalayan massif.

To impress the significance of the many Hindu religious festivals, feasts, and days of remembrance on the children, Gauri always made special sweetmeats for these occasions. For Subotai one year she embroidered a white shawl with a lifelike representation of a king cobra, its hood spread in defensive arousal. Her intricate and artistic craft with gray, brown, and green thread seemed almost to vitalize the embroidered serpent. When she had given the shawl to Subotai on the remembering day of their wedding, they held each other close and laughed over her celebration of his fixation on the snakes and charmers of the Agrayana festivals.

There was still the occasional tension, as was inevitable, but they all learned to take these in stride. There were, for example, the cheetah cubs the Maharawal had given Gauri and Subotai as a wedding gift. They had become the family house pets, and Gauri was as attached to them as the rest of the family, but the older they got the more problems they gave her. At first she only pressured Subotai to keep them out of the bedchambers, but when the energetic, romping cubs turned into full-grown lithe hunting cats, Gauri

decided they must go. She complained that they were too expensive
to keep as house cats, and that it would be better for them to live
out of doors. Dharayan, Subotai, and the two boys, oblivious to the
problems the cats created, simply ignored Gauri's suggestions. The
tension this created between Gauri and her menfolk grew.

The last straw for Gauri was when the two cats, one in hot
pursuit of the other, skidded through her kitchen, smashed ceramics
and sent a bubbling pot of curry crashing against the wall and her
cook screaming out the door.

Dharayan, Subotai, and the unchastened cheetahs were exiled
to the stock and lading yards until the cats were ensconced in a
large bamboo cage. The two men did not return to Gauri's good
graces completely until after they had quietly sold the cheetahs to
a man who trained and traded in hunting cheetahs.

As his life merged with the warm timelessness of India, Subotai
became one of Dharayan's disciples, joining in the evening meditations with Dharayan's inner group of young disciples, those who
shared the Solar Warrior's calm and knowing gaze. For the Mongol,
Dharayan provided a teaching beyond the spiritual leadership he
gave his other followers. Intermittently at first after their trial exercise with sword and lathi, then with growing frequency, and then,
when Subotai's oldest son was about six years of age, on a ritualistic
daily basis, the Solar Warrior trained the Mongol in all the formalized
combat systems of ancient India. To Subotai, the Solar Warrior
seemed under the influence of an urgency which at times assumed
the character of an undeniable compulsion to develop Subotai's pro-
ficiency in the Hindu martial arts. Sometimes Dharayan allowed
even the affairs of the family and the caravanserai to go unattended
in order to allow their training sessions to proceed unimpeded.

From a small locked armory, Dharayan would bring forth the
ancient traditional armaments of classical India. The Solar Warrior's
extraordinary mastery of the weapons, all of them, was beyond the
Mongol's comprehension. In succession Dharayan had displayed his
shimmering art with first the lathi, then with the special swords,
the katar and the pata. The sword arts exceeded in depth and
intricacy even the detailed science Subotai had learned among the
Mongols.

Subotai learned the sword work swiftly, training with an intensity that was new and vivifying. After that came the lances—the bothatee and the subtle and deceptive vita, a light lance with a whippy strangulation cord attached. The theoretical depth of the art of the vita was still a marveling challenge to the Mongol when the Solar Warrior drew him on into the mace, the gada.

Then, sweeping abruptly beyond the closeness and the elaboration of work with the individual weapons, Dharayan coalesced the innumerable, branching techniques of the richly varied fighting arts into a unified, all-encompassing science which was stunning at once in its basic simplicity and in the way it lent itself to limitless variation. And throughout the concentrated and complex interplay of the teaching and Subotai's expanding skills as an individual combatant, Dharayan maintained his emphasis on the use of prana, or Ch'i—the inner energy in the martial arts. Then the Solar Warrior drew together Subotai's meditation and his physical, martial skills until the Mongol's command of the inner power became almost second nature, as natural to him as the simplest movement of his limbs or the flicker of his eyelids.

And there was always more. Radiating and complicated byways of the armed and unarmed combat arts led off into suggestive mental control techniques. And later, all of these man-on-man forms and techniques were used by the Solar Warrior to outline basic and advanced strategic and tactical methods of employing massed bodies of men in warfare.

During a particularly hot exercise session under the blazing sun of the Indus valley, Subotai's attention drifted to cooler memories of the steppes. The Solar Warrior broke into the Mongol's reverie.

"Subotai, the secret of the arts and freedom will elude you as long as thoughts of the light-eyed woman govern your mind."

Subotai had never heard his teacher speak with sharpness before. Even more startling was the Solar Warrior's knowledge of that which Subotai had never spoken of with him. Turning, Subotai expected to see the glitter of anger in the dark eyes, but he saw only the usual poised, detached regard.

"Close your eyes. Focus the mind. Centuries ago the Solar Warrior dynasty dominated the Indus valley because of their ability to actively apply the inner powers in warfare and to avail themselves of natural truths on the field of battle."

When the midafternoon meditation ended, Dharayan began the training period in unarmed military techniques. Here the young and vigorous teacher employed the Indian forerunners of binot and bandesh, not only to instruct the Mongol in the use of jujitsu but to illustrate the traditions of warfare, the ancient military doctrines of the Solar Warriors, of which tradition he had become the sole and last heir.

To Subotai's quick intellect, these fighting methods differed little in their fundmentals from the steppe combat wrestling and fighting of his own people. But when coupled with the conscious use of the inner energy, the more subtle foot movements, and the spinning, circular motions of the body that could lead any attack always around and away from its objective, these methods became almost irresistible. This was particularly true when they were practiced by an expert whose mental state coordinated the physical vector of an attacker with his own body and hand motions and became an implicit integral with the flow of inner energy.

Often Subotai would lie awake in the darkness scanning his own rich Mongol military heritage, seeking some heretofore unapplied method of unarmed attack or technique with spear, sword or cudgel which could possibly discomfit Dharayan. But his thought, his own superior ability in the martial arts, were unavailing against his teacher's warrior skill. Subotai could never achieve even a partial advantage over his enormously more accomplished mentor. The Solar Warrior was so adept, his consciousness so clear, that in all their years of study and association, Subotai never once succeeded in surprising or eluding or overcoming his teacher in their exercises.

Sometimes Subotai and Dharayan strolled together in the late afternoon before the other disciples arrived for the evening meditation and for the Solar Warrior's almost nightly dissertations on the Rig Vedas. During those strolls, Dharayan lectured Subotai, not on the Gita or the Vedas, but always about the lessons and tactics transmitted down through him from the mysterious Order of the Solar Warriors.

On one of these occasions the Mongol remarked in a light-hearted way, "Sir, I am not a great warrior. In my homeland I was only a herder, and sometimes an outriding guard for the encampments. That sword of mine, when the boys are big enough to play with it, I am going to bend the edge so it will no longer cut, or perhaps I'll take it to a smith and have a flat piece welded on the blade's edge, so they can learn with it." With his domestic contentment and the surety of his place in life warming his mind, he went on. "I am satisfied with my life here with Gauri, the children, and you. I like this land, now that the heat is not such a burden to me."

The Solar Warrior stopped, turned, and looked down from his superior height at Subotai with an unblinking gaze which seemed to immobilize the Mongol's very speech processes.

Dharayan did not speak again that evening. Nor did Subotai protest again when the lectures on tactics, starting with one on the use of the circle in envelopments, were resumed on their next walk together.

φ   φ   φ   φ

There was a supper for the disciples some few weeks later. All of Dharayan's closest followers assembled in the hot, early evening for his usual discourse on spiritual matters, but this evening after the meditation Gauri served them a simple meal of chapattis, fruit and rice. The leave-taking by the disciples in the late night hours was one of particular warmth, because of the supper, and because Dharayan, Subotai, and several camel drovers were to leave next morning for the south of India.

It was nearly midnight when the hall was finally left for the servants to clean and straighten, and Subotai was feeling a pleasant weariness after several consecutive days of preparation for the journey and a series of bruising and demanding training periods with Dharayan. He and Gauri shooed the serving women off to bed and finished resetting the lower hall themselves. Then they extinguished the tapers, leaving only one of the large, hexagonal brass hanging lamps alight. They climbed the steps, each carrying a small brass lantern, to their sleeping chamber. Their room came aglow with light when they lit the overhead lamps with long straws set aflare in the flames of their lanterns.

Facing about and blowing out his straw, Subotai met Gauri's eyes. Appraising her thoughtfully, he noted she was more maturely beautiful than the Gauri, his Maid of Fortune and Abundance, he had wed years before. She was slightly heavier with a comfortable voluptuousness; the black eyes were sensibly calm, reflecting pleasure and satisfaction in her family, her home life, and her husband. And Subotai knew at last that this dark woman was his true wife, her loyalty and service and mothering spirit had finally won his troubled and restless soul.

For her part, Gauri was still pleased with the barbarian rawness that remained in Subotai's nature, and with how his heavy handsomeness had contained the burning demands of young womanhood and given her the children she had longed for with an almost frantic desire. His gray-blue eyes were still distant and uncommunicative at times, seeing, she thought, some memory of the unknown sweep and the snow of the country of his origin. Those eyes sometimes changed their color to that of the ice she had once seen on the tributary of the upper Indus higher in the mountains than even the lamasery.

Their evening duties and social and spiritual obligations fully attended to, they took each other by the hand and stood in the mellow light of the burning butter-fat in the lamps, gazing in a complete and ordered fondness at each other. Then without words, as she had done as a bride, she took him into her womanly peace and satisfaction—warm and mysterious India incarnate. When at last they slept, it was in a grace of innocence and total release from the world, as surely had been intended for husband and wife by the Divine.

And it was Gauri, arising before the coming of the sun, who shook Subotai awake and fussed over him and Dharayan to be sure they ate of the warming breakfast she had prepared.

Subotai remembered looking back as he fell into resonance with the slow, rhythmic lurching of his camel. It was light enough to see Gauri's silhouette and the play of her sari as it moved gently in the light dawn wind. Then, dreading the heat of the coming day on the trail, he turned away.

φ   φ   φ   φ

The journey took them through the placidity and the splendor of India. Each night found them welcomed and lodged within a private home in one of the quiet villages. Wherever he went, Dharayan was known, and greeted with great veneration.

Nights in the villages inevitably found a group of the brown people—the aged, the mature, the youthful, and the children— sitting with the Solar Warrior, sometimes listening to his compelling talks, and sometimes sharing his silent contemplation. Subotai, waiting on the master, was caught in the etheric web of the teacher's pervasive vibration, living the precious hours and days of the journey locked into a concentrated consciousness of the present only. Past and future and his obsession briefly put aside, thoughts of his wife and family were only a warmly dim pleasantness in the back of his mind.

Subotai learned that the eternal Indian villages were the source of many of the wares which came to Dharayan's trading venture— of the spices, and of the cloth, homespun by the Indian women out of cotton and jute fibers drawn from the labor of the Indian men of the soil.

They had been gone from Sarghoda nearly three cycles of the moon before they completed Dharayan's trading circuit. All of the camels were now heavily laden with baled cotton, jute, and spices. All of the agreements were safely renewed for another season or so, all the friendships graciously relit, before the Solar Warrior and the Mongol and the camel drovers turned the caravan back toward the north and Sarghoda.

But after several days of retracing their route, Dharayan turned the camel train in a more westerly direction, branching off from the well-traveled and well-marked north-south trade route that connected the southern hinterlands of the Indian subcontinent with the northwest regions.

As they were dismounting from their kneeling camels at the end of that day's trailing, Dharayan spoke to Subotai with anticipation. "We are near the coast. We will go on to the west on foot, a pilgrimage, just the two of us. One blanket each and what food we can carry—enough for a few days only. And one water skin only. Where we are going there are fresh water springs along the way."

They left the picketed camel train and the resting drovers behind in the early morning of the next day. For the first day and into the second, they walked through relatively unpopulated rolling country covered with ferns and thick underbrush which eventually gave way to hot, coastal jungle.

Subotai, more used to the saddle than to walking, had to hike with some resolve to stay even with the long, easy strides of the Solar Warrior's tall, lean body. Sunset of the second day found them within earshot of the murmuring surf of the Arabian Sea. Then they caught sight of the water. The descending orange tropical sun-orb cast a bar of shimmering gold on the evening sea in converging perspective from the foaming shore to the mystical demarcation of sky and sea at the horizon. The striking colors of the sunset especially touched Subotai's ever-present appreciation of natural beauties. The fresh ocean smell and the calls of the sea birds enhanced the vibration he felt when the sun vanished leaving the western Sky still flaming with orange light.

Dharayan led the way to the water's edge. He stopped for a moment as though uncertain of his direction, then struck out toward what appeared to be some grassy mounds a short distance away. Skirting the base of one of the hillocks, they met with a sight which caused the Mongol to blurt out, "Why, it must have been a greater city than Sarghoda!"

The fallen, stone-blocked ruins extended from the very seashore in an astonishing sweep until they were lost in the green tangle of the jungle growth. Not even the long work of the sea tides or the relentless entwining of vines and the insidious patina of fungi had destroyed the elegant geometry of the lost city.

"This is a holy place," Dharayan said. He looked toward the water. "Every other building and stone structure which ever stood on the edge of the sea in this ancient city has been covered by the sand of the ocean, but not the temple." He pointed at a gigantic stone ruin whose rectangular pillars were awash in the evening tide. "It does not sink into the sand, and the tidal swirls bring and remove sand alternately as the moon strengthens and wanes."

The Solar Warrior went into the low surf and waded toward the tall and massive pillars which had once delineated the entrance to the temple. Subotai followed, relishing the sensation of the cooling salt water on his trail-tender feet. Dharayan waded entirely around the perimeter of the ruin, then he and Subotai walked back up onto the dry sand of the beach as the swift tropical darkness began to fall.

They slept that night in the open at the foot of a mighty stone wall from which they had evicted a troop of monkeys. The playful, chattering monkeys swung up the heavy vines and growth the jungle had laid over the ruin. Beneath the immense tropical concavity of the deeply black Indian Sky, the Mongol listened to the ocean swells whisper on the sand and, wondering at the nature of the countless stars in the curved Sky-canopy and the meaning of this ancient temple, fell asleep.

Subotai awoke with a warm and salt-scented breeze on his face. Pushing up on one elbow, he saw that Dharayan was gone, his sleeping mat and blanket rolled up and placed against their bundles of food and their drinking skin. With the morning sun-rays just beginning to show through the congestion of the forest, he set out in search of the teacher.

Subotai wandered in a leisurely way among the stones and the mounded and overgrown remnants of the forgotten city, pausing now and again to stare at some particularly strange carving or to wonder at the size of the structures which must have once occupied the place. Drawn to the sea-washed stone skeleton of the temple, he saw that the morning tide was beginning to ebb, but the flattening waves still reached to the most westerly portion of the huge ruin. And there, seated in lotus posture, his back to the shaded side of a jumble of fallen stonework and shards of faded masonry, was the Solar Warrior.

Subotai quietly sat down on the damp sand beside Dharayan and, closing his eyes, meditated. He felt an extraordinary unity with the morning, the warm sea, and the lilting of the faint breeze on his face and chest. And there, borne on the power of the Solar Warrior's consciousness, he was taken to the edge of the Mystery. And when it was lost to him, falling away into the chaos of his impurity, the aching loss of it seemed to rend his very being.

When he opened his eyes, the sea-vista framed by the pillars of the temple swam through the blurring wetness of his tear-filled vision. Dharayan was standing a short distance away, gazing out over the retreating tide.

Subotai stood up and went to the Solar Warrior. He had not wept since early childhood when the condition of his loneliness and lack of blood kin had burst upon him. He knelt before Dharayan.

"Set me free, Lord. Make me as you are."

There was a look of great compassion on the face of the Solar Warrior. "Your mind is hazy with the incessant pull of the vision of the light-eyed woman. Until you master and throw out that desire, your bondage will only lead you into more pain."

"Won't you take that from me?" Subotai pleaded.

"Subotai...I may not. The dharma is to be accomplished. When duty is complete, then will your freedom come of itself without your asking."

The Solar Warrior turned and walked back toward their little camp at the jungle's edge. Subotai followed after a short while. They gathered their sleeping rolls and food bundles and, without eating and in silence, they went away from the lost city along the route leading away from the coast and back toward the camel train and the long trail north to Sarghoda.

φ   φ   φ   φ

Subotai thought nothing of it at first. But as the trail leading toward Sarghoda became more and more congested, and as the usual trickle of travelers thickened into a stream of cattle-drawn carts with terrified people riding or plodding along beside them, a fearful uneasiness crept over Dharayan and Subotai. Had Sarghoda been attacked by the Kharesmian Moslems in violation of their treaty with the Maharawal while they were gone?

Instinctively Dharayan ordered his own company to keep apart from the fleeing refugees. With Dharayan, Subotai watched the pitiful flood of people straggle by, most with families and hastily collected belongings piled high on carts. Finally Dharayan broke his week-long silence with a single word. "Plague."

After another hour of travel toward the city the atmosphere around them grew thick with the putrid, vomitous stench of sun-ripened dead and decaying man-flesh. They were still more than a day from Sarghoda, and Subotai, thoughts of Gauri and his sons eating at his heart, felt his entrails turn to ice.

Before the afternoon was spent one of the drovers was down with the cholera that was riding on the flood of refugees. They cradled the sick man into a hasty sling and suspended it over the back of a camel where he would swing in his delirium of fever and dysentry and thirst as they pushed the caravan the last few leagues toward Sarghoda.

Before they reached the city it became impossible for them to move against the human tide, the corpses, and the abandoned impedimenta of flight thrown down along the trail by the sick and the dying. They veered off the main roadway and turned west toward the Indus River until they found an untraveled farm path leading in the general direction of Sarghoda. The longer route cost them an extra league and, although they rode on through the night without rest, the morning light still did not reveal the walls of Sarghoda to their straining eyes. The brutal sun of the afternoon simmered above them by the time they were finally close enough to the caravanserai to fling themselves down from their camels and sprint ahead of the tired animals to the dwelling in Sarghoda's south wall. But within, all Subotai could hear were the sounds of his own hurrying feet and his panting breath.

Then he saw the brown, motionless bodies of his sons.

At first he thought they must be the bodies of strange children. They were almost skeletal in their wasted condition. They lay with grimaced teeth and with unseeing, fly-encrusted eyes. The sleeping mats upon which they lay were splashed and fouled with dried excrement. Discarded and befouled cloths and basins full of long-standing water covered with loathesome scum testified mutely to the hopeless battle waged by Gauri and her women against the cholera.

Subotai swayed in a dazed shock of stupefaction. He could not believe that which his senses conveyed to him. And where was Gauri? He hastened to the foot of the stone stairway and saw Dharayan already at the top of them standing still as doom. At Subotai's frantic questioning look, the Solar Warrior slowly shook his head.

Subotai seemed to ring in mind and body with a pained sense of unreality. "It's not Gauri, Lord. We must look again." His voice even contained the timbre of hope. "It is probably one of the serving women."

"Subotai, it is she. All the servants are gone, dead or fleeing this . . . this thing." Dharayan spoke with a harshness meant to refocus Subotai's grief-befuddled mind. He placed a strong hand on Subotai's shoulder and gently led him outside to the well.

Dharayan cast down the stiff leather water pouch, heard it splash faintly dozens of arm-lengths below, then drew it up slowly, hand over hand, by the rope attached to it. He spilled some of its contents while handing the pouch to Subotai. The splash of water made shallow mud and at the same time raised dust. Subotai thought it odd that he had never noticed such a thing before. He drank of the water but briefly, then offered the pouch back to Dharayan. The Solar Warrior slowly and carefully bathed his dusty feet and ankles, pouring the liquid quietly until the pouch emptied, then laid it on the square rock wall surrounding the well.

"They must be bathed and cleanly wrapped," Dharayan said. His words carried with them the inexorable, unretreating process of time. "Already they have lain in the heat and the open for too long. I will go in and bring out the water basins and pitchers. Start drawing up water."

They set about preparation of the bodies. While Dharayan bathed and anointed the pitiful bodies of the children with a fragrant oil, Subotai took a part of the oil and a bronze basin filled with water and went alone into the once happy sleeping chamber he and Gauri had shared.

Her disease-wasted form lay on their bed. With a tenderness strange to him, Subotai bathed away the streaks and stains left by the cholera, oiled the body of his wife, and wrapped it in a sari of blue and wine-colored cloth trimmed with colorful embroidery. He covered the dead face with a napkin of some white material he found among her sewing things. As he finished, the Solar Warrior appeared in the doorway and beckoned.

Each took the body of one child outside and placed it in a small farm cart. Subotai returned, ascended the steps, took up his dead wife in his massive warrior's arms, went out, and laid the corpse in the cart between those of the boys.

It was not difficult to locate the makeshift crematory; the grisly smoke had been a wavering landmark for them from far down the trail. Commercial enterprise had already arrived, and they bought wood for the funeral pyre from one of the opportunists.

The crematory grounds appeared to quake soundlessly with the burning pyres, now obscured by lowering and twisting smoke, now seeming to bend with the wierdness of the light refraction caused by heat distortion in the swimming air. There was an unearthliness here, an overpowering effect amplified by the indescribable odors.

Subotai and Dharayan stacked their funeral wood. Subotai climbed a small ladder he borrowed from a middle-aged man who had come to burn his family of eight and spread a cremation sheet on the top of the pyre. As Dharayan handed up each body in turn, Subotai neatly and carefully placed it on the sheet.

When Subotai came back from returning the ladder, the Solar Warrior was waiting with a lit torch in his hand. He gave it to the Mongol. They looked into each other's eyes, the master and the disciple. Subotai saw a graveness in the mirroring black-brown eyes, but the alert and peaceful centeredness was still in them. He marveled at this. His own grief was staggering and anguishing.

"Have done with it," Dharayan said.

Subotai turned and, without looking upwards, applied the torch to the tinderous material below the kindling. They moved away from the funeral pyre as the fire flamed hotly and reached up to consume the topmost layer of the wood with its mortal burden.

It was dark before the burning down was finished. The jumble of firebrands, the lazing of the flames, and the snap of the burning and collapsing wood stacks marked Subotai's mind with a terrible finality.

The two men walked slowly away. Above them the summer moon of India was hazy, defaced by the funeral smoke.

φ   φ   φ   φ

Subotai sat alone through the hot night, his mind vacuous, his body immobile. The nearly imperceptible lightening that heralded the coming day went unnoticed.

The day itself passed and the light waned, then darkness came over him. His catatonia stripped away his sense of time. The mercuric moonbeams silvering the bedchamber did not register in his consciousness.

Graying light came upon the earth again. Another sun curved across the sky, then sundown, and once more the vacant darkness washed over him. Rigid and statuelike in his fearful loss, Subotai hardly even breathed. In the ending hours of that night he came gradually back to a perception of his body. A stall gate, suddenly sent banging by a hot, predawn wind from the desert, brought his vision and his presence sharply together and he stood up, left the chamber, and descended the stone steps.

He went out and gulped the warm wind like a man near suffocation, steadying himself with both hands against a stone wall. He became aware of his thirst, an inferno of dryness as though his most utter being cried out for water. Ignoring the chaff floating in one of the wooden watering troughs for the camels, he thrust his face into it and drank, then choked, then drank again, this time more deeply and with more control. His mind and body, his very soul it seemed, were sickened with the unbearable hurt. On all fours in front of the trough, he knew himself to be no better than an animal. No, he thought, worse. An animal could not suffer as he was suffering.

Somehow he had to free himself of it. He went into the wall-house, into the bedchamber, and reached up. Strange—it was gone. He always hung it there on the wall, above the boys' reach. He thought he must have put it somewhere else.

He found his packed trail baggage still lying where he had dropped it and searched, but the sword was not there. He combed all the chambers and levels of the dwelling, but the weapon was not to be found. His quest for the sword mounted to a cold fury. He extended his search to the storage sheds and the stock enclosures. The early morning light was not good, but he could see it was not in those places. He returned to the house and climbed back up the stairway, his steps now weary. He stumbled twice, bruising his shins and the top of one foot, before he reached the bedchamber. His anger and frustration at not finding the sword had, at least for the moment, displaced the slurring depression of grief. And then, blessedly, he was spent. Shaking with fatigue, his nerves worn out from the emotional drain of his agony, he sank down on the Siberian tiger skin and dissolved into a deep, black sleep.

The sound of soft footfalls below and on the steps brought him awake. In the midafternoon heat, a blistering thirst tormented him again, drying his mouth and lips.

Dharayan came into the room. Subotai noticed he was still dressed for traveling, and that several of the Solar Warrior's most immediate disciples waited on the stairway. Dharayan offered his hand and pulled the Mongol to his feet.

"We are leaving Sarghoda," he said, indicating the men behind him. "To the mountains for the time being. After that..." He let the words drop.

Preceded by the young men, Dharayan went down the steps. Subotai felt a sudden rush of relief. He walked after them. Speaking to Dharayan's back he said, "Lord, I will go with you."

Dharayan, without a word, turned and gave him a long piercing look. Then, with a negative shake of his dark-haired head, he stepped through the doorway and took up the long walking staff he had left leaning against an outside wall. The blue sword was also there, its hilt propped against the mortared stone wall. Dharayan took it in his left hand and handed it to Subotai.

The tall Kshatriya spoke with great gentleness. "I thought it best to keep you two apart, for a while."

Then the Solar Warrior simply walked away.

Subotai stood rooted in total dismay as Dharayan and the small retinue of his followers strode eastward along the outer wall of Sarghoda. He watched as they turned abruptly north at the juncture with the east wall, and were gone.

Subotai was left alone with the empty lading yard and the empty wall-house. Nothing he drank throughout the remainder of that baking afternoon could assuage his thirst. Somehow he could not follow after the teacher. The pressing, absorbing thirst would not allow him to leave the cool well behind.

The short evening died, but the heat did not abate. Night. And the dessicating desert wind moaned through the abandoned place. The plague-ridden city lay nearly empty beyond the walls. Sarghoda was a shell filled with eerie sounds, its covered byways untrodden, its bazaars unoccupied, its houses and the great Temple of Kali deserted and already filling with fine, red, powdered dirt swept in by the wind and the swirling dust funnels from the eastern desert.

φ   φ   φ   φ

Long before the caravan stirred to muster for the trail, Subotai rose. He draped over his wide shoulders the rich cobra-embroidered shawl his wife had so lovingly made. Stooping, he went through the low flapped entrance of the small tent. A crease of pink and orange in the east signaled the coming of a morning of glory and freshness which would be lost on him. Signing to the sleepy outriders who guarded the camp, he climbed on foot back up to the crest of the rocky pass.

In the stillness he watched the shadows move back before the gaining sunlight across the plains to the south and the east. Putting out a hand to block the sharp emergence of the dawning sun, he gazed intently down upon the Indian landscape.

The wrenching away of his sons, the loss and the honeyed memory of the sweetness and pleasing domestic dominance of his wife, the void left by the sudden departure of the Solar Warrior— these had melded into a gray power which emptied him of life and filled his calm nature with an indifferent fatalism.

He lingered on the stony elevation until he heard, distantly, the bustle and shouting of the awakening encampment. A morning breeze swept up to the heights carrying with it the coolness he remembered from the steppes.

At last he turned his back on the warmth of India, and for the rest of his life what he had known of peace and home was gone.

And time sealed the Gate of Sweet Mercy behind him.

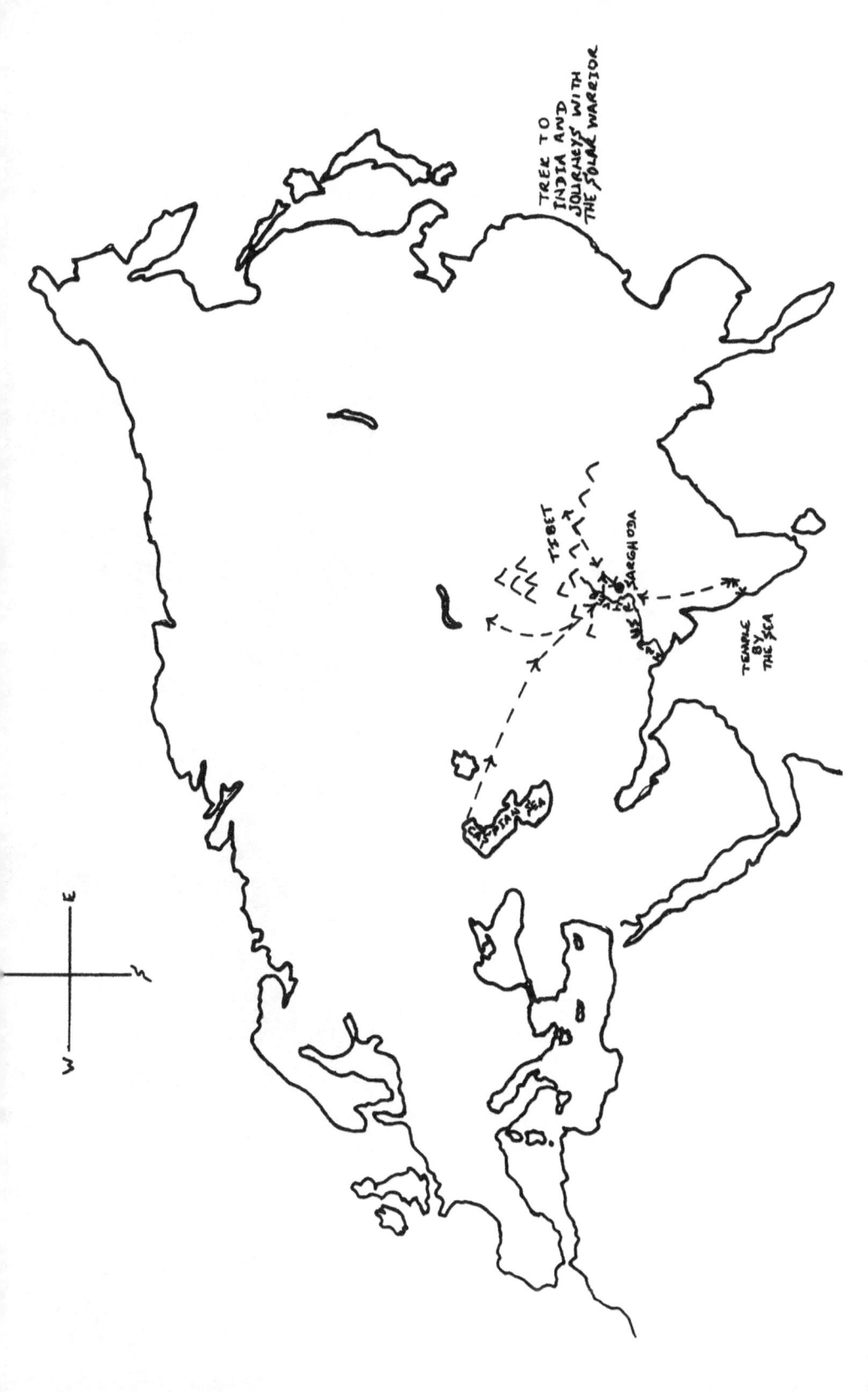

φ φ
THE
KHA
KHAN

The route had turned into a series of dried and befouled watering holes. The caravan had lost its human and animal cohesiveness, and broken down into a long, suffering straggle of thirsting men and beasts. Dead horses and camels marked the trail, and dead men as well, for shallow graves had given way to exposed corpses when the living could no longer spare the strength to inter them.

Subotai's foresight in rationing his water had marked him as the inevitable victim of the growing numbers of those maddened by thirst, and he wondered indifferently if even the blue sword, already caked with the blood of men who had fought him for the precious liquid, would be able to protect his meager remaining supply. Eventually, his eyes spotting from the glare of a sun that turned the southern steppe into a baking pan, he led his mount out of the straggling column, gambling that he would be able to find his way across the waterless desolation and reach water along the southern snow line of the Asian steppe before he succumbed. When he struck out directly north, a number of masterless horses and camels followed his path away from the caravan route, almost as though they recognized his direction as the only survival option. A Persian slave woman also followed, on foot, her olive face draped in a black veil. Doggedly she persevered through the haze of dust thrown up by the cluster of animals trailing to the north with Subotai.

When they came upon the first mud, Subotai fell to with a long stick, digging down to make a hole that gradually filled with murky water. The loose horses pawed at the mud not far away, making their own excavations. Subotai drank first, then scooped up a wooden bowl of the brown water and, as the animals began muscling him aside to get at the water hole, strode toward the black-swathed woman who stood patiently awaiting her turn. Subotai saw that she had thick black brows without any arching, and black eyes which darted fearful looks into his. She took the bowl and, oblivious to the mud suspended in it, drank it down. The black shawl that had covered her face hung, tattered and filthy, over her right shoulder. She proffered the empty bowl to him, but he turned his back on her. Returning to one of his baggage camels, he quickly cut plaited leather ropes into hasty halters. With these he began securing and hobbling the circle of animals as they jostled for access to the dirty water.

The Persian woman retired a short distance away from the water hole and sat down on the ground quietly. Subotai finished hobbling the stray animals, then turned for a long look at the dusty, weary woman nodding sleepily under the hot sun. He had ignored her until they found the mud because he saw no reason to either encourage or discourage her persistence in following him into his unknown fate.

He brought her more water, awakening her to make her drink, but only allowed her to sip the water now. Subotai was glad she had followed him. He had been alone, even in the tumultous, ill-fated caravan, since...since—his mind tried to reject it, but it came through—Sarghoda.

The woman remembered her modesty and started to cover her face with the soiled shawl, but seeing its filth and her aloneness with the slant-eyed man, she tossed it back over her shoulder. She lowered her eyes, partly from modesty and partly because when she looked at the blue-eyed man her hair literally stood on end. The magnetism of his gaze made her fear him, yet paradoxically made her comfortable with him.

On the following day, Subotai, with some effort, herded the

motley assortment of animals away from the watering hole. Then he mounted the Persian woman on one of his baggage camels and set out northward into a land where sparse grass and occasional water could be found.

There Subotai converted his traveling tent into a yurt by butchering three camels and shaping their hides over circular ribs into a conical top. He showed the Persian woman how to cut and dry the camel meat, pack it in pouches with edible greens, and seal it with hot camel fat for winter food. Then he set about arrangements for pasturing the rest of the animals.

The Persian woman knew nothing of the trail tongue, and Subotai could find no basis in the other tongues he was familiar with for spoken exchange to develop between them, but, by putting together various clues, he eventually gathered that she was the slave of a hated mistress who had taken her with the caravan and then died, giving her slave a chance to escape. Why she had elected to come with him, Subotai could not tell. She seemed quite willing to stay, kept to the yurt and kept her silence. Slavery must have wounded her as deeply as the Sarghodan plague had scarred Subotai, for she seemed to mirror Subotai's long, mourning silence. Somehow in their quiet companionship, they assuaged each other's suffering. The Persian woman, though middle-aged, was not unattractive, but the impulse for sexual union never came over them. They existed in a yin-yang of harmoniousness.

During the next four sun years, Subotai kept his yurt on the green uplands below the Hindu Kush during the warm summer months. But before the onset of winter, he would take the Persian woman and, with the yurt dismantled and packed on camels and herd dogs yelping after his goats, leave the higher elevations before snow flew and drift north where, though snows were heavy at times, the winters were warmer.

His stock multiplied, and after rainfall had recharged the vital water holes and wells, he found ways of delivering the surplus to the southern trade route. Sometimes he thought of returning through the Macedonian Gate, crossing the Indus once again, and trailing back to Sarghoda, but each time that happened, he experienced the same intuitive cognition that Dharayan, his warrior-guru, was gone from Sarghoda forever. And then he would feel the bitter loss again—

dreams that filled his nostrils with the stench of the crematory grounds, dreams that made his night a longing for his dark, domineering yet self-sacrificing wife.

He and the Persian woman spent the winters sharing meals and sewing leathern clothing, always in their quiet way. But sometimes the woman smiled to herself, remembering the first smile in her lifetime of slavery, the one she had permitted herself as she drew a silk cord tight around the neck of her thirst-weakened mistress. Even now her brow grew hot with vengeful pleasure whenever she recalled the face of her hateful Kharesmian owner, flushed and swollen with trapped blood, as the life was strangled out of her. All the beatings and scratches and vicious slaps she had endured from those elegant, cruel hands lent her strength as she twisted the cord until the woman's eyes nearly burst from their sockets. That was her first smile, but not her last. When she fled the caravan to follow the strange, silent, blue-eyed man to the north, her smiles of secret satisfaction had split her thirst-dried lips until they bled.

She noticed that Subotai rarely smiled, although his mouth never turned down nor was his manner ever unkind. When they had begun sharing the yurt she often awoke in the night and, without moving, watched the Mongol in his meditations. He seemed more still than even a stone upon the steppe. As the sun-years passed, she came to the startling realization that he slept only briefly in mid-afternoon and just before the coming of midnight. For the remainder of each day he was intensely active with the stock or yurt chores except for his meditation periods.

Then one spring, Subotai did not take her south toward the Hindu Kush, but instead to the north, although sometimes they wandered westward to skirt the foothills of the Tien Shien Mountains. Chinese traders they encountered along the way called the great range the Celestial Mountains.

On this northern trip, Subotai traded freshly slaughtered goat-kid meat for some of the Chin silk the traders carried. A Chin merchant had once demonstrated for Subotai how a weapon, even a barbed arrow, could be driven into silk clothing penetrating the flesh without always piercing the silk, thus lessening the pain and danger when the arrow point was removed. Now, with hand gestures, Subotai set the Persian woman to sewing undergarments for both of them from the soft material.

Subotai spent a great deal of time conversing with the Chin merchants he encountered once or twice more during the northern trip, for during the warmer months the Chinese journeyed toward a juncture with the Great Silk Road. He queried them specifically about star and sky patterns in the different parts of the Chin empire. Once when he asked a group of Chinese about star configurations and their relative locations near Lake Baikal—the Blue Lake—they waggled their fingers at him and laughingly warned him to beware of the barbarians, the Riders of the North Wind.

"We have shut them out with a wall," one of the Chin traders remarked, "so we do not have to do with savages."

But one ancient Chin merchant looked deeply into Subotai's eyes and, recognizing both his spiritual stature and his Mongol origins, kept his silence.

Next morning the same elderly merchant sought Subotai out to show him an Al-Kemal—an Arabian star-board—a simple, flat piece of wood notched on one edge and with a slender knotted cord attached to it. One could, the Chin told Subotai, use it to tell relative positions, north and south. One did it by locating the same star at about the same time each night, he said, sighting it through the notch while standing a known distance from a reference point, then moving the wood either farther away or closer to one's eyes until the bottom of the rectangular wooden board matched with a fixed horizontal line. One then drew back the cord and tied a knot in it to mark the distance from eyes to board. Since northern stars sink closer to the horizon as one moves south, a knot farther from the board indicated that one was traveling south.

Subotai was exhilarated with the Al-Kemal, for now he knew he had a complete navigation system. The sun-stone which the trapper had given him would always sharply define east and west, and now with the Al-Kemal, he could determine relative locations north and south.

In return for this instruction Subotai made the Chin merchant a gift of a bale of lynx furs and an old oil lamp, one he and Gauri and Dharayan had obtained from the Buddhist lamas in the Himalayas. The Chinese bowed deeply to Subotai, and when their lively philosophical discussion—as lively as the limitations of the Eurasian trail tongue and its associated sign language would allow—ended and Subotai walked toward his horse, the merchant walked with him to bid him farewell.

That night when Subotai reached his own camp some distance away and entered the darkened yurt, he found it unoccupied. Thinking back, Subotai remembered he had last seen the Persian woman conversing with a middle-aged traveler, a man with the same kind of prominent Persian nose as her own. The two were standing near a small caravan camped close to the Chinese caravan. He remembered that the small caravan had decamped early the next morning while he was talking with the Chin merchant, and he wondered if the Persian woman had gone with it. Subotai was intending to travel farther north at daybreak, but instead delayed to see if the Persian woman, who had seemingly left of her own accord, would return. Ten days later, he had no sign or word of her, so he packed up the yurt, sorely missing her assistance. He doubted that he would ever see her again. Lives were short, harsh, and tragic in these times.

φ   φ   φ   φ

All that summer Subotai moved his stock, always toward the north. When he established his winter camp in the early fall, he left his goats and dogs for several days while he set a trap line for lynx and sable.

When he came in sight of his yurt, he saw a dozen horsemen apparently awaiting him. As he drew closer they startled him by addressing him in the Mongol tongue. It had been uncounted years since he had heard his native language except in his own thoughts.

"If this yurt is your holding, your stock eats the grass of the Lord Temajin Khan." It was a raw-boned, dark Mongol, apparently their leader, who spoke. Subotai masked his surprise when he heard the name Temajin. "If that be so, you must take up any bows and other weapons you possess and ride with us. The khan makes a war. He requires of you your arms and horses. Or..." the dark Mongol smirked, "you may remain here and gaze up at the sun forever."

Subotai knew military impressment when he saw it. He stepped off his horse and called to his dogs to begin gathering the strays from his flocks in preparation for a move to new pastures. While he dismantled and packed his yurt, he wondered if this khan could be the same Temajin he had met on the winter steppes years before, but dismissed the possibility as unlikely.

With the yurt packed and loaded onto one of his horses—Subotai had divested himself of his camels the previous year—he mounted and distributed his bows and quivers by leather straps across his saddle pommel and settled the blue sword in its soft sheath behind him by looping the sheath's carrying thong over his right shoulder and under his left armpit.

"What clan are you?" the dark Mongol asked.

"Mongol."

"But we are all Mongols," the dark leader replied, but said no more for already he felt the impact of Subotai's presence and personality.

Subotai found himself part of a great mustering representing most of the Mongol tribes and clans across the now vast steppe domain newly come under the leadership of Temajin Khan, known too as the Genghis Khan. He was directed to pitch his yurt in the vicinity of those belonging to the other Mongols without clan affiliations. Many yurts were to be seen all across the grassy steppe, each cluster populated by men from the same clan or tribe who trained as a unit.

Subotai was quickly integrated into an existing regiment of a thousand men. He found that even his rudimentary arithmetic knowledge was adequate for understanding the numerical organization of the Mongol army: squads of ten, companies of a hundred, regiments of a thousand. The largest Mongol military structure was the tuman, the division, made up of about ten thousand men and commanded by an orkhan.

Subotai found himself in the heat of dawn-to-dusk training in the maneuvers and commands used in Temajin Khan's army, an army which consisted entirely of cavalry. Subotai's maturity and his casual superiority with bow and sword, combined with his natural air of leadership and authority, brought him quick promotion. He was a commander of a hundred when the Mongol army broke bivouac less than two weeks after he had arrived to become part of it.

Most of the army formed and went north to seek out the Tartars and the Kuraits. The Merkits and several other smaller nations had already come in under the banner of Temajin. Subotai's tuman was sent east. From the feel of the land, Subotai could tell that his unit was passing far to the south of the Blue Lake as they continued eastward. Word was passed that they were in search of Hsi-Hsia encampments and under the khan's orders to scatter them. In the Mongol army, all ranks were thoroughly briefed before an operation, objectives were clearly outlined, and expected enemy reactions discussed.

Only half a day after they had discovered an abandoned Hsi-Hsia campsite, an arrow rider, one of the khan's military couriers, intercepted Subotai's orkhan. The tuman promptly turned on its axis of march and started back, following the guidance of the arrow rider. The courier's urgency turned it into a forced march, and rumors about their destination spread through the ranks like wildfire. The tough Mongol troopers, under intelligent leadership and spurred by a burning loyalty to Temajin Khan, were like hounds panting after a scent in their eagerness for action.

In the dark of an early morning, the tuman, which had formed into regimental columns, came upon a reach of rugged terrain that forced it to break up into separate lines of cavalry in order to grope a way through twisting watercourses and low, sharp ridges and bluffs.

Subotai heard the murmur of it first. His skin prickled with it. It came and went on the breeze, the haunting, distant, mournful sound of the battlefield. He was at such a distance from it that the noise carried to him with a certain harmony of sound.

When the commander ordered the companies to break off in order to prevent an ambush of his entire column, Subotai turned out of the regiment's line-of-march and led his company to the right. He and his troopers had gone only another league when they came upon it.

It had the smell of butchery and the smell of the latrine. Saddled, riderless horses grazed somberly around the edges. Bloody sabers, bows, and arrows littered it. The bodies of most of a Mongol regiment and nearly as many dead Tartars lay like man-rocks on the ground, the bodies pressing the grass stalks into tortured bends.

Subotai saw at a glance in the now lightening morning the subtlety of the Tartar ambush. He also saw the regimental standard of the dead Mongol unit. Hand-and-arm-signing for the company to follow him, he let his horse pick its way through the corpse-ground. Scooping up the standard, he urged the animal up a steep, sandy embankment where some of the Tartars had lain in wait for the now-dead Mongols below.

From this high ground, Subotai could hear the full, crashing sound and see the dusty melee of the general battle still being waged on the other side of the hill. He could tell the Mongols from the opposing Tartars and their allied Kuraits by the superior unit-cohesiveness of the Mongols. Subotai caught his breath when he saw the great numerical superiority of the enemy. The Tartars and Kuraits were hemming in the khan's hard-fighting army and threatening to outflank it on both sides.

Subotai quickly scanned the surrounding landscape and headed for a low hill, only a mound of earth really, some distance in the enemy rear. His troopers galloped after him as he descended the slope they had just climbed. Circling widely and using all the concealment the terrain offered, Subotai brought them to the top of the mound. As they formed up behind him, he stood upon his saddle and thrust the standard of the lost Mongol regiment into the air, calling for his hundred to spread out in a wide skirmish line and brandish their naked sabers above their heads.

Subotai waited for the precise moment when the shock of his appearance in the enemy rear jerked through the enemy consciousness, then, still standing in the saddle, launched his company down the slope toward the battfield in a wild charge of superb horsemanship. The Tartars, fooled into believing they had been trapped from the rear by a vastly superior force, abandoned the fight, closely followed by the Kuraits.

Subotai, back astride his mount, unhorsed a Kurait with the standard's staff; then he was lost in the flying sword work as Temajin's Mongols surrounded and cut down an enemy formation not fortunate enough to have fled the field.

φ   φ   φ   φ

Subotai dragged the saddle from his weary mount. His sword arm was numb and there was a troublesome gash running half the length of his right thigh. The evening light was failing, but he could see well enough that he had been lucky. The cut was not too deep, and the blood had caked to stop the red flow. The remnants of the Mongol force had dismounted for an open night-bivouac some distance northeast of the battle scene. The day had not seen a Mongol victory, but the Kuraits and Tartars were known to be withdrawing to the northwest, their losses having exceeded those of the khan.

"Are you called Subotai?"

Subotai looked up at the mounted Mongol soldier. The man held a guidon staff thrust into his right stirrup, and from it, fluttering in the light breeze, hung the nine horse tails, the standard of the khan.

"I am."

"The khan, the lord Temajin, requires you at council." The guidon-bearer turned his horse and left without another word.

When Subotai came into the ring of light around the council fire and caught the khan's eye, Temajin stood up. He looked worn and drawn after the ordeal of the day. Like Subotai and all the others, he had bruises and wounds over much of his body. Subotai had seen him on several occasions during the past few weeks, but, as Temajin had shown no sign of recognition, Subotai assumed he had forgotten their encounter during the blizzard on the steppe years before, the pleasant interlude he had spent with the legendary hero, his wife, Bourtai, and their young son. Temajin's first words dispelled that assumption.

"You have come back, Eagle." The two men looked long into each other's eyes before Temajin added, "That trick you did with that squadron of yours—I think we would have been slaughtered if you had not carried it off." Then he looked at his assembled subcommanders and the Mongol noyons, the nobles, arrayed around the fire, and turned back to Subotai to announce in his deeply resonant voice, "I am giving you command of a tuman."

The khan turned and, indicating that Subotai should follow, moved off into the night away from the tattered scene of the Mongols' temporary garrison. The two men walked out on the steppe beyond the roll of the land to where the light from the campfires was only a faint glow. They stood for a long time, the east wind cool in their tired faces.

"My dreams and my faith are as one with the Sky," Temajin said. "Subotai, I call thee Bahadur—the Valiant. All things I will forgive thee. Be faithful to me and to my blood. Thou art the eagle of war sent to me by the Sky."

φ   φ   φ   φ

They were waiting there when Temajin and Subotai returned
to the council fire, the four chieftains of the Kuraits and the khan
of the Tartars.

Temajin's son, Juchi, the youngster of Subotai's steppe memory,
now a full-fledged warrior and his father's adjutant, came forward
and spoke to his father in hushed tones. "They say they are ready
to come in under your standard. I have riders fanning out to the
west and the north to be certain the main body of their army is
not on the march behind them. You have told us often enough of
Tartar treachery."

Temajin exchanged a glance with Subotai. "Come, Lord Orkhan. We shall speak with yonder folk concerning grazing and grass.'"

Temajin's formal use of his new rank sounded strange in Subotai's ears. He almost thought Temajin was speaking to another. He
had come into the khan's service willingly enough, thinking to lose
himself in the army the khan was gathering for a season or two
until he could regain some purposeful course in life, some pretext
to go on living, and had been assigned to one of the guards units
made up of rootless men of the Borjugon Mongols and other clans.
But once in, Subotai had quickly realized that this new Mongol
army was different. There was no longer any scattering of the entire
force after a campaign or a seasonal training passage; the hard cadre
of the army remained with the khan constantly. Other clan units
were allowed to disperse to their grazing grounds when they were
not needed, of course, but were expected to hold themselves ready
for reassembly when the khan summoned them. And when called,
there was a tested framework of experienced leadership to shape
them quickly into an efficient fighting force.

Brief as his service had been, consisting only of the abortive
campaign against the Hsi-Hsia, and now today's battle, Subotai
already felt himself part of that army. His loyalty to the khan,
caught from the seasoned soldiers, had doubled when he realized
that the khan was the Temajin who had shown him such kindness
when he was alone on the steppes. And then the knowledge that
Temajin, too, remembered that encounter combined with the trust

Temajin showed by conferring his new rank to almost overwhelm him. Orkhan, commander of a tuman. He savored the title, then put aside these thoughts to concentrate on the immediate situation.

The air was tensely electric, for only scant hours separated the participants as lethal enemies on the killing ground. Subotai looked the Kuraits over with unhurried interest, then inspected the Tartar khan, a thick man like himself but brown-eyed and with a thin, ragged black beard.

One of the Kurait leaders broke the uncomfortable silence. Speaking in the Kurait tongue, which was closely enough related to their tongue to be understood by the Mongols, he said, "Lord Temajin, I speak for the Tartars and for the Kuraits. We have been the enemies of the Mongols always. But the earth changes. We have all seen the drying of the grass. The land near the Chin Wall is dust, and with every sun, the desert spreads. This very day we have littered the steppe with the bodies of our kin over what remains of the grazing space."

At this point Temajin signed for them to seat themselves at the council fire, whispering to Juchi to bring water skins and whatever food was available to host them with. Subotai started to withdraw behind the Mongol noyons, but the khan motioned him forward.

"Lord Orkhan, Subotai Bahadur, you are at my right side, my sword hand. The left, as you well know, is for the Lady Bourtai alone." Then the khan returned his eyes to the Kurait spokesman. "We agree, at least, that there was ample blood shed this day."

"Lord Khan, Kha Khan . . ." The Kurait let the imperial title linger on the air before he went on. "The swords and the arrows of our people are yours if you will but grant us one condition."

"And that condition would be?" Temajin appeared slightly amused by the Kurait chieftain's tone of negotiation.

"If our clans are to be drawn into the Mongol army, we will retain our hereditary rights to have our clansmen led by their own kind. We will recognize you as the head of the army, but I think you will agree that its effectiveness will be enhanced if each soldier and his immediate leader speak the same language."

Temajin turned thoughtful eyes on the Kurait chieftain for long seconds before he replied, "I cannot argue with the reasoning of that. Will you pledge to me, then?"

"Aye," the Kurait answered.

Then the khan looked at the clusters of his Mongol noyons. "And do you all recognize this as a Kuraltai? Do all here elect me?"

The knots of men stirred and there were muffled discussions, but then, as if on signal, an abrupt silence fell over the assembly and a giant figure stood up from one of the groups of Mongols. Subotai recognized the enormous man even in the scant light of the undulating flames. It was Lariktai noyon, one of the khan's senior orkhans. His voice matched his great frame.

"Lord Temajin, you need not ask of the Mongols. Every man here has shown himself for you more than once on the battlefield. As for the Kuraits and the Tartars, well, we will take them as brothers if they swear to you. I like the grand ring of Kha Khan myself." Lariktai approached the late enemies of the khan and, towering over them, he asked, "What say you, then?"

The Kurait spokesman met Lariktai's fixing gaze with fearless eyes. "Since we have proposed it, naturally we will adhere to this agreement." He turned and spoke in the Tartar tongue to the Tartar khan, who answered immediately in the affirmative. The Kurait started to speak again to Temajin, but the Tartar chief interrupted him, talking at some length and seizing the Kurait's arms from time to time to emphasize some point.

When the Tartar fell silent, the Kurait looked pensively at the fire for some moments before he spoke again. "Kha Khan, your new ally has just, with his typical pointedness, raised again the basic problem which we still face. Now we are allies without enough pasture land instead of enemies in the same situation."

Temajin and Lariktai exchanged a long, knowing glance. Then Temajin said, "There is land aplenty below the Chin Wall."

This utterance brought murmured exclamations from the gathered warriors. The Kurait chieftain knew well the full meaning of Temajin's words, but he parried the hard impact of the statement, seeking to bring the Kha Khan into the open completely. He sought Temajin's attention again. "Many have been to the northern side of the Chin Wall, passing through the parched and dusting Gobi lands. Even I, as a boy, rode by the wall with my father and my kinsman. But who has seen the land of the Chin warlords? Who among us would know of the extent of the Chin empire? And the Chin. They will not open the strong gates of the wall with celebration at our coming, nor slink off like cur dogs, either." The Kurait ceased speaking and waited upon the Kha Khan.

A faint smile fleetingly traced the Kha Khan's handsome tanned face, then his mouth set as seriously as before, but the green eyes, when they caught the firelight, seemed to show, for an instant, luminescently red like a caracal's in the night. "I have been below the Chin Wall, and Lariktai and others of the Mongol noyons. The Chin emperor sent emissaries to us seeking our aid against their great southern enemies, the Sung. They took us to their silken pavilions and returned us to the wall with gifts of bolts of silk and great measures of their rice grain."

Here Subotai spoke up with force. "Lord Temajin, the Chin armies are mighty, and they number as the stars or the blades of grass. And they have held the wall against us for all time as far as we can know. Why would they need our assistance against the Sung? Perhaps this is a great plan of treachery to lure us into an ambush and free them from their long fear of our kind."

Temajin looked approvingly at the stocky orkhan, appreciating the brief incisiveness of his words. "Those thoughts have dwelt in my mind as well, Bahadur. Think now upon this. The bulk of the Chin soldiers we saw were afoot. Not only that, they were shy of our horses. Only their very senior officers were mounted, and that seemed more to show their rank than for the sake of movement. If there is a great treachery there, why, we shall ride away from them and let the snow of our arrow flights float out of the Sky to slow their pursuit. And, once through the gates of the Great Wall, we shall return as we please, since the Chin must bring their grain food a great distance from their wet paddy lands to the wall. We can loiter in wait for them below the wall in the grasslands, mounted and grazing our horses and meat stock."

Something changed in the minds of the warriors just from listening to talk of breaching the Great Wall. An expansive new attitude began to pervade all of those present, as though the wall were already crossed, and the long, serpentine stone structure which seemed to them to have no end no longer bounded one side of their world.

φ　　　　φ　　　　φ　　　　φ

"The Chin have closed the wall, Kha Khan."

The words of the Mongol scout caused Subotai to turn a questioning face in the direction of Temajin. The Genghis Kha Khan waved the weary scouts away and, wordless, he stepped up onto the bed of the yurt-cart he used for a traveling command post. He beckoned for Subotai to follow him as he hunched and entered the yurt. The orkhan propped the felt door-covering on the up-slanting side of the yurt to let the summer air stir inside the hot shelter.

The big green-eyed man spoke, but in a husky whisper as though alone. His vision seemed distant as if drawn within a trance state. "I knew there would be perfidy. Even from here I can detect the wretched smell of their foul cities. It is the twisting way of their fat emperor. Now he thinks he does not need me to break the Sung." The Kha Khan closed his eyes and a gravitous stillness settled over him.

The orkhan, too, drew within himself, letting his mind and memory play across the events of the past sun-years. But even now he dare not let his thoughts cross the high gate, the Macedonian Gate, into that still-seared region of his being. He set the remembered reflection of the Hindu Kush in his mind like a thought barrier to shut him out of that fearful place.

The situation was growing critical. The sparse grasses on the northern side of the Great Wall would soon die with the season, and there were the dry, sandy, and almost waterless Gobi reaches to pass through if they had to retreat back to the steppes. Or— now the Kha Khan's thoughts filled Subotai's mind as well—could they somehow cross the wall to the lush pastures on its southern side? He noticed now that Temajin's head was nodding off into fatigued sleep. He straightened the leader's torso and cradled the brown head as he laid the Kha Khan down on the yurt floor. Then he folded the Kha Khan's fleece-lined winter coat and slid it under Temajin's head for a pillow.

Subotai stepped off the cart and walked slowly through the descending dusk of evening, avoiding the cooking fires, seeking to continue his private musings in the night air. He was challenged then recognized at the horse pickets. Without bothering to saddle, he picked a mount at random, swung up, and rode bareback off into the south.

He eased the beast into a slow gallop and held it there until he could make out the winking of the guard fires like early fireflies on the lookout towers along the Great Wall. He reined up and sat the animal, patting its slightly lathered shoulder and feeding the reins as the horse, stretching and dipping its powerful neck, snorted and recovered its breath. Wherever Subotai could see the wall in the night light, the watch fires gleamed in unbroken regularity. He could find no gaps in the uniformity of spacing between them. Even if the Chin soldiers should doze by the blazes, there was no easy entry, for the gates were few and either heavily barred or blocked-and-mortared behind. The army of the Kha Khan had hauled no siege engines with it to breach this defense. Subotai wheeled his mount and walked it back into the north. The answer was there, tantalizing him in the back of his mind dancing just beyond his conscious reach.

"Gold will carry the mightiest fortress. Its subtle allure is stronger than any force of arms." Yes, that is what the Solar Warrior had said.

The night had slipped by before he turned back, and he reached the horse pickets as the eastern light shafted through low-settled cloud formations. The guard mount near Temajin's cart-yurt snapped erect as the orkhan strode by. Subotai looked quickly into the yurt and, seeing that the Kha Khan was gone, vaulted lithely off the cart and went in search of him. He found Temajin standing with his back to a fire, drinking warmed mare's milk from a stiff leathern cup to dispel the night chill. He joined Temajin on the smoky side of the dung blaze and shook his head when the Kha Khan silently offered him the steaming cup.

"Let us ride back toward the steppes, Lord." Subotai knew what the Kha Khan's reaction would be. The green eyes narrowed to slits, deepening the sun-squinting creases around the eyes and across the brow of Temajin.

"And let the Chin make a joke of us in their putrid cities? Listen intently, Lord Orkhan, you can hear already the jeers and curses of the wall soldiers when the wind carries them rightly."

"Kha Khan, I said let us ride back toward the steppes. I am not suggesting we return to them, only that the Chin think that we have gone. And it would be best, I think, if they were convinced that there has been a bitter quarrel between ourselves and the Tartars or the Merkits."

The green irises were visible again.

"And?"

Subotai scanned about quickly to make certain others were not within earshot, then outlined his stratagem. The Kha Khan heard him out without interruption.

"It's a bold and risky plan, but, win or lose, I prefer it to the empty-handed ride back to the Blue Lake," he said. "We shall begin this very night. You had better get some rest, Subotai. I will get the other orkhans moving."

φ   φ   φ   φ

The Chin soldiers waited for three days before they at last broke and swarmed off the wall to loot and quarrel and fight over the abandoned baggage the nomad army had left among the smoldering remains of their campfires. The Chinese officers had heard the rumors of growing dissension in the ranks of the Tartars and the Merkits. They were not surprised when the nomad encampment became a scene of angry departures, the order of the Mongol army dissolving unit by unit as groups of riders spurred off toward different points, but all in a northerly direction.

The Chinese found the quantities of fermented milk, which had been left behind, a quick intoxicant, and soon, before the sun reached its noonday zenith, even the Chin officers were squabbling over possession of the silk bolts with which their emperor had bought these mercenaries and which had been so inexplicably cast aside. And the Mongols—well, they were gone forever, and if not, the Chin would retreat through the gate they had left standing open and climb their wall to safety as they had always done.

In their clutching and drunken greediness they did not notice the faint trembling of the earth. Here and there a scattering of the more sober Chinese looked away from the looting and revelry to the skyline long enough to see the advancing Mongol skirmish lines when they were just becoming visible. Shock soon reestablished a level of sobriety in the uncontrolled Chin, and they began to flee back toward the security of the Great Wall over miles that suddenly seemed much longer.

As realization spread, they marked their flight with the litter of abandoned booty and the discharge of impedimenta to hasten their escape. The running, undisciplined mob, panting desperately, took hope when they were within reach of the wall, but for moments only. The flare of relief turned into terror when they saw Mongol cavalry units mounted in disciplined order waiting between them and their invincible wall. The Chinese soldiers, who might have overwhelmed the invaders by sheer numbers alone, hung there for what seemed forever to the waiting nomads. Then some of the Chin turned to flee and the contagious panic quickly took over.

Subotai Bahadur, at the head of the Mongol line between the Chin and the Great Wall, gave the simple signal. He raised his bow, drew the white wood shaft to his cheek and, aiming midway between the horizontal and the vertical, released the arrow. Behind him the bowstrings of half a tuman—five thousand of them—strummed the afternoon air.

The Chin saw the sudden broad gleam of strangely reflected sunlight shimmer across the blue Sky. Some of those who were fleeing even stopped their random running to wonder at it. Then the flight of arrows, on the descending side of its arching path, flattened for an instant as the shafts, speeding but still trailing the swishing air noise, enfiladed the Chin. The arrows turned disorderly retreat into a mad scramble for cover.

Subotai saw that the arrows took down almost one in five of the Chinese. He knew that Temajin's saber men would make short work of the rest of the demoralized enemy. He spurred after his troops, riding wildly toward the wall gate. He thought he saw, and his heart nearly sank at the sight, that the gate was closed and barred, but then his leading riders were there shouldering and urging their mounts against the heavy gate. Subotai breathed again as it opened. And the Mongols were through the Great Wall.

φ   φ   φ   φ

"You have seen walled cities before, Subotai?"

"Aye, Lord. In the Hindu regions near the river called the Indus."

Subotai and Temajin looked across the Mongol siege lines at the high and seemingly unbreakable bastion surrounding the great

Chin city of Chung-tu. The morning air was still, as though the chill of the fall season would not permit it any movement.

"We have learned our lesson, Lord Orkhan. But if we return, where shall we come by the means to mount those gray walls?"

Subotai tried to think of an encouraging answer to Temajin's question. He remembered what the trapper had told him about living in the cleanliness of the outdoor steppes and avoiding the filth and corruption of the civilized cities. And he remembered lessons of the Solar Warrior, which he spoke to the wondering Kha Khan.

"My...a man...a warrior I once knew..." Subotai seemed reluctant to share Dharayan's name and his knowledge and experiences directly with Temajin. "He said to learn the tools and ways of your enemies. That when you had done that, you would possess the sure means to victory over them."

The Kha Khan raised one eyebrow. "More riddles. We are about to starve, my scouts tell me the Chin army of the north may filter in behind us, we are not sure we can get back through the Great Wall even if we get that far toward the steppes or the Gobi sands— and you think I should commandeer one of these ancient, white-bearded Chin elders and sit cross-legged at his feet to garner the hoary wisdom of these putrid Chin in order to smash down that Sky-bedamned city's wall over there?"

The orkhan saw that his words had missed their mark. He let a loud stream of air escape through his nostrils to cue the Kha Khan that he, too, was impatient at times. He would have to try another tack.

"You know we cannot break into the city. And, unless our couriers get through to the Blue Lake, there may not be food stock close enough to the Great Wall to feed us when we arrive back there—which will be in a blizzard unless I have totally missed the nature of fortune in our situation. But," Subotai paused for a moment, "there is food in one place we know..." He let the baited words hang with a tantalizing silence.

Temajin sighed with tried patience. "Subotai, your mind is as crooked as that snake you wear on your white short-cloak." Then Temajin became aware of Subotai's meaning. "You must be hungry. The northern Chin army probably has more carts of food than we have troops altogether." But he knew the orkhan was right.

Nearly two days passed before the Chin lookouts on the ram-
parts of Chung-tu learned that the siege excavations of the Mongols
were deserted. The nomad army had left as it had come, in eerie
silence and in the dark of a moonless night, depriving the Chin of
the opportunity to alert their forces on the Yellow River.

φ   φ   φ   φ

"Too bad we could not have caught them on the move, Subotai."
Subotai nodded agreement, and Temajin continued, "They are well
dug in, to say the least."

The center of the great northern army of the Chin had encaved
itself for the cold months on a high salient of land which pushed
the Yellow River into a northerly bend. From the commanding
heights of this peninsula the Chin force faced south looking out of
the land-bridge with the river behind them to the north. By the
time the hard-riding Mongol reconnaissance units had located the
slow, ponderous, but mortally dangerous Chin dragon, the flood of
the Yellow River had moated the Chinese flanks. Blocked by the
river, the Mongols could only gaze across the water at the Chin
positions on hills overlooking the Yellow River.

The Chin commander was no amateur. His entire force was
protected by the interlocking reach of an awesome combined fire-
power: heavy bowmen, catapults, and something utterly confound-
ing to the barbarian Mongols—the weird, shrieking, fire-streaking
weapons. From the dominating heights, the Chin had unleashed
the mysterious fire weapons one night, demoralizing a patrol of
hand-picked men Subotai had selected and led across the Yellow
River paddling on logs to probe the Chin lines. Subotai had had
to rally the men when they panicked at the strangeness of those
fearful, whistling, flame-spouting, death-dealing fire weapons.

Subotai knew the Kha Khan must fight and win here. They
had followed the Chin like the steppe wolves follow their prey. Only
the victors would eat of the Chinese stores of rice and millet, or
even of the chaff and the horse meat which was the inevitable by-
product of Mongol battlefields. Subotai's active mind was constantly
probing for possible weaknesses, and as he and Temajin had studied
the Chin redoubt an insight had come that steadied him and held

him in its grip. He would say nothing of this to Temajin until he could verify it.

He found what he suspected. The Chin, relying on the moating of the river for flank protection, had dug in with their defensive posture facing outward toward the south only. And the arcs of fire of the supporting weaponry on the slopes, including the fire weapons, could swing only narrowly to the left or right of their frontal orientation.

The winter of north China was turning colder, and already the muddy water of the great Yellow River carried ice floes. If the winter were bitter enough, even that mighty river would freeze solid. The very moat that now protected them could become a hardened route to the heart of the Chin dragon. The enemy front would expand to become a circle, a perimeter which they would be compelled to defend on all sides. If it turned cold enough quickly enough, the water would freeze before they could adjust for their error, and the Chin would be undone. Snow and cold wind were the allies Subotai needed. He conjured them in his mind's eye and willed them to swirl from the Blue Lake.

In the bleak dawn after an abortive night probe, Subotai tried to sleep away some of the hunger which now tormented the nomad force from the least soldier in the ranks to the Kha Khan himself. He shivered at the thought that the tide of winter might turn without hardening the river enough to implement his plan. The men were ravenous as wolves now. He shivered again, then began to sweat at the realization of how desperate was his gamble on the north wind and a frozen river. Sleep evaded him. The freezing morning, not quite so damp now that the Yellow River marshes were frozen over, triggered memories of his cold treks with the trapper. Subotai wondered if the Chin fire-streakers he had seen whining out of long, black tubes were the same as the Greek fire the trapper had described. In the darkness those streaking, swift, air-splitting weapons had swept through the night like the shooting stars seen in the summer skies of the steppes.

Ice appeared on the edges of the river. Then the brief haze of time when the river hardened came on and the water crystalled into solidity in the mysterious changes of the winter. Daily Subotai pushed his patrols out onto the ice, testing its thickness and its load-carrying strength. The cat-eyed Mongol general waited until the ice was thick enough to bear the full brunt of the heaviest cavalry squadrons in the nomad army before he approached the Kha Khan with his tactical recommendations.

A few days later, when the river lay unmoving in the bitter dawn of another morning, the orkhan stared up at the Chinese stronghold. He knew that a frontal assault would be hideously costly; the only real hope of success lay in attacking the Chin on the left or right, or in making one of the Mongols' great circling rides to assault them from the rear.

Even though the Chin could not now shift the fields of fire of their heavy weaponry in time to counter an oblique attack, Subotai knew his troops might be forced to come within reach of the Chin superior missile power, for starvation was now rampant in the Mongol ranks. The Chin were well aware of this, and knew the scent of food in the Chinese wagon-larders must soon draw the nomads into the trap of fire.

The snow came later that same morning, swirling from the north and driven by the orkhan's will, and Subotai told the Kha Khan of his plan. They went together to stand on a high point overlooking the Chinese camp. In the midst of the granulated veil of the falling flakes, the two nomad generals stood there like a tableau in time, their wide shoulders beginning to frost with the snow on their fur capes, unmoving and unspeaking, the green eyes and the gray-blue eyes unblinking, spellbound under the sure natural knowledge that the moment was now. They could not turn from the time or the task.

The Kha Khan's voice, when he finally spoke, sounded flat in the snowy air. "Subotai, I will send the Mangudai, the shock troops, against the Chin front from the south. We must draw their big weapons and hold them away from the flanking assault."

Subotai had tried to lock that course of action out of his mind, but he, like Temajin, knew it was an essential, though costly, diversionary tactic, the only way they could hope for success in the limited time remaining before the rapidly decaying Mongol force would be unable to function with discipline and energy. Subotai, trying not to think of the sickening losses the Mangudai would inevitably sustain, drew on another level of intuition to honor the maxim of the Solar Warrior that a general's only real responsibility was to succeed on the battlefield while treasuring the lives of his men. But he could not forget that the wanton death of any man would be wound into the karma of those who had arranged it.

Temajin was speaking again. "Else we shall fail, Subotai, and all will die." The Kha Khan had that disconnected light in his deep eyes again. "Bahadur, the Valiant, you know what must be done while I cross the ice behind their hill. Subotai, I give you the left wing. Guard my heart well, Lord Orlok."

Subotai met the green eyes. "I will, Kha Khan."

This sudden elevation in rank from orkhan to orlok, commander of an entire wing of the Mongol army, did not register in Subotai's consciousness immediately. He anguished as he paced in the snow, his stabbing footsteps kicking up puffs of snow-dust which the brutal, cutting wind violently vortexed and swept away. His heart was racing, his breath hot. He wondered why the cold air was so hot when he breathed it in.

He looked at the Kha Khan's fringed, soft, gray-brown boots, unheeled, and lined with rabbit and wolf fur like his own. There was no need for further words between them; their minds were a unified awareness. Temajin turned his back on the stocky orlok and stepped up onto his horse. Turning the animal away, he rode back toward the center of the Mongol army which was now mounted and waiting in unit formations.

Subotai looked at the Mangudai officer, commander of a tuman of shock troops. He'd known the man since coming into the army, and they had hunted together on several occasions. To look at him today, no one would guess that this officer's serious correctness concealed a suicidal valor. Subotai was annoyed with himself that he could not remember the Mangudai general's name.

"It is you and I," Subotai said.

"No, Lord Orlok..."

"Don't call me that," Subotai interrupted him, "not now when we are about to become sword swallowers. Save it for the council— if we ever sit in one again."

The Mangudai general managed a slight smile. "This is my fate, Subotai. What would I say to the Kha Khan if I had to report that his newest orlok was splattered from here to the Great Wall?"

Now the man's meaning dawned on Subotai, and the reason behind it. Subotai grinned. "We both know that he is always the quickest with promotions when his horse is about to step into a ground squirrel's hole."

The Mangudai general recalled now why he liked the quiet orkan, now orlok—it was because of his relaxed, unassuming manner. "Lord Orlok—no, do not gainsay me—I pay respect where it is due. There is a deadly real reason why you must not assault the Chin lines with us. You see, I want first crack at that Chinese food, and nobody knows any better than I do what kind of devastation you can wreak upon a feast of any size."

The Mangudai general chuckled, and Subotai roared his loud laugh over the icy wind. The orlok's voice still hinted of the sound of laughter as he said, "Brother, that is just why I am going with you."

They mounted and moved southward to a point where the Yellow River, after looping the Chin salient, turned west again, ignoring for the moment the unfortified west flank of the Chin army now exposed by the frozen river. They heard the metallic sounds made by weapons being drawn muffled by the wind, heard the low-spoken prayers to ancestors and oaths to private and fearful gods, gods of Sky, steppe, woodland, and ice, and to vengeful spirits in a score of languages—Mongol, Tartar, Kurait, the hopeless clicking speech of the reindeer people, even some in Chinese.

The cavalry now moved in a disciplined mass, but each man was alone. The orlok turned within to steel himself to the unthinkable which lay only moments ahead. He began to make mantra on the Mother Kali, but somehow in his mind, his efforts to focus on the thought of Kali seemed to phase into the constant and lovely memory of his Mursechen, the mental bondage from which Dharayan had so gently tried to free him. He froze his mind on the image of the Solar Warrior, seeking the one-pointedness to elevate himself above his mortal nature and make himself spherically perceptive in the press of combat.

The hooves of the Mangudais' horses rang sharply on the icy surface as they crossed the Yellow River where it straightened out west of the loop that enclosed the Chin. The hoof-clatter swelled to a deepening rumble as the Mongol horses came up onto the frozen turf on the river's southern shoreline, but the snow was thickening to mute it, and the hard wind strangely began to fall off. Once across, the Mangudai continued briefly on in a southerly direction until Subotai turned them east. They moved east until he sensed they were directly south of the breastworks and trench lines the Chin had built to defend the approach to their land-bridge. With his force lined up roughly parallel to the enemy front, Subotai turned straight back north toward the open maw of the spear-faced mounds of the Chin. It was just as well that snow still hid from them the formidable defensive line they were about to attack.

Subotai could just make out a gray tracery of dark figures racing over the mounds between the heavy emplacements of wooden spears toward the safety of their entrenchments. At the moment of commitment, he drew the blue sword and held it high, a signal and a symbol for the Mangudai behind him. The Mongols used no battle or rallying cries. Theirs was a silent, unemotional commitment to battle born of their terrible evolution in the harsh steppes and the unyielding discipline imposed on them by the Kha Khan's military system.

Subotai and the Mangudai shock troops were at full gallop now, the pounding cavalry charge blotting out the heavy reports of the Chinese ballistas. The boulders of the first salvo fell harmlessly for the most part, only here and there tripping a rider, but the next salvo found the Mongol skirmish line and broke bloody gaps in the Mangudai ranks. Then they were on the spear-barbed mounds.

Subotai's animal, even at full run, seemed to pick its way instinctively through the fixed anti-horse lances and float to the crest of the Chinese trench. Subotai was glad to see the Chinese fleeing uphill toward their next line of defense, abandoning their first trench line without a fight. Then the reason for it became apparent as the air warped under a barrage of the fire weapons screaming down the slope. The flaming comets rammed into the earth mounds with fiery explosions which drove the Mongols off the barricade. The detonations literally blew the orlok off his horse, and sent man and animal sprawling down the embankment. But undeterred, the rear ranks of the Mangudai came up the crest and, urging their mounts to leap the entrenchment, recklessly charged up the hill.

The last line of Mangudai surged over the barricade bringing spare horses with them. Subotai, taking the offered reins, rolled into the saddle with the blue sword still in his right hand just as another salvo of the fire-streakers swish-whined overhead without causing any casualties. One of the fire weapons came in low, seemingly bent on the orlok's destruction, but suddenly shot upward trailing smoke and sparks in a spinning, uncontrolled spiral, then unexpectedly fell silent and, dropping with a slow wobble, landed well behind the point where the Mongols had now breached the Chin's defensive line.

Through the snow, Subotai could make out the lines of Chin archers drawing back in unison, and see their arms drop as they unleashed their shafts. But the aim of their commander was erratic and their arrow volley had no effect on the Mangudai surging upward toward them on steaming horses.

Then the ranks of the Chin bowmen were suddenly decimated by a surprise arrow flight rising from the frozen river, and the Mongol shock troops were on them before the startled Chin could recover and launch another fusillade of arrows. The Mongol arrows fell like snow again, this time creating havoc among the Chin infantrymen who were racing with halberds, spears, and swords to assist the hard-pressed archers now collapsing under the sword-attack of the mounted Mangudai.

The Chinese, recoiling under the shock and ferocity of the Mongols' brazen frontal attack and the unexpected appearance on their flanks of more and more mounted nomad units, halted in mid-stride, then began to break and flow down the northeastern ridgeline of the redoubt they had thought impregnable.

Subotai and the Mangudai were bogged briefly in hand-to-hand work with those of the Chin archers who still had hand weapons and the will to use them. Then the attackers were through these remnants and followed the orlok as he spurred his mount toward the hilltop. Seeing them, the Chin military engineers and artillerymen manning the catapults and the fire tubes scattered into the intricate trenches which most of the Chinese troops had ignored in their desperate attempt at flight, or perhaps in order to attack the Mongol center crossing the ice.

From the hilltop Subotai watched the battle on the ice below.

It was like a shadow play he had once seen during one of the Agrayana festivals. He saw the Kha Khan's Mongols roll back and forth, unit by unit, over the hapless Chinese infantry, saw the countless dark, spreading stains on the ice, and watched in disbelief as the Chin, like driven game animals, grouped, were broken and slaughtered, only to have the survivors, mostly weaponless now, regroup and make the same series of incredibly fatal mistakes again. Then the snow thickened, layering and blocking the light from the cold river below so that he could no longer see the carnage, as though the curtain had been lowered on a drama that had ended.

Perhaps two hundred thousand men perished there on the ice and on the hill. Countless bodies were left on the ice after the victorious Mongols had stripped the dead, both Chin and nomad. And when the ice moved and broke and flowed with the Chinese spring, the dark, frozen corpses of men and horses were swept away so that the early summer floods carried no evidence of the monumental conflict which had been so desperately waged on those same once-frozen waters.

φ   φ   φ   φ

It took Subotai two years to get the Chin engineers integrated into the Mongol columns, two years of warding off sarcastic Mongol opposition to Subotai's unswerving drive. At times even the Kha Khan turned a sympathetic ear to critics of the orlok. Finally the controversy came to a vicious head when one of the junior orkhans, mistaking Subotai's silence for weakness and swollen with the delusion of self-seeking, disregarded rank to openly challenge the orlok in the Kha Khan's very presence.

Subotai, who had borne the man's insults with indifferent silence, started to walk away, knowing that more reasonable men would intervene and temper the man's vainglorious posturing. But the jealous orkhan, a Tartar, stepped directly in Subotai's way as the orlok was leaving the council.

"Bahadur indeed!" the Tartar snarled. "Your courage is as false as your name. Only a man without valor would make war with the Chinese machines." The Tartar unsheathed his sword, a wicked, razor-sharp, white-gray weapon. "If your blood has any thickening to it, take your weapon, Subotai."

The orlok only glanced at the inflamed face as he attempted to walk to the left around his challenger. Then Subotai's time perception altered under the stress and violence radiating from the armed man. He felt the motion of the man's sword stroke without even seeing it. There was a flash of movement, framed in a deadened quiet, speckled with the almost unperceived crackles of the council fire.

The Kha Khan saw the point of the Tartar's sword ram into the turf as Subotai, on the man's outside right, drove the Tartar's sword-wrist down with his right hand. Then the orlok spun in a complete circle to his left, easily evading the Tartar's attempt to grab at him. The Tartar's legs were abruptly flung upward by a will-shattering twist of the orlok's powerful hands which drove the Tartar's chin over the Tartar's left shoulder. The crack of the broken neck sounded with no more definition than the released heat strain in one of the burning firebrands in the council fire.

The assembled council was rigid; only eyes moved to watch the spasmodic shivering as the Tartar went open-eyed and limp with death. Subotai stood without regret over the body of his assailant.

Temajin stood up. His eyes were narrowed, but unspoken approval glimmered in them. "As always, Lord Orlok, you amaze us." Then the Kha Khan's sudden laugh broke the spell still cast by Subotai's spectacular unarmed defense. "Perhaps," he said, "it would be better for us all if we lend all possible support to the Lord Subotai's scheme to use the Chinese catapults and wall-cracking machines against the Chinese capital city." He laughed again. "By the Sky, Lord Orlok, perhaps we shall have that great Chin city."

"Then we must begin drilling with the Chinese who know the use of these devices." Subotai spoke in his usual calm way.

And so through the rime of autumn, the dark snows of winter, and the steppe-sweetening spring breezes, the nomads learned how to support the Chin who had abandoned their land to follow the Kha Khan, learned to disassemble, transport, and aid in the reassembly of the machines so strange to the barbarian Mongols.

And stranger still to the Mongols was the apparent nonexistence of any loyalty in the Chin engineers for their distant emperor. When the catapult-soldiers had surrendered en masse after the destruction of the northern Chin army on the iced Yellow River, Temajin's first inclination was to have them executed. But the orlok had read his intent and managed to intercede before Temajin gave the savage order.

Temajin was indignant. "Spare them indeed, Subotai! So that they may run back to their greedy, fat little emperor and send their fire at us again when we come back?"

Subotai well knew Temajin's attitude concerning loyalty. "I think, Kha Khan, that they have little reason to be loyal to their ruler or to their war lords."

Temajin, still damp-faced with battle-sweat, had wiped at the perspiration running into his eyes with the furred sleeve of his leathern coat-cloak. "I shall spare them then, at your request, but watch out for their skulls rolling under your horse if I ever detect any treachery thereabouts."

φ   φ   φ   φ

When the winter's garrison on the steppes near the Blue Lake was over, the Mongol army grazed its stock south again, through the Great Wall. And the Chin artillerymen marched with them, carried in the wagons along with the war machines or riding on the steppe ponies as more and more of them had learned to do. And this time the passage of the Mongol tumans, the divisions of ten thousand men each, was marked by the sing-song chanting of the Chinese.

Chung-tu lay nearer now, but the orlok saw no signs of desertion among the Chinese, those oddly vigorous men with their straight black hair and their yellow narrow-eyed faces.

It took nearly a year, but the city finally gave way to the hammering of the ballistas, the fire-arrows, the pestilence, and the relentless hunger. The systematic slaughter and the looting that followed lasted for weeks. Makeshift carts and wagons loaded to groaning with booty daily trailed off into the northwest carrying the spoils back to the lair of the barbarians.

The Kha Khan himself had been caught up in the blood frenzy, after the west wall of the city finally had been broken into jagged stone that slammed dusty, ancient mortar upwards in dry, gray sprays as the structure imploded from the months of impacting of battering rams and heavy catapult stones. He joined in the nightmare of indiscriminate murder, burning, and the material madness of the quarrelsome looting which only the true barbarian, schooled by generations of deprivation and wanting, can muster.

Subotai watched the chaos in the tormented Chinese city during the first insane hours after the Mongols broke into the outskirts of Chung-tu, but had no belly for the animal acts being perpetrated there by the savage tumans of the Kha Khan. He commandeered one of the Chin engineers to serve as interpreter and, with his own sober staff, rode off into the southeast toward a distant line of low mountains, leaving word with Temajin's son Juchi that he had gone southward to scout for any Chinese reinforcements that might be coming to relieve the ravished city.

A day and a half down country they came upon a half-wild buffalo and dropped it with lances and arrows. The three Mongol officers and the Chinese engineer, Kua, fell to the task of skinning and butchering the carcass. The languid, humid air of the Chin summer was soon abuzz with flies swarming over the thick-scented blood and the tallowed hide that lay cast aside on the Chin earth.

Subotai found he had little appetite for even buffalo meat. Recalling his years in the Indian heat during which he had scarcely consumed a single mouthful of meat, he muttered that he was going to search for a night shelter and stepped onto his wet pony. He turned the mount and, urging it up onto a farming earthdike, rode the dike, gazing idly at the soggy paddylands which adjoined it and stretched off in all directions into other earthen paddydikes which, in turn, bounded more of the flooded rice fields.

The orlok rode the dikes in a tacking path toward a far, dark smudge of trees blurred by the summer light and bent by the heat and the humidity above the rice ponds. As he drew nearer, he could see a high mud wall set within the shading tree limbs, its entry gate lying where it had fallen when looting war refugees from Chung-tu had torn it from its bronze hinges.

Subotai slow-walked the pony through the open portal in the wall. The house within the compound wall had not been burned, but the looters had crazily torn away everything not integral to the structure of the spacious house itself. The garden and the dying trees had been stripped as well. Subotai, naked to the waist in the hot dampness of the paddyland summer, reined in his pony and listened with the intentness which only the combined severity of a warrior's training and a simple outdoor life can instill. He heard nothing but the slight rustle of dry leaves on the unirrigated trees and the random hum of an insect, but he was aware of the mottled overlapping of harmonious and disturbing vibrations within the looted dwelling. He sensed human presence.

His common sense shrieked caution as he dismounted and ground-reined the steppe pony. Brushing the sweat from his eyes and wiping his palms on his leathern pants, he drew the blue sword from its accustomed scabbard on the upper left stirrup strap. Still he heard nothing. Barefoot, he slipped through the heavy air in soundless stealth, crossing the open threshold as noiselessly as one of the swaying shadows cast by a leafy tree branch. The stone floor was cool on his bare soles. The interior was bright with sunlight admitted through wide casements, but it reeked with the stench of human excrement and sour urine. Picking his path, Subotai glided through another doorway.

The Chin who materialized soundlessly out of nowhere was lean and smooth of flesh tone. The absence of muscular definition on the man's body was the first thing to register in Subotai's consciousness, for he knew this type of physique made the Chin capable of blinding speed. Subotai tried to regain his center, his inner control, but he knew already that in a thoughtless instant he had lost it even before he had attained it. He had met the Chinese warrior's eyes for a flickering moment only, but in that instant he had been drawn into the man's flow of inner power, his Ch'i. Dharayan had warned him. "The eyes of a man are devious pools in combat. Be conscious of his weapons. Avoid eye contact. Men spend a lifetime training not to give away their true intent by a betrayal of eye movement. Some warriors train to fight in a style but train their minds to another method, then employ this deception to overcome even the probing clairvoyance of especially sensitive warriors."

To keep himself from repeating the mistake Subotai looked at everything, at nothing, then hastily scanned the long room he had entered. The Chinese warrior was alone.

Subotai had been holding the blue sword behind him, the wrist of his swordhand braced against the small of his back. His quickness in bringing the blade into guard position evaded the visual acuity of the Chin warrior, who stopped short his own attacking movement and danced several retreating steps to his rear to regain his distance.

The orlok and the Chinese warrior were frozen now, separated by a distance equal to three lance lengths. Subotai had never seen a style like the Chin's before. The Chinese warrior had two short, widebladed swords with rings riveted to the ends of their hilts. He wore a broad, circularly-slotted bracelet on each wrist. Catching the rings in the bracelet slots, he spun the ringswords in glittering arcs, like Buddhist prayer wheels in a high wind.

The Chin resembled a cat testing a pool of water as he stepped one foot forward, touching the toe tips first then slowly settling the ball and heel on the grimy stone floor. Then, like two weights swung from opposite ends of the same cord, the two combatants slid circularly in graceful, floating steps to their right in almost choreographic synchronization.

Subotai strove with all his self-control to pull back his sensory energy, retrieve the stability he had lost in his first surprised involvement with the enemy swordsman's Ch'i, tried to relinquish his feeling for the sweat trickling down his body. He knew he would require all the conscious and psychic powers he could command to emerge the victor from the stone oven he had suddenly found himself in.

Foolishly he glanced at the Chin's hard, rawboned face. He saw the black eyes aglitter with confidence, and recognized the enormous control of the interior forces which only a severe and dedicated lifetime of training can achieve. Subotai knew the Chin was aware of his battle to regain his center, the one-pointedness he would need to succeed in the inevitable flash of violence pressing toward them.

Spinning one ringsword on his left wrist, the other crisscrossing like nearly unseen heat lightning, the Chinese warrior came to the attack. Subotai reacted too slowly. He stumbled back, saving his life by a particle of a second, but the ringsword had gone red as the Chin, like a whirling dervish, passed through his attack. Subotai knew the branding pain would come, and he felt the inside of his left armpit and ribs suddenly go slippery, felt the warmth of newly sprung blood flow across his left hip.

The ringsword stroke had caught Subotai in a backing step

just as his foot slipped on a patch of granular dirt on the stone floor. But even as he felt his right knee slam against the stone, the orlok brought the blue sword scything from right to left in a path parallel to and only a handbreadth above the floor. The stroke took the swiftdancing right foot of the Chin, shearing bone and ligament and muscle and causing the enemy to turn into an astonishingly controlled falling roll, from which he came almost instantly back up onto his one good leg.

Under the driving impetus of hurting, dying hate, the Chin hopdragged his maimed leg and came at the orlok with a battle scream so piercing it made Subotai's head ache from the impact on his ears. Subotai retreated out of the long hall and down the entry steps, his blood leaving a bright crimson trail beneath the blue sword which he held pointed at the deadly twins still blurring about the Chinese warrior's wrists. His breath came with difficulty, his vision skewed, his depth perception expanded and telescoped wildly. Fighting for the strength to make the one last effort, he hurled the blue sword at the lurching Chin. It was a lucky throw; the sword butt struck a glancing blow which dropped the Chin into a greasy welter of his own blood.

Backing toward his steppe pony Subotai grasped his wood and horn bow. Somehow he conjured enough strength to string it and nock a deadly shaft against the sinew string.

The ringswordsman, steadied himself against the doorway for a fanatical pursuit of the Mongol, then saw his error and turned in a powerful, one-legged leap, but he was too late. The arrow whirred behind with greater speed and severed his spinal column just above the shoulders. Almost soundlessly the Chin slid down in a twitching heap just within the doorway.

Subotai looked at the bow, his blood running dark and sticky down upon it. His left arm, now powerless, let the bow slip from his grasp. Overtaken by pain and shock, he sagged to the ground under his horse and closed his now unfocused eyes. As his mind slipped through a hazy region into a black pit of pain and roaring noise, dislocated images danced through his fading consciousness. There was Mursechen, then Gauri in her kitchen—he could smell her curry. Then his bright secret hope for union with the Mother Kali blotted out the others as he lost consciousness.

φ   φ   φ   φ

The Chinese woman and her two female servants, cramped in their hiding place beneath the stone floor of the country house, listened to the sounds of the combat, and even after the silence had fallen, hardly dared to breathe except in shallow clutches at the wet air. When confinement in the stone nook finally became unbearable, the women cautiously ventured out. Trembling, they shoved the stone covering back in place, stifling their cries of fear as it grated against the floor. They found the court soldier whom the emperor himself had assigned to protect them lying dead, an awfulness of jagged white legbone and ragged cartilage showing where his right foot should have been and a feathered shaft in the back of his neck. Then the Chinese woman saw the half-living, bleeding man under the horse outside the door and recognized him as one of the dreaded Mongols. His rough barbarian leathern trousers and fur-lined coat-cloak tied across the shaggy pony were the hateful symbols of the savages who were destroying all she had ever known.

She walked to the horse and looked down at the wounded man, at the face pale from the red leakage she had seen in a spattered trail across the stone floor and down the steps. She noted with surprise that he was clean-shaven, his beard showing black through the skin of his jaws and throat. Silvery-white strands ran through the long black-and-red hair tied back behind his head with a leather cord. The wide intelligent brow covered with the cold sweat of great shock disturbed her.

Then the closed eyes opened for a long moment. She had never seen such eyes—they were like the color of water in the mountain lakes. She assumed he was only a common soldier since he wore no richness nor anything which might be an insignia of rank, but the barbarian's powerful face seemed out of place in the rudeness of the Mongol clothing, out of place almost anywhere. The Chinese woman looked back at the sprawled body in the entryway. The dead Chinese warrior was one of the picked soldiers of the emperor's bodyguard.

The high, sing-song voices of her female attendants were urging her to flee and leave this barbarian to die in a welter of his own blood. They saw what seemed to them an imminent justice. In clipped high tonals, the Chinese woman spoke and the others fell silent. Under her guidance the three of them managed to half-carry, half-drag Subotai's considerable weight through the outer and inner halls into a rear alcove where their travel bundles lay.

The Chinese woman, reaching into one of the cloth-tied rolls, produced a small bamboo vial filled with a narcotic which she forced down the throat of the delirious barbarian. In minutes he had lapsed into a semi-comatose state. She issued curt instructions to her women servants, and they hurried away to do her bidding.

Then she unrolled another of the bound bundles and carefully set out its contents. After arranging the several articles from the bundle, she applied rice powder to her beautiful, young-old face and, dabbing with a slender brush into a small jade dish, she painted her lips a rose-pink shade. After inspecting herself critically in a small reflecting glass, she replaced all the articles in the opened bundle-cloth just as one of her women returned with two heavy buckets of water suspended on the ends of a wooden yoke set across her sturdy peasant shoulders.

The two women rolled the Mongol onto his right side and laid his left arm over his head to expose the long gaping slash on his left side. Blood still issued profusely from the ghastly wound, but the Chinese woman was pleased that there was no indication of the bright red, pulsing blood which she knew would be a sign of impending death by bleeding.

Recalling what she had once seen one of the court physicians do, she thoroughly washed out the wound. Then, drawing on the memories of her country childhood, she selected several handfuls of the various fungi which she had bidden her second serving woman to scrape from the damp walls and crush. These she packed into the open sword wound. She recalled, through the obscurity of the years, that the smaller mold was the best, and sprinkled more of it on top.

Then, disregarding the unconscious flinching of the man-flesh, she sewed the edges of the wound together with a needle and silken thread. She sent her women in search of other fungi, and when they returned with them, she mashed mushrooms and toadstools they brought to her into more of the mold, and spread the new mixture in a layer over one of the bundle cloths. After doubling the cloth over for a poultice, she cut the rawhide Mongol saddle rope into three equal lengths, and used the pieces to tie the fungi-filled pack over the wound, looping each lashing completely about Subotai's upper body and knotting it.

φ   φ   φ   φ

The Chinese woman was holding a black wooden cup of thin egg and rice soup to the orlok's lips when her two women, in a haste of stark terror, burst into the undoored alcove. Wide-eyed, they whispered hoarsely to their mistress. Subotai, weak but alert, could hear horses outside and guessed the identity of the riders. When the handsome Chinese woman rocked back onto her heels and started to rise, Subotai placed a staying hand on her forearm.

The large anterior rooms whispered with the footfalls of Mongol boots, a steel weapon scraped on a wall, and voices cursed the sound. Subotai's Chin engineer and interpreter, Kua, burst in and stumbled over the orlok's sprawled legs.

"Lord Subotai!" Kua shouted back to the others who followed him. "He is here." Then realizing he had spoken in the Chin language, he repeated the call in Mongol.

Subotai's staff officers leaped around a wall corner and crowded eagerly into the alcove. Their smiles turned to serious expressions as they sheathed their sabers. The Chin servant women were as still with fear as if they were confronted with venomous snakes.

Subotai managed a weak smile of greeting. He spoke to the interpreter. "Kua, tell these women they have nothing to fear from us." He kept his feeble grip on the arm of his benefactress, noting with pleasure that she alone seemed fearless in the presence of the big, armed Mongol soldiers.

Kua spewed out a lengthy, rising and falling surge of Chin words. He had apparently embellished the orlok's communication with the rank of the wounded Mongol, for the Chinese woman turned startled eyes on the wan Subotai. Her women still huddled together, but their quick brown eyes ceased to dart with their previous urgency.

The orlok closed his feverish eyes as he asked, "Do you have anything more substantial than the gruel these poor creatures have been sharing with me?"

"Yes, Lord. Some cuts from the buffalo we were butchering when you so foolishly went off on your own." The Mongol officer who spoke was Subotai's aide-de-camp and self-appointed mother-

hen who spared no inconvenience or hardship on himself to assure
the orlok's well-being. Nor did he ever spare the orlok any criticism—
criticism which often tempered Subotai's judgment and helped curb
his ego in the exalted arena of command in which his spinning
karma had placed him.

"Hack down one of those dead trees out there and roast up a
haunch at once. And be careful of these..." Subotai's gesture at
the Chin women was slow and flaccid. "This one braided up my
side and wrapped me in silk like a babe."

Subotai now noted for the first time that the Chinese woman
had replaced the peasant's clothing she had been wearing with a
soiled but elegant silk robe. The courtesan's gown she had on was
ornate with stiff, colorful embroidery representing delicate birds in
flight and a rampant, fearsome-mouthed beast much like a serpent.

Subotai's aide knelt by his side. "We saw your handiwork outside. How in the open Sky did you manage to saw off his foot, then
shoot him in the back? Those tricks alone would qualify you for
command of an entire army."

Subotai grimaced a smile, but the cold, sickly sweat suddenly
dampened his forehead again. "I am not sure which I did first."
He swallowed a rush of nausea and almost desperately said, "I have
to sleep again. Guard this woman and feed her some decent rations.
Leave her women be. You know there will be females aplenty sent
out from Chung-tu for your choosing when we return to the Kha
Khan." And with that he fairly fainted into sleep.

A week passed. Subotai convalesced slowly in the moist heat
of the harvest season. And during this period the Chinese woman
drugged him once again, slit open the silken stitching in his festering side, and cleaned out the great gash. Then she sent Kua back
to the rotting buffalo remains for maggots and loosed them inside
the odorous wound to let them feed on the dead flesh.

Subotai's Mongols watched these proceedings with barbarian
wonder, now and again snapping to the woman's translated instructions to do her bidding. When the putrescence had been eaten, she
took the bloated maggots from the wound to the mud wall and
smashed each of them with a heavy stick. She commandeered some
of the rice wine which the scavenging Mongol soldiers had looted
and poured it generously into the orlok's side. Then, directing that

the warriors hold the unconscious man still, she held a firebrand to the wine-fumes and let the almost invisible blue flame dance for an instant or two in the raw opening. She stifled the burning, knelt and smelled the seared interior. Then she sewed the injury closed again and greased it with a clear salve which she produced from her amazing bundle.

Subotai seemed to weaken after this drastic procedure, but in two days he was sitting up, and in four, began to walk slowly, hunched over, about the dead and littered garden area. Through Kua, he tried to draw out the Chinese woman, but she retreated behind a facade of quietness, answering in polite and uninforming language the queries passed on by the Chin translator.

She asked the orlok's permission for herself and her women to sleep in a private chamber, and to go to a stream which partially irrigated the paddies in order to launder clothing. Subotai did not even bother to try to explain the concept of washing clothing to his officers, but he sent the women on their way, instructing Kua to accompany them but not to intrude on their privacy.

Subotai, his left arm in a buffalo-skin sling, leaned against an open gateway and watched her walk away in her stained courtesan's gown. It was only then that he noticed that she walked with a certain difficulty, and saw how grotesquely tiny her feet were. He wondered how such an incongruity could occur in a woman who, in form, bearing, and every other visible aspect, was almost the perfection of femininity.

Subotai heard a modest giggle when the returning laundry party swept by his alcove, and caught a momentary glimpse of the woman's unmade-up face. There was an instant pull, a drawing-in between them as their eyes met, but the Chinese woman lowered her head and disappeared into her sleeping room. The Chin women kept to themselves thereafter. The orlok saw them only when Kua called them out for meals. Then they would take the sputtering meat offered them on sticks and withdraw from the Mongols into their tight group, facing inward as they sat or squatted, their still undiminished suspicion forming a wall about them.

Seeking to regain his strength, Subotai was cantering somewhat shakily about the ruined wall astride his pony one morning in the early relative coolness when the Chinese woman stepped out through the gateway, garbed in her exquisite, artistically embroidered and clean and mended gown. When Subotai pulled up his mount beside her, she cast her eyes downward and grew as still as the earth itself. Without speaking, without meeting his eyes, she gently and uncertainly stroked the Mongol pony's shoulder. When Subotai reached down and passed his good hand over her smooth forehead, however, she froze. Subotai sensed that her reaction stemmed not from trepidation but from a certainty in her mind that the gulf between them formed by her culture and her conditioning was uncrossable.

Although he knew there were vast differences between their accustomed environments and backgrounds, he could not know that she had spent her life in the imperial schools mastering all the seductive skills expected of a picked concubine, and had learned to please any man. Nor could he know that she had learned, too, the detachment the Chinese courtesan would need when she was at last supplanted by younger women.

Nor could he know that her body ached for the heavy, muscular man above her, that she longed to peer directly into the feline eyes which were, at times, the color of fine blue porcelain. He could not guess that she had once even permitted herself to fantasize how she would conserve his strength for him during lovemaking, even while she knew that was all foolishness. What he did know was that she had heard the hideous tales told by the pitiful peasants fleeing the destruction of Chung-tu by these savages. And he could sense her turmoil.

The awkward moment was broken by a loud burst of voices from within the walled garden area. Subotai walked his mount past the Chinese woman and guided the animal into the wasted garden where his aide and Kua were exchanging animated words. The orlok halted beside the shouting, gesticulating men, raised his right leg over the horse's shoulder, and slid off onto the ground. The aide turned to him for support.

"Sir, this paddy-crawler is telling me the most Sky-crazed thing you have ever heard. If I understand the runty river rat, those women think we ought to teach them to ride horseback and then take them on south with us into the Sung territories. And where would we be if we used all the spare horses we have to mount them?"

Kua, in a jagged torrent of Chin and badly constructed Mongol, managed to interject, "Lord Orlok, the woman saved you from the wound. And she says the Sung lands are not far from here. She says that if we take them close enough, they will go on foot the rest of the way." The young, clear-eyed Chinese engineer looked hopefully at Subotai.

Subotai turned and saw the serious face of the Chinese woman as she came through the dilapidated gateway. He cast a critical eye on her gowned figure. "They cannot ride in those skirts. We will have to sort through our spare leathers and see if we can put them into our kind of clothing." With that, and feeling an onset of weakness, Subotai handed his reins to Kua and disappeared inside for another recovery sleep. Within, he barely made it to his bed-mat before the dizziness overcame him.

The hotness returned. The orlok grew delirious again and the Chinese woman stayed by his side for the better part of two days and a night, cooling him with wet cloths and gently forcing meat broth through his chapped lips whenever the opportunity presented itself, dozing in a corner of the dirty cubicle whenever he slept fitfully.

In the days of his recovery from that setback, Subotai amused himself by watching the Chin women clutch the saddles and manes of horses in terror as they bounced on the Mongol horses while their rude nomad mentors howled and shoved each other in glee. The women looked like children suddenly thrust into adult-sized clothing. The nomad pants and leather tops swamped the women even though they had tried to tailor them down to size.

Subotai sent two of his staff back to Chung-tu, charging them with silence concerning his intent, and on the same day started down country toward the Sung frontier regions with Kua, the women, and his devoted adjutant. Four days they rode roughly south-by-southeast. On the fifth day, Subotai and his party reached an area the women assured him they were familiar with and where they could, they said, quickly find and get aid and comfort from the peasant kin of one of the servant women.

The orlok sent Kua and his aide back toward Chung-tu and continued on with the women for the rest of that day and another. The following morning the serving women awakened him from his sleep before any light of dawn had stolen over the east. The evening before, they had untied their baggage rolls from behind their saddles and piled the saddles on the ground with the other gear when the horses were set out to graze. Now they stood silently beside Subotai with their possessions slung over their necks and shoulders. Subotai made his way unsteadily to a clear, murmurous brook some distance away, got slowly down on his hands and knees, and immersed his face in the cool water. Then he rinsed his mouth and smoothed the water droplets back across his long hair with both hands.

When he slowly rose and turned, he found that both the first light and the Chinese woman had appeared. In the Mongol clothing made for riding and movement she seemed somehow more free. The white rice-powder had been gone for weeks. Her lips and her eyelids were unpainted. Her lovely round face was clearly healthy in the gentle light. The new sun and her nearness lent a pellucidity to her contrasting black hair and the ivory cleanliness of her inviting skin. The high cheek bones and the sweet brown eyes made him thick with a desire that surged through him tidally in consonance with his pulse. His mouth felt dry, his temples throbbed with his need for this utterly feminine creature. He wanted to ask her to stay with him, go to the north with Lady Bourtai, anything to create some possibility that he could be with her again. Why had he sent Kua back to the army? He ground his teeth at his unthoughtful stupidity in thus depriving himself of the tongue to speak to this splendid woman.

She read his unspoken plea in the cat eyes, lowered her own eyes and shook her head negatively. The breeze ruffled some of her shining hair, making her agonizingly alluring to him. Then she turned abruptly and, accompanied by her women, began walking away from him, leaving him with the ponies they had ridden and the saddlery strewn on the ground.

With reluctance Subotai gathered up the saddles and, sweating from the exertion, managed to resaddle the women's horses and secure them to his own saddle by a lead line. As he slowly mounted, his intuition registered the finality of his parting with the Chinese woman. The pain of his wound blended with painful resignation to her departure. Without looking behind, he began to retrace their route.

By nightfall his entire body was aflame with the returned

fever. Dizziness compelled him to ride into a stand of trees, where he was barely able to dismount before he tumbled from the saddle. The fever rekindled, and with it, in the mystery of his being, his desire for the Chinese woman.

Subotai lay alone on the grassy ground in a state of sweetened pain, unsatisfied arousal flowing through him, intermingling with and diluting the festering pain and fever of the sword wound. In a drowzy delirium of hurting and lust, he imagined he could feel her ministering nearness.

He awoke in a warm dawn. Birds were flitting and chirping amongst the shrubs and the tree branches. He could hear the horses cropping the long grass nearby. The creak of saddle leather reminded him he had been too weak to unsaddle or hobble them.

He sat up, the wound dragging his movement, but the fever had broken and the clean air of the dawn filled his lungs and recharged him with returning vitality.

φ   φ   φ   φ

After the sack of Chung-tu, the orlok met with Temajin beyond the Great Wall. The cooling airs of the nearing autumn made their outdoor fire a mellow luxury. As usual, they had eaten quietly beside the blaze, appreciating the silent harmony they experienced together.

Wiping his mouth, Temajin looked with direct interest at Subotai's left side, contemplating the wound which caused the orlok to favor his left arm occasionally. "Kua, your Chin tale-teller, says you downed one of the best bladesmen in the emperor's cohort."

Subotai deflected this subject with a word muttered through a mouthful of horsemeat.

Stretching his long legs toward the fire, Temajin asked, "Can you carry one more campaign for me?" He took a sip of mare's milk, and went on. "Then, if you so desire, I swear I shall rest you for a whole sun-year. And what do you say to a woman? You live like a shaman, or one of those shaven-headed Buddhist monks down there." He gestured toward the distant wall in the south.

Subotai swallowed his bite but remained unanswering. Finally he turned his direct unblinking gaze on the Kha Khan. "You said another campaign?"

"You know I mean Koryu. Go in there and bloody them up.

Stop the intelligence and the supplies they send to the Chin." Subotai waited for him to go on. "And I hear it is all mountains. Don't go in there and chase flies up and down hills. If you cannot bring their main force to battle, take the harvest and burn their capital if you can. I forbid you to take the Chin engines with you. Garrison the Yalu with a tuman when you come out. Be back before the earth turns again."

Subotai laughed pleasantly and, for a change, quite softly. "And what are your orders concerning a woman, Lord?"

Temajin crinkled his brow to subvert his own grin. "Come back from Koryu with the substance of the Koreans and I pledge you my granddaughter, the daughter of Tului, my fourth son." Temajin's eyes twinkled mischievously. "She is only about fifteen or sixteen sun-years, as I recall, but fairly spits with Bourtai's likeness." Temajin sighed. "Too much like each other. They fight with each other worse than the Tartars. The Sky knows I must separate those two before it is too late."

φ   φ   φ   φ

The tumans behind Subotai forded and horse-swam the high Yalu River and began their descent into the Land of the Morning Calm. It was fall, the rice harvests in, and the Mongols found food for men and fodder for the steppe horses. Subotai had directed that all granaries were the property of the Kha Khan, and that army taps of grain would not exceed half of any store except as required in the press of battle situations.

To the Mongols and Chinese installed as regional administrators he spoke briefly on the code of the Yassa, the Law of the Kha Khan. They all knew that deviations from that code were punished in only one way—death.

Subotai led the Mongol force along the ancient invasion route that leads down the center of the Chosen Peninsula from the Yalu toward the city of Songdo. They met no resistance. Below the Yalu the country was one of misty morning vapors floating above green paddylands, steep mountains, and lovely Buddhist temples. Like the Chin, the Koreans were a people locked into a tradition, cemented in a culture.

The weather turned bitterly cold with great suddenness. Icy

winds and snow converted the idyllic autumn almost overnight into conditions very like those of the Mongols' native steppes in winter. Subotai and the Mongol tumans wrapped themselves in their sheep-skins and rode on.

The Mongol scouts had reported the existence of another great river, the Han, near the city of Songdo, not as deep or as swift as the Yalu but wide and now covered with ice in the unbreaking cold of the Korean winter. And the Koreans were anchoring a defensive line around the capital on this river.

The three tumans under Subotai streamed southward on across the frozen Imjin River well to the north, drawn on by the magnet of the capital city and its potential plunder. The Mongol scouts had seen few horses with the enemy army that had been dispatched from Songdo, and Subotai knew now that he would have to contend only with infantry, infantry of unknown quality. His reconnaissance patrols described them as turtles, meaning they were heavily armored troops. And probably very good in hand-to-hand combat and close weapon work.

The orlok knew full well that at least as many of the Koryu troops remained behind the inner city fortifications as had marched east along the Imjin to form the outer defensive perimeter. But the greater part of Songdo was unwalled, and Subotai, at Temajin's order, had brought none of the Chin siege engines, nor had he any inclination to build them even if he had had engineering troops with the necessary skills to do so.

His strategy was simple: first destroy the Korean army in front of the city approaches, then demand the city's surrender. If it did not capitulate, Subotai, carrying no illusions about the nature of war and the demands the Kha Khan had levied upon him, intended to avoid the city's strong points and instead burn the papery acres of the peasant houses and waste the land from Songdo to the Yalu.

He knew that his force was under constant surveillance from lookout stations on the tops of the rugged mountains. Intelligence of his every movement was being passed back to the Korean warlords by means of the glimmering signal fires he saw on the lofty, snow-covered peaks at night. But they would not see the orlok's last and decisive move.

In the dead of a frigid night, their horses' hooves squeaking and crunching in the crusted snow, the Mongols moved out of their camps, leaving the cooking fires to burn and the warming yurts to glow like great lanterns. One tuman slanted toward the west to cross the frozen Imjim River above the city and come up on the southwest of the enemy positions. Another tuman, under Subotai, moved toward the southeast so it could turn and attack the Koreans directly from the east. The third tuman, the Mangudai shock troops, rode straight down upon the Koreans and struck at the defensive line in a mounted frontal assault timed to occur just before the other two tumans appeared.

The Koreans bitterly contested the defensive works against the frontal attack which came upon them in the freezing darkness. Both sides suffered severe losses on the slippery breastworks, but the sudden flights of fire arrows launched into the Korean reserves by the two flanking tumans announcing the surprise assaults on their left and on their right sent the Koreans reeling in a mind-seizing shock. The clear, cold sunrise saw the forces of the Koryu streaming in panic back along the river toward Songdo.

Subotai unleashed his tuman orkhans to harry the fragmented Koreans with bow and lance. Few of the Korean troops managed to elude the precision of both the Mongol arrows and their mounted pursuers to escape into the ramshackle outskirts of Songdo. The orlok gave the unavoidable orders to drive the pitiful inhabitants out of the clustered slums. The unselective slaughter of the people of Songdo was almost an act of mercy, sparing them the inevitable agonies of frostbite, starvation, and the horror of a scene of unbridled death.

But the soldiers manning the inner fortifications of the death-cleared city ignored the Mongol envoys' offering of life for surrender. A hard cadre of Hwa Rang warriors manning the strong points threw back the Mongol probes against their works with desperate savagery, unsurpassed courage and weapon skill.

Mongol siege lines already encircled the trapped Korean soldiers, and Subotai ordered back the attempts to storm the Hwa Rang strong points. As the orlok was contemplating the Hwa Rang fires from his campfire site on the river bluff, an arrow courier galloped through the Mongol garrison, his saddle bells announcing him through the frosty air. Subotai saw the courier hesitate at a

Mongol campfire across the river, and, after apparently receiving directions from the soldiers around the warming fire, spur on across the glistening surface of the ice straight toward the command post.

When the courier pulled up and jumped from the saddle, the orlok saw the wood-and-hide tablet strapped to the light saddle, and saw, too, that the man was nearly collapsing from cold and fatigue. Scooping a cup of hot barley soup from his camp pot, Subotai squeezed it into the frostbitten hands.

After a few gulps of the broth, the man followed Subotai into the command yurt. Grimacing as though to loosen his mouth and jaws from the cold so that he could speak, he said, "Lord Orlok, you see I carry the Kha Khan's tablet of authority?"

"Aye, tied to your saddle."

The courier took another deep draught of the barley broth. "The Lord Temajin bids you disengage from Koryu. You are to bring your entire force—that is, disregard his earlier order to leave one division at the Yalu—and return to the Blue Lake."

The arrow-courier was starting to doze off in the relative warmth of the yurt, but Subotai slapped him along his lower spine to bring him from his drowsiness. "Does the Kha Khan mean for us to come immediately?"

"Yes, Lord Orlok."

Then Subotai let the trail-spent man fall into a deathlike sleep.

φ   φ   φ   φ

"The bastard slaughtered my envoys, Subotai!" Temajin spoke as if the orlok were entirely privy to all the goings-on of his newly initiated diplomatic enterprises.

"Who?"

The Kha Khan, surly from events and in his cups, did not hide his irritation at Subotai's flippant one-word question. "You know damn well who, and don't pretend that you do not. My arrow-courier has already informed me that you drained him of all he knew on the way back from Koryu."

Temajin paused for a drink of koumiss, an intoxicating beverage fermented from mare's milk, then resumed his tirade. "And even if he hadn't mouthed it, you have those Hindu mind tricks. Don't deny it. I've seen you literally wait for words or events that you already knew were forthcoming."

The orlok reached for the skin filled with koumiss which was hanging from the yurt frame and started to refill Temajin's cup, but the Kha Khan pushed it aside, causing some of the drink to slop on the yurt's felt carpet.

"And don't try that on me, either. I have also noticed that whenever you want your way, you try to liquor me up so that I will sleep on your advice." After another swallow of koumiss, Temajin spoke through a prolonged belch. "One of these times I may startle you by disagreeing with you when I wake."

"What about your promise of wiving your granddaughter to me?" Subotai asked to steer the Kha Khan's mind in a different direction.

"That will wait, too," Temajin said gruffly, "until we return from the Kharesmian lands. If we return."

Subotai dropped all pretense of lacking knowledge of the Kha Khan's plan to attack the Kharesmian Empire. "Juchi and Ogadai say you have already sent a dispatch to this..."

"Muhammad Shah," Temajin interjected.

"...and told him of your intent to make war upon him. Wouldn't it have been wiser to just do it and forgo any warning? Now they will be in arms and ready for us."

"You think like the Chin, Subotai. The Sky will determine the victor. I want the Kharesmian to know he has brought this upon himself."

Subotai wanted to remark that perhaps the rumors of the wealth of the Kharesmian cities had brought this upon the shah, but he saw that Temajin's mood would not bear it.

"While you were in Koryu, I set out the staging posts between the Blue Lake and the edge of the dry steppe north of their two great cities, Samarkand and Bokhara." Then Temajin asked thoughtfully, "In that great wandering of yours, Orlok, did you come across the lands of the Kharesmians?"

Subotai's gaze seemed to flicker inwardly for an instant. Then he answered, "Yes, easterly from Bokhara. I have never seen the cities, but our caravan came along the edge of their planted fields which seemed to stretch as far as the eye could see."

A little more thoughtfully now Temajin said, "But we have

the Celestial Mountains and their deep snows to cross before we see that steppe."

The orlok noted the season. It was midsummer, but the warmth would die quickly in a scant few weeks. Subotai rubbed his stubbled chin, then stated more than asked, "We march for Kharesmia soon, then."

"Yes. Juchi and Jebe—he's the orlok you nicknamed 'the Arrow'— are already scouting a way through. Incidentally, they are hauling bridges to get us across the mountain chasms and gorges. Kua and his troops constructed the spans, then disassembled them into portable units."

"And we follow the way they are pioneering?" Subotai asked.

"Aye—you will. Bring up with Juchi, but leave him in command and advise him closely. And see to it that that youngster of his, Batu, is blooded on this expedition."

Subotai waited a long moment, then asked, "And you, Lord?"

"I will take the right wing and go westerly, then cross toward the southern steppes through the Sarayan Mountains. My intent is for you and Juchi to lure the shah out of his walled cities to fight while I filter in behind him to block his retreat to the cities—as you did with the Chin when we breached the wall—then bring him to battle on the open steppe. I have no reason to believe that we will not be outnumbered even worse than we were in China."

Temajin appraised Subotai's relatively thin appearance, so different from his usual robust stockiness. "Are you ready to go down after Juchi and the Arrow? Or should you wait a moon before you ride?"

Subotai weighed the merits of delaying against the unknown span of time involved in making the traverse the Mongol armies were forging through the Tien Shien Mountains, which he knew rivaled in some places the Roof of the World in their dizzying heights. "The day after tomorrow. I'll bind myself like an arrow rider and start then. I assume that courier way-stations are being established to mark the trail?"

"Yes," Temajin answered. "I have been receiving reports almost every other day."

"And, Lord Orlok..." The words caused Subotai Bahadur to turn as he was leaving the Kha Khan's yurt. Temajin said nothing for a long moment, then the tension and the slight inebriation seemed to lift from his face. "Subotai, you have striven much for me and mine. And only the Sky knows what the outcome of this great war will be. Perhaps our campaigns will end before long. If our eyes do not meet at the mighty citadels of Samarkand or Bokhara..." Temajin hesitated. "...we shall be together as Sky-brothers when the Door of the North opens, when what we have come to do is at last complete."

φ   φ   φ   φ

"You have found no signs of any people living in this valley?" Subotai's question rang with incredulity.

"No, Lord Orlok."

Subotai again looked out over the sweep of lush, grassy meadows, the swift, sweet streams coursing through the grasses, and the clumps of evergreens which gradually thickened into forested slopes blanketing the heights which rimmed the pristine valley. Above the greenery and the cold water, the Celestial Mountains were white with a high chastity seemingly unsullied by men or animals.

The orlok breathed in the chill mountain air. Again he turned to the lone Mongol scout riding with him. "And no signs of herd animals or things grown by men?"

"Only the tracks of wild animals, Lord. Wildcats and deer aplenty, General."

"This is not the way Juchi, Batu, and Jebe came, then?"

The Mongol soldier was quiet with fear, but Subotai knew the answer. In this valley was none of the residue the tumans always left behind showing that a great nomad force has passed. The orlok spoke softly to the young soldier.

"I knew they did not come this way. We must have lost our way when we came through the pass up there." With a gesture that relieved the strain he pulled the young man's fur hat over his eyes and squinted toward the setting sun, its rays suddenly broken into bars of light as it touched the western heights of the Tien Shien peaks. "We must have drifted east of their trail by a mountain range or so."

The scout spoke up hopefully. "But I am certain that cut in the peaks is the same one Lord Juchi went through. He called it the Gate of the Bones because we found some human skulls up there."

"Then we'll go back up in the morning. I hope your trail coals are still smouldering. Let's fall to and build a night fire. There are snow tigers and snow leopards hereabouts, I'll wager. And when we leave this peaceful valley, son, there is only battle ahead of us."

In the cold autumn night beneath the snowbound Tien Shien, Subotai and the scout listened to the darkness. From high up came the faint, coughing snarl of a snow leopard hunting through his white domain. A great gray-white moon illuminated the valley, its reflection in the restless streams cutting the mountain meadows with dark silver.

Leaving the young soldier to feed the fire, Subotai strode away from the fire and climbed on up the slope above his camp. The wind gently slurred the night quiet in its subtle play among the pine tops. Subotai sat down and, in the manner he had been taught by the Solar Warrior, spent a long, deep meditation above the mystical, virgin valley.

Afterwards, he wondered on the great desires of his life: the blue-eyed Mursechen, for whom he still ached after all the swiftly passing years; his long-dead Gauri, whom he still reached for in the nights; and the haunting idea which the Solar Warrior had instilled within him, the strange, inner surging and mental reaching for the Living Mother Kali.

Someday, he thought, when this war is finished, he would come back to this valley. Perhaps with the wife Temajin had promised him. The winters were probably not too severe in the valley, and the hunting and the grazing would be good. Yes, a quiet and good place for an old man.

Had he thought that? Old? Once he had not thought it possible that he would grow old, but now he was already passing his middle years. Still, he smiled to himself, except for a slice or two, he was nearly as strong as he had been in his youth. And if he lived, if he got through again, and if—so many ifs, he thought. If—again— Kali Ma, if it were her will, he would come back to this valley and to peace.

φ　　　　φ　　　　φ　　　　φ

Juchi and Jebe had met with near disaster at the hands of Muhammad Shah when their relatively small force had come upon close to a hundred thousand Kharesmian Turks of the shah's host. And now the shah's spy network, moving clandestinely along the high Asian caravan routes, had divined the intentions of the Kha Khan.

Subotai and his eager young scout located the remnants of the Mongol spearhead on the down-slopes of the Tien Shien range where Jebe had been desperately trying to reorganize his decimated tumans. The orlok found the discouraged Juchi sulking, leaving the command duties entirely up to Jebe.

"How will I be able to face the Kha Khan?" Juchi's hair was matted and his face marked with fatigue.

"You have done nothing wrong," Subotai said, seeking to enhearten the young man. "Think, lad, unless I miss my guess, Lord Temajin will be nearing the western side of the Kharesmian lands. You have drawn the Turks out, and perhaps they think they have met the entire Mongol army." Subotai pulled Juchi to his feet. "Head up now, son. Give Jebe a hand. You engaged the enemy, and from what Jebe tells me of the odds against you, you nor anyone else could have done better. You are guilty of nothing but working your father's stratagem against the shah. But now we must be quick about it. We must be back at them with every man who can ride. Leave the wounded here. The ones who can will have to lay in firewood and forage for game for the others."

The orlok pushed Juchi back to his neglected duties. "Now, lad! We must keep them out on the steppe and away from their great cities. When they discover your father at their backs they will be somewhat less formidable than if they are manning the high walls in Samarkand."

In less than a day Juchi's revitalized contingent rode again, the orlok staying close to Juchi to stiffen his young spirit. With the other half of the regrouped point force, Jebe and Batu wheeled into the west. In three days they located the Kharesmians again, and began harassing their bivouacs with swift-striking ride-bys to shower the Turkish tents with naphtha-soaked fire arrows by night, and by day retreating before the hard-riding Turks.

Then Juchi, with Subotai and Jebe guiding Batu in his first

command, brought the troops together once again and, like steppe wolves, they cut off and nearly annihilated a major flank unit of the Kharesmians before the Turks could send reinforcements. Riding through the butchery left behind by the silent northern barbarians, the shah suddenly felt the chill of the distance between himself and the safety of his fortified cities, but before he could turn his forces around, Temajin, with the bulk of the Mongol army, smashed into the Kharesmian rear.

Muhammad Shah and perhaps two-fifths of his troops escaped the ghastly debacle on the steppe. They fled insanely southward, arriving at the gates of Bokhara only minutes ahead of the pursuing Mongols.

φ   φ   φ   φ

"The assault on the north wall was not to begin until daybreak." Subotai was hoarse from days of shouting over the battle din and from the smoky pall overlying the city. Mongol fire arrows were taking effect on the wooden and straw frames and rooftops in the poorer sections of the Moslem city. He could hear the sounds of combat on the Kharesmian wall above him.

"He's up there!" The Mongol soldier, a big black-bearded man, one of the Kha Khan's picked guards, was gesturing wildly, pointing up at the wall in an exasperation of confusion, indecision, and helpless concern.

Subotai dropped his reins and rubbed his smoke-smarting eyes, then spoke through a cough. "Who is up there?"

"The Kha Khan, Lord Temajin. When the boy was hit by a fire ball, he just went berserk. He grabbed one of the climbing ladders and started dragging it. Everyone who saw him joined in, and they all started up. I was knocked off by a boulder." Here the soldier seemed to choke up as he spoke. "The ladder fell back and broke after the Kha Khan and only a few others reached the top of the wall," he sobbed.

The orlok swept the scene with watering eyes. By the light of the flames now beginning to lick at the sky above the walls of Bokhara, he could make out a pair of burn-blackened little legs showing in broken awkwardness from beneath a bloodied and grease-stained leather raincloak which had been hastily thrown over a small figure. It was the boy, Tarmai, the much-loved great grandson of Temajin.

"Kali Ma," Subotai whispered to himself. Then, to the soldier shivering with shock, "Just what was the boy doing so close to the walls that a Moslem catapult shot could hit him?"

The soldier sat down heavily on the ground beside the little boy's corpse. He rubbed his temples brutally with the heels of his hands. "The Kha Khan brought him to the base of the walls—said he wanted the boy to become accustomed to the sound of war and the smell of a burning city—said something about our destiny, his destiny..." Here the man's voice trailed off.

"Get up, man! We've got to have another ladder for that wall. And muster an assault party." Subotai was walking his horse nearly onto the soldier as he urged him to action.

Others had seen the ladder fall beneath Temajin and were moving more swiftly than Subotai. A group of Mongols and Tartars ran past the orlok with a scaling ladder, followed by a growing body of men who seemed to sense what was happening. Then the giant Lariktai Noyon, Temajin's boyhood and boon companion, thundered up, took in the situation in a single, commanding glance, and spurred his great war-horse after the haphazard assault group. Subotai rode on behind the imposing silhouette of the huge Mongol general mounted on his immense animal.

The scaling ladder had not even touched the stonework before Lariktai was scrambling upward, his heavy, curved and wide-bladed Chin headsman's sword held point up in his right hand as he climbed. The orlok was so close behind that Lariktai's booted feet kicked him in the head several times on his way up.

Near the top of the ladder, Lariktai paused to look down at the orlok and shout, "You jab me in the rump one more time with that damned fancy sword of yours, Subotai, and you will be the first one I take care of on the walls."

"I'll have to watch that," Subotai yelled to the ascending feet above him, but it flashed through his mind how easily Lariktai held in only one of his great paws a Chinese headsman's sword. And not only hold it. Lariktai had demonstrated many times how effectively he could use it with both grace and skill.

The first of the hastily forming group of Kharesmian defenders at the wall-top were slaughtered by a single, hellish, scythelike sweep of Lariktai's titanic war sword. Subotai smelled the ugly gore as it spattered over his steel-capped fur hat, and felt its grisly warmth as it slid down his open-throated leather shirt. It greased and slimed the metal and laquered-leather studs armoring his leather clothing and greased the ladder rungs so that he almost lost his footing.

Then they were atop the battlements. Even in his mad dash to keep up with the amazing Lariktai, Subotai was struck by his first sight of the great Moslem city spread before them, lit by a russet dawn and by the fires now leaping wildly from roof to roof. Slim minarets shone with both an eye-entrancing coherence of peaceful sunlight and the gaudy reflection of the lapping flames climbing into the morning sky.

Lariktai still in the lead, they sprinted toward the clashing sounds of a melee somewhere west of their point of ascent. Rounding one of the towered defense posts which studded the walls, they ran into the rear of a Kharesmian press which was hemming Temajin against a stone balustrade. The Kha Khan and the few who had been able to follow him into this maw of death were fighting furiously. Only the Kha Khan and two or three others were still on their feet, entrenched behind a growing semi-circle of Kharesmian dead.

Hardly breaking stride, Lariktai swathed his way through enemy backs to the Kha Khan's side. So swift was Lariktai's action that Subotai had to twist around and leap over bodies which hesitated as they fell because their owners were not entirely certain if they were dead or alive.

More Kharesmians swarmed in behind to overpower the Mongols, though, and minutes later there was only a quartet maintaining the desperate defense: the tall Kha Khan, the formidable and now blood-streaked Lariktai, the broad and stocky Subotai, and one remaining imperial bodyguard already grievously wounded in the upper thigh and groin. And even as Subotai noted the discouraging tally he saw the guard sink down on one knee, his head nodding off sleepily as his lifeblood drained away.

"We can't stay here," Subotai yelled with a quick glance at Temajin and Lariktai.

"You are right, little brother," Lariktai responded for himself and Temajin.

Subotai backed another step toward Temajin, the blue sword, which he held in a two-handed grip above his right shoulder, seemed to disappear in a down-diagonal stroke which took off a Kharesmian's right hand and sent an enemy sword clattering on the stone. The Kharesmian went down on both knees, shivering with shock, as Subotai's backhand stroke all but severed the man's head from his body.

A moment later the Kharesmians drew back. In the brief respite Subotai yelled hoarsely, "We have got to push them toward our people coming up after us." He added quickly, "It's better than going like a rabbit with a ferret down its hole."

Lariktai nodded, and the two of them leaped at the surrounding Kharesmians, dealing death with the ease of spring butchers among lambs. The Kharesmains fell back before the combined onslaught of the gory giant with the sword more than twice as large as it should be and the stocky devil with the blue blade. The Kha Khan moved up from behind, still in his murderous rage of grief over the boy.

Like three creatures from hell itself, they hewed and thrust and spun and slew, the orlok a dazzling flame, his mind shocked by the combat into one of the highest states of consciousness he had ever experienced, his feet gliding like the Solar Warrior's to negate the movements of enemy swords and maces. The blue samurai sword glistened in the climbing sunlight of the morning with the fresh-drawn red dew of life. Even with the sun in their eyes and hopelessly outnumbered, the three were gaining ground. Temajin's natural skill and his almost supernatural anger at the death of the boy, Lariktai's overpowering physical presence, and the orlok's near-mystical mastery of the slash and thrust of the contest brought them slowly but inexorably toward the Kharesmian guard tower.

Then the crash of arms was drowned in an uproar as the main Mongol assault opened against the north wall of Bokhara. Subotai dragged Temajin down as a wave of catapulted boulders sheared across the wall-top. Following the catapult barrage with nerveless closeness, the invaders swarmed onto the wall and overwhelmed the late-arriving Turkish reinforcements that had been sent hastily from the east wall where the main attack point had been expected.

φ   φ   φ   φ

Only days later did the Mongols learn of the flight from Bokhara of Muhammad Shah and his son, Jelal ad-Din. Their escape cast a shadow over the celebration of victory on the steppe and the capture of Bokhara, and over the welcome report of Tului's conquest of Samarkand.

Gazing out across the vast, well-irrigated fields, Subotai was struck with the memory of how Gauri had loved gardening her little melon patch, and the moist, lush satisfaction of the fruits it had produced under the hot sun of the Indus Valley.

"But horses and flocks cannot feed on those melons, nor graze among those tangles." Temajin spoke as though trying to explain a simple fact to a backward child. The Kha Khan ran his powerful fingers through his thick, gray-streaked brown hair. "Subotai, you would have us dismount and live as these soft Kharesmians do. We know nothing of their ways. The Sky has given us their lands for our flocks and our women. Have you forgotten the dryness of the northern pastures? Or the hunger and sickness we went through?"

The orlok did not respond. Temajin turned his mount back toward the Mongol camp outside the smoking shell of Bokhara.

"Subotai, you must obey me in this. Let their crops waste as we have wasted Bokhara and Samarkand. Then our flocks will have new pastures and the young people will be fed."

Subotai knew his pleas had been useless. He guided his mount up to Temajin's right side. The Kha Khan looked sideways at him and went on. "And we cannot tarry here. We must take up the trail of the shah and his son before they are lost to us. You know as well as I that it will not be finished until we put an end to the both of them."

They dismounted at the Mongol yurts pitched below the east wall. Waiting by the largest of the campfires were the orkhans, leaders of the Tartar, Merkit, and Kurait tumans. The Kha Khan's sons were there as well: Ogadai, Juchi, Jagadai. Only the fourth son, Tului, was missing. He remained at Samarkand supervising the systematic looting of that other conquered Kharesmian city. Batu, the son of Juchi, was standing near his father. Batu had shown

up well in this campaign, his first, although Subotai could discern
no hardening of his character to indicate what his nature would be
in maturity when his wild youthfulness was worn off.

At Temajin's signal the officers sat down on the ground. Water
and wineskins were circled among the group. Courtesy demanded
silence until the Kha Khan had spoken.

"You all know what must be done. Our scouts have found signs
of mounted military troops leaving the refugee trails south of here.
Two groups. Apparently one turned east and the other group continued on toward the southwest. I need them dead." Temajin's
greenish eyes had a strange deepened light in them which chilled
even Subotai. "I want the world to know what passes when I make
war. When that is known, then our task will be easier. Befriend
those who submit. Slay those who resist."

The commanders waited in dead silence. Temajin looked in
Subotai's direction. "Orlok, take Jebe and Batu and six tumans and
ride down the Kharesmians who went westerly. You started that way
once before, years ago, as I remember."

"Yes," Subotai replied, "but I never quite got to the Kipchaks,
whoever or wherever they may be."

Subotai's mind warmed with memories of his gypsying youth
on the Caspian steppes, and he thought again of Mursechen, her
eyes, her blondeness. Then he began passing on to the others the
trail lore he had garnered in his search for her, his memory sweeping
across the vastness he had experienced in his travels through regions
all the way to the edge of the black earth in the far western steppes.

"Muhammad Shah is more than likely heading toward Persia,"
Subotai concluded. "He will probably seek refuge among any kinsmen he might have there. And if he has no kin in Persia, well, they
are all Moslems like the Kharesmians, so he will likely find all the
succor he needs, maybe even be able to raise a new army against
us." Subotai paused thoughtfully, then he continued. "But, even as
far as the Sea of the Ravens, which you have all heard of, they are
Moslems, and even into India."

Subotai guessed the Kha Khan's intent and, meeting his eyes,
said, "If you follow the band that went easterly, they will attempt
to reach the Indus River, the western reaches of India where there
are now many Moslem warlords who might protect them. Lord

Temajin, it will be very dangerous to follow them farther if they once succeed in crossing the Indus."

Temajin listened with half an ear as he silently appraised Subotai and the other orlok, Jebe Noyon. Temajin had never spoken it to any man but he knew instinctively that the heavily built man now drinking from a waterskin—Subotai Bahadur—was the greatest general in all the world.

The younger general's youthful and arrestingly handsome appearance contrasted with Subotai's plainness of dress and somewhat heavy but very masculine appearance. Jebe, the Arrow, as he was sometimes called since Subotai had given him the nickname, was richly garbed. Except for the traditional leather trousers, his clothing represented a cross-section of the haberdashery in Mongol conquests: sable cloak from the northern Tartars, a blue-and-gold sashed shirt from the empire of the Chin much like a shortened surcoat, silver girdle belt, and silvered sword in a bejeweled scabbard from the Kharesmian empire. Golden coins and finely crafted pins and bangles replete with light-catching precious stones adorned the Arrow's fur hat, which was peaked with a steel helmet. A heavy, studded, leather drop fell behind the helmet to protect his neck.

The Arrow was nearly as tall as the Kha Khan. His hair and flowing, luxuriant mustaches were solid, unrelieved black. Intelligent brown eyes were set within the lean, narrow and pale-skinned face. The almost perfectly symmetrical face was subtly good-natured, but totally without seriousness. It lacked the gravity and the deep mystical eyes the Kha Khan saw when he shifted his gaze back to Subotai.

Subotai had set his helmeted, fur Mongol headgear aside. His stomach was lean now from campaigning, but Temajin could see that the orlok might drift into obesity in later life. Like Jebe he wore leather riding pants. And as the sun rose higher, Subotai slipped off his lambskin vest, opened the throat of his silk shirt, and untied a cord which wrapped the shirt about his belly and pulled the overlap of the shirt apart for ventilation, revealing his broad upper chest. The orlok's hair had thinned slightly from its youthful fullness, but its color was a rich mixture of gray, black, and russet tones. Under the open sky, his eyes, lighter now than in his young manhood, were washed by the sun to a uniform blueness with little trace of the gray they had shown in years before.

The two orloks, so different in age and appearance, were yet, Temajin thought, like father and son, especially in the way that Subotai had recognized Jebe's talent early on and had tutored and promoted the young officer.

Temajin sometimes wondered about Subotai's deep and secretive nature. He knew of the orlok's continuing obsession with the lost Mongol woman—what was her name? Subotai had told him once, but he had forgotten. He wondered how any man could be so foolish over a mere woman, especially a man like Subotai.

Temajin looked again at the Arrow, and chuckled inwardly as he mused. Now Jebe, he never hesitates to take his pick of the women when the fight is finished. Temajin would never understand that story he had heard about Subotai and the Chin woman. Damned attractive, Chin women, in their slant-eyed way. After she saved Subotai's life—and she had other motives than just saving her skin, he was sure—Subotai had given her escort to the Sung frontiers. But what those other motives of hers might be, well, only the Sky was privy to things like that. The Kha Khan knew that women were a mystery to themselves, let alone to a man, however wise he might be.

Temajin took many women, but he would ever be married only to Bourtai. He thought now of her, that blending of folly and wisdom, silk and steely courage that Bourtai was. Even now she held the grasslands for him in the north with only women and crippled or aged men. If not yet in title, she was in fact already the Empress of the Chin lands. The handful of Chinese administrators Temajin had allowed to remain in their posts had been quick to discover Bourtai's talent for government and no-nonsense decisiveness. They trekked constantly to the steppes where Bourtai held her impromptu courts, seeking her guidance and intercession in matters that would ultimately preserve Chinese civilization.

Temajin knew about this, as Bourtai knew of his profligate sexual behavior. Though they shared a yurt whenever he returned to the Blue Lake, Bourtai had turned him out of their bed.

And the time was near when he must designate heirs. Only the sons of Bourtai would follow in the Kha Khanate. He would send Bourtai to Chung-tu when he finished with the Kharesmians, and have her recognized as empress to prepare the way for his successors. Face, as the Chin put it, would be saved for both of them in this way. And there would be no more opposition from the only quarter that mattered, from Bourtai, to his fancy for women, especially the courtesan, Houlon, whom he intended to take into his yurt when the empress was gone to her Chinese followers.

φ φ φ φ

At first light the two orloks led their tumans south-by-south-west away from the death and ruin of Bokhara. Temajin, departing with the bulk of the Mongol army a short time later, went easterly from the destroyed husk of the once-proud Kharesmian city.

Subotai and Jebe knew that an immense desert region lay ahead, its reaches entirely unknown to them. The baggy stomach linings of slaughtered camels had been hastily converted into makeshift water bags for the expedition. If these gave out, blood would be drawn from the living horses, just enough to keep men from succumbing to the craze of thirst.

The Kha Khan's briefing had been terse: run to earth Muhammad Shah or Jelal ad-Din, whichever was in the southwest trailing group; slay him if his capture proved impractical; go as far and as long as it would take but do not return until the thing was done.

Two days out, the Arrow and Subotai separated their commands to ease the demand on the skimpy grazing and the insignificant, shallow, and too-few watering holes they found in the great aridity of the baking plain before them. Contact was casually maintained between them by rotating scouting parties which would ride out from one column, reconnoiter the area ahead of the line of march, and return to the other to report.

The heat astonished the Mongols, accustomed to the coolness of the northern steppes. It blasted into them and their horses, soaking them. To Subotai the heat brought back the sweet and the painful memories of India, but to some of the shaggy steppe ponies and Mongol soldiers it brought death.

In a week they came upon the edge of salt flats that stretched to the horizon in the south. Subotai fixed himself against the stars and shifted the direction of the tumans westward, guessing that the refugee Kharesmians would avoid the salt and the thirsting death which awaited any man or any army foolish enough to venture upon it.

The trail of the Kharesmians appeared and faded during the weeks that followed. In the north of Persia, the Mongols scattered part of an enormous Moslem army and rode by the bulk of that sluggish host. The Mongols were startled to find that the Kharesmians had not taken refuge with the Persians, but instead had fled on through hills and desert to the west.

Then, on a sweltering afternoon, the tumans came upon a vast, salty expanse of water. Subotai recognized it, but to be sure, he queried by signs a fisherman his men had captured by the shore. When the man had signed that this was the Sea of the Ravens, and when the orlok had determined that the coast curved away into the north on either hand, he reckoned he had arrived at the most southerly point of the great, land-locked sea.

Then the fisherman startled Subotai by speaking in the trail tongue. "Are you the Mongols who pursue the Turks from Bokhara?"

Subotai did not try to conceal his surprised interest, but quickly responded in his rusty trail talk. "Aye. If you can send us in the right direction you will have more than gold. You will have the gratitude and the protection of the great Kha Khan, Temajin."

The fisherman was poor, his lean, nut-brown frame and his scarred and hardened hands testament to the grinding struggle that had been his life, but his eyes were clear and their brown depths were heavy with character and with his religion.

"I carried the Lord Muhammad Shah out to an off-shore island only yesterday. He died there before afternoon ended." The Moslem paused and looked into Subotai's eyes, now silvered and blued with the reflections of the Caspian light. "But before he died, he bade me return and await your coming. He gave me words which are for the great general who conquered China. He said that one would be called Subotai, and that the word along the caravan trails was that this general was a just and selfless man."

Subotai knew that the fisherman knew, but he said the words. "I am Subotai."

The Moslem pursed his thirst-cracked lips, and Subotai sent an aide scurrying for a water bag with a silent directive from his eyes and a slight nod. Subotai took the water bag from the man's mouth when the Moslem choked on the flow. He let the fisherman cough, then handed the bag to him again.

The fisherman wiped his mouth gratefully with his ragged sleeve, then squinted at the orlok. "The Lord Muhammad Shah said to tell you that you will die as alone as he was dying. He said,..." and here the man felt for words in the childish trail vocabulary which would carry the appropriate meaning, "...that One whom you know appeared to him and told him that you will lose yet another son." The thin, brown man fell silent.

"Was there anything else?" Subotai asked.

"No, Lord, except that he said the Mongols would probably kill me." The fisherman looked away out over the Caspian waters with resignation.

The orlok drove out the sudden shudder of memory of the crackling funeral pyres in that hot night of India so long ago, but the pain orbited on the periphery of his consciousness. He swallowed hard and turned to his aide. "Free this poor devil. Is his boat hereabouts?"

"Yes, sir. It's down the shore a way."

Subotai looked at the pitiful yet quietly dignified man. Without the wars and the Kha Khan, perhaps his own life would have been much like this fisherman's, except that he would be following his dwindling flocks through drought and blizzard in his ragged lambskin until...until...well, it all ended the same way. Every desire he entertained, every imagined pleasure of love or companionship or safety, that greatest lust of all, ended in the same way, didn't it? But to be immune from that end, to be safe, to know that that dark inevitability lying at the end of every man's life could be denied or avoided or—something.

Then Subotai roused from his momentary reverie. He knew instinctively that the Moslem fisherman was thoroughly honest. Facing his aide, he said, "Bring me half a hand of Kharesmian silver." But then he remembered the harassment he continuously suffered from the Kha Khan's Chin paymaster over the accounts and corrected himself. "No, see Kua for a couple of silk shirts."

The Mongol aide rolled into the saddle and spurred away from the beach. Subotai went to his own mount and drew out a small necklace of gold coins strung on a delicate silver chain, walked back to the fisherman, and handed the chain to him. "Part of its value," he told the man, "is for the burial of the Lord Muhammad Shah. You may keep any residuals when you trade the rest of the coinage."

The fisherman got up from the sandy beach as Subotai's aide galloped up holding a handful of Chinese silk. "No shirts, General," the aide said, "but here is a length of raw silk."

Subotai took the material and gave it to the Moslem, whose astonishment shone through the dignity he had maintained throughout the interview, and gestured him to be on his way. Now the orlok's mind slipped again to the final words of the dead shah. "Another son..." Perhaps, Subotai thought, perhaps he had meant that symbolically. As a Mongol corps commander, an orlok, he had many sons in his soldiers. But the shah's warning was specific and ominous. Long ago it had been the warning of the shaman, and now the Shah. Damn them both. His sons were already dead, already dead.

φ   φ   φ   φ

Kua half turned in his saddle and raised his arm in salute to Subotai and Jebe the Arrow. The Chin engineer rode beside the dust-raising, slow-trundling carts and wagons which bore the timbers and lines of the dismantled Mongol siege engines. They had brought the ponderous gear from Bokhara and Samarkand, following, with staggering difficulty, the route of the reckless advance of the two orloks and their tumans across Persia. They had caught up with the Mongol army on the southern shore of the Sea of the Ravens, and accompanied it to the Caucasus. Now they were headed back, retracing the excruciating route.

And this time, the carts were even heavier laden, carrying, along with the siege engines, the weapons, the mail coats, the helmets, and the saddlery taken from the chivalry of Georgia.

The courage of the Georgian knights had been their undoing. Subotai had led the Mongol tuman probing into the Georgian valleys while Jebe delayed with the bulk of the cavalry behind Subotai's reconnoitering screen. The valiant Georgian knights knew only one method of combat: linear. Subotai's lighter, mounted bowmen, spurring fearlessly close to the big, heavily armored mounted knights, had lured them piecemeal into close, savage pockets of hand-to-

hand fighting. And the Georgians, exulting in their quick domination of the combat, had broken out of their self-supporting little
clusters into wild, pell-mell pursuit when the Mongols, feigning a
loss of heart for the bloody little battles, had fled before the measured
gallop of the huge Georgian warhorses, keeping always just beyond
the weapon range of the knights.

When the knights were well strung out, Jebe's ambush, launched
by Mongol detachments with heavy lances against both flanks of
the slow-maneuvering Georgians, had whip-sawed both ends of the
Georgian column. Then Subotai's fleeing squadrons had faced around
and with bow and saber downed, one by one, the knights who now
had no choice but to fight singly and without coordination. So few
were the Georgian survivors who had lumbered away on their ponderous and weary warhorses that the orloks did not even bother to
pursue.

And now Kua with his Chin contingent, at Subotai Bahadur's
order and with the arms and booty won from the Knights of Georgia,
was retracing his tortuous way back to the main Mongol force
encamped near the ruined Kharesmian cities. The orlok had requested
and received permission from the Kha Khan to continue on along
the western side of the Caspian Sea toward the north.

The barrier of a steep mountain range confronted the Mongol
tumans. Deep white gorges, sprayed with plunging mountain rivers
and nearly vertical slopes, constrained their line of march into plodding, serpentine trails of ascension and slippery, slow descents. Even
in the midst of summer, snow patched the stone-littered passes and
mountain spines.

Subotai breathed his mount under a noonday sun. For the first
time in nearly a moon-cycle he could see the blue sweep of the Sea
of the Ravens lying northeast in the distance below the windswept
summit in the Caucasus mountains. And directly ahead a seemingly
unending steppe spread into the northern and northwestern horizons.
From the altitude at which Subotai was now viewing them, the flat
yellow-brown plains seemed undistinguished by any relief of elevation or contrasts of color.

The Arrow had already dispatched reconnaissance patrols down
toward the steppe. If the early and mild fall weather held, the Mongol
columns would continue on northward, keeping close to the western

shores of the salt sea.

By nightfall most of the Mongol force was encamped in the northern foothills of the Caucasus range. But the orlok, turning troubled eyes into the darkening north, gave a quick order to cold camp; the long-range patrols were still out and an ominous pre-monition gripped his mind. The great steppe, which had seemed so inviting and empty after the strenuous crossing of the rugged mountains, suddenly seemed alien and dangerous. And the mild weather in the high mountains would surely worsen before many more days passed, which would make retreat back through the mountains impossible.

Subotai's mental state denied him any sleep that night. He spent the time wandering from guardpost to guardpost, checking bivouac security. But the night passed quietly, and, after the cool of night had freed the dew, morning was a blossoming light-shower which glistened off the dampened bushes of the Caucasus foothills and the unmeasured reaches of the steppe before the Mongol tumans.

φ   φ   φ   φ

"We were scouted, Lord Subotai. Riders like ourselves. They had several mounts for each man, and they spelled their horses by shifting from animal to animal, as we do. They bolted as soon as they saw us, and our own horses were so spent we could not come up with them." The Mongol scout paused to drink from a water bag, then went on. "And there is more salt water," he swung his arm to show the direction, "off to the west. Water as wide as the Sea of the Ravens."

Subotai dismissed the senior scout and his reconnaissance squad. He and the Arrow sat unspeaking by their campfire throughout the late afternoon until the snap-thrown sparks flared brightly in the descending night air. The ominous feeling which Subotai had first felt weeks before in the northern foothills of the Caucasus Mountains still hovered in his mind. With the Caucasus range snow-locked behind him, he was leading the Mongol tumans on to the north, always keeping the waters of the Caspian in sight to his right, but an early winter steppe blizzard had forced them into winter camp.

At dusk, both men got up and withdrew into the small, light garrison-yurt they shared as quarters and as a command post. Jebe carried a brand in from the outside fire and lit an oil-pot. The silent, low-hovering flame from the oil quickly heated the yurt's interior and lit the black felt walls.

Then Jebe voiced the thought that dominated both their minds. "We had best keep our patrols active and as far out to the north and west as we can reach."

Subotai nodded in agreement. "Aye, there is a presence out there. I shall be glad when the warm wind comes to dry the steppe. Then we will turn east along the north shore of the Sea of the Ravens and trek back toward the Blue Lake."

Gray winter weeks followed with a freezing sameness which made the dismal days interminable. To defeat the morbid dreariness of cold inactivity in the camp, Jebe and Subotai often joined the hunting and foraging parties and the far-ranging patrols.

The frigid darkness of yet another winter night was inking the background of the Mongol cooking and warming fires when the Arrow, returning with one of the patrols which constantly ranged into the northwest, pulled his mount up in front of the command yurt where Subotai was rousing himself from a nap beside the oil-pot. The tall young orlok strode into the yurt, took off his sword and silver girdle, and tossed them carelessly aside. His body and clothing carried the chill of the outer air.

"We saw what looked like smoke all along the far line where the Sky weds the land," he said, "but it was beginning to blow up a blizzard." The Arrow strained at one of his damp boots, freed it, and thrust a bare white foot toward the warmth of the oil-pot.

Subotai saw the haggard lines of fatigue and the winter gauntness of Jebe's face accented by the firelight. "Did you send anyone on to scout?"

The Arrow did not answer immediately. He drew his forearm across his brow in a motion of cold weariness. Then he said as he lay back on the felt carpeting of the yurt, "No. We were at the limit of ourselves and the ponies. We will have to send another party out to see." Then the young general was gone in blessed and warm rest after nearly two days and a night in the saddle.

Subotai covered the Arrow, stepped out into the night-snow, and strode through the concentric arrangement of yurts to the one where the evening guard mount was forming. The orlok summoned the watch commander and directed that the guard be mounted on the earthworks thrown up around the bivouac. If the normal watches were put out in the storm and on foot, the night and the blizzard would yield only lost and frozen dead men.

When the blizzard passed he would send riders out to investigate the mysterious smoke, but until then he would rest the tumans as much as possible. The haunting premonition seized him again. Somehow, the orlok could not construct it in conscious thought, but he knew without thinking it that the great climax, the highpoint of his life, was upon him. For the first time he feared the future, but he knew the spiraling eddy of time which moved his life would carry him to it, fear or not.

After the blizzard had passed, the steppe lay like a carpet of gray dust, the new snow's luster rescinded by the unbroken, sunless Sky. Subotai dispatched a long-range penetration party of hand-picked riders to scout the distant columns of smoke the Arrow had seen before the snowstorm. Then he waited out the anxious days until the scouts at last galloped back into the Mongol camp.

The scouts brought back captives who were dull but cooperative. From them and from the scouts, Subotai eventually learned that news of the swiftness and the formidable prowess of the Mongol army had drifted with the steppe winds to places along the Dneiper River and to the gold-domed city of Kiev, and that a great army had gathered against his tumans. The army they faced was the army of the Rus. Subotai knew now that most of the great princes of Russia had set aside their hereditary feuds and quarrels to unite, at least temporarily, against the Mongol peril. It was hard for Subotai to learn exactly how large and where this army was since all the verbal reports were couched in awed superlatives.

On a gray, brutally cold afternoon, Subotai set out alone, taking only the blue sword, his bow and one extra horse. Travelling briskly in the westward direction indicated by his scouts, he crossed the upper reaches of the River Khalka three days later. For six more days he rode on, stopping at night to rest. Each night he scavenged for dried dung and whatever other fuel he could find for a small fire to save himself from the agonies of frostbite.

On the day that it did not get dark, he knew he had reached his goal. The gray Sky usually hid the brief daily passage of the winter sun so that the exact time of sunset could not be determined, but he had the sun-stone, the trapper's gift to him, to help him maintain his sense of direction as he rode. But on this day, a mighty illumination reflecting from the low-hanging ceiling of clouds continued throughout the hours of night. He turned to his right and rode to a just visible cluster of low hillocks about a league away.

He grew extra watchful, keeping the blue sword in hand, for surely the Rus would have set lookouts and even pickets this close to their army. He left his animals at the base of the rise and went on foot to the top. He forgot the unrelieved cold and his gnawing hunger when he saw the gigantic Russian encampment below him, the source of the artificial illumination. North and south as far as he could see stretched a panorama of great and small campfires, so numerous that, even from Subotai's vantage point, they lit up the surrounding land.

He was too far away to discern many details of the huge garrison, but the human smells mixed with the taunting smell of cooking meat carried to his sensitive nomad nostrils. His years of contact with the higher cultured, bathing peoples of the Indus and eastern Caspian regions made the foulness the wind carried to him repugnant, almost sickening.

He sat down cross-legged on the snowy ground and let his eyes scan and his mind roam freely across the immensity of the Rus army. His first conscious reaction was that this was another great, sluggardly army which could be avoided, simply ignored. After all, Muhammad Shah was dead; it was time to take the tumans, or what was left of them, back to the Kha Khan.

When he had absorbed as much as he could from the scene, he cautiously retraced his route back down the slope, then stepped onto his pony and turned away from the Rus firelight. He would leave the tumans where they were in winter camp, and perhaps he would send envoys to the Rus princes with the message that the Mongols had no warlike intentions or designs on the black earth of the Russian steppes, and that he would depart in the spring.

φ   φ   φ   φ

"I hope they were dead when the Rus did that to them." Jebe's voice had a sickened tinge in it. Subotai's jaws were set in a hard line which the Arrow had never seen before. Although Jebe, like the others, had heard the stories of Subotai's legendary fighting spirit, he had thought the older orlok above any display of anger.

Subotai drew in and exhaled several deep breaths before he spoke. "They weren't." He breathed noisily again. "I thought..." The words trailed off. "...flayed them alive, both of them."

Jebe looked into the orlok's eyes. They were lit with an inner anger like a steady, undiminished light shining forth from precious stones.

Subotai looked again on the bloody rags lashed to the backs of steppe ponies—all that was left of the envoys. "I want every man in every tuman from every tribe to see this. I want no questions when we ride against the Rus."

The orlok retired into his command-yurt, sharpening the blue sword to vent the furnace of his fury. But the day-long sounds of the mounted Mongol warriors filing past the obscene man-carcasses laid on the snow added to the storm seething in his blood. He tried to meditate but he could not gain control over his rampaging emotions. He noticed that his body seemed angered all over, his entire being a blazing sense of fury. And the strength of his rage carried him into a near-trance state. When Jebe and one of his Mongol soldiers entered the yurt, they were unnoticed by the orlok. And the Arrow, knowing something of the deep nature of the senior orlok, directed the soldier in a whisper to be seated. Then they waited in silence for the orlok to again take notice of his surroundings.

When Subotai finally stirred, he turned his eyes immediately on Jebe's as though expecting his presence in the yurt. Jebe nodded to the soldier, who stood up. "Lord Subotai, the Rus have broken camp. They are on the march. We picked up signs of their scouting parties just to the west of the River Khalka, then we located their columns about two days' ride from the river."

Subotai's jaw muscles rose and fell. It was the wrong place, nothing felt right, but his way was set. He managed to speak calmly to the soldier. "Son, get yourself and the rest of the troops some hot meat, then sleep for a while." Then he said for the benefit of the soldier and the Arrow, "Let's have all the available food cooked tonight. I want all but the guard mounts to sleep inside the yurts tonight, and I want every man fed as much as he wants. You," he gestured toward the scout, "get your scouting parties out before daybreak." Suddenly he felt more positive. "Jebe," he smiled at the Arrow, "we will move at first light. Leave the auxiliaries to break and pack the camp. They are to take our baggage out to the steppe just north and west of the Sea of the Ravens. Send the Tartar tuman with them. They are to remain in contact with us by means of arrow riders, but they are to wait northwest of the salt water."

His sudden revival of confidence and purpose was contagious. Jebe and the Mongol scout left the yurt briskly. And that night the cooking fires sizzled with spitted game. Along with the hot rations, each man received his trail issues of dried meat and milk curds. Before the tumans bedded down for the night the larders were nearly depleted.

φ   φ   φ   φ

It must be the third day. Or is it the fourth? Subotai's questions to himself were blurred in a brew of pain and deadly, sapping exhaustion such as he had never known before. How can they be so strong? How can it last so long? His mind spun with a fatigue that seemed to sicken and dizzy him. They are like stone; the arrows rattle off them; they strike down my soldiers, horse and rider with a single stroke; they bleed but they do not fall. If only it would snow, then he would know what to do.

He tried to focus the wavering cloud of weariness in his mind. If he could only trap the tiredness, then he could move it away like a hooded falcon on a cadge, and then he would know what to do.

For the first time, Subotai knew gut-weakening, uncontrollable, will-stealing fear. He fought to conquer his growing awe for these Russian warriors, for their powerful physiques, their wild courage, their ugly, vibrating war cries. Their fierceness turned his insides watery and raw with terror. His mouth was foul with the foamy retch of his fear. He looked to the gray Sky, but it was not the familiar, light-sheeting Sky of the northern lights. If only it would snow, then he would know what to do—he thought it again and again as though he were incapable of any other thought. He locked and wrapped his mind in the meaningless hope.

And in this way his own panic was stayed. The Mongol soldiers, now drawn off the massed Russian positions by the whistling signal arrows Subotai had ordered, looked back at their great general and saw only what they had always seen—the implacable, unrevealing face gazing at the battlefield. It brought back the veteran confidence of men who had never known anything but victory.

Why had he attacked? And then he remembered; he attacked because he couldn't draw them out. His mind cleared for a few brief moments. What had the Solar Warrior said? "You must turn the enemy's power back into himself. The strength of a direct attack is subordinate to the power of the circling reply." The orlok was suddenly irritable with his thought. The power of the circle! Well, it hadn't worked this time because whenever he tried for their flanks the Rus always moved that heavy Kipchak cavalry out. He had known he would find those damned Kipchaks someday.

He could not make them move in a straight attack. They were going to sit behind that trench, behind their shields, until the spring mud swallowed him up. Somehow they knew that he was only feigning his retreats to get them out, and they would not come.

There are always too many, he thought. If he had learned the Hindu way of counting he could tell how many there were. He nearly smiled. Better that he not know. But he knew there were always more than his army.

Then as he visualized the Solar Warrior his mind lightened, inundated with new energy. Ordering the signal to withdraw once again, the orlok began to ride slowly into the east. In the terrible silence which characterized the Mongol army on the field of battle, the squadrons, regiments, and tumans of nomadic cavalry broke contact with the Russians and quickly fell into the disciplined, guarded marching order that was now more than their second nature, had become the natural condition of their seemingly ever-moving existence. As the moments passed and the Mongols moved farther and farther away, the taunting, bellowing shouts of the Rus warriors echoed around their heads.

Subotai began to move into a slow gallop. As easily as in his youth, he slipped onto a fresh horse galloped alongside by a soldier from the Mongol herding detachment. Throughout the Mongol flying column as it moved in quiet, orderly retreat, riders shifted onto fresh mounts. Badly wounded and totally spent horses had their throats cut. The Rus might find some food, but there would be no transport left behind for them.

On they rode through the gloom of the afternoon and the swiftly falling darkness of the winter north. On and on, ever eastward. Subotai dozed and slept in the saddle with the rhythm of his mount's motion as did all the Mongol troops. Hour upon hour they moved in an alternation of the easy gallop and then long, resting walks over the hard-frozen ground of the Russian steppe. The short daylight came and went. Mounts were exchanged again and again, the riderless horses falling back into the unmounted galloping herd of spare mounts as their riders shed them.

Just before dark they saw the colored lanterns of the auxiliary camp on the steppe. Then the Chinese auxiliaries were spurring through the nomad combat columns with hot meat, chunked and spitted on sticks and spears and swords. The ravenous cavalrymen seized the food, slicing mouthfuls off with deft strokes of knives and biting into its warmth while remaining in the saddle.

As ravenously as the least soldier in the ranks, Subotai gratefully tore at the meat offered by the camp riders circulating through the tumans. The Chinese auxiliaries had not been idle. While the battle raged to the west, they had skimmed and hunted the country, restocking the limited food stores, keeping the Tartars at rest in the yurts. And now the Tartar tuman stood in arms, mounted, a powerful reserve of which neither the Rus princes nor the Kipchak khan had any knowledge.

Jebe galloped up to Subotai followed by Temajin's grandson, Batu. Batu had proven himself in every way along the long march from Bokhara. The trio bridled their mounts inward to face each other. Darkness had settled once again, but there was to be no rest for the Mongol army.

"Lord Batu, you are to take the Mangudai straight back along the way we have just come. Engage the Rus and hold them on the steppe until we arrive."

"Aye, Lord Orlok."

Subotai looked at the Arrow. "Son, son..." He said the word twice. "Lead your tumans south until mid-dark, then back toward the Rus. I will do the same, but into the north with my units and the Tartars." Subotai slapped Batu on the shoulder in his fatherly way. He extended his hand to Jebe and their eyes locked in an instant of knowingness, as though a sliver of eternity passed between them.

The Arrow turned his animal and vanished into the midst of his own staff and his troops. Batu kicked his horse into a quick sprint, shouting for the Mangudai troop commanders. The orlok held his own mount, listened for a moment to the snorts and heavy breath of the animals, the rustle of thousands of harnesses, and felt the remorseless cold of the Russian night gathering about him once again.

Subotai could only estimate how far away the Mongols now were from the Rus. He guessed that he had brought the tumans more than three hundred Chinese li—more than a hundred English miles—in the unrelenting cold and with only this short resting stop and the scant but blessed food to sustain them. He signaled the tuman leaders and led them into the black north where, at midnight, they would wheel once again into the west, back toward the mighty Rus army.

φ   φ   φ   φ

In the thin light of early morning, Batu's Mongol squadrons ignored and flowed past the Russian vanguard. Subotai's instructions had been explicit, and Batu came upon the very situation the great tactician had described to him. The huge, ungainly army of the Rus was strung out for nearly a league in an uneven series of clumpish camps, slumbering for the most part in a drunken contempt for the Mongols who had slunk back before their might and their pursuit. The Russians and now their Norse-descended nobility had been the hereditary enemies of the steppe nomads since before the memory of man, and the nomads had never quit a field this easily before. Only a handful of Rus, suspicious of the Mongol withdrawal, remained watchful.

Batu controlled the hot battle-urge of youth at least momentarily and issued simple and curt directives to his subcommanders. He well remembered the maxim of his grandfather, the Kha Khan, and of the wise Subotai, that only simplicity can succeed in war.

As each major group of Rus warriors was encountered, units from the tumans peeled off to engage them while the bulk of the force galloped on to the next enemy concentration. Most of the Russians roused themselves and recovered with extraordinary speed, only a few succumbing to the shock of the Mongols' sudden reappearance. When the Mongols had shot away nearly every arrow in their quivers, the battle was rejoined with hand weapons at close range.

Batu, riding on past the advance enemy contingents at the head of the Mangudai, the shock troops, those that belong to the Sky, slammed into the re-forming center of the Rus army.

Then ensued combat so fearful that the birds fled the winter Sky and all the wild ground animals raced away in unknowing terror from their steppe burrows, away from the crashing, numbing tumult of thousands of arms, axes, swords, spears, and the thunderous roaring war cries of the Rus army. The Mongols, Turkomen, and Merkits were silent in their grim fury. In their hate for each other, warriors on both sides, almost to a man, lost the fear of death and wounds as they were borne relentlessly into the grinding, blood-drenched maelstrom of the battle. In the grip of a great and irreversible evolutionary impulse, they struggled and slaughtered and died with the sickening breath of man-killing in their lungs.

No matter that it had gone on now for nearly seven days, the fighting reached toward superhuman exertions. Men who had thought themselves masters of their weapons met their equals and died before their superiors in that horrid place. The battlefield was veiled with the steaming breath of men and animals in the brittle air. The agonized, terrified, honking gasps of wounded and stricken horses added to the hellishness of the thing. There would be other battles between Mongol and Russian, but they would pale before this merciless cauldron of blood and desperate carnage.

Waves of Russian warriors on foot engulfed the Mangudai, halting their horses' movement with the swamping, suicidal press of their own bodies. Batu was hauled into a clustering center of veteran Mongol shock troops, the rare ones who had somehow been through combat like this before and lived to be here now. The murderous weight of the Rus press wielding their long spears and heavy axes inflicted savage butchery amongst the Mongols, but the Mangudai gave as good as they received. The ground was a quivering litter of bloody bodies, severed limbs, shocking white bone ends thrust out of wounds, suffocating casualties, and riderless horses alimp with sliced tendons or legs gone altogether. And still the

Russians poured in, a score of men waiting outside the violence to fill each gap the Mangudai made in the circle surrounding them. The huge Rus force now faced the melting enclaves of trapped Mongols. Locked in the blood-hysteria of mortal close combat, they had only to wear down the ever-decreasing Mongol pockets.

With an almost miraculous simultaneity, Subotai's and Jebe's pincers converged in a double envelopment from the north and south onto the field of battle. The Rus, taken from their right rear and their left flank, recoiled in rippling waves of shock and confusion which rolled through their ranks then rebounded and rolled back with what seemed a natural periodicity. Panic grew in their lines. Some of the haggard and worn Russian troops assaulting the Mangudai turned to engage the new Mongol onslaught; others joined the first trickles of deserters fleeing the field. The few surviving Mangudai, Batu among them, caught their tortured breaths as the press about them faltered.

Now the orlok, seeing his entire force committed, his tactical control of the issue exhausted, unsheathed the blue sword from beneath his left leg and urged his mount into the deafening melee. The battle pulsed to a peaking crescendo of indescribable violence before the stab of the two Mongol prongs finally broke the Rus formations apart.

When the fresh Tartar division struck the Kipchak cavalry and broke it, the khan of the Kipchaks, himself seized by the panic which the Mongol counterattack had struck into the Russians, led their flight from the field. The Tartars harried the Kipchaks across the Khalka River. Subotai, coming free of the slashing drive through the mass of Rus warriors, spurred after them, leaving the mounted Mongols to harvest the scattered Russians from the steppe. Ahead he saw Jebe and some of his troops joining with the Tartars.

There was a sudden flare of steel-ringing combat at the near edge of the river, where a Kipchak rearguard tried to delay the onrushing Tartars long enough for the main Kipchak body to cross the treacherous ice of the frozen Khalka before it was overwhelmed. Subotai could see that the Kipchak maneuver was succeeding, and spurred toward the frozen river. He hauled up on his reins when he saw the Arrow's tall body sag in the saddle, then weave too deeply toward his mount's flanks and slide off heavily onto the river bank.

Even from the far side of the ice, and with only one eye to serve him, Kotyan, khan of the Kipchaks, knew as though pierced by truth that the stocky, cat-eyed Mongol kneeling beside the wounded nomad soldier was the one. He spat out the blood from his slashed face. Yes, he was the one. The one that Mongol witch, his wife Mursechen, had taunted him about. But the Kipchak khan could not tarry. The time gained in negotiating the treacherous ice was seized, and they fled across the gray steppe.

φ   φ   φ   φ

Subotai was powerless to contain the darkly crimson flow of the Arrow's great wounds. Attempts to staunch the blood only sopped the rough woolen wrappings. Somehow the Chin woman had been able to stay his own bleeding. If only he knew how!

The young general grew weaker before Subotai's anguished eyes. When the Arrow managed to speak, the words were maundering and incoherent. Subotai had seen vast, dreadful panoramas of death, but the sight of the young man, his rich and colorful regalia soaked and stiffening with the redness of his young life, moved him to a great helpless pity. His sons would have been about the age of Jebe. He remembered their eyes, like the Arrow's, had been the same beautiful brown as the eyes of their lovely Indian mother.

Shortly after midday, Subotai's grim watch ended. The Arrow was silent in death, the handsome face distorted by the uncoordinated set of the open eyes, which the deep Russian cold gradually covered with a thin, opaque layer of ice.

Subotai had the richest cloaks stripped from the bodies of the princes of Russia. He selected several martin and sable fur cloaks of great heaviness and helped wrap Jebe's body in them. The grave was dug deeply in the frozen ground to thwart the wolves already feeding without fear on the battlefield. Subotai and Batu gentled the body into the excavation, Subotai smoothing the furs to cover the dead Jebe. The whirling fates had struck the younger of the two supreme commanders of the Mongol armies, leaving the survivor to grieve and wonder on the logic and justice of it. Subotai's loss was the loss of a great companion, almost of a son. Jebe, the Arrow, had been vain, unbridled, and reckless, but a true friend and a remarkable leader, and a courageous man. The orlok stood numbly, watching the burial party chink and slide the cold, knotty earth back into the grave. Boulders were emplaced above the torn earth, heavy stones that required two men to move.

He heard the words behind him, coming like the hissing of a snake. "Smash them. They should have come over to our side. They ride like us and their weapons and language, what I could hear of it, are like ours." Batu's face seemed like a mask set round with frozen sweat and blood.

Kaidu, Temajin's great-grandson, had quietly joined them. Hearing Batu's words, Kaidu sought out Subotai's eyes and said, "They were the ones. You saw them strike down Jebe after the Rus were finished, when it was already won." Kaidu, his face red with the righteous passion of youth, spoke in great heat. He was even younger than Batu.

Batu was shaking with rage. "Remember what grandfather says. Any who offer resistance are to be wasted, scattered."

The orlok stood silent, seemingly deaf to their anger. Their furious demands were buffered by Subotai's drifting mind. Even there in the cold beside the Arrow's grave, he could once again feel the compelling urge that had driven him up and down and across half the known world, sense anew the soft warmth of the feeling which had filled him when he first saw Mursechen beside the pond. It was possible that she was still alive somewhere in the tents of the Kipchaks, but he had to admit that it was improbable; nomad women, even those married to nobles, did not ordinarily live to great age.

With a wrenching effort he choked down the order for full-scale pursuit of the withdrawing Kipchaks. Now that the Rus forces were broken, the Kipchaks were not a military threat to the Kha Khan. His duty was clear: to return as many tuman warriors to Temajin as possible. He could perhaps catch the Kipchaks, but he had seen their valor, and knew they would fight again. His own forces had suffered enormous losses; had he the right to risk them in the swirling uncertainty of a cavalry clash with the desperate Kipchaks? And what of Mursechen herself? If she lived, she would be in the Kipchak encampment. And when his Mongols defeated the Kipchaks, could he find her, recognize her, in time to save her from the random slaughter his own troops would inevitably inflict on every Kipchak they could find?

As though to finalize his harrowing decision, he heard the winter wind heighten and felt the first wet flakes of an oncoming snowstorm. With every circumstance of fate conspiring against him, he had to accept his impotence over the moment. Powerful and powerless, what a cursed thing he was!

Subotai laughed out loud, to the consternation of Batu and Kaidu, who thought he was deriding their arguments to pursue the fleeing Kipchaks. "We go to the east. To the Kha Khan. Give orders to despoil the dead before they are snow-covered. I want every banner, symbol, coat, and weapon carted back to the Lord Temajin."

When Subotai spoke in this way, argument gave way to the quickly-spoken Mongol equivalent of "Yes, sir." There were no doubts, not even among the grandcubs of the Kha Khan, about where the ultimate authority of the Kha Khan and his code, the Yassa, still resided.

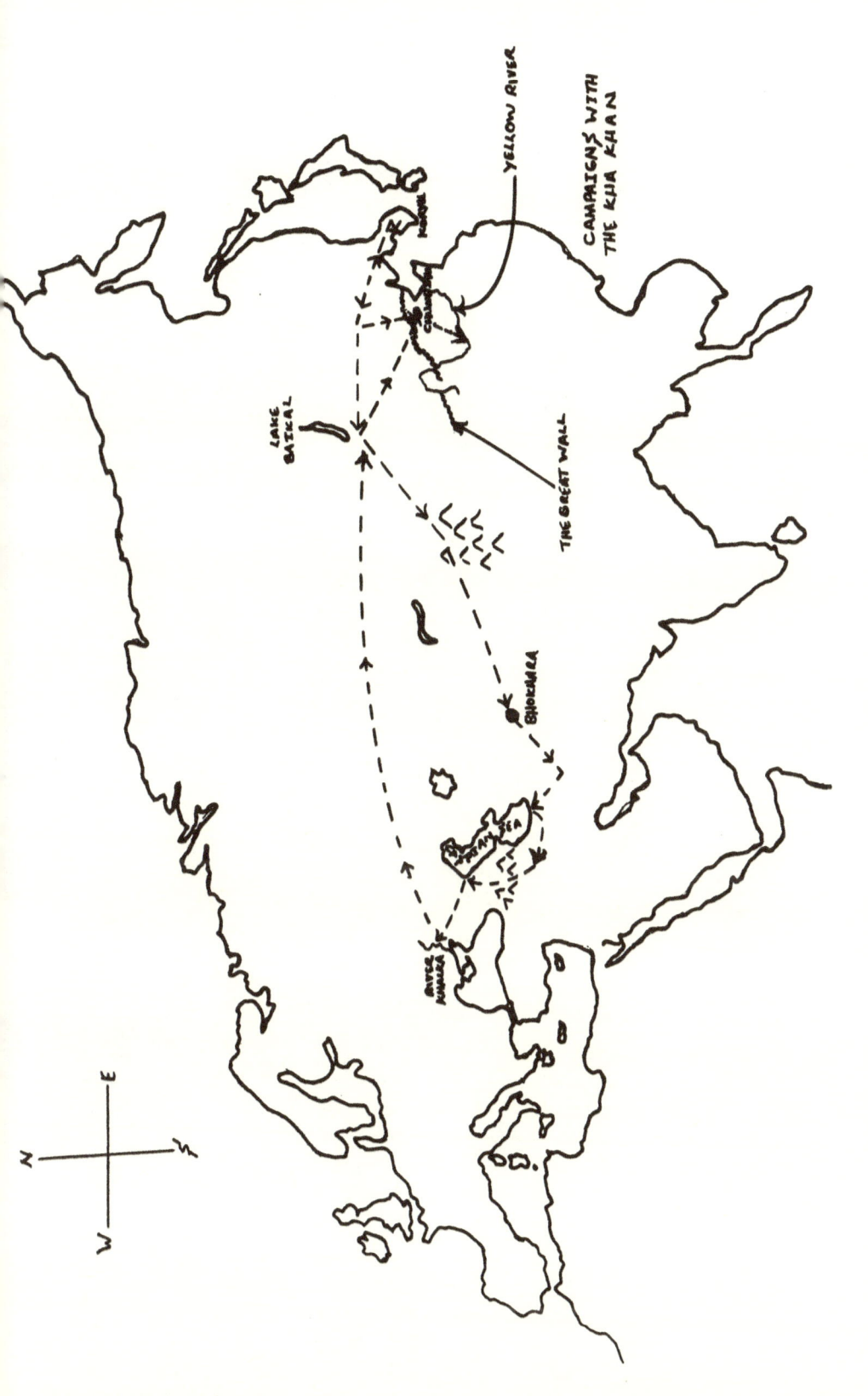

CAMPAIGNS WITH THE KHA KHAN

YELLOW RIVER

KARAKORUM

SAMARKAND

LAKE BAIKAL

THE GREAT WALL

BOKHARA

ARAL SEA

BATTLE KHALKA

N
E
S
W

φ φ
THE
WAR
MASTER

*T*he orlok was leading his Mongol tumans home.

The Rus war standards, weapons, and the stacks of Eastern Orthodox icons with their flat religious likenesses were unloaded from the wagons and placed outside the Kha Khan's big steppe pavilion.

Among the trophies the orlok brought was a herd of uniformly brown, white-nosed horses abandoned by the Kipchaks. Subotai himself led the herd stallion as a gift for Temajin when he dismounted to meet the Genghis Kha Khan who was approaching the orlok on foot with a leather cup of foaming mare's milk.

Subotai dropped to one knee, his face warm and smiling broadly. "Lord Temajin, we are returned at last."

Then the Kha Khan lifted him to his feet. Temajin's hair was gray. His voice quavered slightly with age, but still rumbled deeply as he said, "Lord Subotai, Orlok, once I called thee Bahadur, the Valiant, but now I call thee the Victorious."

It was more than two years since that hot morning when the tumans had ridden away from Bokhara toward Persia in pursuit of Muhammad Shah. They had swept, unchecked by human valor or force of arms, across some five thousand miles. The overwhelming Mongol victory on the Khalka River had extended Genghis Khan's

271

Golden Empire onto the Russian steppes.

The returning force was far from intact. Word of the Arrow's death had preceded them, borne by the swift, mounted, relaying couriers who kept the lines of communication open between the Kha Khan and the orlok throughout the epic Mongol ride around the Caspian Sea. Batu had left the army to stay on the Volga steppes newly won from the Rus. Subotai rode with almost the last contingent of what remained of the sixty thousand men he had led away from Bokhara. Only two in four of those Mongol soldiers had lived to see the Gobi or Lake Baikal again. In addition to the heavy battle casualties, there had been the inevitable toll exacted by disease and accident during the long trek.

With a studied but genuine deference, Temajin led Subotai into the spacious felt pavilion. "Subotai, I would hear the entire tale from your own lips. And as you speak I shall have the Chin scholars make their scroll writings to keep a memory of your ride and of your great battles beyond the sun-place in the west." Temajin motioned for Subotai to sit, and both men, ignoring ornate Chinese chairs, sank down in the Mongol way on the felt-carpeted earth.

The warmth of the homecoming broke through Subotai's normally taciturn behavior, and for almost a moon-month he and Temajin talked. Over their evening meat and into the late night hours, Temajin recounted the events of his chase of Jelal ad-Din into India and the destruction of the last remnants of the Kharesmian armies, and the orlok described the vast circuit about the Sea of the Ravens, Jebe's death, the death of the Shah, the battles, the pale, light-haired Rus, dead, left for the scavengers on the steppes.

Then one evening the tales were suddenly completed and both of them were quiet, keyed to the gentle ruffling of the pavilion's top in the warm night wind of the steppe summer. The orlok had revived something of the emotion and the enormous tragedy of the savage battle with the Russians. The wearing years on the long trail coupled with the emotional drain had left him in a lingering depression.

The Kha Khan had caught Subotai's mood. He absent-mindedly toyed with the meat scraps on his laquered Chinese plate. He surveyed the orlok, saw the withdrawn gaze and the motionless man. Then he broke into Subotai's painful reverie. "Someday you must take the tumans back into the west. The work is not yet finished there."

The words caused Subotai to turn a startled look in Temajin's direction. Then, almost in whisper, Subotai, not bothering to mask the angry questioning in his voice, asked, "What work? Lord, you speak in mysteries to me. A work? Can that be what this long agony has been? A work?" Then his voice swelled with his feelings. "I am sick of the death, sick of the fighting. You—you are dying of the long campaigns. Once you said your purposes were to see your enemies smashed and to have their goods and their women. But that is not the reason. I see what you have."

Subotai narrowed his eyes and sought to pierce the veils Temajin had drawn over his consciousness. "You took the woman, Houlon, and set aside the Lady Bourtai—no, I am not condemning, I am saying that that is all I have seen you take for yourself. You are no better off than the night I stumbled onto your yurt in the storm. It all goes back to the army for more expeditions."

At the mention of Bourtai's name, Temajin met Subotai's eyes. "I gave China to Bourtai."

"Perhaps, Lord,"—Subotai's voice was grave—"she did not want China."

The Genghis Khan was silent. To Subotai, Temajin and the Solar Warrior were the two great enigmas of his life. It was only now that he noticed how much they were alike—the same deep look of inner knowledge in their eyes, the same willful but unvoiced purpose of being. His own purpose, the blue-eyed woman, had never been enigmatic to him. She was at once spirit, desire, hope, perhaps even a fanciful image of the mother he had never known, or the Mother Kali. She was as real to him now as the day he had first seen her Nordic Scythian beauty.

And yet he knew she was unreal. He knew now that his reasons—the exhausted army, his fears for Mursechen should she be caught in potential combat between her Kipchaks and his Mongols, and the onset of the snowstorm after the battle on the Khalka— were not the only or even the most powerful reasons why he had not sought her in the enemy yurts. He knew now that his precious image of her was of a woman who no longer existed, perhaps had never existed. Part of him had been afraid of what she might have become after all the sun-years, if she had survived at all. And part of him knew that his long-held memory of Mursechen had dissolved, years ago, into his inner longing for the Mother Kali.

The orlok spoke softly now, the long lonely years since the death of Gauri, the years of the tormenting memory of Mursechen echoing in his speech. "I have spent many sun-years of my manhood at war for your sake. Won't you tell me what has been the purpose of this thing?"

The Kha Khan remained silent. The orlok rose to leave, but then Temajin spoke, his words catching at Subotai.

"Lord Orlok, I bid you stay. You shall sleep here this night. And in the morning I have gifts from China and the Moslem lands for you." Here Temajin smiled in the way that attracted the loyalty of all he came near. "And something else. When the couriers arrived with the news that you were coming east from the Sea of the Ravens, I sent to China. Bourtai and I have given our granddaughter for you to wife. The girl has held herself in readiness at my bidding. You shall be joined in the dawn, under the Sky when it gleams like the gold plate we took from the Chin." Temajin waited for Subotai's reaction, which was long in coming. Then he said, "Do not look so distraught. She is the one I told you of. She bears a remarkable resemblance to Bourtai. And just about nineteen seasons, I think."

"You have never told me her name," Subotai said.

"Kralyan." Temajin knew he need not say it, but he wanted it to be right for the great soldier, the great mover behind his triumphs. "You must remember how strict Bourtai has always been. The young woman comes a virgin."

The words turned Subotai's mood. "I have not forgotten how much I owe to you and your family. Lord, you honor me past recompense by making me kin to the Golden Family."

φ   φ   φ   φ

In the dawning, Subotai waited while the Mongol shamans slowly divined the exact point of direction for the ceremonials to face in order to acquire the most propitious blessing, the hooded figures turning slowly like Chinese weather vanes, haunting silhouettes against the lightening Sky. The emergent sun was beginning to smear the line of the east on his right shoulder when the Mongol women, all with birchbark adorning their hair, led the bride forward. Her fresh face was unveiled, her dark hair was plaited into a single thick and long braid behind her shoulders and secured with a bright silver clasp and slender silver Chin eating stick. Kralyan wore an unadorned gown of plain silk colored lightly with green and an overblouse of layered silk vividly embroidered with bands of colorful patterns, leaflike and swirling, such as were affected by the women of the steppes whenever they could acquire the means to adorn themselves.

The group of women held themselves in a protective cluster apart from Subotai, Temajin, and Kralyan's father, Tului. One of the shamans knelt and drew a handful of whitened bones from his charm bag. The shaman cast the bones on the ground several times. He grunted sagely from time to time at particularly significant orientations of the cast bones. Finally he rose and went directly to the women, took the full sleeve of Kralyan's blouse, and brought her to the orlok's side. Subotai had been watching the pretentious behavior of the shaman with a patient smile, but now, as he saw the girl's features and eyes in the intensifying light, his smile fled and a pleasingly surprised look of mild shock came over his broad face. Kralyan's similarity to Bourtai was uncanny. Her beautiful and intelligent face seemed to be golden-hued in the dawn's illumination. Her eyes were brown with a hint of flecked gold within them which scintillated with light when she turned her head and caught the radiance of the east.

Kralyan caught her breath when the orlok's magnetic eyes seized her. Bourtai had described him to her, his hard, muscular stockiness, the black and russet and gray hair, but she was unprepared for the aura of strength and dynamic power about him. And the blue eyes, steady and calmly centered beneath the thick eyebrows.

The shamans circled about the couple and made outlining passes over the bodies of the man and the woman with their hardwood wands. When the ancient steppe purification rite was finished, the women brought meat for Subotai and Kralyan to share. The moment they touched their lips to the brim of a sacred cup of mare's milk, a great shout rent the morning air. Smoky streamers lined the sky as a fusillade of fire arrows winged from the bows of an honor guard of Subotai's troops.

Tului and Temajin held Subotai fast while, in the old Mongol tradition, some of his line soldiers gleefully poured rice wine and fermented milk into the orlok's mouth. Only when he was in actual danger of drowning did they relent and let the choking Mongol general free to reclaim his breath. Tului, already drunk, set about assuring that the entire Mongol settlement, thousands of souls, would be drunk too before mid-morning.

Kralyan was carried about from yurt to yurt for the greater part of the morning, receiving gifts and pledges of stock and goods. Custom required that she at least sip from each of the proffered beverages which the seemingly endless sequence of well-wishers thrust up at her. Despite her concentrated efforts to imbibe as little as possible, she grew dizzy from the confusion and the heterogeneous qualities of the primitive liquors she sampled. Her head was swirling with inebriation and the turbulent spirit and noise of the gigantic wedding celebration. Then it seemed she was being passed from arms to arms in an endless human carousel. She had closed her eyes and let her head fall back, then fallen drunkenly asleep before she was finally deposited in Subotai's arms.

Subotai was still reeling somewhat from the enforced and lengthy wedding toast, but he managed to carry the sleeping Kralyan through the back-slapping, roaring throng of celebrating Mongols. He took her into the marriage yurt which had been especially prepared for them and laid her gently on a raised wedding pallet which was draped with an assortment of thick furs that served as bedding. The crowd was pelting the sides of the yurt with stones and dragging sticks along its ribbing. In spite of the din, Kralyan manifested no sign of reawakening, and Subotai, his head pounding, stretched out beside his new wife and fell asleep.

It was dusk when he awoke. Kralyan was not beside him on the pallet. As he swung his legs over he saw her. She was dressing her long, softly dark hair by the light of a Chinese oil lamp with her legs tucked beneath her. She heard him stir on the furs that covered the straw pallet and turned her head with a seductive smile.

"You are awake, my Lord. I feared that after your long drink you would not awaken until tomorrow."

Subotai went to the far side of the yurt and splashed water from a drinking skin into his hands and onto his face. He dried his hands and face, then drank thirstily from the water bag before he turned and scrutinized his young wife thoughtfully. She had removed her colorful overblouse and her slim, tanned arms were bare. Their feminine motions about her hair competed for his attention with the soft, full rounding of calves and thighs revealed when her skirts rode upwards. She neglected to readjust them.

"Am I pleasing to you, Lord Subotai?"

The orlok felt the mental bands he had locked about his cravings begin to dissolve at the sight of Kralyan's youthful voluptuousness. "Aye." He dredged his mind for a compliment, but the words would not come. He had been too many years at war. He had scarcely been near a living, breathing woman, aside from the hopeless and broken captives in the jetsam of the Mongol conquests, the long, uncommunicative time with the Persian woman, and the painful frustration of his encounter with the Chin woman.

They met in the yurt's center, pausing at arm's length to search each other's eyes. Wordlessly they embraced. Kralyan's mouth was wet and warm against his neck and cheek. Her unstayed breasts under the sensual silk against his bare chest funneled his powers into his lower parts. He worked her skirts upward hand by hand until the backs of her golden thighs were uncovered, then he caressed them with his powerful but gentle hands. Their mouths melded, her pelvic undulations braced by his hands pressing against her rounded buttocks.

He half-turned her and dropped his left arm to the back of her luscious thighs, then lifted her in his arms and carried her to the furred pallet. They were both breathing heavily now, and they joined, with her gown hiked up above her tawny hips. Her softness beneath the silk was an almost forgotten sensory experience for the orlok, and her ready young femininity absorbed his manhood and drew the power of his loins. His undiminished mature lustiness at last satiated the Mongol maiden and it was complete.

φ   φ   φ   φ

Kralyan's pretty face was set in an artificial and teasing pout. "Oh Subotai, please take me back to China. You will see how much you will enjoy the life at grandmother's court. No more cold yurts and going weeks without a warm bath or hot food."

The orlok turned his eyes from the renewing green of the spring steppe to his young wife. They had wintered virtually alone, away from the Kha Khan's new and still sparsely settled capital of Karakorum. "Were you cold or hungry here with me?"

"No, but you are always so quiet. I shall be a good wife for you, but I long for the sound of the Chinese flutes and the talk of women my own age."

Subotai's only weakness as a general was his lenience in disciplinary matters and the mental anguish he had undergone arising from his attachment to and concern for his men. As a result his losses had always been light, and he was adored by his soldiers, but the years of concern and his enormous private suffering and grief over the deaths of his troops had worn him inwardly. Now he displayed the same patience and interest in Kralyan.

"If I had known you desired to be near the Lady Bourtai, we would have followed after Lord Temajin when he led the tumans back into the Chin lands last fall. I could have taken the sun's leave the Kha Khan allowed as well in Chung-tu as here."

Kralyan jerked her head with annoyance. "I do not want to return to Bourtai's court just to be near her." Kralyan narrowed her eyes. "Do you know what she did to me once? When you and all the men had gone to Kharesmia, she took a saddle strap to me when I told her it was beneath a granddaughter of Temajin to herd the stock as we had done before we took the Chin lands."

Subotai said nothing and kept a grave countenance, but he warmly remembered Bourtai's practical nature and common sense.

The next morning Subotai hitched the oxen to their lumbering cart-yurt and set the nomad land-ship creaking on its way toward Karakorum. After a muddy trek of some weeks, the yurts and the growing numbers of mud-walled buildings hove into view. The couple paused only long enough for Subotai to replenish their traveling stores and obtain a pair of saddle horses, which he rein-tied to the end of the cart. Then they followed the now well-traveled road toward the Great Wall.

As they traveled, Subotai kept a lazy watch over the oxen's progress from the front of the cart-yurt, while Kralyan busied herself within, sorting and packing all of their clothing as she planned for each of the Chin court festivals she remembered. She knew that the Empress Bourtai had adopted the Chin custom of wearing yellow silk gowns at official functions. Surely she, Kralyan, as the only wife of the great orlok, Subotai, would have the privilege of wearing violet or blue silk gowns. Then, pridefully, she thought that she, too, should also wear yellow. Her self-smile was one of satisfaction. Subotai did not have official obligations to Bourtai; he answered only to Genghis Khan. Yes, she as well as her grandmother, must have the rank to wear yellow.

Carefully she began to set stacks of silver plate and cups into the bottom of one of their big wooden, steel-hinged chests. Then she took the blue sword down from the peg where Subotai left it to hang, planning to place it in the chest with the plate and their other metal possessions.

The blue sword was lying on the floor next to the chest when Subotai stepped inside. "What are you about?" He tried to keep his voice softened despite his displeasure at seeing her handle the sword.

Kralyan looked up with an unconcerned smile. "I'm putting away all the things we won't need for a long while. Everything of iron, steel, or silver goes into this chest. Your sword should be at the very bottom—you aren't going to need it again, ever..." Her voice trailed off when she caught sight of the hard look on Subotai's face. The meaning of that look swamped her emotions as she watched him seize the sword roughly and replace it on its peg. Her eyes widened in horror. The faces of the young men she had known who had left for Kharesmia and never returned flashed suddenly through her mind, making her fists clench with fury. "I will not have it!" she shrieked.

"That sword, like myself, is the property of the Kha Khan." Subotai put his arm over her shoulders. "If he calls me, he calls for my sword as well as my arm. Kralyan, I am and you are what he has made of us." Then he tried to mollify her. "But think, I have been granted my leave while he and Mulagi have gone back into the Chin hinterlands with the army."

Calmer now but still furious, she turned knowing eyes up to him. "There will be other wars, other campaigns. With him,"—she nodded toward China—"there will always be another war."

"Wars start and end by themselves," he said, but she did not believe him.

One morning, when they were still not yet in sight of the Great Wall, the orlok awoke before dawn with a start, as though great wings had drafted a chill breeze through the sleeping corridors of his consciousness. He dressed silently, drew the quilts up to cover the warm, breathing breasts of Kralyan, and stepped out into the now-lightening morning. The land grew more distinct as the day subtly spread across the steppe Sky.

He stared intently toward the south. His feeling grew even stronger now. When Kralyan brushed his arm, he took her under it. She shivered despite the quilt she had drawn about her and despite the warmth of the summer dawn. The morning was still, the birds and insects were hushed, no animals stirred. They breakfasted without speaking, buried their small fire, then set the oxen in motion for the day's travel. The ominous feeling persisted in Subotai's mind for several days, and Kralyan's irritation at his inordinate silence grew. Her words were sharp when she spoke to him, but he seemed not to care.

Then, under a blue afternoon sky, they heard and felt the trembling reverberations of thousands of horses' hooves, although the land was still empty before them. It was not until the next morning that they finally saw the long lines of nomad horsemen approaching from the south. Kralyan looked fearfully into Subotai's grave eyes. He jumped off the cart and hauled up on the lead oxen to halt the wide-wheeled wagon.

A group of riders detached themselves from the main body of horsemen and rode toward the cart-yurt. Several of them recognized the orlok and saluted with lifted sword arms as they halted their animals. One of them tried to speak, but grief silenced him. The army had been expected to be in China for several sun-years during the campaign, and Subotai knew without asking why they were returning to the steppes so soon.

He saw the wagon with the long, black teakwood casket on it. The thousands of troops of Temajin's tumans were utterly silent. They rode by with only the sounds of leather, the softened impacts of the animals' feet, and the oddly melodious jangle of harness and trappings.

Kralyan saw the stricken look on Subotai's face and set her lovely jaw in a hard line. Now she knew she would not be in China for a long, long time. Even in his death, her grandfather had managed to thwart her desire for the elegant life of the court there.

φ   φ   φ   φ

The Genghis Khan, Temajin, was laid to rest near the Iron Mountain in the region where he had spent his outlaw youth. The Mongol mourning lasted for nearly three moon-months. Subotai himself had set the watch over the conqueror's grave and commanded the ceremonial guard detachment personally for the first moon-month.

And, true to the Kha Khan's will, Ogadai, his second son, succeeded him as Kha Khan. Juchi, the eldest and most rebellious of Temajin's sons, was already a year dead. Batu, Juchi's son, sent grieving emissaries to the Blue Lake but remained away himself, secluded in the western steppes.

When Subotai returned to the funeral encampments near the Blue Lake, Kralyan ended his moon-month's celibacy with her young woman's demands. For once she seemed sympathetic with Subotai's unspoken needs in his grief over the death of his great friend, and she pampered him with cooked delicacies which she did her best to create in the Chinese manner with whatever greens and shoots she could gather in the wet woods. She drew on the rice stores brought as tribute from China, and mixed tender young meats and spices into steaming and succulent meals for the orlok. And in the nights she tantalized and burned and climaxed his still full manhood. Her tutoring under the Chinese women of Lady Bourtai's court and her own imaginative variations in the arts springing from her urgency spurred both of them into day- and night-long bouts of love-making.

The incandescence of their renewed relationship dwindled in a single quarreling afternoon when Kralyan grew petulant and jealous over the growing amounts of time Subotai was being required to invest in advising the new Kha Khan. She expected—hoped—Subotai would beat her for her viciousness in the argument, but he lapsed into his silence, a silence she mistook for indifference. She could not have known the terrible conditioning, the flaming years of battle and march, which his silence reflected.

She knew from the gossip passed among the serving women

that Ogadai was planning new wars in conformance with the will
of Temajin, but to her anything would be better than this. She was
bored with Subotai's company, bored when he sat gray-faced from
the pain of old wounds through the cold nights, bored when he
came from the Kha Khan's pavilion in the early morning hours and,
ignoring her, flung himself down in fatigued sleep. She was especially bored with his incessant meditation. Why did he not go to
one of the monasteries in China? She brightened. Or even to Bourtai's
court? Bourtai always had soothsayers and monks about her to guide
her and the Chin administrators in the government.

Subotai said nothing during the following spring and summer
when she hunted and rode with the other young people, even seeming to overlook her overt flirtations with the young Mongol and
Turkish officers.

She entered their yurt late one afternoon attended by a circlet
of idle, laughing young people to find him sorting through his
meager belongings. Then with scarcely a glint of recognition in his
deep eyes, he hastily said a farewell and disappeared. He was gone
for more than two years, on another campaign deep into China.

φ   φ   φ   φ

When the orlok returned to the Blue Lake his army columns
carried with them the booty of the great Chin city of Hai-feng.
Ogadai Kha Khan received the miles-long wagon trains of loot with
the indifference of one who expects such voluminous wealth as a
matter of course. He received Subotai with abrupt courtesy, but his
mind wandered and his eyes dropped in the virile presence of the
orlok. Subotai knew that the Kha Khan was sunk in the night
sweats of brooding paranoia, was debased and unnaturally under
the influence of his sexual appetites, draining his vitality into the
endless pools of concubines the Mongol conquests had tapped.

After a series of uncomfortable silences, the Kha Khan finally
said, "Lord Subotai, I give you one in ten of all the stock and horses
you have brought out of the Chin lands." He waved his hand weakly
in the general direction of the entrance to the royal pavilion. "Yes,
and be certain your wife has her pick of the rich cloth."

Subotai accepted the dismissal for what it was. He left the
imperial pavilion, glad to take in the fresh steppe air outside the

presence of the corruption which had befallen Ogadai.

Kralyan had hastily ejected her current paramour when she learned that the orlok had been shown into Ogadai's pavilion. She felt a sudden gladdening that Subotai was returned. Her mirror showed her what she did not want to see: the aging about her eyes and the widening of her hips brought on by the indolence she had lapsed into with the leisure and plenty provided by the loot and by tributes from the vast lands conquered by Temajin and Subotai.

She snapped at her servant women while she searched for a gown special enough for the meeting with her husband. Her hair was still a crowning darkness, and she capitalized on its healthful and shiny thickness. She thanked the Sky that she had at least heeded Bourtai in the matter of drink. Her body would not have the reek of sour wine about it and, with a subtle application of an alluring Kharesmian perfume, she felt sure she would be desirable to him.

Then she waited in the soft light of the yurt lamps for him to come. But the flames of the lamps were low and Kralyan was dozing by the time Subotai finally drew aside the yurt's door-curtain and entered. Kralyan came awake with a start. The orlok said nothing as he divested himself of the blue sword, then rubbed his eyes with the heels of his hands. When he turned into the light, she could see he looked older and that the lines of his face were more pronounced than she remembered.

At last she found her tongue. "Have you eaten, my Lord?"

"Aye. I fed at the tuman fires before I came." His jaws tightened. "There are so many wounded now. Sometimes I think the old way was better, when we dispatched the more seriously injured. The Chinese doctors have a way, though."

She was at his side now, letting her soft, devilish fingers work their way beneath the rim of his leather trousers. She knew intuitively that he had been celibate. In her woman's way it pleased and angered her at once. Her growing nymphomania and her now more experienced techniques brought her the desired results. She plied him past the death of the lamp oil until the day began to break.

During the days that followed they rode together in the daylight after the furnaces each night in their bedding, and for a few weeks it was good again. Subotai even grew talkative at times, always avoiding the acrid memory of the siege of Hai-feng. Sometimes they rode afield to watch the Kha Khan's falconers course wolves with the golden eagles, sometimes they galloped wildly after a speeding gazelle which they had not the slightest chance of overtaking. Then horses and riders panting with the exhilaration of the chase, they would watch the gazelle until it was a dusting dot in the distance.

But one night, when a rare summer rain was pounding sleep into the yurt, Kralyan awoke to find Subotai standing in the open doorway watching the lightning turn distant night clouds into gigantic sky-lanterns. He was sipping from a mug of warm goat's milk and seemed unaware of her stirring on the furs and quilts of their bed. She watched his unmoving back for a long time. She used men carelessly, but this orlok, nearly old enough to be her grandfather, he was like a young man, oblivious to the multitude of scars that covered his dense, steely body. She could imagine the jagged storm-light reflecting in the clear, deep eyes.

Then without turning he said, "You will have to go to the Lady Bourtai in China after the winter, when the grass makes the land passable."

She did not know why she even asked, but she blurted out the unnecessary question, "Why?"

He faced about toward her and a flash of lightning inked his broad silhouette against the open entrance. "Because..." he was uncertain of how to say it, "because I must complete the work of Lord Temajin." Thunder raked the rainy steppes outside the Mongol yurts. The crashing night made Kralyan's skin bump with chills of fear. The orlok waited for the reverberations to die out. "And many of us will not return from this great war."

"But where will you go, Subotai?" She asked the question with honest naivete. "Does not all the world already belong to us?" She could not see the orlok's patient smile in the darkness.

"No. There is a land a great distance to the west where the people have very light skins, eyes as blue as mine, and hair like sunlight." His own words brought the thought of Mursechen to him. He walked to the wide, raised pallet, knelt, and placed his elbows on the furs so that his stone mug rested its pleasant warmth on the quilting covering her lap.

"But I thought Batu already held the steppes in the west," she said.

"Yes, but the land reaches on a very great distance beyond the Rus steppes," he replied.

She pressed him now, although she really did not care. "Why must there be more war in these western places, my Lord?" She waited for his words, finding pleasure somehow in the steady, measured breathing of this extraordinary man.

He stood up. "Because it was Temajin's will that it be so." He went back to the entryway to watch the rain. "As for more than that, well, there is no other reason."

It sounded utterly stupid to her, but she held her words. The snugness of the yurt and the warm bed with the rain's sound outside made her seek the security of the cozy quilts and heavy bed furs. She slept and was awakened when Subotai slid his cooler body beneath the bed coverings. The night rain was steady and gentle now. She started to slip into sleep again, but he began to talk. About a lost and mysterious valley somewhere in the Celestial Mountains near a place he called the Gate of the Bones.

How unusual, she thought. It sounded very much like the tale she had heard from that attractive young commander of a hundred. Kralyan wondered if they could be talking about the same valley. Probably not, she concluded, loitering in that half-state between wakefulness and sleep, listening mistily to Subotai's deep, soft voice describe the wondrous valley.

Then it was the same tedious way it had been before he went into China to take Hai-feng. His attitude grew distant again, and again there were late nights of planning and staff work, this time with Ogadai's son, Kadaan, and brilliant and warlike grandson, Kaidu. His meditation reintensified as it had before. All the behaviors that infuriated Kralyan's young and sensitive ego were resumed.

Then Subotai vanished with Kadaan to ride from tribe to tribe carrying the Kha Khan's tablet, the Mongol symbol of authority passed down from Genghis Kha Khan, and issuing mustering instructions for each levy of troops from the nations sworn to the Yassa. And each tribe and each standard immediately designated warriors to man the courier stations which would link the long road Subotai had marked on the steppes leading from the Caspian lands to the Blue Lake and to Karakorum. Then the couriers, the arrow riders, carried the intentions of Subotai and the warrior princes of the Golden Family westward to Batu Khan on the Volga steppes.

φ   φ   φ   φ

Kadaan and Subotai were gone for several weeks, and autumn had sharpened the steppe air when they returned from forming the elements of the tumans. Command and staff groups of other Mongol expeditions came and went continuously from Ogadai's encampment. Nomad armies under Mongol leadership were being formed for the opening of the Sung territories and for the renewal of the assaults on Koryu begun years before by the orlok.

It was after nightfall when Subotai and Kadaan finally reined in within the outer fringes of the yurt clusters not far from the piney heights overlooking the Blue Lake.

The startled looks on the two young faces bordered on terror when Subotai swept into his brightly lit yurt. Kralyan usually had ample warning from the imperial pavilion whenever Subotai was returning, but something had gone wrong this time. And this time it was different. She threw herself in front of her lover with the glare of a leopardess in her gold-flecked eyes. Her expression turned into one of astonishment when the orlok did not even bother to reach over his heavy shoulder for the blue sword. Instead, he carelessly dropped his saddle bags and bow near the entranceway.

"Put clean quilts on the bed, Lady Kralyan," he said in a voice seasoned with a dispirit she had never heard from him. "Then both of you get out." The orlok looked at the ruggedly handsome young man. There was something familiar about him, but he could not place it. "You seem to care a little bit about this one."

Kralyan spit out the words like a panther's snarl. "And why should I not? You leave me here alone for moon-months, even sun-years. I never know when or if you will come back. And when you speak it is only concerning new wars you and Kaidu are planning. I waited for you even past the time you said I should depart for Bourtai's court in Chung-tu, and still you did not return." Her eyes were triumphiant. "And does this suit you as a homecoming, Lord Orlok?"

Subotai did not even bother to reply. She was right, of course. It would have been better to give her a steadier future, especially as the time at the Blue Lake was about to end.

The young Mongol officer had taken advantage of their quarreling to dress quickly. Now he came to Kralyan's side.

Subotai looked again at him. "Oh yes, you were the disoriented scout who tried to lead me over the Celestial Mountains."

"Yes, sir." The younger man's bearing and speech were respectful but without trepidation.

Then it struck both men at the same instant, and Subotai set it into words. "Do you think you could find that secret valley once you are on top of the Gate of the Bones?"

"Aye." The answer was eager.

Then Subotai put his deeper thoughts into words. "After the command units leave to gather their tumans, this place will be nearly deserted. Pack this very night and both of you be ready to start down the road toward the Chinese Wall in the morning. I will issue the covering order." He looked at the man who had so blatantly cuckolded him. "When you deem it right, turn toward the Celestial Mountains, but only after you stop in at least two or three of the manned way shelters along the trail." The orlok was thoughtful for a moment, then added, "The season is late. No search for any traveler who fails to appear at the next way stop on the trail to China will be undertaken until the spring weather warms the land." A strange note of urgency and caution came into his voice. "Get over the Gate. You must stop for nothing. Only within that valley will you be able to winter without freezing." Then Subotai added, almost as a rejoinder to the unspoken thought in their minds, "You know that the Chinese intrigue at Bourtai's court will not allow you to be together without compromise."

The orlok raised the ornate ivory chop Kua had engraved for him over his head by its thong. He wore the chop always about his neck now to counter the occasional forgetfulness which plagued him at inconvenient times. He went to his old campaign chest and took out a leather sheet, then rummaged in the depths of the chest to find a hard block of marking material. The end of the chop block where the Chin ideograms were incut he pressed onto the marking material until he could see the imprint of the ideograms in the almost solid ink, and then he set the seal to the leather.

Without turning he handed the authorization to the young

Mongol officer. "Be sure you take a light garrison yurt on one of your baggage animals." With that the orlok left the yurt. He sought out a guard yurt and fed from one of the army pots before he went to sleep among the weary bodies of the guard mount.

φ   φ   φ   φ

With the rations and equipment vouchered by Subotai's chop, the young man and Kralyan hastened down the well patrolled trail toward Chung-tu. When the Celestial Mountains to the west shimmered pink in the dawn, they abruptly left the roadway to China and rode without rest toward the peaks.

They were almost frozen before they topped the Gate of the Bones, and they made one false descent into the wrong area, but after they climbed back up to the Gate, the way was clear to him. They could feel the warmer air when they located the sharp slope that fell away into the snowless valley below. Kralyan saw at last what Subotai had been trying to describe to her—its unspoiled secrecy, the meandering rivers, here and there a small herd of deer bouncing into a stand of trees. Suddenly she wished he were here with her, but she knew the gate to her past with Subotai, that strange, silent, meditative man, was closed.

Kralyan looked back once, but behind her lay only the harsh heights of the Tien Shien Mountains and her unrewarding marriage to Subotai. She reached an affectionate hand to the man who rode beside her. It seemed that all her desires for rank and court life in China had been deliberately blocked, partly by her grandfather, partly by her own actions, and partly by Subotai who, she suspected, had foiled them many times for reasons she could not understand.

The young Mongol officer squeezed Kralyan's hand, then, bridling his mount closer, patted her fur-clad shoulder. They both laughed aloud, sharing the knowledge that he was now a deserter from the Mongol tumans and she, for all practical purposes, was the run-away wife of an imperial orlok. There could be no turning back from here; those labels ended their former lives forever. The realization solidified the already strong bond between them, the surprising bond that had grown out of their casual flirtation. Kralyan was, for the moment, content. If she had learned one thing as the wife of a Mongol orlok, it was that the position was not worth the strains and demands it imposed. But before night fell that bitter day, she was troubled again. Something—yes, even now she felt the vague sense of new life in her belly. And she could not gainsay her woman's intuition that this was Subotai's child.

They let their animals pick their way slowly down toward the inviting landscape below, while the winter blizzards closed the passes of the Tien Shien mountains behind them.

φ   φ   φ   φ

In the darkening hours before a sunrise which would illuminate but fail to warm the unvarying cold, Subotai and Kaidu saddled and mounted. The genius of the union between Temajin and Bourtai had leaped two generations and come into fruition in Prince Kaidu. He swung his long form, taller even than Temajin Khan's had been, into the saddle. Brown eyes with hints of lightning in them like those in Bourtai's surveyed the snowy landscape before the two riders. Wordlessly, the tall Mongol prince and his stocky mentor walked their horses through the sleeping imperial encampment, then let them into a gallop through the shallow snow.

Behind them more than a hundred thousand Mongol warriors began to gather and stage down through the utter cold of high Asia toward the distant peninsula of Europe.

φ   φ   φ   φ

Batu Khan and the orlok listened with a mounting interest to · the tales told by the more gregarious of the Russians now thronging to Batu's court. Their numbers swelled as more and more of the Rus nobility sought Batu's protection. Batu, now the recognized Khan of the Golden Horde, as Juchi's followers had come to be called, had been designated by Ogadai Kha Khan as the nominal leader of the Mongols' assault on Europe.

Now one of the minor Rus princes, a man who apparently basked in Batu's radiant reign for the primary advantages of unlimited koumiss and food, was holding sway. "Novgorod is the richest city of all the Russias." Here the Rus belched loudly and broke wind magnificently before going on. "Why, they have traded, without interruption,"—he reswallowed a sudden ballooning of wine fumes from his stomach—"with the Hanseatic cities for centuries, and they have had an open access to the Baltic, along with its fish and the wealth along its shores."

Subotai, always ready to absorb information, especially when it concerned geography, queried the Slav. "This Baltic you speak of, is it a salt sea or a big lake?"

"A salt sea." And here the Russian was deferential to Batu even though he and all the rest of the assemblage knew that the victories and the slashing strategies had been Subotai's. "The princes of the Rus cities and lands you have just won were descendants of the Rus Vikings who originally came from the other side of the Baltic Sea, from Scandia. They used to come down the great rivers trading and trapping as they went. Many of them would make the journey to enlist in the Varangian Guard of the Byzantines, at least that is the tale I have heard."

The orlok sat unspeaking, showing some of the fatigue of the hard winter campaign he had led through the Rus lands north of the steppes now held by Batu and the Mongols. He had used the winter as the trapper had taught him to do: attacking across the hard frozen lakes and rivers, striking and burning the Rus's log cities. He had encountered little organized resistance, for the Rus had been quite sure that no one would think of making war in the harsh forest cold.

Musing over the factors that had determined his success, the orlok wondered what had been the fate of the trapper, a descendant, he knew, of those wandering Vikings. He thought once again of the strangely expressive language he had learned, a little of it at least, from the Englishman, and remembered the Norman and Saxon and Danish folklore the big trapper had entertained him with beside the campfires during their matchless adventure together. It struck him that the myths and the thrilling legends of the European north about gods and goddesses were remarkably similar in many respects to the aspective deities of the Hindu mythology. This turned his mind to the Solar Warrior, who had convinced him that all deities were Aspects of The One, and it puzzled him that the trapper's legends gave no indication that the Norse Wotan, the Universal Father, embodied also the love aspect of Freya, the goddess whom Subotai equated with the Mother Kali of the Hindu philosophy. Were the differences between those who spoke different languages too great for Temajin's dream of a universal empire?

Batu was speaking to him with an edge of irritation in his voice. "Lord Subotai, I find that you drift more and more like an old man musing over his lost youth."

Subotai almost let this bruise on his ego show, but only an instantaneous glittering of his blue eyes betrayed any loss of balance behind the heavy white-black eyebrows. Without any courtesy to the Khan of the Golden Horde, Subotai signalled for the Mongol guards in attendance to clear the yurt of the Russians. He knew he would have to be decisive. He looked over the group of Mongol staff officers with his unblinking gaze and said, "We will move on Novgorod as soon as the snow begins to melt."

Batu smirked. "The entire army?"

Subotai met Batu's eyes, let his superiority of consciousness show through just long enough to make the arrogant Batu drop his gaze. "No," the orlok said with soft calmness, "just you and two of your tuman-bashis—and myself." Then his voice lightened with his simple and genuine sense of humor. "I would like to see this Baltic. Perhaps I will catch a fish for your dinner while you hammer away at the log palisades of Novgorod like a good little soldier."

The insult was not lost on Batu. Any Mongol would rather starve than eat a slimy fish. Subotai waited with a bemused expectancy on his face for any retort from Batu, but the younger man let it pass.

ϕ   ϕ   ϕ   ϕ

The winter mists lingered over the bogs and woods they had to struggle through to reach the prize of Novgorod. The northern sun was a dim white ball seen only now and again when the diaphanous, floating veils thinned ever so slightly. The Mongol bowstrings were limp with dampness. The orlok could not get his reconnaissance units far enough afield to monitor adequately the flank and point safety of the two Mongol tumans as they labored north through the wilderness which barricaded the great trading city.

And when even the steppe horses began to sicken from the labor in cold swamps and clinging snowbanks, Subotai ordered them back toward the drier southerly steppes. Batu said nothing, appearing as ready as any to retreat out of the dismal and soggy and dispiriting land.

φ   φ   φ   φ

Standing as unmoving as one of the great rooted pines, Prince Alexander Yaroslavevich watched the rear point of the Mongol cavalry fade in the unrelenting rain. Had they continued on for but a day or two longer, his trap would have sprung on them, but their thickset general had sensed something. Yaroslavevich had recognized him easily, even as he and his forest squads shadowed the Mongol column from a distance in the glades. The Mongol general's straightness of spine, his unresting watchfulness—yes, that Mongol had known the Rus were there. He had seen the broad Mongol commander suddenly turn his mount and ride to the edge of the band of forest where the Rus, in masterful camouflage, were waiting to cut him down as soon as he passed the first tree. The Mongol had reined his horse up short of the trees and stared with extraordinary stillness into the woods. Yaroslavevich had broken the basic rule of concealment—"Never look at the quarry"—and stared intently through the wisps of fog, but he had not been able to make out the features of the wide, Asiatic face. He thought he detected, even at that distance, a shadowed smile crossing the Mongol's obscured countenance. And it was then that the slant-eyed Mongol general had turned his mounted invaders back, away from the poised Rus ambush.

φ   φ   φ   φ

Kotyan, now a widower for many years, received the Mongol emissaries with cold civility. The old Kipchak khan listened with an attentive and serious demeanor to the dictatorial tones of the Mongols as they urged him to bring his people under the protection of the laws of the Yassa of the dead Genghis Kha Khan. Kotyan appeared to nod his head in sage acknowledgment of the advantages afforded to the vassals of the Mongol empire.

He hid both his fear and his hatred of the eastern devils. They had cut his left eye out and whitened half of his face with scar markings those long years ago, and there had been that half a lifetime he had spent under the cold contempt of his Mongol wife, Mursechen.

When the Mongols ceased talking, Kotyan took the opportunity to ask, "If I seek the protection of Batu Khan, will my military levies be enough?"

The senior emissary, sensing the success of his coerciveness, smiled. "The matter of your military support for our ventures would best be discussed with the Lord Batu and his orlok, Subotai Bahadur."

Kotyan stiffened at the mention of that name. The Kipchak's head began to ache with hateful tension. What a plague that name had been upon his life! Mursechen had taunted him over the years with intimations of a hidden love—purer, more sacred in its uncomsummated state than the carnal mating offered by her brutish husband.

And once, just once, he had seen the specter that had haunted his yurt, seen him through his one remaining eye across the cold ice of the Khalka River. Kotyan stayed his vengeful smile. He had learned later that it had been Jebe the Arrow they had struck down, and that it was Subotai he had seen abandon the pursuit when the Arrow fell. But the blue, cat's eyes of the man were still registered in his memory.

Then the Kipchak spoke, but before the last word died he knew he should have held his tongue. "Will we be required to ride with Lord Batu when he moves toward the Carpathians and the Danube?"

Sickly looks came over the faces of the Mongol envoys at this revelation that Kotyan had knowledge of the secret intention to move the Golden Empire farther west, but the emissary caught his balance and said, "Another matter for you to negotiate with the Lord Batu."

But the Kipchak knew the Mongols were now aware that he had been treating with the Rus who still opposed the Mongols, and he did not ponder his alternatives for long. Before a moon-month had passed, Kotyan gathered the Kipchak nation and marched westward toward the Hungarian plateau and the Danube basin. And Europe was warned of the Mongol coming.

φ   φ   φ   φ

The orlok stood alone in the darkness. Behind him, lighting the black Sky above the Russian steppe, the flames of the burning city of Kiev marked the passage of the Mongol army. Kiev was nearly half a day's ride behind them now, but he could still see the fires that showed its fate. To the Western world and to history, Kiev was a proud center of culture, its destruction an act of barbarism. To the Golden Horde, it was simply one more obstacle to be burned and forgotten, its total destruction a pragmatic guarantee against its becoming a threat to their rear.

Subotai listened to the night sounds of the Mongol war camp around him. The distant challenge of a circling guard picket, the hooves of a passing column of riders bound on a scouting mission toward the Carpathian heights in the west, the sing-song of Chin voices in the work detachments. It was beyond the familiar to him now, it was an ingrained mode of life scribed into his consciousness by decades of war.

The garrison yurt occupied by Batu was lit like a Chin fishing lantern. The sounds of loud laughter and the dull, metallic sounds of gold and silver wine cups in salute came from its interior. As usual, Batu had ceremonially invited Kaidu and Subotai to the victory celebration, and as usual, it was unspokenly understood to be only a gesture. Neither the prince nor the orlok was welcome, and it was well known that neither desired to attend.

The night was bitter and the snow crust crunched beneath the orlok's feet as he walked to his command yurt, which was mounted on a cart frame. Within, charcoal braziers bayed the cold at the cart-yurt's ribbing. He lit an oil lamp with a fodder straw set aflame from one of the glowing braziers. Then he brought out the rough maps he had sketched in ink on leather, maps of the lands west of the Rus steppes based on intelligence of the eastern Europeans and their territories gleaned from traders and spies. Prominently demarcated on one were simple markings representing the Carpathian mountain range and the Danube River. In some places on the maps Chin ideograms denoted the location of towns and cities. The orlok had come late to his literacy, developing his own coded notation based on the patient schooling in the Chin language and writing systems Kua had provided for him.

Old Kua. Subotai smiled, then was startled to remember that the brilliant Chin engineer had been dead these long sun-years. The orlok thought it odd that he had forgotten Kua was dead, that it was even an effort for him to sort through his memory in order to recall Kua's death. Then it was there, as though he were again standing right beside Kua on the wooden assault tower as it had been moved up to the wall around Hai-feng. Once again he heard Kua's warning scream as the Chin defenders thrust out a long pole with a flaming pot on the end of it, and once again he smelled the explosive smell of the Chin fire-pots. Into his mouth came the same taste that had fouled his tongue when he smelled Kua's burning body as the Chin engineer was blown off the tower.

Subotai spent long moments swallowing down that taste until the remembrance of Hai-feng was gone, then put aside the maps with sudden disinterest. Batu's envoys and his Russian informers had brought word that the Kipchaks had gone, abandoning the ancestral grazing lands which they had held for centuries. Since the land east and south and to the north of them was under imperial Mongol control, there was only one direction they could have taken. There would be no need for covertness now, or clandestine reconnaissance. Somehow Subotai would have to convince Batu to move across the snow to the eastern slopes of the Carpathians and from there to watch for the Europeans to form their armies.

Kipchaks. What a curse they had been to him. He wondered if their khan, Kotyan, was the same noyon who had taken Mursechen so long ago. But there were probably many Kotyans among the Kipchaks. He wondered about the nature of his obsession for Mursechen, its undiminished power over his conscious mind even after all these sun-years and after Gauri and Kralyan. He had internalized this as devotion for Kali, yet his man's nature still hungered for the humanness of the youthful Mursechen of his memories.

The cart-bed creaked and swayed. Subotai came from his musings as Kaidu stepped into the yurt. In the semi-light of the warm yurt, with his face obscured by the darkness, Kaidu easily could have been taken for Temajin. The Mongol prince carelessly cast aside his fur cloak and seated himself beside the yurt's central brazier across from the orlok. He lifted the drinking skin that was slung over his shoulder, ducked his head under its rawhide thong to bite out the plug, and offered the skin to Subotai. The orlok accepted it and swallowed half a mouthful of the clear, fiery Russian liquor. It warmed his innards and dispelled the night chills of his age.

Kaidu reclaimed the skin and took two consecutive swallows before replugging the pouch and setting it aside. Then he stared through the dim light at the chunky Mongol general. "From the howling over yonder, it sounds as though cousin Batu, our great Sain Khan, has convinced himself that he arranged another victory."

Subotai smiled. "Now we are going to have to convince him to keep going toward the Danube. I am afraid that now that Kiev is in ashes, he will think his little steppe domain will be as snug as a squirrel burrow."

They both turned their heads slightly at a fresh outburst of revelry coming from the khan's yurt, and Subotai remarked, "What he doesn't know is how much the Rus hate to bring him his tribute every sun, and how easily they could persuade the western Christians to come to their aid against him."

Kaidu nodded in agreement. "I think your plan to move up to the Carpathians before the winter ends should be followed," Kaidu said. "Then we will be able to rest the troops and horses before we face the western Christians."

Subotai looked into the glowing brazier, and the light of the coals blued in reflection from his eyes. "If we can credit the tales told by our trading friends, the Europeans are too sluggardly to take the field in cold weather."

Kaidu took another pull at the drinking skin and offered it to Subotai once more, but the orlok refused it this time. Kaidu recognized the dry, concise edge in the orlok's voice as Subotai said, "From this point on, I want wide reconnaissance sweeps rotated up to the Danube. These...what are their names?"

"Poles, Germans, and Hungarians," Kaidu prompted.

"I think they will be much like the Rus," Subotai said, making his thoughts into words. "If we let them gather in strength, they will be able to make very stubborn defensive stands. Should they assemble in great numbers, we will have little choice but to avoid them or draw them out. And if we waste our strength at exercises like those we went through against the Rus on the Khalka River, we will face disaster."

Feminine shrieks were now added to the riotous cacophony disturbing the cold night. "From the sound of it, I am tempted to join in myself," Kaidu said.

Subotai, recognizing it would be fruitless to voice any more of the objections he had been raising for years, feigned an approving interest. "I noticed those strong, blonde Rus noblewomen you sorted out for yourself at the Kiev walls. Ample companionship, I'll wager, for a night as cold as this." He tried to conceal the suggestion that Kaidu leave him for the night.

Kaidu looked upon the orlok with the regard of a respectful grandson, but he said, half humorously, "If it please you, Lord Orlok." He stood and resumed his cloak. "I shall have the older one sent here for your comfort this night." Kaidu was gone into the night before Subotai could fabricate an excuse to avoid the woman, and he knew Kaidu would do just as he had said. Pointless to dispute it. Subotai laughed under his breath. Damned Kaidu, an incarnation of the devil of the wind. Just like Temajin and, yes, like Bourtai. Subotai was setting spitted meat to roast over the brazier when he heard the knock on his cart-frame. He called out permission to enter, and two Mongol soldiers thrust a Russian woman into the yurt. They saluted, and the orlok dismissed them.

The woman cowered against the felt yurt-wall, head down and with her eyes tightly closed. She was voluptuous in the manner of women who bloom into a mature beauty in early middle age. Her hair had been brightly blonde once, but it had browned and grayed slightly with the years. Her face was wide and strong, with cheek bones almost as high as a Mongol's. Her heavy bosom heaved with the breathing of fear and of shame.

Subotai could see she was cold. His face impassive, he got up and covered the crouching woman's shoulders with his heavy fur coat. He noticed that two of her fingers were bleeding where jewelry had no doubt been torn from them. The sizzle of dripping fat made him to go the brazier to turn the meat before he went to his war chest and lifted the hinged lid. Then he stood and reached for one of the hanging lamps, took it from its suspension and set it on the open chest lid. When he found the precious little clay jar of ointment, he rehung the lamp and let the chest lid drop with a bang. The Russian woman jerked, and her green eyes locked open with shock and terror. Her jaw muscles set, as though by this she could hold at bay the horrors she had gone through and was expecting.

Subotai took off his wide girdle-belt with its dagger and hung it above the war chest. No point in giving her an easy opportunity like that. Then he went to the stricken woman and sat down next to her wet boot toes which were showing beneath her full, blue velvet skirt. She locked her arms about her knees and riveted her head downwards into their fold.

She stopped breathing when he touched her. He seized her left thigh, digging his iron grip into the back of her knee to straighten her leg, and pulled the soaked boot free. Glaring at him with a sudden return of her woman's pride, she struck at him when he dug into the nerves behind her right knee to take off the other boot. Subotai ignored her slaps until the boot was off her other foot, then he caught her left hand and, turning his left thumb under her down-turned knuckles, lifted it toward the yurt ceiling with her elbow bent and locked by his arm in an excruciating hold. She breathed loudly and viciously through her teeth, but the slaps stopped. Then she whimpered and looked pleadingly at Subotai, mutely begging him to release her hand.

Subotai maintained the cruel lock, but spoke softly in the Rus he had learned from the Russian turncoats who fawned about Batu. "Are you hungry, my Lady?"

The violence had seemed to dispel some of her fear. The emerald eyes were not as wide now. "Yes," she said softly and breathlessly.

Still he did not release her tortured hand but reached with his other hand for a luxuriously soft sable cloak which had recently adorned the back of a Russian merchant and began to dry one of her feet.

When Subotai let go, she rubbed her strained hand, and then, for some reason, drew up her skirts to her knees to let him finish drying her wet, cold feet and ankles. Her white calves were fully and heavily alluring. She was very quiet when he took the hand he had so recently and brutally twisted to dab the soothing ointment onto the torn flesh where her gold rings, her portion from her father, had been.

Then the broad, powerful, gray-haired man got up and turned his back to her. He lifted the spits and, looking over his shoulder, he said, "Come."

She came slowly and watchfully and sat facing him, reaching for the hot meat on the spit he held out to her.

"No," he said, "here." She obeyed his gestures and sat next to him, relief from fear and from searing memories of the Mongol sack of Kiev beginning to show in her face.

She waited respectfully for him to start eating first, then she bit ravenously at the food, and once even sobbed in relief from her terrible hunger. Seeing her famishment, Subotai paused after a few bites and replaced the empty spit in her hand with his own which was still heavy with succulent goat meat. She thanked him with her wide-set eyes and finished the meal. Subotai filled silver cups with scooped snow and set them beside the brazier and they quenched their thirst with the melted snow.

She wondered which rich family in Kiev had been robbed of the cups, which were exotically designed in a way unknown to her. From time to time she stole glances at the man beside her. He seemed much older than she, yet his eyes were youthful and his skin was firm and healthy. And already, in only a short time, he had shown her more kindness and consideration than her husband had shown her in half a lifetime of wedlock. She knew the powerful man beside her was a soldier of great authority among these savage barbarians, yet he was pleasing beyond words to her. She shuddered at the memory of her husband writhing out his life impaled on a Mongol lance, but the recollection of his greed and his miserliness dampened any feeling of loss she had carried away from the flames of Kiev. Thank God there had been no children; he had been too grasping to consider feeding additional mouths, seldom sleeping with her even in the long, cold Russian winter nights.

While she looked to the past, the orlok sought out the future. He now realized that the years he had allowed for subduing the western lands were more than the years remaining of his life. It would be left to Kaidu and Kadaan, if they survived, to carry forward the immense and detailed operational, occupational, and logistical plan he had conceived for conquering the fabled city of Rome and even the island of Britain. Since most of the strategic approach to the Mongol assault on Europe was recorded only within his mind, it would be necessary for one of the Chinese scribes to begin taking the plan from him by dictation.

Then another complication: who among the Mongol leadership could decipher the written Chin language? Kaidu was brilliant, but in a wild way that Subotai could not imagine being harnessed long enough to learn even the rudiments of the ideograms which Kua had so patiently taught the orlok. Kadaan? Subotai rubbed his jaw thoughtfully. Kadaan had the same almost insanely reckless courage as his nephew Kaidu, but sometimes Subotai had noticed him in thoughtful and withdrawn moods. Perhaps he would become the living repository of the plan of conquest Subotai was about to put into operation.

The plan carried the hallmark of his own innate military genius. The Genghis Kha Khan had developed the operational guidelines for it before his death. And some of the Chin auxiliary officers had contributed the concepts of their great military theoretician, Sun Tzu, to the plan as well.

Letting his thoughts return to Kadaan, Subotai decided to look for a diplomatic way of persuading the young Mongol prince to undertake the study of the Chin ideograms. But now, with the handsome Russian woman near him, Subotai felt once again and nearly as powerfully as in his earlier manhood the flow of his Ch'i and procreative powers.

He sensed that her tensions had subsided. Her thick hair was tangled, and Subotai, moving to sit behind her, gently began straightening the gray-brown strands. The feel of the woman's hair in his hands amplified his arousal. She turned her head slightly to facilitate his care of her tresses, then reached across his lap with her left arm and offered her moist lips up to his. He steadied her head with both hands, gently gripping her magnificent hair, and kissed her full mouth. Her kiss moistened even more when he slid his strong hand upwards beneath the rich skirts to caress her soft and heavy thighs. His only concessions to luxury were the numerous and rich furs which covered the floor of the command yurt, and these now provided the warm mattressing where he and the Rus woman came together, the sensual velvet of her skirts adding an extra dimension to his pleasure in her.

For several days thereafter she was cloistered in Subotai's command yurt as it creaked across the Ukranian steppe toward the setting sun. He came to her only once after that. And in the dark of the following morning he consigned her to another of the huge rolling cart-yurts, one of those bound for the Mongol stronghold in high Asia. They parted in silence after a Russian interpreter explained to her that the leather scroll Subotai had tied to her waist beneath her clothing bore his special seals and elaborate instructions entrusting her to the court of the Empress Bourtai.

The Russian woman knew she was being sent out of the war zone along with other women captives. As they traveled eastward, she tried to control her own fear and comfort the scores of younger Rus women when the column of cart-yurts passed by the crow-circled ruins of Kiev. Her fear and bewilderment grew when they crossed the ice of the Dnieper River and, days later, the Volga.

The Mongol soldiers convoying the women followed their strict orders and stayed apart from them and from the Mongol women who chaperoned and guarded them. In time the Rus women and the Mongol women began to eat together and even to communicate. On the long journey the handsome woman of Kiev became aware of the deferential treatment accorded her by the Mongol women. When, after long, slow months of travel across the boundless steppes, she had learned enough of their tongue to enter into conversation with the Mongol women, she was told the identity and the rank of her military benefactor. She was also told she was bound for the north of far China, and that the orlok had already sent a message with the arrow couriers asking the empress to take the Rus woman under her protection.

She had never seen the face of her protector in the daylight, only by the weak light of the yurt lamps. The strongest memory of him she carried was of the last morning when he had wheeled his horse in the darkness and, sending snow flying, had galloped away, the cold vapor of his mount's breath disappearing in the indistinct dawn.

φ   φ   φ   φ

The mountain streams on the eastern slope of the Carpathians were trickling with the first loosenings of the spring melt. Subotai, Kadaan, and Kaidu had pushed and coaxed the reluctant Batu across the Rus steppes, but the movement of the Mongol army had been delayed by the Sain Khan's lagging spirit. The three Mongol commanders stood in the orlok's command yurt scrutinizing the rough map of the Danube and Carpathian region. They knew that by now the Europeans were nearly ready to move against them. Their intelligence and spy system had located the mustering points for at least five major armies gathering to oppose them beyond the Danube.

"Lord Kadaan," Subotai looked at the stalwart young Mongol prince. "You will take the southern spear. Ride down the Magyar army but,"—and here the orlok raised his hand in emphasis—"if they are horse-archers as we are, lead them into the west but do not bring them to battle. Then you must return to the rendezvous point at the western side of the Carpathians where the Magyar gate-trail begins in the foothills east of the Danube."

Subotai pointed at three small horse symbols on the war map. All three lay just east of the Carpathian range: one at the eastern entry to the Magyar gate, the central pass through the range; one north of the gate at the Vistula River; and the third one south of the gate where a narrow plain opened between the southern Carpathians and the Grecian mountains. "Rotate couriers back to the post stations and inform me daily of your tactical situation. I intend to go with the northern spear which you, Kaidu, will command. Batu Khan will have to clear a way over the Magyar gate."

The orlok saw their young yet seasoned eagerness, and added, "We all know that the largest army is forming among the Hungarians. By our three-pronged attack around and through the Carpathians, we should be able to draw the Hungarians across the Danube, and once there, it will be absolutely mandatory that we be able to reassemble and bring our full power to bear on them."

Subotai glanced toward the snowy Carpathian slopes. Batu's tumans were already route-marching toward the Magyar gate. He looked queryingly at the Mongol princes, but both of them seemed confident, and clear about his strategy. He rolled up the map and tied it with a rawhide thong. They stepped out of the yurt and onto their saddled ponies, Kadaan turning toward his tumans which had formed up to the south of the encampment, the orlok and Kaidu together signalling for the tuman commanders to order the march toward the north.

Kaidu's division rode with the orlok's urgency. Three separate and numerically powerful armies were gathering to come together and confront them along the front of Kaidu's route.

φ   φ   φ   φ

Henry, Duke of Silesia, took the hard-crusted bread which the priest thrust into his hand. The Liegnitz cathedral was filled. Beside him the grand master of the Teutonic Knights joined in the kneeling mass. There was a steely rustle of mail and the sounds of helmets and sword scabbards scraping against the stone floor as the communion bread passed among the ranks of Knights Templar and Teutonic Knights kneeling at prayer-benches near the altar. The square outside the church was a mass of Polish and German troops, horses, and supply carts.

Henry listened to the droning Latin. He had never understood the mass, but he had always felt a comforting pleasure in hearing the soft Latin, so different from his native Polish and German tongues. He looked up at the wooden image of the tortured Christ on the cross above him, then glanced over his shoulder. Damn. Why were the priests taking so much time? The Mongols were near. And it had been only three days since the stragglers of the Polish armies of Boleslas and Prince Miestislas had appeared, nearly crazed with fear and babbling their tales of the speed with which the Mongols had divided and broken the Polish knights and men-at-arms.

How could the Mongols have come so swiftly? The Oder River should have slowed them, but already they were reported nearly upon Liegnitz. The duke stood up without waiting for the priests to finish the rite of the wine-soaked communion bread. The German bishop made the cross as the duke and the knights filed out of the sanctuary and, taking reins offered by squires, novices, and men-at-arms, mounted their heavy war chargers. Henry kicked his horse into a walk and led the army through the portal in the east wall of Liegnitz. Somehow they must join with the Bohemians marching from the south under Wenceslas. If they could cover the open ground between Liegnitz and the hills to the south before the pagan cavalry appeared, they could form on the heights and then let that slant-eyed devil try. What was that strange name the bishop had read from the letters of King Bela of Hungary? Yes, Subotai—that was it. Subotai was not the king of the Mongols, but his military reputation filled the Latin letter the bishop had translated.

The April morning was sunny and the Germans and Poles marched enthusiastically behind him. Surely they would encounter King Wenceslas and his troops before nightfall. Wenceslas' reputation as a reveler and a lover of his cups and table were the talk of

Europe, but he had mustered his army readily enough to meet the pagan threat to Christendom. Duke Henry assured himself that Wenceslas' troops, at least, would be welcome comrades-in-arms.

The duke noted the irregular band of dark against the landscape to his left and assumed it was a line of trees. Then he saw that line waver, and for an instant what he had taken for vertical pine caught a whiteness in the sunlight. The band of trees suddenly granulated into horses and riders with long ashen lances held vertically to the blue spring sky. The veteran grand master left the duke's side and, issuing harsh, Germanic commands, turned the disciplined Teutonic Knights in one smooth flanking movement to face the oncoming Mongols.

The Germans set their mounts into a three-ranked, thundering charge across the open, untilled earth. Without the stylized discipline of the knights of the German military order but with a matching martial ardor, Henry spurred after them, packing closely in with his own Polish and Silesian knights. His view blocked by the charging Germans, the duke did not see the Mongol skirmish line split, then melt away in front of the European lances. The Poles and the Germans wheeled ponderously after the fleet Mongol lancemen, but a great shout behind him shocked Henry with the knowledge of his fatal underestimation of the pagans. Other Mongol units had appeared behind him and now they systematically began to butcher the European infantry with volley after volley of arrows. The terrorized infantry fled toward the knights who were now scattered and were attempting to regroup. The battlefield became a chaos of running infantry seeking the protection of the mailed knights from the rattle of unseen Mongol shafts.

Then, impeded by the foot-soldiers gathering to them, the mounted knights were struck along their disorganized longitudinal axis by quilt-padded, heavy Mongol lancemen astride horses as aggressive and nearly as large as the European warhorses. The lancemen struck against the knights like a single pulse, then turned away as volley after volley of arrow flights broke the Europeans into a mob running insanely back toward the supposed safety of the walled city of Liegnitz. The Mongols harried them for miles. And when the fleeing Europeans encountered more Mongols blocking the route back, they turned in despair. By the time the sun reached its noon position in the sky, they had fallen almost to a man.

φ   φ   φ   φ

The orlok rode slowly through the blood and the wildly scattered disarray of equipment in the aftermath of Liegnitz. The flower of the Teutonic Knights had perished on this field under the Mongol swords and arrows, their classical German courage scarcely a consideration against the genius of the orlok and the veteran nomadic cavalry which was his weapon.

The Germans were big men, he noted, even bigger than the Rus. He got down to look at several of the dead knights at closer range. One in particular caught his eye, a man younger than most of the others, helmetless, with blue eyes startled in the unblinking gaze of violent death, and blond hair streaked and matted with dried blood. Subotai stared at the corpse of the young German warrior, unable to look away. Something about the face, the contrasting black and red stubble of the beard against the sunny hair, or was it something else?

Then with an emotionally shattering echo, it came ringing down the years to him. The blue of the glazed eyes, the gold of the light coming off the man's head—they were the same as those in the treasured image he had carried of Mursechen in his mind since his youth.

In that moment, Subotai Bahadur, Orlok of Temajin, the Genghis Kha Khan, conqueror of a sixth of the earth, began to grow old. The emotion of the freshened memory of Mursechen now drained and shook him. How it might have been with them! He conjured up once again the nearly forgotten desire he had had for a life with her in the olden, simple ways of the nomads. Somewhere along the way he had forgotten that he had never even spoken to her.

Subotai realized at last that the Solar Warrior had been right in saying that he would suffer because of the desire he carried for the light-eyed woman. Then, as though by some instantaneous triggering of a biological mechanism, Subotai's extraordinary mental faculties began to phase away from the conscious control of his great will. His aged body, the healed and unhealed wounds, the weary, aching trials of the unending campaigns through the freezing sleet and snow, the merciless sun, the thirst, the unnumbered cares and duties of command, the hunger, the shocks and the uncompromising demands of combat across two continents and always against superior numbers—they all rose up in a hammering plague in that moment. All of the old pains and traumas he had so carefully controlled now came upon him like jackals sensing their triumph at last.

"Lord Subotai." The weary arrow rider grew frightened when his repeated words did not break the distant and unwavering set of eyes of the still-standing man. "Lord Subotai?" Still the orlok was statuelike, his vision locked. The courier gently touched the orlok's arm. "General, sir, are you wounded?"

Subotai jerked his head, then said in a voice cracked with uneasiness, "No, I am not wounded."

"Sir, Lord Kadaan sends word that he has smashed the Magyars. They are scattered, Lord."

It took an enormous effort, but the orlok drew his mind back to the messenger. His own speech sounded distant and fuzzy in his ears. "And Batu Khan, is there any word from him?"

The courier did not answer immediately. Then he dredged up his courage and said, "Lord, the khan sends no word, but,"—and here the arrow rider swallowed hard—"the khan's tuman commanders bade me tell you that the Hungarians have a great host of Germans with them and have begun to cross the Danube. And, Lord, the khan does not stir against them." An expression of breathless relief crossed the young man's face after he had blurted out the message.

Subotai wished to the Sky that some of Temajin or Bourtai had carried into Batu. He looked at the worn courier and asked, "Did you come directly from the khan or were you relayed from the post stations on the Rus side of the mountains?"

"I rode directly, Lord."

"Did you mark your path as you came so that you can lead me straight back the same way?"

"Yes, sir."

Subotai turned his back on the messenger and began to unsaddle his horse. He looked once over his shoulder at the soldier and said, "Find Prince Kaidu. Tell him we are going back to the central column. Also, you are to tell him not to forget about the Bohemians. When he is finished with the city of Liegnitz he is to engage them or maneuver them out of our way, at least until we have dealt with the Hungarians." He pulled the saddle off and simply let it fall to the ground. It seemed heavier than it had ever been before. "When you have delivered your message to Prince Kaidu, return to me here, but let me sleep until dark. Do you understand all I have said, son?"

"Yes, sir." The arrow rider swung up onto his swift pony. But he jerked his animal up short in the middle of turning it away from the Mongol general and asked with a shivering note in his voice, "Are you going to sleep right here, Lord Subotai?"

The orlok threw an old army quilt and a ragged fur on the ground between two dead Teutonic knights and, without turning, he answered, "Aye, lad. Right here."

And in his great weariness the orlok sank in sleep, unaware of the flies that buzzed about the fresh man-blood or the sun's warmth steeping his own body which had somehow aged and tired in a single morning. His consciousness subsided into a partial darkness which had a drifting and subtle screen of changing shades about it which altered and held him aware of its presence. Then he tasted the great thirst he had experienced in India once, but the dream's vision was a snow-covered steppe. He stooped to take some snow to cool his dryness and quench the unbearable thirst, but the snow became the hot sand of the Hindu desert in his hand. He let it trickle through his fingers and watched it become snow again as it fell. He looked up when a man's shadow moved across the face of the snow. Even before he saw the face he knew from the fringed boots and the long shanks that it was Temajin. But when he lifted his eyes to the man's face the face was dark and the locks of hair were deepest black.

Subotai heard his own voice say from afar, "Oh my Lord Dharayan, have you come for me at last?"

The Solar Warrior reached and also took up a handful of the snow, but the flakes did not become grains of sand. The brown hand squeezed the snow, and a clear torrent of water gushed from the Solar Warrior's fist. Subotai let the water flow into his open mouth, and it drove out the thirst and brought back the enormous vitality of his young manhood.

When at last Subotai ceased swallowing the water, Dharayan

lowered his hand. The Solar Warrior began to walk away as he had so long ago after the great plague in Sarghoda, but he stopped once, turned and looked back at Subotai, and spoke. The face and the voice were Dharayan's, but the words were Temajin's. "The work is not yet finished." Then the Solar Warrior smiled and the ground shook so that Subotai could no longer see him.

"Sir! Lord Subotai! You must wake up, it is growing dark. You said to let you sleep only until nightfall."

Subotai sat up, still befuddled with sleep. The night air of the German spring seemed unusually cold to him, and he shivered. The arrow rider went to the orlok's saddle and untied his fur coat and brought it to him. Subotai got up and slipped into the coat all in the same movement. "I appreciate it, son. Did you by chance lift some rations from Kaidu's larders?"

The soldier grinned conspiratorially. "Yes, sir. I sure did."

"Good lad. Let's fall to and start our ride on a full belly, then straight to hell with the rest of it, eh, lad?"

"Yes, sir," the boy said, suddenly liking the warrior legend he was now standing beside.

φ   φ   φ   φ

"They are encamped on the other side of that river, Lord Subotai." The tuman orkhan who spoke was a seasoned campaigner. "Do the Hungarians have a name for that river?" Subotai asked.

"They call it the Sajo, sir."

Subotai surveyed the gigantic circle of armored wagons in the distance. The Hungarians, Germans, and more of the Knights Templar were there—a huge host, as though all Christendom had come in arms against him. "And they hold that bridge over the Sajo?"

The tuman commander's jaw muscles set. "Aye, Lord."

Subotai was quiet as though deep in thought, but he had lapsed into his worn condition once again. The long breakneck ride from the battlefield at Liegnitz to the Sajo east of the Hungarian cities of Buda and Pest on the Danube had exhausted him. Fortune had favored the Mongols, though, for Batu's inactivity had encouraged King Bela, who, as Subotai had hoped he would, ferried his entire force across the Danube and marched toward the Mongol garrison at the western foot of the Carpathians where the Magyar gate debouched not far from the Sajo River.

"What word has been received from Prince Kadaan?"

"We do not expect his column to appear before tomorrow, Lord."

"Then we must move before the dawn tomorrow." Subotai heard his own words, but they seemed to emerge from somewhere apart from himself. "Kadaan's force, when it arrives, could have the shock effect we may need. I want to lock them into their wall of wagons and hold them there until they would rather die than stay within that laager. But," and strength returned to his speech as he went on, "that bridgehead must be taken in the morning. No paths of attack are to be left to them. I will take your tuman and two more and cross the Sajo north of the bridge tonight. We must have the bridge and have their laager encircled before sunrise." Subotai turned his eyes from scanning the smoky enemy camp to gaze on the tuman orkhan and asked, "Who do you suggest to lead the assault on the bridge?"

The orkhan was about to answer when a voice behind them interrupted. "I will lead the assault."

Startled, they turned and saw Batu coming up to them. It was a different Batu they saw, sober and clear-eyed, intent with purpose. As though reading Subotai's thoughts, he said, "They will be ready to run back to the Danube after a day or so of naphtha and flaming arrows and catapult stones raining on their golden heads."

For the first time in years, the Sain Khan and the orlok gripped each other's hands.

After dispatching Chin work parties to throw a hasty bridge across the Sajo far above the outermost Hungarian pickets, Subotai napped away the remaining daylight hours. He awakened at dusk and felt an incandescent return of his old strength, drawn up from the excitement and uncertainty of the great battle that was almost upon him.

Now the young arrow courier, who had been attached by Subotai as his personal aide, handed the orlok a mug of warm mare's milk. "Lord, the tumans are already starting across the log bridge the Chinese have built."

The orlok saluted with his milk mug and his old readiness rang in his voice. "Then we shall not be far behind. Let's get mounted and after them, lad."

The three divisions, the orlok with them, were across the river before midnight. Batu, charging closely on the heels of an intense Chinese catapult preparation on the Sajo bridgehead, felt a resurgence of his former battle craze. Under his leadership, the Mongols overwhelmed the hard-fighting Hungarian knights and men-at-arms who were holding the stone causeway. By first light the European wagon laager was totally encircled and under arrow and catapult fire.

Some of the Hungarians and Templars sallied out at mid-morning against their tormentors, only to meet the arriving tumans under Prince Kadaan who had been riding insanely to the scene of the battle.

The interior of the European laager was beset with panic as the Hungarian charge was routed and thrown back to the defensive wagons.

Then Subotai ordered the encirclement broken to the west of the huge defensive laager. The opening drew the terrorized Europeans out of their wagon-wall riding and running to escape the unrelenting fire arrows and the burning catapult shots that were hurtling down in the midst of the Hungarian camp.

The Mongol sabermen leisurely isolated pockets of the fleeing Europeans and slaughtered them in the woods or on the wide plain. Few of that proud Hungarian and German host ever saw the Danube again. Perhaps more than a hundred and fifty thousand men died in the bitter retreat between the Sajo and the Danube. Subotai's losses amounted to less than five hundred men, most of whom perished at the fiercely contested battle for the bridgehead.

φ   φ   φ   φ

The orlok had planned and commanded a lightning campaign that in less than a month had utterly destroyed four major European armies sent against him and driven off a fifth, the Bohemians under King Wenceslas. Now the Mongols awaited the appearance of other western forces, especially those of the warlike and spirited Holy Roman Emperor, Frederick II of Hohenstaufen, but no European armies took the field during the warm months after the Christian disaster at the Sajo River.

In the days following the battle on the Sajo, Subotai spent the warm afternoons sleeping in the Mongol camp near the Danube. He awoke one afternoon to find Batu sitting quietly near his yurt's entrance. The Sain Khan held a golden tablet on his lap. Subotai turned questioning eyes on the khan. "Ogadai?" Then he answered himself with another question. "He is dead?"

Batu nodded. "We are ordered back to the Kirultai to elect the new Kha Khan."

The arrival of the golden tablet of khanate authority with the news of Ogadai's death, carried across Eurasia from the Blue Lake, sealed the end of the western march of the Mongol armies. To Subotai it had come as a blessing. He was tired now beyond caring. He had sustained Temajin's will to the end of his vigor, and now he knew that for him, the work was at last finished.

Subotai, Batu, and the princes, Kaidu and Kadaan, conferred briefly. The Mongol columns west of the Danube were to be notified to ride past in view of the German cities, even Vienna if possible, before following the general retirement toward the far steppes.

The Mongol columns appeared, always in the dead of night, at the fortified, walled cities and, through captive interpreters, shouted that the army of the Sain Khan was called away, that the Germans were to be spared war—for the time being. After calling up to the watch at each town or city, the Mongols would vanish, leaving even the more seasoned German commanders shaken and sweating in their watch-towers, and to all of Europe a legacy of fear that would haunt the western world for generations to come.

And as the Hungarian dusk settled on the evening before he would begin his journey east, the orlok rode toward the Danube. The night was warm, but the air cooled steadily as he approached the banks of the river, its surface silvered by a bright, moonlit Sky.

Subotai stepped off and ground-reined his animal at the river's edge. He sat down on a soft clump of grassy sod and listened to the quiet river slip past him. He meditated in this setting of natural peace until the damp river air of midnight brought him back. Then he arose, walked back to his slow-grazing mount and took the blue sword from the saddle scabbard, and returned to the river.

Even in the waning moonlight, he could make out the gray, warped streaks in the fine steel. He hefted the beautiful weapon, swung it in three wide, air-whispering circles over his head, and let it sail away out over the water, its trajectory faintly revealed by uneven, spinning scintillations of reflected moon and starlight. He heard it splash into the Danube.

That sword. He had found it when Mursechen was given to the Kipchak noble, and it had become his life's companion. What a cold wife that steel had been.

φ   φ   φ   φ

"Who is this broken-down old camel?" The young Mongol soldier snatched off Subotai's now dilapidated fur hat. The orlok had long since put aside the steel cap which had armored the old headgear. Others of the special troop detailed to guard Temajin's grave joined in the harassment with delight.

"I don't know," said another, "but from the look of him, he must have spent the Kha Khan's wars herding stock with the womenfolk here at home. See, not even a bow to his name."

The ragged hat flew through the air from rider to rider as they galloped menacingly around Subotai in a wild game of buz kashi. Finally tiring of the sport, one of them plunked the dusty relic onto Subotai's balding head.

"What do you want, old lynx?" He had noticed the slanted, blue cat's-eyes of the old man.

Subotai spoke with tired patience. "Only to visit the Kha Khan's grave for a little while."

Hoots and yells greeted the softly spoken words, but the troop commander who now rode up, an older man, no doubt a veteran, heard Subotai speak. "Let the old man be." And to Subotai, "Go on in, but be certain not to disturb so much as a leaf. We are charged with this shrine. The grave is yonder under the tallest trees of the grove."

Subotai rode into the trees and dismounted in the damp, cool air. The grave, marked by a full-sized, ornate wooden yurt and encircled by heavy granite boulders, was shaded in the late afternoon sun by the advancing shadow of the Iron Mountain to the northwest of the clump of birch and evergreen trees. He walked completely around the stone-lined perimeter of the monument. Here in the silence of this green glade, the Genghis Kha Khan slept the death-sleep that comes to all men, even to the destroyer of nations and empires. Temajin's tall frame was now part of the earth beneath the moist, grassy soil.

Subotai had thought to pray here for his Kha Khan, his friend, but his mind seemed content enough with the peaceful, green setting. Surely the Mother Kali had set them on their path for Her own purposes. It was not that Temajin had gained from it, or himself. He was out of the army now, alone and unheeded even as he had been as a boy, forgotten and discarded by the new Kha Khan. Cycles of life, Dharayan had said. And the old orlok grinned to himself at his hopeless condition.

The troop commander, his back to an evening fire, noticed the old man ride out of the burial grove into the twilight and become lost to view.

One of the Mongol soldiers watched, too. "Do you know him, sir?"

The guard officer squinted into the dusking light. "He reminded me of someone—but, no—it could not have been him."

ᛣ   ᛣ   ᛣ   ᛣ

He knew from the gathering cold of the lengthening nights that autumn was upon the land and the end upon his life. He wondered how old he might be, but he had no way of reckoning it. The teal, the geese, and the great swans would soon come from the land above the Taiga, the tundras, which were already the raucous scene of departing flocks, the swift and beautiful peregrine falcons preening and ready to follow after the waterfowl.

On the morning of the day, his warrior's intuition, that high consciousness which had saved the Mongol army on so many desperate fields, had bade him make ready. He felt himself in the grip of an overpowering inner compulsion to meditate upon the spiritual state, and upon the remembered image of the Solar Warrior as the guardian and guide of his Way. He spent the bright hours motionless, eyes closed.

The chill of the windy afternoon vanished into the bitter onset of a night of great stillness. He took the bridle from the white-nosed mare, a descendant from Temajin's own herd, and set the animal loose. He limped painfully into the lonely yurt. The ragged shelter was filled with the unreal, shadowy light-play of a single stone lamp nearly empty now of its oil.

He looked slowly around. The lamp, the small pile of furs on which he slept, a cooking pot. No weapons. Nothing to bring him back. Except—and his loud laugh broke the empty night—except the thought of the blue-eyed woman.

He limped into the darkness. Instinct turned him toward the east. He could not feel the cold as he moved.

When at last he knelt down, his soul swept upward within him. The blessing of the Mother Kali engulfed the war-master as his lifeless body lay easily outward upon the cold ground of the steppe.

An eagle owl drifted over the darkened earth, then an unbroken quietude descended. Beneath the infinite sky, a soft snow began to fall, and soon the whole steppe was silent and covered with clean whiteness.

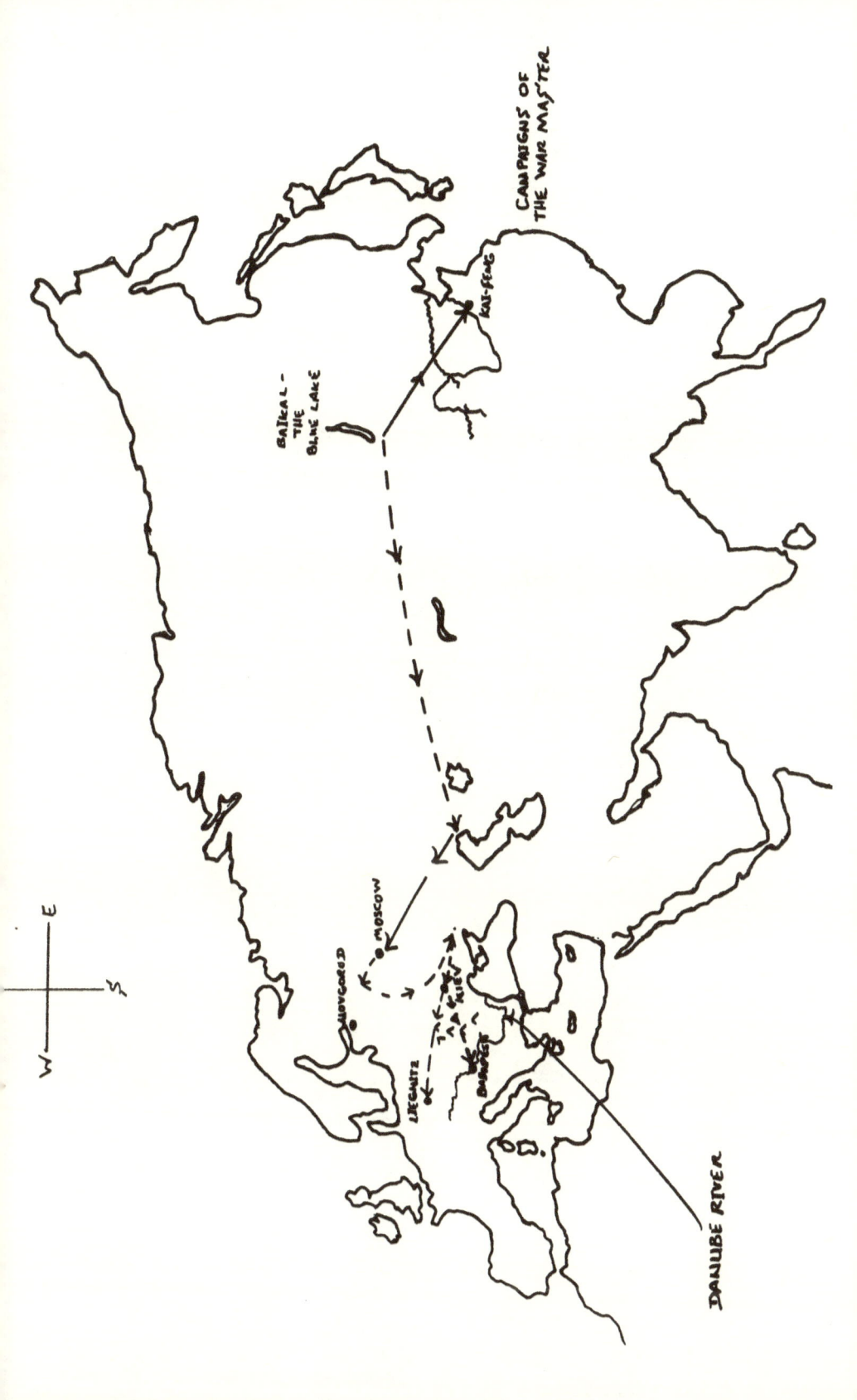

CAMPAIGNS OF
THE WAR MASTER

KAI-FENG

BAIKAL –
THE
BLUE LAKE

MOSCOW

NOVGOROD

LEGNITZ

KIEV

BUDAPEST

DANUBE RIVER

EPILOGUE

The Empress was glad to be free at last, at least for the remainder of the day, from the endless administrative duties. There was a rare lull in the constant stream of emissaries and tasks and demanding decisions which came to her almost daily from the near and distant regions of the Golden Empire of the Yassa—from the Russian lands, from Koryu, from the steppes which reached down to the Hindu Kush, from the hinterlands of China.

And her mind returned, as it had more and more for quite some time now, to the thought of him. She knew from the empty feeling she had experienced some moon-months past that he was gone.

She had seen him many times since the cold night when he had come upon them strangely out of the blizzard. The winter when Temajin, for some unknown reason, had taken her from the Yakka encampment onto the steppe by themselves. She remembered the lovesick boy she had fed in the little cart-yurt. The tales she had been regaled with over the years of when he led the Mangudai against the Chin fire weapons, of his great ride around the Caspian Sea, of the epic battle with the Rus, and of his astonishing campaign into the eastern reaches of the Christian lands—they seemed to be about someone apart from the cold, wet, lonely lad she always remembered. She left the imperial wing and strolled into the palace gardens.

The Russian woman did not hear her quiet approach. "Oh!" she burst out, "you startled me, my Lady," and quickly moved from the place where she was sitting in order to kneel.

The Empress waved her up. Bourtai's hair was now white and gray, but her eyes were still piercing, their brown and jagged yellow coloring adding power to her calm, commanding presence. "Where is the boy?"

The Russian woman smiled affectionately at the great Mongol lady. "By the lake. He likes to throw things into the water to see the reflection of the clouds change and then return. Shall I call him?"

"No, let us walk down to the water and watch him."

The gardens were green and breezy in the summer's afternoon.

The lake was blue and tracked in places by wind and temperature gradients. The little, brown-haired boy was laughing as he chased a flock of white ducks which finally eluded him in a congestion of honking and fluttering across the water. The boy stopped at the water's edge, looking sad as he watched them paddle away. Then his ebullience returned and he ran, barefoot and shouting, through the shallow shore water, soaking the legs of his Chinese silk trousers. His torso was bare and sun-browned, and showed the heavy bones and wide shoulders of his heritage.

The boy bent down, picked up a stone from beneath the clear water, and threw it, then froze in a sudden silent fascination as the rings of ripples smoothly expanded from the splash. He turned and, seeing the Empress, ran straight to her with a loud laugh to be taken up by Bourtai into her strong nomad woman's arms.

Bourtai braced the child on her hip and smoothed his hair, noting as she always did how striking the boy's face was with the eyes the slanting shape of his father's and with the green of his mother's in them. She sat on a stone bench and settled him on her lap, listening with delight as his little-boy stories poured out in quick Chinese.

The Russian woman placed herself on the grass at Bourtai's feet and happily watched her son chattering and hugging the Empress. But the Rus woman's green eyes were suddenly overcome with a sign of worry. Catching Bourtai's eyes, she asked, "Will he be a warrior, my Lady?"

Bourtai did not reply for some moments. Then, without taking her adoring eyes from the happy, restless child on her lap, announced, "No. The son of Bahadur, of Subotai the Bold, he shall be a scholar."

AFTERWORD

As a general—in his unparalelled success on the field of battle—Subotai is rivaled only by his lord, Genghis Khan. The conquests and the marches of Alexander of Macedon and Julius Caesar pale in comparison.

According to history and to tradition, Subotai was victorious in more than fifty battles. He was an amazing tactician and a near-global strategist in the modern sense.

But the sole adequate description which can be applied to this strange and shadowy historical force, this Subotai, is in the words of a dying Chinese general who had asked to see the great nomad general. When he had seen the Mongol orlok, he closed his eyes and spoke. "Having looked upon you, Lord Subotai, I am ready for death. You are come from the Tao."

If you enjoyed reading this book, here are some other books from Pineapple Press on related topics. To request a catalog or to place an order, visit our website at www.pineapplepress.com. Or write to Pineapple Press, P.O. Box 3889, Sarasota, Florida 34230, or call 1-800-PINEAPL (746-3275).

THE HONOR SERIES

"Sign on early and set sail with Peter Wake for both solid historical context and exciting sea stories." —U.S. Naval Institute Proceedings

The Honor Series of naval fiction by Robert N. Macomber. Covers the life and career of American naval officer Peter Wake from 1863 to 1907. The first book in the series, *At the Point of Honor,* won Best Historical Novel from the Florida Historical Society. The second, *Point of Honor,* won the Cook Literary Award for Best Work in Southern Fiction. The sixth, *A Different Kind of Honor,* won the Boyd Literary Award for Excellence in Military Fiction from the American Library Association.

Adventures in Nowhere by John Ames. A boy in 1950s Florida wrestles with adult problems and enjoys the last days of his boyhood in a place called Nowhere, sometimes fearing for his sanity as his family falls apart and he watches a house change shape across the river.

Seven Mile Bridge by Michael Biehl. Florida Keys dive shop owner Jonathan Bruckner returns home to Sheboygan, Wisconsin, after his mother's death. What he finds leads him to an understanding of the mystery that surrounded his father's death years before.

The Bucket Flower by Donald Robert Wilson. In 1893, 23-year-old Elizabeth Sprague goes into the Everglades to study its unique plant life, even though she's warned that a pampered "bucket flower" like her can't endure the rigors of the swamp. She encounters wild animals and even wilder men but finds her own strength and a new future.

My Brother Michael by Janis Owens. Out of the shotgun houses and deep, shaded porches of a West Florida mill town comes this extraordinary novel of love and redemption. Gabriel Catts recounts his lifelong love for his brother's wife, Myra—whose own demons threaten to overwhelm all three of them.

Black Creek by Paul Varnes. Through the story of one family, we learn how white settlers moved into the Florida territory, taking it from the natives—who had been there only a few generations—with false treaties and finally all-out war. Thus, both sides were newcomers anxious to "take Florida."

Confederate Money by Paul Varnes. In 1861, as this novel opens, a Confederate dollar is worth 90 cents. We follow Henry Fern as he fights on both sides of the war. Through shrewd dealings, he manages to amass $40,000 in Confederate paper money and finally changes his paper fortune into silver and gold.

For God, Gold and Glory by E. H. Haines. The riveting account of the invasion of the American Southeast from 1539 to 1543 by Hernando de Soto, as told by his private secretary, Rodrigo Ranjel. A meticulously researched tale of adventure and survival and the dark aspects of greed and power.

Nobody's Hero by Frank Laumer. Based on the true adventure of an American soldier who refused to die in spite of terrible wounds sustained during the battle known as Dade's Massacre, which started the Second Seminole War in Florida.